THE LITTLE VILLAGE CHRISTMA

Sue Moorcroft writes award-winning contemporary fiction of life and love. Her last Christmas novel, *The Christmas Promise*, was a #1 bestseller. She also writes short stories, serials, articles, columns, courses and writing 'how to'.

An army child, Sue was born in Germany then lived in Cyprus, Malta and the UK and still loves to travel. Her loves include: writing, reading, watching Formula One on TV and hanging out with friends. She's worked in a bank, as a bookkeeper (probably a mistake), as a copytaker for *Motor Cycle News* and for a typesetter – but none of these jobs made her as happy as her current one of 'author'.

You can follow Sue on Twitter @SueMoorcroft and find out more by visiting www.suemoorcroft.com.

The Little Village Christmas

Sue Moorcroft

avon.

This novel is entirely a work of fiction.
The names, characters and incidents portrayed in it are
the work of the author's imagination. Any resemblance to
actual persons, living or dead, events or localities is
entirely coincidental.

AVON

A division of HarperCollins*Publishers*
1 London Bridge Street,
London SE1 9GF

www.harpercollins.co.uk

A Paperback Original 2017

2

First published in Great Britain by
HarperCollins*Publishers* 2017

A catalogue record for this book is available from the British Library

ISBN-13: 978-0-00-826001-9

Typeset in Sabon LT Std by Palimpsest Book Production Ltd, Falkirk, Stirlingshire

Printed and bound in Great Britain by CPI Group (UK) Ltd, Croydon CR0 4YY

MIX
Paper from
responsible sources
FSC **FSC™ C007454**
www.fsc.org

This book is produced from independently certified FSC™ paper
to ensure responsible forest management.

For more information visit: www.harpercollins.co.uk/green

Acknowledgements

Every author needs help along the way and this is where I get the opportunity to show my appreciation for the help, time, expertise and experiences of so many wonderful people.

Heartfelt thanks to those who helped with vital research: Mark Lacey, independent member of the parole board and retired detective superintendent of police, for his help on prisons and law; Keith Martin for putting right my plans for a bank scam (it's OK – we're both ex-bank staff); Michael Matthews for teaching me all I know about construction; Jo Askew of Icarus Falconry for her advice on all things owl-related, reading the manuscript and pointing out where I was endangering Barney's life; Giulia Lunghi, Andrea Crellin and Julie Vince for their views on and experiences of TV; Heather Korbey and Lord Bungle for advising on what Alexia needed to know about setting up a café; *Homes Under the Hammer* for keeping me occupied when I couldn't use my left arm for a couple of weeks; and the Offenders' Families Helpline website for so many small details that it was important I get right. Also, Facebook and Twitter friends for their views of whether Ben should turn Lloyd in and the correct treatment of ornery old ponies; Paul Matthews and Ashley Panter for vital advice on current social trends and mores, including knowledge of Betty Boop.

Huge thanks to my faithful beta readers Mark West and Dominic White. Their commentary on an early draft provided its usual valuable insight on the male point of view, especially when they saw hilarious boy-jokes in what I intended as innocuous lines.

Thanks to the stalwart members of Team Sue Moorcroft for their endless support. Special mentions for Mark West and Joanne Baird for help with the naming of characters.

I can't tell you how much I appreciate the publishing industry professionals who work with me and help me write the best books I can: my lovely agent Juliet Pickering and all at Blake Friedmann; along with fab editor Helen Huthwaite and the entire Avon Books UK team.

I consider it a privilege to earn my living as an author, so **thank you,** lovely readers, for reading my books, following me and sending messages via social media. Every book's for you.

To Mark West and Dominic White.
Thank you.

Prologue

'Are you *serious*?' Ben stared at his mother.

Penny twisted a tissue in her hands. 'I'm only telling you that Dad said if you hadn't taken up with that girl then none of this would have happened. Lloyd wouldn't be . . . where he is.'

Ben sank onto his parents' floral sofa, the cotton cold beneath his sweating palms. '*That girl*'s name is Imogen.'

'In a way, I can see Dad's point. Everybody in Didbury knows her family. The Goodbodys breed like rabbits, live off benefits and their garden looks like a scrap yard. They're like something from a reality TV show.'

'Imogen's never claimed a benefit in her life. She's put in long hours in a demanding sales environment, in spite of her background and in spite of people badmouthing her.' Ben wasn't sure whether he was more outraged by his parents' prejudice or by being put in the position of defending Imogen.

His mother didn't let his dig deter her. 'The Goodbody men are chancers and the women are slu—' She flicked Ben a glance and chose a primmer adjective. 'The women

1

are man-eaters. If she was supposed to be on a spa weekend with an old uni friend, why was she in a car with Lloyd in the middle of the night? Dad warned you you'd never have a quiet mind if you married her, so why did you insist on working away so much? You're such a decent, straightforward man, but didn't you see that it was like throwing petrol and a match together? At least Lloyd's single. Imogen was married to you—'

Ben leapt to his feet. 'Lloyd's my *brother*!' He ought to have been used to being the second child in all senses, but no way could he get his head around his mother holding him in any way responsible for this mess.

Penny buried her face in her hands. 'And those aunties of Imogen are going round painting her as an innocent victim and you as a callous husband!'

'Do you think I don't know? The Auntie Mafia never pass me in the supermarket without asking what happened to "For better, for worse".'

And his petition for divorce had goaded them to literally hiss at him in the street. He hadn't wasted his breath defending himself because he understood Imogen's family's loyalty lay with their own. They'd never heard Imogen's words: *I don't think we're going to get past this, Ben. If you can't forgive me then divorce me.* Her pain when he'd demanded to know how he could forgive her when she refused to tell him what had really happened that night had been too deeply personal and painful a moment to share with anyone but her.

Penny gulped. 'And now the Goodbodys are giving you a hard time and you're selling up and leaving Didbury.'

Her words reminded Ben of the depressing task that had been interrupted by this conversation: dismantling their home. Stilted phone calls to Imogen about what she wanted packing into her brothers' vans, his heart convulsing as he imagined her, white-faced, trying to be brave.

The very same heart that couldn't forgive her.

He turned wearily for the door. 'I'm not leaving because of Imogen's family, Mum. I'm leaving because of mine.'

Chapter One

Over the course of the wrecking party, enthusiastic villagers had shifted the rubbish of decades from the once-splendid Angel public house to the skips outside. Most of the Victorian building's fabulous period features had been dismantled.

Alexia clambered up on a stepladder in what used to be the 'Bar Parlour' of The Angel to make an announcement above the hubbub. 'I declare the "wrecking" over! Now let's party!' Jumping down amidst cheers and calls of, 'Thanks, Alexia!' she ignored the surge of people towards the cool boxes of beer and instead she gazed

5

around the long-neglected room. The lovely old door with its etched glass had been moved to storage along with the once-polished Victorian bar. Dozens of flickering tea lights had been lit in place of the industrial lights rigged for the stripping-out.

Someone had brought a docking station for their iPod and music began to echo off walls freshly stripped of red flock wallpaper and nicotine stains. Dusty people chattered around the mood boards that depicted Alexia's vision of the pub's transformation to The Angel Community Café.

Alexia's best friend, Jodie, appeared at her side, her long dark hair overlaid with a cobweb, and pushed a cold can into Alexia's hand. 'Here. You deserve a drink.'

Alexia pulled the ring tab with satisfaction. 'We all do. I love this village. Forty people have given up their Saturday to help us.'

'They want a community café and they like free beer!' Jodie raised her voice to match the increasing noise. 'Shane says he's stowed the mirrors, tiles and etched glass screens upstairs so there's nothing to damage if folk let off steam. He's gone to fetch the burgers and sausages from your fridge. Shall we find someone to help us set the barbecues up? Seb's around somewhere.'

'Not Seb,' Alexia protested. 'I don't need my ex breathing down my neck. There must be someone else mug enough to sacrifice drinking time in favour of carting more heavy stuff.' Alexia's gaze shifted to the only person in the room she didn't know, a man with tousled corn-coloured hair. She'd watched him help take up the black and white tiles to be stacked in the back of Shane's truck and moved off-site to be cleaned. Most people had joked and chatted as they worked but the fair man had offered only the occasional reply if a remark was tossed in his direction.

Now, T-shirt and jeans dusty, he was alone, leaning on a wall. 'Him,' she suggested.

Jodie followed her gaze. 'Two minutes single and you've got your eye on the brooding stranger?'

Alexia grinned. 'It's four weeks. And what's the point of being single if you can't show interest? Come on.' She cleared the dust from her throat with a swig of beer before threading her way towards the man who was idly watching a group of four laughing women trying to dance on the mortar where the floor tiles had been. His gaze focused in on Alexia only once she was standing in front of him.

She introduced herself and gave him the benefit of her best smile. 'I'm project-managing the refurbishment of The Angel. And this is Jodie, who'll run The Angel Community Café when it opens.'

'I'm Ben.'

Alexia disregarded the economy of his reply. It was probably overwhelming to be the only person here who didn't know every other person here. 'Thanks for helping. Aren't you Gabe Piercy's nephew?' Gabe had been uncharacteristically reticent about why his nephew had turned up on the edges of Middledip village and then kept almost entirely to himself.

'That's me.' His hair slid over one eye as he nodded.

'Gabe's probably told you that he's bought The Angel because the village can't sustain a coffee shop unless it has some community value—'

Ben finished for her. 'So he's set the rent low to make the café viable and the book club and all the other local groups are going to bring business in.'

Alexia took a step back. There was 'brooding' and there was 'abrupt' and in her eyes Ben had just crossed from one to the other. 'Sorry if I'm being boring, but this is such an amazing building, I'm excited to see it brought back to life. And,' she added tartly, 'in case you're worried that your uncle's being ripped off, the village has raised money towards the refurb. Gabe will end up with a sympathetic restoration, and a share of the profits from the café that's far in excess of what he'd earn if he kept his money safe in the bank.'

She prepared to turn on her heel and find someone friendlier to haul barbecues around for her but Ben put out a hand, looking rueful. 'No, I'm sorry. Like Gabe, I'm a bit of an oddball and, worse, I'm an oddball having a bad day. My mind was on something else when you came up.' He managed a faint smile. 'Let's begin again. It's a great community effort and Gabe tells me you're not charging for managing the project.'

Before Alexia could protest about Gabe being termed an oddball or explain why she was working *gratis*, Jodie jumped in to claim a vicarious share of the accolades. 'And my boyfriend Shane's doing the building work for "mates' rates" because I'm in partnership with Gabe for the business side of the café. By the way, thanks for taming the jungle at the front so we can actually see The Angel from the road for the first time in decades.'

At this reminder, Alexia forgave Ben his earlier instance of gracelessness. Twice on site visits she'd enjoyed watching him dangling from a harness, not above wondering what his face was like without his hardhat and visor. 'In that case you're practically one of us boring community volunteers so I don't feel so bad about hitting on you to help drag barbecues about.'

A brief pause as he stared at her. Then, 'Hit on me? Lead the way.'

'Great.' Blushing, sure he knew it had been accidental-ly-on-purpose that she'd said 'hit on you' rather than 'hit you up', Alexia led him through groups of chatting villagers to one of the doors to what had once been the kitchen, evidenced by a pair of white pot sinks, both cracked. The borrowed barbecues were lined up in the middle of the floor as if waiting to be invited to the party. 'That big green one's on wheels. The other two have to be carried.'

'You wheel, I'll carry.' Ben wrapped his arms around the sphere of a battered steel kettle barbecue and heaved it from the floor while Alexia and Jodie began dragging the green barbecue into the hall and over the steps of the side door. Ben had fetched the second barbecue in the time it took for them to manhandle it across the weeds that heaved up the aged tarmac.

They were selecting the most even ground when Shane drew up with the food Alexia and Jodie had shopped for yesterday.

'Shane!' cooed Jodie, throwing open her arms to take up what was these days a familiar position – wound around her boyfriend.

Shane was good-looking, Alexia acknowledged. His short hair and square jaw went with the kind of body that reflected his physical job. He wasn't the stable influence Alexia would have chosen for her lifelong friend, though.

'No Tim?' Alexia enquired.

'Nah, he's gone off somewhere. C'm'ere, gorgeous.' Shane swung Jodie, lifting her off her feet, making her squeal.

Alexia could imagine stolid Tim preferring to go home than come to a party. Shane chattered enough for both of them, anyway.

'Right. This is Gabe's nephew, Ben, who—'

Shane pumped Ben's hand without waiting for the rest

of Alexia's introduction. 'All right, mate?' Brimming with bonhomie, he joined Ben in hooking up the gas bottles that fired the barbecues and dragging a battered table out of a skip to bear the food.

Seeing Shane opening another beer for Jodie, though she was protesting and giggling that one was enough, Alexia glanced from the packs of food to Ben, who hadn't vanished at the first opportunity as she'd thought he might. 'Fancy manning a grill?'

He shrugged. 'OK.'

It took twenty minutes for the grills to become hot enough and they could take up their stations flipping burgers. Ben looked after the grill to Alexia's left while Jodie cooked to her other side, when she wasn't giggling with Shane. She seemed tipsy already so she probably hadn't stuck to her intention to only have one drink.

Alexia frowned. 'You should take more water with it, Jodie.' She tried to sound jokey rather than judgy, but Jodie was already trying to play Jenga with the sausages.

Shane used his beer can to wave Alexia's concern away. 'She's fine, aren't you, darlin'? She's grand. She's lovely.' He nibbled Jodie's neck, prompting an explosion of giggles.

Jodie allowed herself to be smooched off into the shadows and Alexia rearranged the Jenga sausages so they could actually cook. She sighed. 'Jodie's going to have a sore head tomorrow if she keeps this up.'

Ben's eyes remained on his grill. 'It's her head. People make their choices about drinking and have to put up with the consequences.'

Alexia wasn't sure if the slight edge to his voice was disapproval of Jodie's tipsiness or of Alexia's grumble. But as she was in danger of being landed with Jodie's grill as well as her own, she felt justified in lifting her voice in mild protest. 'Hey, Jodes, I thought you were the cook around here? Shane, any chance you could start slicing bread rolls? This food's going to be ready soon.'

Reluctantly, Jodie swayed back to her post. Shane sent Alexia a dark look, but reached for the bread.

Gabe stepped out of the porch. Behind him, the once impressive front door, currently beribboned with peeling varnish, squeaked on its hinges. Gabe sniffed the air. 'I smell sausages and my belly's rumbling.' Known for his silver ponytail and mismatching sartorial choices, today, along with his hungry expression, he wore a button-down shirt tucked into jogging bottoms.

Alexia grinned. 'We're just about ready with the first lot of food.'

Gabe turned with alacrity. 'I'll call everyone out.'

In seconds, hungry villagers were pouring out to grab paper plates to heap with carbohydrates and cholesterol. Fat sizzled and Alexia's eyes began to sting as the press of bodies left the smoke nowhere to go. 'Ouch.' She tried to wipe her face on her sleeve.

'Here.' Ben passed her a sheet of kitchen roll with a smile that flashed so briefly she almost missed it.

It chased away his frown lines and almost made her forget the waiting queue. 'Thanks.' She smiled back. Maybe Ben simply took a while to relax around people and warm to them. Maybe—

But then a familiar voice claimed her attention. 'Alexia, you're looking good.'

Alexia jumped. She hadn't noticed the tall man who now hovered in front of her barbecue. 'Seb! But I look as if I've been living in one of the skips.' She tried not to feel guilty at laughing her ex's compliment off. 'Burger?'

11

'Yes, please.' Sebastian held out his plate. 'Shall I walk you home later?'

Alexia's heart sank. Seb always reminded her of a genial bear with his brown hair and burly shoulders, but he acted more like a sheepdog. 'No need.'

'So you're going on somewhere?'

'I don't know.'

'I'll check back with you.'

Alexia fought down the urge to snap, 'You can't act like an over-protective boyfriend now you're not my boyfriend!' Instead she tried to let him down lightly. 'Thanks, but you know nobody needs walking home in the village.' She smiled past him at the next person in the queue. With an air of reluctance, Sebastian moved on.

Ben clicked his tongs and popped sausages onto plates passing on their human conveyor belt. 'Plaintive expression from him; guilty tension from you. Ex-boyfriend carrying a torch?'

Alexia checked Sebastian had moved out of earshot. 'Good guess. He's a lovely guy and I've known him forever but . . .' She shrugged, not sure how to say, 'Too nice, too smothering, too settled, too *unexciting*' in a way that didn't make her sound like Ms Heartless. 'I'm in a wing-spreading phase and hope to be leaving the village to work on new projects in London. Whereas Sebastian . . .'

He shrugged. 'If you don't want to be with someone, you don't. No justification necessary.'

Alexia paused in opening a new pack of burgers, trying to read his suddenly shuttered expression. 'True,' she replied carefully. 'But also not true. At least not to this particular "someone", because he apparently needs to be freshly convinced each time we meet.'

'It'll be easier when you leave.' Ben returned to doling out sausages.

The villagers Alexia had grown up with filed by, offering snippets of gossip or teasing remarks. Meeting both with good humour, Alexia kept them moving. Until a small woman planted herself squarely before the grill, regarding Alexia balefully from beneath a blonde geometric bob. 'No fish?'

Alexia smiled, hoping this wasn't going to turn into another awkward encounter. 'Hello, Carola. No, sorry. Nice of you to come and help.' In fact, Alexia hadn't seen any assistance from Carola, who'd been a thorn in their sides during the fundraising, and was pretty sure she was only here to turn her nose up.

'I don't eat much meat.'

'Veggie burger?'

'No. I'll have two sausages – if you've got any that aren't overcooked.'

Deciding not to point out that the sausages weren't veggie, Alexia simply slapped two on Carola's plate and the line moved on. And on.

'Well now, Alexia!' said a jovial man with a long and lugubrious face.

'Mr Carlysle. Sausages?' Not many people in the village called the owner of the local Carlysle estate by his first name. It was always 'Mr' or the whole mouthful of 'Christopher Carlysle'. He was another who'd come to the party for reasons other than to work. In his case it was to 'show his face' at an event to which he had vague connections.

'Lovely, lovely. And one for Mrs Carlysle, as well, please. She's around here somewhere.' He held out his plate before having a few words with Ben and then moving on.

Some people came back for the second or third time. Alexia became used to Ben's presence alongside her. Villagers tried to get him talking but, although he was affable enough, he somehow kept the conversation superficial.

Alexia tended her own grill and Jodie's, as Jodie seemed more into exchanging tongues than wielding tongs. All three grills had emptied again before the line of hungry people abated.

Shane and Jodie, arms clamped around each other as if they were running a three-legged race, staggered back, Shane beaming. 'I'm taking this beautiful woman to her bed, 'Lexia. Apologies in advance. Know what I mean?' He gave an exaggeratedly lewd wink as he began to steer Jodie down the drive.

'All too well, unfortunately,' Alexia muttered, watching them weave off towards Cross Street. She transferred her attention to her grill, dropping the last few burgers and sausages onto its glowing rack. 'Just enough left for us.'

Ben turned off the other two grills and stuck his hands in his pockets as she arranged the sausages like sunrays around the burgers. 'You didn't look too thrilled at Shane's remark.'

She flicked him a glance. 'Jodie lives at my house at the moment.'

'Ah.' Laughter lurked in his eyes.

Her cheeks heated up. 'But at least it means they've left Shane's truck here rather than trying to drive to his place.'

Any trace of amusement faded from Ben's face. 'Driving and alcohol is a bad combination. So you and Jodie house share?' He seemed prepared to chat now there were fewer people about.

'For the last few months, since Jodie's marriage ended. We've been friends most of our lives.' Under the guise of

14

tearing off a fresh sheet of kitchen roll, Alexia glanced around to check Sebastian wasn't one of the shadowy figures finishing up a burger in a corner before adding, 'Seb was making moving-in-together noises so inviting her to live with me worked for us both. I hadn't bargained for Shane, but Jodie says their hot and heavy "thing" is a good way of getting over her husband.'

Ben's eyes narrowed thoughtfully beneath his unruly hair. 'Does that work?'

Shrugging, Alexia patted a burger with the flat of her spatula. 'She took it hard when Russ left, and Shane does seem to have cheered her up. I just wish he wouldn't encourage her to drink so much. He must've stashed beer out here, I think, because I didn't see either of them going in and out for cans.'

She didn't add that Jodie was subject to mood swings and when Alexia had explained to Shane that alcohol made the tendency stronger he'd snapped at her not to be a worry-arse.

Ben began slicing rolls to place on the plates. 'That food looks good. I'm starving.' He pulled two chairs, minus their backs, from the skip, dusting them with a flourish of an imaginary handkerchief before disappearing indoors and returning with two cans of beer.

Alexia sank onto the chair, realising how much her feet were aching. Although almost everyone else had gone indoors to escape the evening chill the residual warmth from the barbecue made it pleasant to dine al fresco. She sipped the fresh beer. 'This must be my last.'

Ben paused, a hot dog halfway to his mouth. 'Don't think I'm trying to get you drunk. There's lemonade indoors if you want it. Your ex glared at me when he saw me taking two cans.'

She laughed and then groaned. 'I hope he doesn't come out to check up on us! Every time I see him I realise how much I prefer being single.'

Ben gazed at her for several unsmiling seconds. 'You're giving me lots to think about tonight: rebound relationships as a good thing and the joys of being footloose and fancy-free.'

There was such a strange expression on his face that Alexia just gazed at him, not knowing how to answer.

Obviously divining her confusion, he smiled faintly. 'My wife and I split up a while ago. Learning to like being single could make things easier.'

Chapter Two

Alexia put down her burger. 'I'm sorry if anything I said was smug or insensitive.'

He smiled, if a little painfully. 'It was refreshing. It's easy to keep viewing things from the same old perspective.'

'You've taken off your wedding ring.'

'Rarely wore it. Safety hazard when I'm up a tree with a chainsaw.'

They lapsed into silence, chewing smoky food and sipping beer. People began to emerge from The Angel to call their goodnights, the more thoughtful among them depositing their rubbish in a skip as they passed. Alexia returned the farewells, wiping up her ketchup and licking her fingers. Though surprised to realise it was past eleven, she felt no immediate need to move.

Sebastian emerged and hesitated.

'Night, Seb,' she said brightly, not wanting a repeat of the 'can I walk you home?' conversation.

With a brief 'Night' Sebastian melted away down the darkened drive. Alexia felt a pang at the despondent set of his rounded shoulders. Ben was probably right that things would be easier when she could carry through on her plan to leave the village.

Gabe appeared, carrying a box of empty cans. 'I'll take these to the recycling.' He glanced back in the direction of the building. 'It looks frighteningly bare in there. You are going to put my property back together again, aren't you?'

Alexia laughed. 'Just give me till Christmas. It's bare because Shane and Tim have been so conscientious about keeping period features safe.'

He beetled his brows at her in mock ferocity. 'The Saturday *before* Christmas. That's our grand opening.'

'The Saturday *before*,' she agreed with a grin. 'The tiles will have been relaid and the fireplaces restored. I'll make gorgeous Victoriana Christmas arrangements of holly and dried oranges to stand on the mantels. The Victorians loved Christmassy things made of lace and beads as well – it will look gorgeous!'

'I knew I could rely on you,' Gabe acknowledged, patting her shoulder. They said their goodnights and Gabe strode down the short drive.

Alexia glanced at Ben. His face, lit only by the lights of the kitchen windows, was shadowy. 'You can go with him. I'll finish up here.' To give Shane and Jodie time to fall asleep she'd gladly linger to explore the newly bared Angel, excited by the metamorphosis to come. Tomorrow she'd bring her camera and take work-in-progress pictures for her portfolio. It was an important project for her and it would be good to properly capture this swept-clean moment.

Ben wiped his hands. 'I don't live with Gabe. I'm staying in a cottage on the Carlysle estate.'

Alexia put on an interested expression, though she'd

already known. Everyone in Middledip knew everything. 'A cottage on the home farm?' The Carlysle estate employed many of the villagers and a few of lived there.

'No, Woodward Cottage, near the lake. I was able to persuade Christopher Carlysle that it goes with my job. "The woodward" was the old name for someone who looked after woodlands.'

'I haven't been to Woodward Cottage since I was a teenager. It was so tumbledown it's hard to imagine it as habitable.'

'Apparently Mr Carlysle was able to get a grant to do it up. His idea was that the estate bailiff would move in but the bailiff decided to marry a woman with two teenaged kids and there's only one bedroom. I've been there about six months.'

'Six months? I'm amazed Gabe hasn't introduced us. I haven't even seen you around the village, except for dangling in the trees out front.'

He rubbed his nose. 'I've kind of kept to myself.'

Alexia could somehow imagine solitude suiting Ben. He had the air of someone who could take people or leave them. 'I think you were the subject of conversation at the pub the other day. Do you have a pet owl? The guys decided you're a wizard.'

He grinned faintly. 'Barney's a rescue owl. Owls aren't pets. Gabe found him on the edge of the wood. He'd fallen from the nest and damaged his wing. He'll never fly or hunt, so I've given him a home. When not looking after Barney I'm a tree surgeon. I used to have my own business but I sold up when I moved here. The woods haven't been managed as well as they could have been so Gabe put in a word for me with Christopher Carlysle and now I'm employed by the Carlysle estate. I was in the mood to be

19

left alone to do my thing and that's the kind of employee Mr Carlysle likes.' Ben rose and returned his chair to the skip.

Reading this as a full stop to the subject, Alexia rose too, collecting paper plates while Ben disconnected the barbecues from their gas bottles.

They moved indoors to find that the last stragglers were ready to yawn off into the night. Alexia switched on the main lights and went round blowing out the guttering tea lights. 'I declare the Middledip Wrecking Party a success.'

He ran his finger down a gaping crack in the plaster. 'Does work start soon?'

'The electricians and plumbers arrive on Monday while Shane and Tim get on with cleaning up the tiles to be reused. Luckily the windows and doors are OK and most of the plaster mouldings, too.' She gazed around the Bar Parlour, its missing fireplace and bar making it look like a mouth with gaps in the teeth.

Ben drifted over to the mood boards still standing at the end of the bare room. 'And this is how the place will look?'

She joined him, casting him a quick glance to check he wasn't just being polite – not that he struck her as someone who'd bother. 'Yes, this is the storyboard for the project beginning with photos of the building as it was when Gabe bought it, to my vision of the finished article. My 3D drawings are called rendered models and the 2D are the floor plans. The colour swatches make it look pretty.' Her heart gave a tiny kick of excitement that the project was finally underway.

'It's a Victorian building and must have been quite grand for a village. When Middledip was bypassed by better roads in the eighties it couldn't support two pubs, and the more

20

homely The Three Fishes was the one to survive. After The Angel closed, the landlord died and the landlady lived here alone for more than twenty years. She eventually died without a will and distant cousins had to be tracked down to inherit. It was a long time before it could be put on the market and then nobody seemed to see its potential.'

She lifted her gaze to the beautiful plaster ceiling roses where big glass lights had dangled until Shane took them down to protect them. 'I'm amazed nobody bought the place just to get the period features and sell them to a reclamation yard. The moulded brickwork on the front elevation alone must be worth a fortune. Maybe the grounds were so overgrown that everyone forgot The Angel was here.'

'Until Uncle Gabe decided his tree surgeon nephew would love to take out all the overgrowth.'

'It does seem as if you've been handy,' she agreed, glad to see the faint smile return. His default expression seemed so grim. 'Luckily, Gabe not only knew The Angel was here but was willing to invest in the building to give the village its coffee shop if additional funds could be raised to see it restored. Otherwise, The Angel would probably have fallen down from neglect.'

'Generous of the village to contribute.'

'What swung it was that the village hall had to close because the roof timbers are rotting. They'll cost a massive amount to replace, much more than to fix up The Angel. The village hall committee's obliged to slog through applying for grants and asking the county for money. We were able to just spring into action.'

He quirked a brow. 'Bad luck for the village hall.'

'I do feel disloyal. I've been to the hall to so many parties and stuff. But accommodating all the groups that used to meet at the village hall meant Jodie and Gabe could call it a community café and start fundraising.' Alexia led him through a doorway. 'This was the poor-relation bar. It says "Public" in the glass in the door – when the door's hanging where it's meant to be.' She flicked a switch as she stepped into the room and the strip light flickered into life. A couple of stray slivers of 1970's woodchip wallpaper lingered up near the ceiling, suggesting the Public hadn't been deemed worthy of the red flock of the Bar Parlour. 'It's where pub customers used to play skittles and darts. It's not as grand as the Bar Parlour but will work brilliantly for groups.'

Ben gazed around the big empty room with its scarred floorboards. 'I'm surprised that whoever orchestrates things at the village hall didn't say the funds you raised ought to go to them.'

'I'm afraid that's exactly what's happened,' Alexia acknowledged ruefully. 'The village hall committee's headed up by the formidable Carola, the one who demanded fish at the barbecue. She's vehemently opposed to the community café and says the villagers should never have been asked to raise money for a building and a business that belongs to an individual. But nobody had their arm twisted. The village hall and The Angel Café have no relationship to each other, and Gabe, Jodie, me and your boss, Christopher Carlysle, who accepted responsibility for The Community Café fund, aren't about to hand over the dosh to Carola.'

A suspicion of a twinkle lit Ben's eye. 'If I hadn't come from a small town myself I'd be astonished at the politics.' Then his phone beeped and he pulled it out to silence it. 'Interesting as this is, I'm going to have to get home. That's the alert to remind me that Barney needs his dinner.'

'You must feed him.' Alexia felt a tiny prickle of disappointment at losing his company, not to mention an opportunity for her to spout about her pet project, but told herself not to be so idiotic. 'I'll hang on here for a bit longer before I lock up.'

He hesitated. 'On your own?'

She rolled her eyes. 'Don't you start! I could run around Middledip at night with my hands full of cash and nothing bad would happen. Honestly, I'll wander home when I'm ready.'

'Giving your friends time to quiet down?' He half-smiled, his eyes bright in the overhead light.

She felt her cheeks heat up again. 'That would be the plan.'

'Can't you just tell them to be more considerate? It's your house.'

'I could. But if I can move my career in the direction I want to then Jodie's hoping Shane will move in when I move out. Two lots of rent will smooth my way considerably.'

Grey eyes thoughtful, he considered her. Almost offhandedly he said, 'I can't leave Barney hungry. He's so young he needs feeding three times a day. You could come and meet him, if you want? It would fill an hour before you go home.'

Alexia debated quickly. It wasn't that she couldn't find something to keep her occupied for an hour or two at The Angel but, truthfully, she was intrigued by the idea of a late evening stroll through the woods with this man. He termed himself an oddball like his Uncle Gabe, but Gabe just happened to be one of the nicest men she'd ever known. Going over her plans for The Angel could wait. 'I'd love to meet Barney and see how Woodward Cottage has turned out.'

They ferried the cooling grills into the kitchen in case of rain, then Ben waited as Alexia locked the big front door before they stepped together into the quiet night-time village.

Ben paused. 'We could walk down Little Lane and hook back on ourselves up the track to the cottage, but it's about three miles. It's quicker to take the footpaths, if you're not scared of the dark. I have a torch on my phone.'

Alexia laughed at the idea she might be scared. 'I grew up here. I know my way around the bridleways and my phone has a torch, too.' A feeling was fluttering about inside her. But it wasn't fear.

Angling right and crossing Port Road, Ben lit up his phone ready to leave the pavement and take the bridleway. Beside him, Alexia followed suit. The bright white lights illuminated the path and the vegetation that soon replaced the fences on either side. Insects flitted through the beams as if anxious about what the humans were up to.

What *was* he up to?

He glanced at Alexia. 'Certain you don't want to go around by the road?'

In the backwash of the light he saw her brows lift. 'What, walk three miles instead of one? The bridleways are safe.' She reminded him of the cartoon character Betty Boop with her dark curls and mischievous smile. And her curves.

She also possessed the easy confidence and self-sufficiency that made him see why, by trying to look after her, her old boyfriend had been doing exactly what was most likely to aggravate her.

'OK, if you're sure.' He set off again, deciding to accept it all as part of this strange ending to an odd day.

It had begun badly.

Opening his mail, he'd discovered he'd been granted his *decree nisi*.

Just plain white paper with typing on, he hadn't even realised what it was at first. He'd stood on the old flags of Woodward Cottage reading the words that symbolised his failure and loss. Grief had risen up and made him want to break things, which was the only reason he'd given in to Gabe's urging to attend the wrecking party.

He'd hurled stuff into the skips as if each bent curtain rod or cracked mirror had caused the end of his marriage. He'd only meant to hang about for one drink to wash the dust from his throat but then Alexia had arrived in front of him with big eyes and a wide smile and launched friendliness at him like a missile. When he'd tried discouraging her with boorishness he'd found himself apologising the instant hurt and dismay had filtered across her features.

When her infectious smile forgave him it had been as if she'd released one of his inner knots of tension.

Fun seemed to radiate from Alexia at a time when he'd all but forgotten what fun was. It had made him feel the first inclination to reclaim that distant, half-forgotten Ben, the one who'd liked a good time.

As the evening had progressed he'd found himself enjoying her company, wanting to know more about her, being interested in what she had to say.

Finally, she'd made him think about the *decree nisi* not as a symbol of failure but of liberty. A strange topsy-turvy instinct had seemed to pop the invitation to Woodward Cottage out of his mouth and he'd probably looked just as surprised as she had.

Maybe it was just basic need, but now a startling question was revolving in his mind. Could he still pull? It had been eight years since he'd made love to anyone but Imogen. Then for two years he'd gone without sex in a daze of pain and grief. Strange that the urge should flood back today but it was swamping him, compelling him to ease the need.

This woman beside him, with her smile and fitted T-shirt, was paying attention to him. It wasn't that she was the only woman who'd done that since Imogen and Lloyd had ripped his guts out . . . just the only one he'd responded to.

He was man enough to admit to himself that her being commitment-averse and aiming to get out of the village at no distant date was attractive, too.

He cleared his throat. 'So tell me more about your career plans.' He might be rusty but he was pretty sure asking a girl about herself was a safe conversational gambit.

Alexia gave a little skip as if the subject put springs in her heels. 'I'm an interior decorator.'

'Painting and wallpapering?' He could envisage her up a ladder wielding a paint roller. She'd seemed completely at home getting her hands dirty at the wrecking party.

'No, that's a painter and decorator. I do some of the same hands-on things but also project manage, come up with ideas and overviews, and produce some one-off and bespoke decorative items. In DIY, a householder decides on the look they want, sources the materials and carries out the decorating. I'm kind of the alternative option, working with clients to give them ideas and help them decide what they want. Then I create it, either via sub-contractors or by doing the work myself. Sometimes it's a redecoration of a single room; sometimes it's a much bigger project, particularly refurbishments. I've made it my business to build up a fantastic network of tradesmen who like

26

working with me because I listen to them and properly utilise their skills. Do you know how vastly tradesmen are underrated? Especially by certain architects and designers.'

Taking the right-hand fork in the path, she climbed the stile that marked the beginning of Carlysle land, dropping down lightly on the other side. 'My friend, Elton, started training at the same time I did. He stayed the course and became an interior designer, making him vastly superior to me – *he* thinks.'

He swung himself over the stile in her wake. 'But didn't you just say you *are* an interior designer?'

'No.' She came to a halt as if she couldn't make him understand while she was in motion. 'I'm an interior *decorator*. An interior designer has a professional qualification, a degree. As Elton never ceases to remind me, I dropped out of uni.' She sent Ben a conspiratorial grin. 'But I put up with his superiority because he's working for an investment property developer. He wants to concentrate on acquiring the properties and he's looking for someone else to oversee projects – which could be me! So I'm working hard on getting my portfolio and website "looking great and up-to-date". Elton won't present me to the investor until he's completely happy.'

They started off again, Ben following Alexia along the narrow path, and soon approached the point where the path curved round the small lake. Ben realised he was training the beam from his phone onto Alexia's behind, and angled it down to her feet. 'But it's all dependent on one money man?'

Glancing over her shoulder, she sent him a look of slight reproof. 'Money *woman*. She's made a lot in industry, apparently, and now she's making more by investing her money via Elton and telling him to spin it into gold.'

'I can see why you'd want to be part of that. Will your parents mind you leaving the village?'

'Mum lives in Bettsbrough and Dad moved to Bolton with his new wife.' She stopped short as the path swerved to the left. 'Wow!'

They stepped further into the clearing where the silent cottage waited in the moonlight. Ben had permission to make a garden in the clearing if he wanted but he liked the woodland floor as it was, the great horse chestnut trees rising up from a leaf-mould carpet.

Alexia gazed at the tiny building. 'I can't believe this is Woodward Cottage! When I used to come here you could see more ivy than walls. There were no windows or doors, the stone was crumbling and in the end the roof fell in. What a great renovation! It looks as if it came from a fairy tale.' She took her time, studying the stonework, admiring the dormers in the roof. Then, wandering on past the log store, she paused where a framework leant against the back of the cottage, a roll of netting on the ground alongside. 'What are you building?'

'Barney's aviary. He'll be ready to move in to it in a few weeks.'

'But it's enormous.'

'Not compared to the entire wood, which is what he should have been flying around.'

'True. Loss of mobility means loss of freedom.'

His throat was suddenly dry. 'That's right.'

She turned to give him a smile. 'Gabe must think a lot of you to trust you with one of his animals.'

He nodded. 'My uncle can usually find room for a creature in need.' When Ben had been unable to stay on in Didbury, where everything he'd thought was his was his no longer, Gabe had provided a refuge. When Ben had been a kid in the shadow of his golden big brother, Gabe had given him time. If anyone had stopped Ben turning his second-child grievances into teenage troublemaking, it had been Gabe.

'Come and meet Barney,' he suggested, turning on his heel and almost mowing Alexia down in his haste to get away from his personal darkness and into the light.

Alexia had to hurry to keep up with Ben as he led her to his front door and directly into a sitting room.

She blinked as he hit the light switch. Revolving in the middle of the room, she admired the beams, the staircase rising up from one corner, the black woodstove on the hearth. Two chairs that didn't match stood either side of the fire on a rug of silver grey and willow green. 'The inside doesn't disappoint.'

'Make yourself at home. Coffee?' Ben went on into the next room.

'Tea, please.' Alexia heard a tap run then the unmistakeable sound of a kettle beginning to heat up.

'Can we light the stove in here?' she called. 'I know September's a bit early but I love firelight.'

'Go for it. Matches on the mantel. One thing I'm not short of is firewood.'

The stove door screeched when Alexia opened it. Crouching, she swiftly made a bed of screwed-up newspaper to criss-cross with kindling from the basket in the hearth. There was something satisfying about striking a match and watching the blackening newspaper shrink as the flames grew brighter and bigger.

Ben arrived with two mugs, a whisky bottle and two glasses. 'Nightcap?'

'Definitely.' Alexia settled on the rug with her back against an armchair so she could feed the dancing fire as Ben poured the whisky.

He settled himself against the opposite chair. 'So you're completely done, you and Sebastian?'

She was suddenly conscious that his legs had come to rest close to hers. She took a sip of the neat whisky, feeling its fiery kiss in her throat. 'Completely. Jodie always said I'd settled for him because he was nice and kind. Maybe she was right.'

Ben snorted. 'I'm pretty sure most men would hate that description. Might as well say "dull and boring".' His eyes glittered at her over the rim of his glass, the reflection of the fire flickering like flames in the whisky.

She took another sip, feeling lassitude weigh her limbs as it combined its effects with the beer she'd drunk earlier. 'Aren't you "nice and kind"?'

'Not so you'd notice. Why did you "settle" for Sebastian?' He shifted slightly and their legs brushed.

Alexia felt a tightness in her belly. Was he doing it on purpose? 'The boyfriend before him was "high maintenance and awkward". It was exhausting.' She circled back to the question he'd side stepped. 'I'd describe myself as "bright and bubbly". Your turn.'

He screwed up his face in a mock-ferocious frown. 'I'm "prickly and disorientated".' The frown faded. After several moments he added, thoughtfully, 'And horny.'

Alexia, taking a sip of whisky, choked.

Ben flushed fierily, giving a laugh that ended on a groan. 'And cringingly out of practice! Sorry, that was dire. Wipe it from your memory. I've obviously forgotten how to do this.'

Alexia giggled. Despite his show of embarrassment, she

noted that his gaze didn't drop entirely, hinting that he was interested in her reaction.

His legs still grazed hers. Heat reached her through the fabric of their jeans, a heat Alexia doubted came from either stove or alcohol – though the latter probably encouraged her to be more airily direct than she would usually have been. 'You haven't, erm, put in any "practice" since your marriage ended?'

He sobered. 'I needed recovery time. And now I'm floundering.' He smiled ruefully. 'Hints and clues gratefully received.'

Alexia was entertained by his frank request. 'Well,' she mused, lounging a little more deeply against the armchair. 'Bringing the tea and whisky on one tray was smooth but not pushy, allowing me the opportunity to choose whether to drink more alcohol. And mirroring the way I'm sitting is supposed to be the right thing to do to make me trust you, isn't it? So you've got that right as well.'

'Ticks in two boxes.' His eyes smiled.

Alexia turned her expression reproving. 'But, seriously, if you invite a girl home to see your barn owl, you really ought to have one.'

He jerked upright. 'Barney! He's in his box. I haven't fed him yet.'

He dumped his glass on the tray, scrambled up and shot into the next room.

Rolling to her feet more slowly, possibly because the room was getting a little fuzzy, Alexia followed him into his kitchen in time to see him ease an open box of translucent white plastic out from under the counter. An indignant rustling came from within. Carefully, Ben positioned the box on the red quarry tiles. 'Alexia, meet Barney. Barney, you just wait in your tub for a minute while I get your supper. Alexia's going to keep you company.'

Ben busied himself elsewhere in the kitchen while Alexia sank down beside the tub and peeped inside. 'Ohhhhhh . . .' she breathed. Peeping back was a pair of round black button eyes topping a hooked beak that looked way too big for the little plate-flat face and ball-of-fluff body. One wing hung badly, like an empty sleeve.

The beak opened and emitted a surprisingly loud *HEHHHH*, like gas leaking under pressure.

Delighted, she laughed. 'You are so *gorgeous*.' Extending a cautious finger, she touched the off-white fluff of Barney's chest. 'As soft as down.'

'I suppose it is down. He's a bit young for feathers.' Ben was still occupied with whatever he'd taken from the tall white fridge. 'Look away if raw stuff upsets you. He eats mice and chicks. I buy them frozen from a pet food supplier.'

'I'm a country girl. I know animals have to eat and that they eat each other.'

Ben returned to kneel beside her, in his hand the red lid of a sandwich box covered in chopped meat. Delicately manipulating a pair of tweezers he lifted Barney out, and touched a tiny piece to Barney's beak. Barney, with a bob of his head, grabbed it quick and scoffed it down with much chomping of his beak.

'Cute!' The slightly acrid smell of Barney warred in Alexia's nostrils with the much nicer man-and-whisky smell of Ben as he patiently fed the youngster. Barney bobbed energetically and made little breathy noises that sounded to Alexia as if he were trying to squawk with a sore throat.

Ben murmured soothingly as Barney's supper vanished, addressing him solemnly as 'little guy'. Alexia watched, fascinated by the contrast of Ben's strong tanned hands and the tiny ball of fuzz snatching at every morsel of food that came his way.

Finally, Ben put down the now-empty lid and pulled a towel from a drawer. He spread it over Alexia's lap where she sat cross-legged on the floor. 'Now, little guy, you look after our guest for a few minutes while I do your house-work.' Gently, he scooped up the baby bird and transferred him to the hands Alexia instinctively cupped to receive him. 'Put your hands low on the towel. Relax your fingers and let him putter about.'

Alexia marvelled at the almost weightless warmth in her hands. 'Barney Owl, you're so soft and cuddly.'

Barney breathed *hehhh* companionably and peeped all about the kitchen, head twitching this way and that as his gaze fixed on each new thing, one stumpy wing waving. Alexia breathed a sad sigh over the other, broken, wing, but then if Barney hadn't been injured she would never have known him, never felt his tiny talons scraping across her skin under his dandelion-clock fuzz.

Filling a bucket with water, Ben removed a soiled towel from Barney's tub to drop in it then retired to the sink to scrub his hands. He returned to carefully relieve Alexia of the near nothingness of the young owl's weight, their fingers touching as Barney made it from one to another. Then Ben sat beside her on the floor and set Barney on the flagstones to stretch his legs and explore. Alexia giggled as Barney pecked at drawer handles or paddled his feet on the floor as if finding it odd beneath his feet. 'He's so cute!'

At length, Ben took the towel that had been draped over Alexia's knees to line the tub before collecting Barney up. 'Bedtime, Barney. Maybe Alexia will come back and see you another day.'

'I'd love to.' Alexia rose reluctantly. While Ben slid the tub back in place with Barney in it she glanced around the kitchen, noting the natural oak cupboards and drawers, the plain worktops. 'Did you really fit this kitchen? It has a charming lack of artifice.'

He shrugged. 'I'm not the kind for fads or frills.'

'So I see.' Everywhere were unfussy lines, no pictures and no ornaments. She wandered back into the equally sparse sitting room. All the shape and movement in the room came from the minimal furnishings and the unevenness of the walls – warm but making 'plain' an art form.

Following her in, Ben stopped in front of the stove and fed another log into the flames, though the room felt warm compared to Alexia's recent perch on the kitchen floor. 'Do you want to see the upstairs?' His back remained to her but his voice held an undercurrent that made Alexia's heart trip on its next beat.

Did 'seeing the upstairs' mean simply viewing what he'd done with the upper storey? Or something more to do with his hesitant move on her, the interest in his eyes whenever he looked her way?

She was quite confident that if she responded, 'I think I'd better go home,' he'd just nod and walk her back to the village.

But being with him was like being in the thrall of an absorbing film: not knowing what would happen next and gripped by the urge to find out. She decided on a neutral reply. 'That would be interesting.'

Ben turned away from the fire with a smile of what might have been relief. Flipping the light switch at the foot of the stairs, he stood back to allow her ahead of him. The practical, mushroom-coloured stair carpet looked new and, remembering that she'd spent the evening

34

disturbing dust and spiders, Alexia kicked off her trainers before treading up the stairs.

At the top, she halted as she found herself on a postage stamp of a landing under a slanting ceiling. The uncurtained window framed a rectangle of black night. 'Bijou,' she observed. A door to her left was closed, then the landing simply opened out into a bedroom. Much of that bedroom was taken up by a double bed. Two small windows in the wall beyond it rose either side of a stone fireplace laid with newspaper and kindling.

As Ben reached the landing too she could feel his warmth crossing the few inches of air between them. He cleared his throat. 'At least the bed's made. Kind of.'

Alexia glanced at the forest green quilt dragged untidily up to a heap of pillows and had no idea what to do next. It felt equally wrong to barge through the closed door or lead the way into Ben's bedroom. There was no room to stand back and let him go first yet if she suggested they go straight back downstairs he'd probably think she was feeling worried or threatened.

She wasn't . . . she was feeling warm and swimmy. And it was more to do with his presence behind her than whisky or beer.

From his stillness she suspected he was processing similar 'what now?' thoughts. The silence grew until Ben broke it with a sigh. 'I think in the old days I used to plan some kind of lead-in. That saying about buying dinner first can't have come from nowhere.'

Though reassured to realise that he seemed to be feeling all the uncertainty she was, he sounded so disgusted with himself that Alexia felt laughter brewing. She turned, meaning to make a joking remark, but he seemed to move at the same time and her forehead clonked his chin, making his teeth click audibly together. 'Ouch, sorry!' She clutched her forehead, which felt as if it bore the imprint of his jaw. His look of ludicrous dismay released her laughter into the air. 'I'm no more prepared than you. I'm so dirty.'

Laughter sprang into his eyes and she began a mortified backtracking. 'I meant dusty, *dusty* from the wrecking party and I must smell of sausages and—' She clutched her forehead harder than ever. 'And I can't believe how much I just over-shared.'

Slowly, he reached out and opened the door that had been closed. He pulled a cord and light sprang out to greet them. 'Help yourself.'

Alexia gazed into the room in wonder. It was as if Ben had made up for the unfussiness of the rest of the house with a bathroom of floor-to-ceiling opulence. A blindingly white corner spa bath and one of those shower cubicles with jets from all angles gleamed invitingly between walls and floors of polished tiles.

'Ooh.' She stepped into the room, forgetting their mutual embarrassment. A small sigh of longing escaped her. 'How *gorgeous*. It makes me want to wallow in the bath.'

His expression focused now, rather than mortified, he stooped to push down the plug and pull up the lever on the shiny chrome tap. The room began to echo with the thunder of water. A dollop of bath foam from a tall green bottle soon added a froth of luxurious light-reflecting bubbles.

Alexia gazed at the steaming water then back at Ben. 'Are you sure? It looks blissful.'

His hands were looped loosely into his pockets, his gaze steady. 'Absolutely sure.' His smile was pensive. 'What I'm uncertain about is whether I'm staying. It's been so long that you're going to have to give me a sign. One that's not too subtle.'

She breathed in the sharp smell of the lime bath foam in the steam that was rising to prickle her skin. Or perhaps the tingling was actually the excitement of being wanted, of being fixed in the tractor beam of his gaze. She had to lick her lips before she could speak. 'Your bath's big enough for two. Is that clear enough?'

His smile flashed. 'Even for me.' He hesitated no more, lifting his hands to rest lightly on her shoulders before dipping his head to kiss her, letting the kiss deepen as they learned the taste of each other. Then he touched her body slowly, as if exploring a new land.

Heart pounding with every new caress, she let him undress her before she reached for him, unfastening the dusty denim of his jeans, releasing him. Enjoying his shudder as she caught him in her hand, savouring the brush of his body hair, the heat of his skin.

Somewhere along the line he'd paused to turn off the tap. Now he tested the water then lifted her, stepping over the bath side, sinking down into the delicious bubbly warmth until the foam threatened to overflow.

Their bodies slipped and slid familiarly, as if they'd known each other for years. He cupped his hands and rinsed the dust and cobwebs from her hair, sending it streaming back from her forehead. Then he turned his attention to her body and soaped her from top to toe, stoking her desires until it was all she could do to concentrate on soaping him in return, learning the shape of him and what made him close his eyes and groan.

Finally, she straddled his body.

His eyes flipped open as if in sudden pain. 'I have no condoms.'

She halted with a groan. 'Neither do I.'

Then he surged to his feet, taking her with him, reaching

37

for the towels. 'Let's take this into the bedroom. A little imagination . . . a lot of possibilities.'

Wrapped in towels and sketchily dried, they padded into the bedroom and he paused to put a match to the fire, crouching on the dusky red rug to feed the flames until they danced high, bathing him in flickering golden light. Alexia sank down beside him. 'I've never seen an open fire in a bedroom. Are you a caveman?'

He turned his head, reaching out to flick her towel open. 'Sounds impressive but actually I get free firewood.'

Then he secured the guard around the fire and reached for her again.

Alexia didn't know whether it was the heat from the flames or his hands and tongue that scorched her skin. Every touch just made her hotter, want harder, a wanting he took as his mission to fulfil until, finally, they made it onto his bed to sleep.

In the darkness, Ben ricocheted out of his dreams, heart bouncing against the walls of his chest.

He blinked, trying to force open his burning eyes. Nightmares. Again. Sucking in a breath he tried to remember what he'd been dreaming about. It had involved fear and pain. Imogen. Again. Panic. Again.

His clock's illuminated figures told him it was 04.13. Night after night it was as if his body awarded him a single cycle of sleep and then slapped him mercilessly awake.

With a shock of desire, he became conscious of the naked woman curled up against him. Still half-trapped in the web of sleep, he traced the curve of her hip, the dip of her waist until his hand found her arms nestled between their bodies. He snatched his hand away.

Not Imogen.

Reality crashed back.

Alexia. Bright, vivacious Alexia with her rounded body and naughty smile.

Right on cue, the insidious voice of negativity slunk into his mind. *So your head was turned by a mischievous smile. You think this is OK?*

Sweat broke like a stripe of shame down his back and he eased his flesh from hers, heart still thumping. He tried to remind himself that it was just another middle-of-the-night anxiety attack; the bombardment of worry, guilt, regret and pain would ease.

But the voice wouldn't leave him alone.

You've got it easy compared to Imogen and Lloyd. And now you're in bed with a naked stranger. Can you imagine Imogen's pain if she saw you now?

We're getting a divorce.

So you pick up a local girl for a one-night stand?

Alexia's leaving the village soon—

But not right away. She's going to expect things from you. Calls, texts, dates. You seriously think you can do that? YOU? The fuck-up who lives like a hermit?

The choking fingers of panic closed around his throat. The slaking of his desire had transported him briefly out of the bleak place he'd inhabited. Maybe he wouldn't feel so bad if he hadn't enjoyed it so much, but her smile had made him feel better, more worthwhile, and her enthusiasm had poured into the air like a rainbow on a grey day.

Desperate not to wake her and have to rationalise these warring emotions, he eased backwards until he could scoot out from under the covers.

Yes, go. That's how you cope, isn't it? By being alone.

Alexia stirred, muttering in her sleep. He groped his escape across the little landing and down the stairs.

In the kitchen, breathing came easier. He pulled clean clothes from the tumble dryer and fumbled into them, heart beating too loudly for him to hear whether Barney rustled in his tub. Grabbing the rechargeable torch from its holster on the kitchen wall he cast around for his boots.

Then he crept out of the front door, refusing to look at that sheet of paper headed *decree nisi* on the table by the door, lying as it had landed when he'd flung it from him this morning.

The period between nisi and absolute exists for a reason. It's for last efforts, second thoughts. For now, Imogen's still your wife.

He stumbled through the door and out of the clearing, the torchlight lighting the path unevenly, the same path he'd trodden along with Alexia a few hours ago; a woman he'd wanted. A woman who'd excited him.

For two years his libido had been sulking, but last night Alexia had unleashed it and it had flown out, fizzing and spinning.

Now, the memories of all the mornings he'd woken wrapped around Imogen's body swept in.

You've been unfaithful.

It can't count. We're nearly divorced and—

And your heart and your guts are telling you that you've been unfaithful.

Like one of the animals that wandered the night Ben trudged around the path edging the lake, where the water lapped and the breeze stirred the leaves.

The negativity always won in the dark hours.

He should have remembered that before he invited Alexia to share his night.

Chapter Three

Alexia woke slowly, languorously stretching sleep-heavy limbs. Through the windows she could see patches of blue sky hung with hurrying clouds. But it wasn't her window.

The events of last night rushed back at her.

The Angel. Ben. Coming back to his enchanting little house in the woods.

The ashes in the grate were grey and cold now but last night the fire had roared up the chimney as she and Ben enjoyed each other's bodies, the shadows dancing across his skin as he rose above her.

It had been a damned shame that neither of them had had a condom to allow them the satisfaction of the final act. Still. Hands and mouth had provided a fine substitute.

She glanced at the other side of the bed, but already she knew it would be empty from the absence of warmth stealing towards her along the sheets. She yawned, then stopped and listened. The house was quiet.

'Ben?'

No answer. She felt a little as Goldilocks might have done if there had been no bears, waking alone in a strange bed in a cottage in the woods. She rolled out of bed and wandered to the head of the stairs. 'Ben?'

Silence. Shrugging, she entered the bathroom, glancing at herself in the mirror and laughing at the way her hair was sticking up. Last night's dusty clothes lay on the floor but she stepped over them to try Ben's upmarket shower, experimenting with the buttons that controlled the jets. Enjoying the hot water, she thought of Ben's hands on her last night. Maybe he *was* a wizard. He'd certainly worked a little magic on her body. Her limbs still felt heavy and relaxed. Sated. She smiled gently at the memories as she allowed the hot water to sluice the scent of Ben from her body. Then she borrowed his towel and had little choice but to climb into yesterday's clothes, combing her hair with her fingers.

'Ben?' she called again as she ran down the stairs. It didn't take long to check the ground floor. In the kitchen she pulled out Barney's tub and crouched to peep at him. 'Where's he gone, Barney? Did he have to work today? It's Sunday. I thought most of the estate workers had weekends off.'

Barney's beak flipped open. '*Hehhhhh.*'

Rising, she gazed out of the window at the clearing and the tree trunks crowding beyond it. The silver truck she could see was presumably Ben's. Briefly, she debated hanging on to see if he returned but then decided he wouldn't be so rude as to leave her to wake up alone unless he'd gone out to work for the day. Maybe an elm had needed urgent surgery. She glanced at her phone to check for texts before remembering there had been no reason to give him her number.

'He could have left a note, eh, Barney Owl? But maybe he told me last night – parts of it are a little blurry. Never mind. He'll come back to feed you so tell him I said bye.'

'*Hehhhhh*,' remarked Barney, tilting his head.

Alexia let herself out into the brisk September morning and headed up the path to the village, hurrying to keep warm until she left the tree canopy and made it out into the sunshine.

In fifteen minutes she emerged from the bridleway and crossed Port Road, electing to traverse the playing fields to access Main Road rather than taking Cross Street, which would mean passing the village shop. 'News and Booze' for many years had been A & G Crowther but now Gwen Crowther's niece, Melanie, had taken it over and made it an off-licence. Melanie was even more beady-eyed than Gwen had been and Alexia could just imagine her throwing open the door and yelling, 'Where have you been to get your jeans dirty this early on a Sunday?' Her huge friendly smile wouldn't in the least prevent her from later sharing Alexia's reply with every customer to enter the shop.

So, crossing the village by way of the playing fields, Alexia waved at a couple of people she knew who were pushing their children on swings and spared a glance for the sad sight of the closed-down village hall.

Her trainers were damp from the grass by the time she got home. Like Ben's cottage, 44 Main Road was made of stone, but there the similarity ended. Long and low, its windows peered out from under its slated roof. Grandpop, Alexia's grandfather, had left the cottage to Alexia and her brother, Reuben – bypassing his son, Clifford, their dad, because he knew its proceeds would be swallowed by the insatiable maw that was Clifford's finances.

Alexia, who hadn't inherited the rubbish-with-money gene, had taken on a mortgage to buy Reuben out, who, living happily in Germany with his wife Hanna, had been delighted.

43

It was Alexia who'd been close to Grandpop anyway, spending hours with him in his workshop at the side of the house 'making sawdust' as he'd called it. Her workshop now, Grandpop's tools mingled happily with her sewing machine and paintbrushes, the perfect place for the projects that brought her touch to her clients' homes.

She let herself in, acknowledging wistfully that though she planned to take down all her lovely handmade Christmas ornaments early in the holiday this year, she'd be packing them along with everything else ready to move out in January. It would cause her a pang to leave number 44, even knowing Jodie and Shane would look after her little house and that Alexia could return. But Grandpop would have understood her leaving Middledip for a while to give working with Elton a try. 'Upwards and onwards,' he'd have said.

The house was silent, though it was past ten o'clock. Shane's truck wasn't outside so presumably it was still where he'd left it at The Angel last night and he and Jodie were still upstairs, oblivious.

Enjoying the peace, Alexia ran up to change her dusty clothes before embarking on weekend chores – doing laundry, humming gently to herself as she ironed, wondering, occasionally, whether Ben would get her number from Gabe.

As the hours went by with no sound from elsewhere in the house, she revised her opinion about Shane and Jodie. They must have got up and gone out before she came home, which was pretty hard-headed of them considering how drunk Jodie had looked the night before.

By the middle of the afternoon she was seated at her kitchen table, happily emailing Elton an update on The Angel.

I've allowed twelve weeks for the project from tomorrow,

but there's a time contingency built into that. IF everyone turns up when they say they will AND we hit no snags I'd like to complete the refurb in ten. I'll keep you posted . . .

A sudden noise caused her to cock an ear towards the kitchen ceiling as what sounded like Jodie's footsteps crossed between bedroom and bathroom. She must have been sleeping off her heavy night all along.

Alexia returned to her email.

. . . and also get my portfolio and website absolutely spot-on to include loads of pix of The Angel. Maybe that would be a good time to resume the conversation about involving me with your investor's portfolio of properties?

Evidently Elton was online too, because his answer pinged into her inbox in minutes.

You know I'm waiting for you with open arms, woman. Just get your crap together and give me something I can show my investor!

Alexia had typed back – *You'll have to give me till Christmas to get The Angel up and running, then, hopefully, in the New Year* – as Jodie trailed into the kitchen wrapped in a past-its-best blue-striped bathrobe. Flopping down at the table she propped her head in her hands. 'Bleurgh,' she groaned piteously. 'Have you seen Shane?'

Regarding her friend's waxy pallor with sympathy, Alexia shook her head. 'I assumed he'd be with you. He's not working at The Angel today, is he?'

Jodie gave a tiny shrug, palms dragging her cheeks down. 'Dunno. I'm dying, I feel horrible. Can you make me feel better?'

Sportingly, Alexia closed her laptop and picked up the kettle. 'I'm surprised to see you quite so hungover. I know you had several beers but—'

'I only had one beer!' Jodie protested. 'But it did go to

45

my head. Shane had some lovely lemon stuff his auntie had brought him back from Sorrento and he said it would set me right. We took it up to bed.'

Alexia's hand tightened on the tap. '*Limoncello?*' Seriously? Shane had poured liqueur down Jodie when she was already drunk? His brain must have begun to rust from spending too much time outdoors.

'Yes, that was it. I loved the limoncello,' Jodie added, fairly. 'But it didn't make me better. I started to be sick so Shane got me a bucket.'

'And cleared off?' Alexia felt anger bubble up that Shane wasn't responsible enough to stay and ensure his girlfriend was OK when he'd quite obviously encouraged her to get drunk. What kind of shitty boyfriend did that? She set a mug of coffee before Jodie. 'Don't you mind that he didn't stick around?'

Groaning, Jodie slowly collapsed until her arms pillowed her head. 'He stayed till I went to sleep. Will you make me some toast?'

Deciding today wasn't the day to demand the magic word, Alexia did so, scraping only the thinnest coat of butter across the warm surface so as not to upset Jodie's stomach. She set the plate alongside the coffee beside Jodie's head and settled back down to her work.

She'd just reread Elton's email and decided she'd been right to step up her preparations for an exciting move down south when her phone began to burble.

'*Urrghhhh*,' groaned Jodie as if the noise had given her physical pain.

Alexia read the screen and answered, 'Hi Gabe,' scrolling to the foot of the email with the hand that wasn't holding the phone. She wondered suddenly whether Ben was with Gabe. He could easily have had plans with his uncle. The thought made her feel better about waking up alone this morning.

Gabe's precise voice came loud in her ear, sounding puzzled. 'I didn't think there was any work going on today.'

Alexia clicked 'reply' on the email ready for when the call was over. 'Is Shane at The Angel? Jodie was just wondering where he was.'

Jodie lifted her head from her arms, face already shaping itself into its 'Jodie loves Shane' expression.

'No, Shane's not here. But neither's the roof.'

Alexia laughed. 'Have you looked on top of the building?'

But humour was sadly lacking from Gabe's voice. 'The front of the building's perfectly normal. But at the back? Fresh air where there used to be slates. If Shane has stripped the roof then why hasn't he put a tarpaulin over the timbers? It's already spitting with rain. We'll have the damned place down around our ears with damp.'

Slowly, Alexia's hand fell away from her laptop. Unless Gabe had been eating strange mushrooms, there was something going on. 'There's no reason for the slates to be stripped. The roof's sound.'

'That's what I thought.'

Alexia's unease grew. 'I'd better come down to the site. Be there in five minutes.'

'What's up?' Jodie managed to prop her chin on her hands as Alexia ended the call.

'Gabe says the slates have gone off the rear aspect of the building.'

Jodie eased her head back down onto the table saying, 'Can't have,' before once again closing her eyes.

After dragging on a jacket, Alexia strode along the uneven pavement to The Angel, casting about for an explanation

47

that would account for Gabe's astounding revelation. Leaving Main Road, she broke into a jog along Cross Street, passing the row of cottages known as Rotten Row before turning in to Port Road where many of the village's redbrick Victorians were grouped together as if the rest of the village wasn't quite good enough for them.

Where Shane's truck had been outside The Angel last night was now an empty space. Gabe paced up and down the drive, silver ponytail flirting with the breeze. With his usual smile absent there was more resemblance between him and Ben than Alexia had hitherto noticed.

Wordlessly, Gabe led her to the back of the building.

She didn't have to go far down the overgrown garden to see the naked roof timbers and daylight where the slates should have butted up snugly to the bricks of the gable end. 'What the hell?'

She gazed around the jungle of the garden. No sign of stacked slates. Nor were they tucked between the skips in front of the property.

Fishing out her keys she hurried towards the building. And jerked to a stop when she rounded the porch.

Gabe did exactly the same. 'Where's the *door*?'

A long snake of fear began to uncoil itself in Alexia's tummy. She ran through the gap where the door ought to have been, into the Bar Parlour and then the Public. Having checked every room downstairs with a mounting feeling of doom, she raced across the foyer and through the doorway to the stairs.

It seemed more like a mountain than a staircase but she made it up to what had once been the living quarters of the pub, darting from bedrooms to bathroom to sitting room. When she could no longer dispute the evidence of her eyes she ground to a halt. Over the pounding of her heart she could hear the slates at the front of the building shifting uneasily as the wind prodded their unprotected undersides.

The noise receded and then flooded sharply back, mixing with the sound of men's voices floating up from downstairs. She held her breath, hoping to hear Shane explaining why he was busy with unplanned work.

She did recognise the voice. But it wasn't Shane's.

On jelly legs she trudged back downstairs to find Ben standing in the foyer beside Gabe.

Absently she noted that he didn't smile. He didn't step forward to greet her or express concern about what was going on. There was no air of awareness of last night or this morning.

In fact, it seemed to Alexia that his eyes were unfocused as if he weren't quite looking at her.

That was the least of her worries right now though. She turned to Gabe. 'Everything Shane stowed upstairs is missing.' She slumped down on the bottom step. 'And everything of any value. Every original feature – doors, radiators, even the cast iron toilet cisterns. Someone's stripped the place. I presume the only reason they left the roof slates on the front was to disguise what they'd done for as long as possible.'

'Someone?' asked Ben. 'Like who?'

Alexia shook her head. 'I'll try and ring Shane.' Her voice seemed to echo in her ears.

Gabe began to speak but was interrupted by the ringing of his phone, which he answered with a 'tsk' of irritation. With fumbling fingers Alexia pulled up Shane's name in her contacts list and pressed 'call'. It went straight to voicemail. Trembling, she tried his mate Tim's number too. Same result.

'But how the hell . . . ?' she heard Gabe demand of his caller.

She paused to raise her eyebrows hopefully and mouth 'Shane?' at him. Gabe gave an abrupt shake of his head and held up a hand to indicate he needed to listen to the person on the other end of his line.

Desperately, she tried Jodie who did, at least, answer.

Alexia took a steadying breath. 'Has Shane turned up?'

'Not yet. I tried to ring him but—'

'You got his voicemail,' Alexia finished for her. 'Does he have a landline number because—'

Then she dropped her phone, ending the call hastily as Gabe made a strangled noise and reached out to steady himself against the wall. Ben got to his uncle before Alexia could even begin to move and in an instant he'd lowered Gabe down to sit on the steps beside her.

Gabe was grey, clutching his phone with a shaking hand. 'That was the bank. The money's gone.'

The room seemed to do a huge swoop around Alexia's head. She couldn't force words past the lump of fear that had jumped into her throat at Gabe's words.

'What money?' Ben crouched before his uncle, his expression granite-grim.

'The money in the community account and the business account. It's been moved out of the accounts in a series of transactions, raising a red flag with the bank.' Gabe passed a shaking hand over his face. 'It's the money the village raised and the start-up money Jodie and I put into the partnership.'

Ben swung a grey gaze on Alexia before returning his attention to his uncle, his voice hard and rapid. 'Who has access to the bank accounts?'

Gabe pressed his forehead as if forcing himself to think.

50

'For the community account Alexia, Jodie, and Christopher Carlysle and me. Jodie and I for the business account.'

'But it takes two of us to sign to get money out of the community account,' Alexia croaked.

'Not on Internet banking. We all signed that it was OK, if you remember.'

Ben's face was a mask as he studied the evidence on Gabe's phone. 'The accounts are showing nil balances. And my uncle's property has been stripped out and devalued with no means of refurbishing it.' Slowly, he raised his gaze. 'Can you shine any light on this?'

'Me?' Alexia's eyes felt ready to pop out on stalks as she gazed at Ben in fresh horror. '*Me?*'

'Well . . .' Ben hesitated at the shock in her dark eyes, conscious that his thoughts hadn't translated into quite the right words.

He'd been so angry at the grief and shock on Gabe's face, this good and genuine man who'd always been on Ben's side, that only half his thoughts had been on the current situation. The other half had been a shame-filled reflection on what Alexia must be thinking of him after his middle-of-the-night desertion. All day he'd been plagued with images of her in his arms. But they'd warred with images of Imogen until he wasn't certain where he should lay guilt and over whom he felt regret. He tried to explain. 'You have the knowledge of how much the original features are worth and where someone might sell them. You were telling me last night about your contacts.'

'Ben!' Gabe protested sharply. 'You sound as if you're accusing Alexia!'

Ben groped for better words. 'No, I was asking for insight—'

But Alexia was already climbing to her feet, turning on Ben a look of dazed repugnance, lifting a shaking hand as if to keep him at a distance. 'We'll have to come back to that discussion. I have to ring one of my *contacts* and get a tarpaulin on that roof.'

Gabe clambered to his feet too, pulling her into a comforting, avuncular hug. He looked to have aged ten years in ten minutes but at least the torpor of shock seemed to be fading. 'Are you OK to handle that? I've got to ring the police.'

Over Gabe's shoulder Ben watched Alexia close her eyes as if she couldn't bear to have to look in his direction. 'I can do it. You report what's happened.'

Then Ben ceased to exist – at least so far as Alexia was concerned, anyway. Her gaze didn't rest on him once. She moved into the Bar Parlour to make her call while Gabe remained in the foyer to make his.

Ben found himself hovering between the two, unable to contribute and with plenty of opportunity to wish his words to Alexia unsaid. He cringed at what she must think of him – the man who last night had savoured her body and today sounded as if he were accusing her of wrong-doing.

Through the doorway he watched Alexia slide down the wall as if her legs wouldn't hold her, pinching the bridge of her nose as she spoke into her phone. 'Dion, I know it's a huge favour –'

'I'm afraid I have to report some thefts –' Gabe said into his own phone from Ben's other side.

'– it's not my property but it's my project –'

'– it seems like a finely calculated scam. Much of the property was removed last night under the guise of –'

'– I'll really owe you if you can get it tarped tonight. I

hate to ask you on a Sunday evening but you can invoice me, obviously –'

'– I know what was in the bank accounts but fixing a value on the rest at this moment is difficult –'

'– and I need someone to put a temporary door on, too. Oh, would you? That would be fantastic.'

Gabe finished first. He came to stand silently with Ben while Alexia began another call.

'Jake, a project I'm on has been done over.' She hunched a shoulder as if feeling Ben's gaze on her. 'Can I list some of the stuff that's been stripped out? Then if you could let me know if any of it's offered to you . . . It's all mid-Victorian. A load of roof slates, mahogany doors and screens with etched glass, two mahogany pub bars – probably dismantled – Victorian mosaic floor tiles, black and white with a border tile . . .' She pushed herself up and began travelling from room to room, slowly listing what she could remember of what had been in them. She remembered a lot. Her voice went on and on, growing fainter as she progressed.

Gabe turned a steely gaze on Ben. 'You must apologise to her.'

Ben felt slightly sick. 'I will. I didn't mean it the way it came out.'

'Then you need to control the way things come out. She must think you're a shit.'

Gabe almost never swore. In fact, Ben couldn't remember seeing him angry before, but now his bushy brows were meeting over a sharp crease between his eyes. Like a naughty child, Ben squirmed through the only lecture, in fact the only criticism, he'd ever received from Gabe, who wound up with, 'I know you've had a bad year, Benedict, but to say I'm mortified is understating the case. Alexia's

53

not only a dear friend, she's donated all her work to this project.'

'It honestly wasn't meant to sound that way.' Ben was unable to summon a better explanation or admit that he'd had only half a night's sleep, again. 'I'm not proud of myself,' he muttered in the end, which had the virtue of being true.

Before Gabe could reply Alexia returned to the room, white and shocked but otherwise composed.

Ben lost no time in trying to put things right. 'I'm sorry if I sounded as if I was accusing you, Alexia. I was angry on Gabe's behalf and I was just trying to get information. I offer an unreserved apology.'

Alexia's gaze remained on Gabe. 'A roofer, Dion, is coming to tarp the roof and he says he'll hang a temporary door while he's here. What did the police say?'

Gabe glanced at his watch. 'They're sending someone.'

'OK. I'll stay and see them with you.'

'Alexia,' Ben tried again.

Alexia turned her back.

Ben spent the rest of the evening fermenting in a mix of shame and irritation as Alexia continued to elaborately ignore him but bestow fervent thanks on Dion when he turned up with rolls of blue plastic sheeting and the scaffold tower he needed to protect the roof from the worst of the weather.

When black-clad Police Constable Arron Harris arrived, Alexia gave a factual outline of her part in things and agreed to make a full statement at a later time, nodding along as Gabe and the police officer discussed how best to proceed with the bank. The same bank of which Gabe had once managed a branch.

'So the contractors, Shane Edmunds and Tim O'Neill,

you don't think they could have simply put in extra hours?' asked PC Harris, reviewing his notes.

Alexia shook her head. 'Not to remove items we'd agreed to store, and there's no valid reason I know of for them to strip the slate from the back of the building. Neither Shane nor Tim are answering their phones and Shane's not with my housemate, though they're in a relationship.'

PC Harris nodded, making new notes. 'Any other contact details? An address, maybe?'

Alexia felt sick. 'My friend should know. I'll ask her.'

'No rush for the moment. Let's deal with what we've got. You're clear that the money should be in the bank accounts?'

'Crystal clear.' Gabe began to detail the access arrangements on each account.

Finally, PC Harris arranged that a detective constable would ring Gabe on Monday then departed to knock on the doors of the neighbouring houses in case the occupants had seen anything useful.

'We mustn't jump to conclusions.' Gabe's face was furrowed with worry as he watched the police officer leave.

'No. But I'd feel a lot more comfortable if Shane hadn't disappeared.' Alexia paced nervously.

Gabe nodded. 'Especially as we have to accept that the money and the materials are likely to have been taken by the same person. It would take a massive coincidence for it to be otherwise. And experience in banking tells me that when money vanishes from accounts there's usually someone involved who's connected to the account holders.'

Alexia couldn't have looked much more miserable without bursting into tears. 'Do you mean you know how it happened?'

Gabe blew out his lips. 'I have a few ideas but fraudsters

have a lot of weapons in their armoury. We'll have to see what the police turn up.'

Alexia passed a shaking hand over her eyes. 'Why didn't I just stick to one of my normal contractors?'

'It's not your fault.' Gabe's gaze flicked to Ben, though he continued to address Alexia. 'Shane was Jodie's boyfriend so we took her personal recommendation. I had no misgivings about it and she's a partner in the business side.'

Alexia hugged her arms around herself. 'When Dion's finished, I've got to go home and talk to Jodie.'

'I think we ought to go together. I'll ring Christopher and advise him of the situation while we're hanging about.'

As Gabe stepped away to make his call, Ben cleared his throat. 'Alexia, please let me apologise—'

Alexia didn't even look at him as she turned and strode into the Public. If her nose had tipped any further in the air she would have given herself a crick in her neck.

Then Gabe ended his call and returned. Ben turned to him. 'She won't let me apologise.'

The older man sighed. 'She probably isn't too bothered about your feelings right now because she's facing the prospect of confronting her best friend about the boyfriend going missing at the same time as money and valuables. And when bad things happen to Jodie she can find it hard to cope.' After a pause for this to be digested he added more gently, 'You get off home, Ben. Give her time to calm down.'

Dismissed, Ben had little choice but to trail off in the direction of Woodward Cottage, zipping up his hoodie against the evening wind that had an edge on it for September, crossing Port Road and entering the quietness of the bridleway under the familiar weight of negative emotions.

But this time he knew exactly where his guilt and regret lay.

Chapter Four

Alexia's feet felt like lead weights, heavier with every step she took towards home.

Gabe seemed in no more of a hurry, scuffing gloomily through drifts of golden leaves. Alexia tried to rehearse what to say to Jodie but her thoughts kept flying back to the rage on Ben's face as he'd questioned her. Though he'd tried to back up, her anger and disappointment had refused to let her listen.

When they reached the cottage she silently unlocked the glossy blue door, finding Jodie, still in her dressing gown but looking less hungover, lying on the sofa, tucking into what she always termed her 'poorly food' – salty crackers and Pepsi. She looked up from the TV as Alexia trailed into the room, Gabe on her heels. 'So what's going on with the roof?' She was grinning, obviously ready to be told some funny story about why Gabe had phoned Alexia with news of missing roof slates.

Falling into a chair, Alexia was no nearer knowing how best to approach Jodie than when she'd left The Angel.

Thankfully, Gabe took the lead. In his deep, precise

tones he explained to Jodie what had happened at The Angel.

Slowly, Jodie sat up, belting her dressing gown more tightly, frowning. 'So someone's broken in and *stolen* the old radiators and tiles? They've taken the slates *off the roof*?'

'We can't tell if they broke in, or whether they had a key, as the door's gone.' Gabe's voice held the cautious note of someone pussyfooting about a subject.

Jodie's gaze flicked between Gabe and Alexia. 'What do Shane and Tim say? Have they seen anyone lurking around?'

Gabe fidgeted. 'We haven't been able to contact them. Have you heard from Shane?'

Jodie shook her head, but slowly, as if moving it too decisively might disturb something delicate.

Gabe glanced at Alexia but Alexia felt frozen, as if she were watching an oncoming car speeding towards them and was unable to suggest they jump out of the way.

Gabe turned back to Jodie. 'I'm afraid there's worse to come,' he said gently. And he told her about the missing money. 'I take it you have no knowledge of these transactions?'

Jodie gasped, clutching at the neck of her dressing gown as if holding herself together. 'I haven't had any reason to look at the accounts for days. How can the money have gone? Who's taken it? It's nearly £30,000 altogether. It can't be gone!' She scrabbled in her pocket for her phone and began to stab wildly at it.

Slumping more deeply in her chair, Alexia watched hopelessly, letting Jodie have her moment of denial but miserably aware that no amount of checking the bank balance was going to make the money miraculously reappear. She felt exhausted. It wasn't until Jodie lurched into a high, keening sobbing as she tried fruitlessly to ring Shane once more that Alexia dragged herself over to the sofa to slide her arm around Jodie's quaking shoulders.

'What are we going to do? How can it have happened?' Jodie wailed.

Alexia felt hot tears ooze from her own eyes. Whether they were for Jodie, Gabe or herself, she couldn't have said. But, used to Jodie's emotional reactions, Alexia patted her back while Gabe made hot drinks and fetched tissues. There was nothing to do when Jodie was locked in grief but to allow her to cry it out.

Eventually, when the storm had lessened, Gabe accessed the recent bank account transactions to show them that the money had disappeared in a series of withdrawals – cheques on Friday, when they'd all been preoccupied with preparing for the wrecking party, and the rest via Internet banking either side of midnight Saturday/Sunday.

'You can see the name of the payees!' crowed Jodie, hope dawning on her red and blotchy face. 'Look, this one's a company called Oatwood 2k Ltd. And this one's —'

But Gabe was already shaking his head. 'Don't get your hopes up. Whoever did this is clever. They'll have hidden their tracks. It will lead to a dead end.'

'But how can it?' Jodie demanded, expression bewildered. 'It's *there*, the name of the company—'

Gabe's lips thinned. 'If my experience is anything to go by the money will have been transferred out already and will have disappeared into a network of companies and individuals. The addresses of some will be rental properties and the current tenants will never have heard of Oatwood 2k or any of the others. Some will be legitimate entities, often blissfully unaware that their identities have been stolen and used to open bank accounts. Somewhere along the line the money will be drawn out in cash.' Jumping up, he started to pace around the room. 'There's a very practised hand on the tiller during this voyage of deception, let me tell you. They knew precisely which gambles were worth taking. I, for one, was kept very busy on Friday and Saturday and had no reason to check the accounts.'

'Same,' said Alexia, picturing Shane 'marshalling the troops' as he called it while they'd all helped to get ready for the wrecking party. She curled up on the sofa as Jodie tried over and again to ring Shane. Alexia might not have Gabe's banking experience but she was shrewd enough to know that whoever took the money must have had an in. 'Jodie,' she began gently. 'Do you have an address for Shane?'

Knuckles whitening around her phone, Jodie began to bluster, brown eyes furious. 'Honestly, Alexia, I can't imagine why you'd bring up such a random question now, when we've got this to worry about. He lives in Manor Road in Bettsbrough, but I've only been a couple of times and I didn't exactly note down the door number.'

Alexia glanced at Gabe. He gazed gravely back, compassion in the depths of his eyes. She tried again. 'The police want to know. Someone has taken this money. Shane isn't answering his phone so they need to find him—'

'*What*?' Jodie physically jumped away from Alexia. 'Are you accusing my boyfriend? The bank accounts have been hacked. Obviously! It happens all the time. It's random! Don't you dare—!'

Gabe interrupted, voice soft. 'But slates and doors, fireplaces and tiles . . . how could a hacker remove those?'

Jodie stared at him dumbly, horror written on her face.

Alexia swallowed painfully. 'Has Shane had access to your Internet banking app, Jodes?'

With a wail, Jodie leapt up and fled from the room.

Alexia covered her eyes. Could this day get any worse?

That night, Alexia tossed and turned long after Jodie had shut herself in her room and Gabe had gone home. Though she was exhausted, her gritty eyes refused to stay closed and her brain wouldn't sleep. It flipped from anxiety to disbelief to guilt. She was one of the people the village had trusted with the money they'd raised. And now the money was gone.

With a need to do something constructive, she sat up and switched on the light, then balanced her laptop on her legs to type an exhaustive list of what had been stripped out of The Angel. Together with the 'before' and 'during' photos she'd taken of the building, the list would go to the police, and to every reclamation yard she knew of in Cambridgeshire.

As she laboured on in the still hours, the phrase '*All the money's gone*' echoed through her mind, last heard fifteen years ago in her mother's horrified whisper. They hadn't needed the police on that occasion. The culprit had been well known to them. Alexia's dad, Cliff, had run up debts faster than Heather, Alexia's mum, could pay them off.

To prevent his credit card companies taking the family home Alexia had had to stop attending uni and let her mum use her student loan. A debt Alexia was still repaying as Heather wasn't well-off and Clifford was on to a whole new lot of debts, probably. Unless his current wife had him well in hand.

61

Her parents' marriage hadn't made it past the crisis and Alexia and Reuben had been more relieved than distraught when Clifford had moved out. They'd all suffered by being hitched to the same financial wagon as him but at least he'd accepted Heather's rejection, just at he'd later accepted Grandpop leaving his cottage to Alexia and Reuben, philosophically acknowledging his total lack of money management. It was an endless mystification to his children that he could apparently see the truth yet never mend his ways.

Alexia and Reuben heard from him mainly on birthdays and at Christmas now.

Last night had felt like a return to the old financial nightmare and as Alexia grimly tapped at her keyboard she made a series of fruitless wishes.

That Jodie had never met Shane. Jodie might have been resolute in refusing to join the dots of the money and goods disappearing at the same time as Shane and Tim, but Alexia didn't believe in that kind of coincidence.

That Alexia had never agreed to Shane and Tim being the main contractors at The Angel. But once they'd shown her their work was good enough she'd decided to give them a chance. It hadn't occurred to her to ask for evidence of their honesty.

If she had access to unlimited wishing wells, fairy godmothers and wishbones, top of her wishiest wishlist would be the wish that she hadn't spent Saturday night in Ben's bed. On his rug. In his bath.

She *so* wished that.

But he'd seemed likeable in his offbeat way – what was it he'd called himself? An oddball? – and she'd been attracted to his dishevelled good looks and slightly brooding air. The tenderness he'd exhibited with Barney had made her feel all warm and fuzzy, as had his vulner-ability over his divorce and bashful confession that he'd forgotten how the seduction game went – though he'd pretty quickly got the hang of it again.

Alexia had been a prize fool. Carefree with singledom, she'd seen no reason for caution. She'd never before indulged in a one-night stand but, hey, they were adults.

It had felt like a triumph every time she'd made him smile. He hadn't looked at her then as if he didn't know who she was. It had been a special connection! It had! Though new and exciting, they'd seemed to know each other in the private world they'd created in his cottage in the woods. It had even led her to assume there would prove to be a perfectly good reason for him leaving before she woke.

That should have been a clue to what kind of man he was, because who *did* that?

Benedict Hardaker. That was the name he'd provided to the police officer. His relationship to Gabe Piercy must be on his mother's side. Fancy him being related at all to lovely warm Gabe, familiar to everyone as he clippity-clopped through the village with his blue cart and little black pony, Snobby.

Benedict gitty shitty Hardaker, she typed into her list after *4 Victorian toilet cisterns, black*, thumping the keys so hard it made her fingertips burn. Then she went back and deleted the words with slow, deliberate taps. Gone. She wished he'd go as easily from Middledip, or at least crawl back into his lair in the woods so she never had to see him again.

It was light by the time she'd finished so she gave up on sleep, freshened up under the shower and trailed down-stairs to make a huge mug of tea.

She tried to put some hours in on her real job, the interior decorating she actually charged for and which paid the bills, but couldn't concentrate. She should be putting the finishing touches to the scheme of works for a basement kitchen-diner conversion with utility room and shower room, the old ground-floor kitchen being knocked through to the sitting room to make 'a generous living space'. She'd thought it would be the last substantial job she'd schedule before leaving the village, but now she wondered if what had happened to The Angel would put her new role with Elton back a bit.

In any event, her heart wasn't in it today. She grabbed the key to The Angel's temporary front door, which Dion had dropped off, picked up her jacket and went out.

She found The Angel dreaming under a sun that glowed through the merest suggestion of September mist and paused outside. The front view was misleadingly intact. The thieves had been smart enough to resist even the beautiful moulded brickwork between the windows so their crime wouldn't be immediately obvious. She supposed she ought to be grateful for small mercies instead of standing in the road, her heart a tonne weight. Now she was here she found it hard to go inside and confront again the indignity the gracious old building had suffered.

She reversed her route and crossed back to Main Road, ignoring her own home and taking instead the track that led to Gabe's.

Gabe was feeding his chickens and collecting eggs, a waistcoat over a shirt that used to have a collar. He took one look at her and said, 'Want to take Snobby a couple of carrots for me? He's a good listener.'

Alexia laughed. 'Do I look woebegone enough to need Snobby's listening ear?' But she took three carrots from the feed store by the back door and set off for the paddock. Snobby, black all over, his long mane blowing in his eyes, looked like the pony equivalent of an emo. Planted in the middle of the field he regarded her unmovingly until she waved his snack and he knew it was worth the trip to the gate to meet her. He arrived with his neck extended and his mouth already open.

'Life sucks,' she told him, holding a piece of carrot in her palm and feeling his velvet muzzle shiver over her skin as he hoovered it up. 'And I think it's going to get a lot suckier.' Breaking the carrots into the smallest pieces she could, she fed the thick-coated pony slowly, running her free hand down his smooth neck, letting his coarse mane slither soothingly between her fingers as she told him her woes. Snobby's ears flicked back and forth as if paying close attention. Until the carrot supply dried up, then he tossed his head out of her reach and ambled back into the middle of the field to graze.

Alexia sniffed. 'So now you've had what you want, you don't want to know me? Reminds me of someone else I know.' She stayed for a while, deriving comfort in Snobby's serenity as he tipped up one hoof to rest his leg, tail streaming in the quickening breeze.

At length she headed back, finding Gabe still in the chicken run. He passed her a rake. 'And how's Snobby?'

She surveyed what had once been grass before the chickens got at it. 'Behaving like a man.'

Gabe grunted as he scraped the chicken litter from the hen house into a bucket while Alexia raked up chicken droppings, wishing she could rake up the poo in her life and discard it as easily. Then she took the bucket out to Gabe's compost heap while he dusted disinfectant powder around the hen house and added fresh bedding.

Accepting her help unquestioningly as he moved through his morning's chores, Gabe didn't ask Alexia why she was there. It wasn't because he didn't care, she knew. Gabe just had an uncanny knack for letting people be.

It wasn't until they stopped for elevenses of homemade mint tea with Eccles cakes, consumed leaning companionably on Snobby's gate, that he enquired whether Ben had spoken to her again. Snobby rested his head on Gabe's arm because Gabe was the one person he'd come to without a bribe.

'Nope.' She sipped her steaming drink and stroked Snobby. 'Looks like his coat's thickening for winter already.'

He nodded. 'Probably it will be a hard one.' He sighed, making Snobby sigh back. 'Alexia, I'm not excusing Ben's clumsiness but he has had a dreadfully shitty thing happen to him. He pretends he's coping but I can't tell you how unBen-like it is to isolate himself in the woods.' He gave Alexia a nudge to encourage her to look at him. To read the sincerity in his brown eyes. 'All the people he loved most let him down. He's full of anger and he doesn't know how to let it out. I think I understand why he was so maladroit yesterday and then didn't seem able to retrieve the situation. It was like he was a boiler with a tiny crack. The steam that escaped was under pressure.'

Alexia put down her Eccles cake as she relived the stomach-plummeting feeling of being made to feel like a criminal by the man whose body she'd caressed. 'Are you talking about his divorce?'

Gabe hesitated. 'It's a hard thing to face, not being able to keep your wife. But there's so much more to Ben's situation than that.' He finished the final bite of Eccles cake before continuing. 'I've always had a special relationship with Ben. I see him as a bit of a kindred spirit. For most of my life I tried to conform. I let my parents influence me into joining the bank, a very stuffy institution in those days, just because I was good at maths. I tried to give my wife the kind of marriage she wanted, with dinner parties and a modern box of a house. I was thrilled when the bank gave me the opportunity to retire early but she was horrified that I wanted to get an allotment and animals. I wasn't trying to winkle her out of her precious six-bed detached in Orton. I would have carried on with all that nonsense if she'd given me a bit of understanding, but she wanted me to fritter away my days on bridge parties and coop myself up on cruises. We had the most extravagant rows about it.'

His laugh held an echo of an old relief. 'When we finally gave up on the marriage, I came here to the simple outdoor life I'd always wanted and my wife was happy with that as long as she got the lion's share of the money in the divorce settlement. Ben was the only one of my family who seemed to understand, who glowed as he explored every inch of the place, asking question after question. The rest of our family looked down their noses and said they were wearing unsuitable shoes.

'In time, it was me who supported Ben's wish to study arboriculture instead of whatever boring subject my sister Penny had earmarked for him. Because I recognised a square peg in a round hole when I saw one.'

Despite herself, Alexia was interested. She still tried not to show that her interest extended to Ben, though. 'Do you think of your wife much?'

He gave her a wink. 'I called my pony Snobby, didn't I?' With a last squeeze of her hand he rose. 'Shall we pick those beans?'

Before they could, his phone began to ring and he slid it from his pocket. As he listened, the laughter died from his face. Presently he said, 'Hold on a moment. Alexia Kennedy is with me. I'll ask her.' He took the phone from his ear. 'A detective constable from Bettsbrough Police. Would we like to go in and make our statements this afternoon?'

The sun went behind a cloud as reality made itself felt again. Alexia sighed. 'I suppose. Let's go together. Get a time and I'll pick you up, because I don't suppose the police station has a hitching rail for Snobby.'

Chapter Five

Ben remembered Alexia telling him she lived in Main Road, but not the number of the house. As he didn't particularly want to ask Gabe in case it provoked another lecture, he asked at the village shop.

'Number forty-four, blue door,' the well-upholstered lady behind the counter responded promptly. 'Caught your eye, has she?'

'Um, thanks.' Put off by such outright nosiness he hurried out before she could invade his privacy further.

When he located Number 44 he realised it stood quite close to the entrance to Gabe's track. He must have passed it dozens of times. Squaring his shoulders, he strode up the path and rapped with the black doorknocker.

The door was opened by Jodie, wearing a tatty cardigan and a half-hopeful expression. 'Oh. Hello,' they said in unison, each sounding disappointed to behold the other.

'Is Alexia here?' Ben felt on edge. Last he'd heard, Jodie's boyfriend had been proving difficult to contact just when a lot of people wanted to speak to him urgently.

Jodie shook her head.

'Right.' He tried to prompt her. 'Any idea when she might be home?'

Jodie just shook her head again.

Good manners made Ben thank her, though he wasn't sure what for. He turned and wandered up the track to Gabe's but found the house locked up.

While he decided on his next move he watched the chickens pecking peaceably, placing each clawed foot as if fussy what they trod in. Though the autumn sun fell on his shoulders there was no real warmth to it. It made him wish he'd spent some of the summer at Gabe's place instead of letting Gabe come to him while Ben did the hermit thing in the woods.

Shaking himself free of such pointless regrets he tried Gabe's phone. No answer. He strode back to the shop, where he'd left his pick-up, and drove around the corner to The Angel. He might as well do something useful.

He carried his kit around to the back of the property where the yellowing grass was up around his thighs and neglected shrubs had linked arms as if to keep humans out. His target was an old apple tree with a decided lean. The bare branches on one side and the shelf fungus on its trunk told Ben there wouldn't be a good end to its story so Gabe had agreed it had to go.

Hardhat, visor and ear defenders in place, he paced around, treading down the grass and deciding on the best place to drop the tree. Then he turned to the wall of shrubs, alternately using his saw and his hedge cutter until he'd cut a path through them. He dragged aside the resultant heap of brush to go through the chipper later.

He turned back to inspect the tree. It would be unsafe for him to get up into it to reduce the crown before felling, so, after a check of the blade and chain, he started up his chainsaw to lop what he could reach from the ground without it falling on him. Guided by his even strokes the glistening blade sliced through the wood in a fountain of chippings as the motor wailed *yeeeeOOwwwwww*. He cut up the branches as they fell, clearing the brush and stacking the timber.

Then he pulled back the grass and weeds to get a good look at the base of the trunk. He eyed the line on which he wanted the tree to fall then returned his chainsaw and ear defenders to the truck and picked up his axe.

Hefting it, he mentally marked out his target then began to chop, first a pilot cut on the side the tree would fall, then settling in to cut slightly higher on the opposite side, his swinging axe eating methodically through the trunk. Despite gloves, his palms stung and his shoulders ached, but somehow the regular blows gave him satisfaction.

He paused to shrug off his jacket and wipe the sweat from under his visor, checking that his line of fall was still good. That was when he realised he had an audience.

A woman who reminded him of Betty Boop was standing back, watching. He pulled off his hardhat and visor. 'Alexia!'

The deep blue jacket and skirt she wore with heeled shoes made her look more grown-up than the jeans and T-shirt he'd so far seen her in. And out of. She tilted her head. 'You're using an axe when you have a chainsaw in your truck because . . . ?'

He glanced back at the tree, only a few strokes away from succumbing, the cream and brown heartwood exposed. 'I wasn't prepared to wield the chainsaw on a trunk with no one around to get help if I got into trouble. Anyway, it seems fitting that such an old tree meets its end by hand.'

71

Her eyes narrowed. 'You looked like you were beating it to death.'

Face heating up, he felt as if she saw right through him. But he pushed the thought aside, wanting to make the most of their return to conversation rather than frozen silences. 'I really need you to let me properly apologise—'

'It's OK.' Her expression didn't change.

'It wasn't OK! I was incredibly crass, doing a vanishing act while you were asleep then sounding as if I was accusing you of having something to do with what's gone missing. I've hardly slept for wondering what you must have felt.' Hardly sleeping wasn't new, but he'd passed a bad night even by his standards. 'You must have *something* to say.'

She stared. Finally she nodded. 'I'm glad we didn't have condoms.' Then she turned and vanished around the corner of The Angel.

He stared after her, insulted, as he knew he was meant to be.

Turning back to the apple tree he pulled on his hardhat and visor and weighed the axe in his hands before swinging the glinting glade once more. Ten strokes and the tree creaked and whined. He stood back and watched as it seemed to fall in slow motion, landing with a thump that travelled up from the earth and into his legs.

It lay exactly where he'd planned. At least he was good at something.

Chapter Six

Alexia let herself into her house and found Jodie once again lying on the sofa, staring at the ceiling while *Family Guy* blared out from the TV.

Alexia hung her jacket on the doorknob and flopped into an armchair, scooping up the remote to switch off the TV, too heartsick and hollow to worry about niceties. 'We need to talk.'

Slowly, Jodie turned to look at her. 'I was watching that.'

Alexia declined to get involved in an argument about what constituted 'watching'. She suspected that even the most optimistic of girlfriends must by now be seeing the writing on the wall but was unsurprised Jodie was putting off reading it. She wasn't exactly one of life's copers. 'Gabe and I have been to give our statements to Detective Constable Fitzhugh at Bettsbrough police station.'

Jodie's eyes shimmered with sudden tears.

Compassion triumphing over her own grey mood, Alexia hauled herself up and went to kneel on the floor beside her friend. She softened her voice. 'Have you been able to reach Shane?'

Jodie shook her head and a tear skated from the corner of her eye.

'The police have confirmed they're looking for him, Jodes. I'm so sorry. According to a neighbour's CCTV his truck made several trips to and from The Angel between eight and ten on Sunday morning. It was fully loaded each time it left. Shane and Tim don't seem to exist, according to the police national computer, so DC Fitzhugh wants you to see him to provide what details you can. Give him pictures of Shane from your phone, and his truck's registration number.'

More tears followed the first, plunging down Jodie's cheeks. 'I don't remember his number plate.' Her mouth stretched around a sob. 'Shane's *my boyfriend*. I've been with him for months, he almost lived here—'

'About that.' Alexia clasped her aching forehead. 'You know some of the money in the community account was cleared by cheques paid into a few different accounts?'

Jodie gave the tiniest of nods.

Alexia stroked her friend's arm through her dressing gown. 'Gabe and I have an appointment with the bank tomorrow and we're hoping you'll come.' She cleared her throat miserably. 'The thing is . . . the cheque numbers relate to the cheque book we keep here so a likely scenario is that . . .' About to say *as he got so close to you* she looked at the misery and pain on her friend's face and changed it to, 'as we let him pretty much run tame here, he had access to it.'

Slowly Jodie's face crumpled. 'How *could* he?'

Although she knew Jodie was beseeching her to explain how Shane could treat Jodie that way, Alexia shied away from any discussion that might lead to the conclusion that Jodie had been a mug. 'The DC said it's possible Shane's a confidence trickster. Obviously time's been invested in pulling together his plan and it probably won't be the first time he's done it. By sharing space with you he got access to your laptop, your security gadget from the bank and the cheque book.'

With a howl, Jodie lost what was left of her composure. 'All the cheque books. My private bank accounts are empty too-oo-oo!'

Shock swept through Alexia. 'Oh, *no*! Oh, Jodes. For some reason that hadn't occurred to me. Have you called the police?'

'Noooo-oo-oo,' Jodie bawled, flinging her arms around Alexia and burying her head against her shoulder.

'Then tell DC Fitzhugh when you go and see him. And you'll have to notify the bank.' She slipped her arms around Jodie's quaking body. 'Do you want me to come with you?'

'Yes plea-ea-ease!'

It was some time before Jodie stopped howling. Alexia hugged and patted her and passed her tissues, stunned by the cruelty of her friend's humiliation. Ben's disappointing behaviour paled into insignificance when compared with the cynical way Shane had used Jodie.

'Th-thank you for not being cross,' Jodie hiccupped eventually.

'Of course I'm not cross. You're the sister I never had, remember?' Alexia referenced the phrase they'd used as teenagers. Jodie, older by two years, had always been ready with teenage wisdom at important moments, such as Alexia's 'first time'. *At the end the boy goes 'ruuuhhhhh' and falls on you but he'll be OK after a minute.*

In their twenties it had been Alexia who'd blossomed, following her star despite not being able to complete university, determined not to stagger from one financial crisis to another like her dad, nor to rely on a man, like her mum. Jodie, less driven, had been content with working in cosy coffee shops popular with customers who liked a chat as well as a well-risen scone.

Alexia had been surprised when Jodie agreed to join with Gabe to run The Angel Community Café. Responsibility didn't feature large in her comfort zone – in fact it was a prime cause of anxiety for her – but probably Gabe, with his innate good sense and decades of financial experience, had made it seem nice and safe.

Now everything had gone wrong. Alexia and Gabe were struggling for a grip on the nightmare of being the victims of crime. Jodie had gone to pieces. Christopher Carlysle, who'd only ever lent his good name to The Community Café fundraising account, was making it plain he had not expected to be dragged into the fallout from theft by deception.

And how the hell was this whole ugly mess to be explained to the villagers? So many had joined in the fundraising—

Jodie thumped the sofa cushion, jolting Alexia out of her unhappy reverie. 'You're supposed to be the business-woman, Alexia!'

Alexia, her legs aching from crouching for so long, wobbled dangerously. She'd thought herself inured to Jodie's lightning changes of mood but this one caught her by surprise. '*What?*'

Jodie's face was blotched red but her mouth was set in a stubborn line. 'You obviously didn't check Shane out, did you?'

Alexia hauled herself to her feet, rubbing her knees to bring the circulation back. 'One of the ways I check contractors out is to go on personal recommendation from someone I trust! In this case, the person I trust would be *you*. FYI, you're also the reason he's half-lived here, eating us out of house and home while, it turns out, he poked his nasty nose into our private things, stole anything he could get his shitty hands on including a lot of money we were responsible for, and left us to face the music.'

Though understanding it was fear that made Jodie snap and snarl like an injured animal, the attack left Alexia feeling sick and trembly. 'I'm going to have a few drinks at The Three Fishes. Coming?' The invitation was tacked-on with little enthusiasm.

'I just want to stay here.' Jodie turned her face into the cushions.

Alexia gazed at her, shoulders quivering under a mantle of unbrushed hair. 'Do you want to phone DC Fitzhugh before I go?'

Jodie's voice came out muffled. 'No.'

Trying to persuade Jodie in this mood was like trying to cajole a timid dog out from under a bed – it was best for everyone to wait until she felt safe. Alexia shrugged wearily back into her jacket and let herself out of the front door. Her days didn't usually involve being in the pub at six o'clock, but sod it. Her days didn't usually involve fraud, theft, betrayal and a horrible throb of panic beneath her breastbone, either.

It was only a five-minute walk to The Three Fishes but it was chilly enough that Alexia was glad to push open the door into the pub's bright warmth and make for a stool at the bar. Janice the barmaid appeared from the back regions as Alexia propped her elbows wearily on the polished wood. 'A very big glass of Sauvignon blanc, please.'

Janice reached for a glass. 'Your wrecking party took

all our trade on Saturday night, by the way, so you're on Tubb's shit list.'

'Unfortunately, the landlord being cranky doesn't even make the top ten of "Alexia's things to worry about" right now.'

Janice laughed as she placed the frosty glass in front of Alexia along with a tumbler of ice, not needing to be reminded that Alexia liked to pop ice into her wine no matter how well chilled it was already.

Alexia took a big gulp of wine to fortify herself before reaching for her phone. She hadn't wanted to rub salt into wounds by checking her private accounts in front of Jodie but she was almost shaking with trepidation as she opened her banking app . . .

Phew. She took another big gulp of wine in relief. Both personal and business accounts were intact. Though he might have been able to find her Internet banking security device in her drawer, Shitty Shane hadn't had the opportunity to look over her shoulder and catch her passwords as he probably had Jodie's.

Grateful for small mercies but feeling decidedly un-chatty, she kept her eyes trained on her phone screen as she worked her way steadily down both her wine glass and her email inbox.

An enquiry about a small decorating job: lounge with garden room opening out. Two newsletters, which she deleted unread. Offer of £5 off if she took a train to London before the end of October. And an enthusiastic email from Elton about a property they were completing on in Wimbledon, *The sort of thing you could so go to town on, rejigging the space for best effect and greatest profit.*

The thought that she'd yet to tell Elton how spectacularly pear-shaped her project had gone made her feel queasy. Unless, she thought, regarding her now empty glass, that was due to pouring one-third of a bottle of wine into a stomach that had scarcely seen food today. She caught Janice's eye and ordered cottage pie. And another glass of wine.

While she waited, she googled Shane Edmunds and Timothy O'Neill. If the police national computer hadn't thrown anything up then her Internet search wasn't likely to, but she had to try *something*. Predictably, all she dug up was their social media accounts, presumably as phoney as they were, and social media accounts of different Shane Edmundses and Timothy O'Neills.

Her dinner arrived and she felt better for eating it. She was just deliberating between another glass of wine or a more sensible cup of coffee when a man she didn't know strode into the pub and came to stand just around the corner of the bar. Tubb had replaced Janice as server and he ambled over to hover expectantly.

'I'm hoping you can help me,' the man began loudly. 'I'm looking for someone called Benedict Hardaker. Ben.'

Alexia gave him a second look. The man had thin sandy hair and a forehead that looked as if it saw a lot of frowns.

Tubb shrugged. 'Sorry, mate. Don't think I know him.'

The man's frown dug deeper furrows. 'He might be staying with his uncle. Gabe Piercy.'

Tubb gave his odd smile, the corners of his mouth turning down instead of up. 'I know Gabe. Not been in here tonight, though.'

'He's not at home either. Neither he nor Ben seem to have been answering their phones lately.'

Tubb looked sympathetic. 'Bad signal round here sometimes.'

'Right.' The man's cheeks were mottled red. 'Perhaps if

you do see Gabe you could give him a message to pass on to Ben? It's very important that Ben sees his brother. Tell him Imogen really needs his help, too. Oh, and we'd actually appreciate knowing that Ben's OK.'

Tubb began to move off to serve a customer. 'If I see Gabe I'll try and remember the gist.' He didn't look as if he'd try very hard. Probably the man ought to have at least bought a drink before demanding favours.

Alexia pinned her gaze to her phone screen. Should she speak up and say that Ben was fine – if you didn't count being moody and changeable? But Ben might be hiding out in the woods for a reason.

On the other hand . . . the messages had sounded as if they could be important.

The 'buts' continued to circulate in her mind while the man drummed his fingers on the counter then turned and left.

Tubb paused in front of Alexia on his way to the till. 'Have you seen Gabe today?'

She nodded. 'Think he was going out this evening.' He'd been going to see Christopher – they'd taken one awkward interview each: him Christopher, her Jodie – so maybe he was still there.

'Gabe's nephew is the wizard in the woods, isn't he?'

Alexia nodded, unsurprised. Tubb knew a great deal about the village and everyone in it.

Tubb grunted and went to the till, frowning. Alexia had known Tubb since she was a child being brought into the beer garden for lemonade and crisps on a summer's afternoon. Despite his often dour façade he had a code so far as his pub was concerned. It was the village's oasis and people deserved to be able to relax there unhounded. Ben was a prospective customer by virtue of having chosen to live in Middledip, even if on its very edges, whereas the man asking after him was an outsider.

In following the possible workings of his mind, Alexia found herself making a decision. 'I'll make sure the nephew gets the message. I can ring Gabe.'

'Thanks.' Frown disappearing now that someone else was taking responsibility, Tubb moved on to another customer without even making the anticipated complaint about the Middledip Wrecking Party taking all his business last Saturday.

Alexia fished out her phone and dialled Gabe's number, but the call went straight to voicemail. She sighed.

What now? Nobody would blame her for filing this under 'not my business' and simply passing the messages to Gabe tomorrow, but something about that solution didn't sit well. She had a strong feeling Ben should be warned about the man looking for him. Maybe it was because the man had sounded closely connected with the family and Alexia remembered what Gabe had said about everyone who Ben loved letting him down.

Also . . . her conscience kept nudging her that her remark about the condom had been malicious and, from Ben's expression, hurtful.

They were both aware that when she realised neither of them had a condom, she'd been so frustrated she could have screamed. Actually, she had screamed, just a tiny bit, and he'd laughed and applied himself to relieving her frustrations in ways for which no condom was required.

She glanced behind her to the window. Twilight. She sighed and gave up on the idea of coffee.

*

81

If Ben was surprised to hear a knock on his door in the middle of the evening he was downright astounded to open it and find his caller to be Alexia Kennedy.

'What an unexpected pleasure.' He was aware of sounding sarcastic but this afternoon's interchange had stung.

'I came to tell you something.'

He looked past her into the darkness. He hadn't heard the approach of a car. 'Don't tell me you've walked here.'

'OK. But I've had two large glasses of wine so I didn't drive.'

It was hard not to notice how she hugged her thin jacket around herself. He took a tentative step back. 'Do you want to come in to tell me?'

Equally as tentatively, she stepped inside.

As she seated herself in one of the armchairs he shook from his mind the image of the laughing, eyes-dancing Alexia lounging on the floor on Saturday evening, back propped against the same chair as she drank whisky. And, later, naked and glistening Alexia exploring his body with inquisitive hands.

Glad he'd already lit the fire in view of the way she extended her hands to it, he took the other chair. 'What's up?'

She wasted no time on small talk. 'A man was looking for you at the pub. He said it's important that your brother sees you, that Imogen needs your help, and that "we", whoever that is, would like to know you're all right. I decided that some of those messages might be important and as I don't have your phone number I came over.'

'Thank you for going to the trouble.' Part of him wanted to consider why she had. Her collar, he noticed, bore small white polka dots, an unexpectedly frivolous detail of the same otherwise no-nonsense outfit he'd seen her in earlier.

She narrowed her eyes as if trying to measure his muted reaction. 'The man was in his sixties with thin sandy hair—'

'I know who he was.' He rested his head on the chair back, knowing he had to prioritise. 'It is possible that one of those messages might be important.' Not the one about his brother, Lloyd – or, at least, he doubted it would prove to be anything new.

But Imogen . . .

'Would you mind hanging on while I make a quick call?' Without waiting for an answer he jumped up and made for the kitchen. There, he opened his contacts list and tapped on *Imogen*.

She answered after two rings, voice breathy with surprise. 'Ben?' She sounded so familiar that for an instant he felt as if the past had slipped into the present, as if he might be calling to say he could get home on Friday so they could go out to dinner. He could almost hear the reply she would have made: *Or we could stay home, just the two of us . . . and then you never know what you'll get on the table*, her slight Berkshire burr caressing the words 'could' and 'never'. He'd have laughed and lowered his voice to suggest . . .

He snapped his mind back to here and now. 'Yes, it's me. Are you OK?' It made something in his chest feel odd to voice the commonplace, caring question he'd asked a thousand times.

'Yes. Well, so far as . . . you know.'

'Yes, I know,' he answered awkwardly, compassionately, hearing what she wasn't saying.

'Why are you calling?' Was that a thread of happy anticipation in her voice?

Guiltily hoping it wasn't, he kept his voice steady as he

explained. 'I think it's just Dad being Dad, but I got a message and wanted to check you weren't in any trouble.'

'I won't ask what's going on between you and your dad this time, but thank you.' A pause. 'Did you get your . . . you know, the divorce . . .?'

'The *nisi*? Yes.' He cleared his throat. 'Obviously you did?'

'Yes.' Another pause. What was she waiting for him to fill the silence with? *Had* it been hope he'd detected in her voice? If so, when she spoke again she'd smoothed it carefully away. 'It seems odd to discuss it so casually. But I suppose it's good that we're not at each other's throats.'

'Yes.' They never had been at each other's throats. Cold anger on Ben's part and bitter remorse on Imogen's had been how they'd seen off their marriage. Maybe he'd have felt better for a few screaming matches. 'Well, sorry to disturb your evening. I just wanted to . . .'

'I'm touched you did, but I'm fine. And you—'

'I'm fine, too.' He didn't want to prolong the call. Before he slid his phone back into his pocket, however, he sent his parents a one-line text assuring them that they needn't worry about him.

Then, gingerly, he examined the state of his heart. The usual swirl of grief and guilt about Imogen had been absent as they talked. Not long ago the call would have been enough to plummet him into a black mood.

As if movement would keep the darkness at bay, he crossed to the door to the sitting room and gave it a tiny push. He could see Alexia sitting where he'd left her, fidgeting and casting glances at the front door as if considering using it. He pushed the kitchen door properly open and cleared his throat. 'Want to feed Barney?'

She turned, an uncertain smile following a moment of surprise. 'OK.'

She joined him in the kitchen and while he dealt with the necessities of preparing supper for a baby bird of prey she gently slid Barney's tub into the centre of the floor. Out of the corner of his eye Ben watched her crouching alongside the downy little bird, chuckling at his loud, wide-beaked *hehhhhhhh*s and his half-hops, half-flops around his tub. 'Hello, fluffball.'

'*Hehhhhhh*,' replied Barney.

Once the meal was prepared Ben joined them, settling himself on the floor so that Barney's tub was between him and Alexia. He offered her the tongs.

Her big brown eyes flipped up to gaze at him. 'What do I do?'

'Get a piece of meat and offer it to him. Touch it to his beak. He'll do the rest.'

'*Hehhhhh*,' rasped Barney encouragingly.

Gingerly Alexia used the tongs to select a morsel of chicken and approached the business end of Barney.

'*Hehhhhh*-nom-nom-nom.' Barney did his bobblehead thing as if to shake the food down inside him. '*Hehhhhhhh*.'

Alexia laughed. 'The rest's coming don't worry.'

'*Hehhhhh*-nom-nom-nom.'

Ben looked on, holding an old plastic plate that had become Barney's dinner service as each morsel travelled from it to the young owl's ever-open maw. Alexia's attention was all on Barney, eyes smiling as she gravely exhorted him to mind his manners. 'You'll be putting your elbows on the table next.'

Eventually, she lifted up empty hands to show the little owl. 'It's all gone.'

'*Hehhhhhhh*.' Barney cocked his head sceptically.

She showed him up her sleeves. 'Look, empty.'

Discarding the plate on the floor and pulling out a clean

bedding towel, Ben slid careful hands into the tub and scooped Barney up, offering him to Alexia, who shook the covering out across her lap and made a baby owl sized hollow in it.

While she continued to chat to Barney, Ben donned disposable gloves to clean out the tub then returned to sitting on the chilly floor, reluctant to suggest moving to a more comfortable spot in case Alexia took it as an opportunity to leave. Although he shied away from actually acknowledging that part of the reason he'd wanted to check on Imogen was to leave him free to talk to Alexia, he was aware of some level of contentment watching her with Barney. He didn't want a polluted atmosphere to continue between them.

They'd shared a bed and it was completely his fault that it had gone so badly wrong. Until the trouble with Imogen, Ben had considered himself a decent bloke who knew how to treat women. For his own sake, if no one else's, he wanted to rediscover that person.

He drew in a breath. 'Sorry to leave you to your own devices just now but I needed to make that call. The man who was looking for me was my dad.'

She flicked him a glance under her thick dark lashes. Then she returned her attention to Barney, still exploring her lap and noisily declaring, '*Hehhhhhhh*'.

Ben ploughed on before he could change his mind. 'Imogen's my wife. Ex-wife when our divorce becomes final in a few weeks. She's fine. Dad's obviously trying to flush me out.' He paused to marshal his thoughts. 'My parents know how close I am to Gabe so I suppose Dad guessed I might not be too far away from Middledip. Annoying that he's right.'

Alexia raised her eyes to look at him properly, though

86

her arms still formed a pen for Barney. 'They don't know where you're living? They must be worried about you.'

He extended a finger to stroke Barney's delicate foot. 'I have a difficult relationship with my parents and it's particularly troubled at the moment. My brother, Lloyd, he's their golden boy and when he screwed up they sort of blamed me.'

'*Hehhhhhhh,*' added Barney, looking wise.

The expression in Alexia's eyes melted into one of compassion. 'Was it your fault?'

'I can't see how.' Ben, to his surprise, found himself feeling better for bringing even a small part of the story out. It was a bit like being horribly nauseous but feeling relieved when you could actually throw up. 'There was an accident. Lloyd was driving. He was drunk. Imogen was his passenger. She'd been drinking too.'

'Oh, no,' Alexia breathed.

He nodded jerkily. 'There was no reason for them to be together in the early hours of the morning. Lloyd – well, he's single and he can be with anyone he likes in the middle of the night. *Except my wife.*'

'Do you mean they . . .?' Her eyes darkened with dismay.

'Imogen denies it. Lloyd's been strangely silent on the subject.' He coughed. 'Sorry. I don't usually unburden myself like this. I started out meaning to give you background on why I acted the way I did on Sunday after . . . well, Saturday.'

'I suppose it explains some of your moodiness.'

He flinched, but he understood why she felt able to be that direct. Copping the fallout from a situation in which one felt blameless did tend to make for carelessness with the feelings of others.

As he watched, Barney began to cuddle bonelessly into

the crook of Alexia's arm, his eyes slowly closing. Ben could remember slipping into sleep with the same arms across his naked chest. 'Imogen and I, we agreed the only option was to end things, but I didn't cope well. At *all*. Had to be pulled off Lloyd. Refused to forgive Imogen. Her family was completely on her side, which I admire, but we lived in a small town so battle lines were drawn.'

Gently, Alexia lifted Barney and the towel off her lap and back into the tub, returning it to the dim recess under the worktop where he could sleep off his dinner. Then she shuffled herself a few inches closer to Ben. 'Didn't her family acknowledge that you were the innocent party?'

His swallowed. The sympathy in her big brown eyes almost undid him. 'Imogen was disfigured in the crash. Her left arm's massively scarred and damaged. She won't regain full use of it. She has some scarring on her jaw and neck, too. Her family say that I only wanted her when she was fit and beautiful. Their family name is Goodbody so they said stuff like "No use for a Goodbody now she hasn't got a good body, eh?"'

She looked appalled. 'They don't consider the – the other circumstance?'

'That she was involved with my brother? Not so much.'

'Wow.' She frowned, chin on fist. 'But if your brother wants to see you, can't he come looking for you himself?'

'Not really.' He had to force the final words past a sudden obstruction in his throat. 'Lloyd's in Spring Hill open prison. The poor blameless lady in the car his vehicle ploughed into died. He does get short visits to the outside on Release on Temporary Licence, now his sentence is well underway, and so long as he keeps his nose clean. Although as one of the purposes of a "ROTL" can be to maintain family ties he has to submit a plan for where he'll be and who with. I won't co-operate with any plan that involves me. I don't think there's anything new to say.'

'You don't visit him?'

'I don't want to see him while he's in there.'

Silence. Then her hand crept onto his leg. Warm. Comforting. Non-sexual. 'So there's some positive feeling between you.'

He stared at her hand, small and delicate against the coarse denim of his jeans. 'There's feeling all right, but you're only assuming that it's positive. I can't analyse it. What if subconsciously I want to gloat?'

'*Seriously?* You'd do that?' She sounded shocked but she didn't move her hand.

'I don't think so,' he admitted, 'but I'm frightened just at the possibility and what that would make me.'

'He might want to apologise and explain.'

'He had time to do that while he was awaiting trial. What I got was silence.' He sighed. 'Sometimes I fester with resentment.'

'I can imagine. You have a lot to deal with.'

He gave that half-laugh that came out all choked and didn't sound like him. 'I'm still trying to get to the bit where I explain why I was . . . as I was with you. The other night – that was the nearest thing to normal I'd felt since the accident, even though I'd gone to your wrecking party angry because I'd received my *decree nisi* that morning.' He held up a hand as she opened her mouth as if to interrupt. 'Yes, it was me who had instigated divorce proceedings so it might not seem reasonable that it affected me. But you have to remember that until the night of the accident I thought I was a happily married man.

'Then you blew in, all smiles and enthusiasm, involving

me, being nice and uncomplicated and fun. I was drawn to that. To you.'

He went on, gaining confidence from her air of concentration. 'I was desperate to feel normal again, to remember what fun was. I rationalised that my marriage was over all bar one last piece of paper. You and I were both up for an encounter. If you were having liberation sex and I was having angry sex I didn't see it as an obstacle – although, looking back it would have been better if I hadn't kept you in the dark about the anger.'

Her brows flipped up to her hairline. 'You weren't angry.'

'I was raging. Just not with you.'

'If you were angry with Imogen, I'd call that revenge sex, not angry sex.'

It actually made him smile that she'd make him pause in the middle of his confession to argue semantics. 'It wasn't revenge for what Imogen did with Lloyd. It was more self-orientated than that. I was trying to lose myself. In you. Blot out everything that was making me furious and bitter.'

Her mouth made a silent 'O'.

He shifted, trying to find a position on the quarry tiles that didn't make his legs cold and numb. 'It worked. Until I woke up in the middle of the night and felt horrible. It was like my own mind had turned against me. All the anger had turned to guilt, I felt that I'd been unfaithful to Imogen and hadn't been honest with you. The guilt and anxiety and everything . . . I was in a cold sweat. I felt compelled to get away from what I'd done. So I left you alone here. I'm sorry.'

'Are we talking about a panic attack?'

'Probably,' he admitted, hoarsely. 'I feel as if I'm making wimpy excuses—'

'Anxiety's a powerful thing. I've seen it all with Jodie

because she suffers from anxiety. It takes her over. She withdraws and doesn't seem to have the capacity to care about things she ought to care about. She might go into retreat from a situation or lash out blindly – you can't anticipate which it'll be because her emotions are chaotic. I can understand how it would happen to you in the circumstances. It wasn't fun for me but I can see it.'

'I'm sorry,' he repeated. Her let his hand touch hers. 'The anger came back – but at myself. It consumed me. When the thefts were discovered at The Angel I turned it on whatever shitty bastard has done this to Gabe and I didn't think what I was saying. I didn't mean to sound as if I were accusing you.'

'I'm glad you explained,' she said softly.

'I'm glad I got this opportunity. I'm not trying to excuse myself. I just want you to know why, when you were so great, I responded like a creep.'

'You've been let down. That's hard to deal with.' She unfolded her legs and shifted around to lean on a cabinet door beside him. 'Thank you for telling me. I think it was hard for you.'

He was aware that her hand was no longer resting on his leg but somehow her proximity eased some of the tension from his shoulders. Maybe he felt forgiven. 'I should be thanking you for letting me spill my guts.'

'That's something that can make any of us feel better.' She hesitated. 'You know, there's this theory . . . I don't know if it's just psychobabble but it makes sense to me. Women have affairs with the brother of their spouse because they get whatever attracted them to the spouse in the first place but without the day-to-day worries or gripes the spouse brings along.'

'That's offensive.'

'I don't suppose it's meant to be a compliment. More of an explanation.'

He managed a weak grin. 'I meant offensive to suggest Lloyd and I are alike. He's a smooth, hotshot lawyer who loves to party and who's never been in a relationship for more than six months.'

Her face cleared as she got that he was joking. 'And you're a wizard who lives in the woods caring for a baby owl. You're right, you don't sound much alike.'

As joining in a joke definitely counted as an improvement in the temperature between them, and as she'd been generous in letting him get everything he needed to off his chest, he turned the conversation. 'How are things with you? Gabe's been keeping me abreast of developments so I know there's no good news.'

She stretched and yawned, then clambered stiffly to her feet. 'It just gets worse. Jodie's just admitted that Shane cleared her personal accounts too. I need to get home.'

He rose too, wincing as the blood returned to his legs in a storm of pins and needles. 'Let me drive you. Not because I think you can't walk home in the dark on your own,' he added, remembering her objections to Sebastian, 'but because you look cold after sitting around on the kitchen floor and it's late. You'll only get colder.'

When she looked undecided he added, 'You have to let me because it's evidence that I'm trying to be a better person.'

Her eyes sparkled for a moment as they had the night of the wrecking party. 'Oh, OK then, if I'm helping you along the path to redemption.'

When he'd driven her into the village and watched her hop out of his truck outside her cottage with its old stone wall and her car parked outside, Ben drove back to Woodward and slept all night for the first time in months.

Chapter Seven

October blew in like a dragon, which meant Alexia had to keep running to The Angel to check the tarpaulin was still nailed to the old roof timbers.

She attended to her day job despondently. Her major project was a townhouse refurb in Bettsbrough where walls were coming down to make the loo and bathroom into one space and the kitchen, utility room and dining room another. It was all systems go because she'd scheduled various tradesmen for the three-week period when she could promise the clients would stay with family, out of the way. She reminded the client how much dust and inconvenience there would be, just to make sure.

At the same time – or on the same loan – the clients had ordered new windows and chose the last minute as the perfect time to go into mourning for the original stained glass. Alexia dashed to the site to take photographs and rubbings to enable a specialist glazier to make up replica double-glazed units. Just as she was ready to leave for the glazier's workshop she received a text.

Gabe: Everybody who needed to give police statements

or provide consent to close old accounts and open new ones has done so. Some of the dust could be considered settled.

Gabe had taken the lead in dealing with the bank's fraud department, grumbling that it had to be by telephone to some remote location instead of in their local branch with an actual person. With a bit of 'not like in my day' harrumphing he was spending hours jumping through the tedious and frustrating hoops that needed to be jumped through for both bank and police, and marshalling Alexia, Jodie and Christopher Carlysle as necessary.

Alexia closed the door of the client's sitting room against the noise of a disc cutter from the bowels of the house and rang him. 'There's a lot more than dust to be settled – the police haven't found Shane and Tim!'

Gabe's short laugh echoed in her ear. 'I think they know we've seen the last of the slick little weasels.'

Alexia rubbed her forehead. A band of pain above her eyes tightened with every bang and clang from the kitchen. 'So the police don't think they'll be able to pin them down?'

'They haven't been able to discover a thing. When I question whether they can do more I'm told, "It's a matter of resources". I'd like to pin down Shane and Tim – or whatever their real names are – with their own nail guns.'

'So –' Alexia heard her voice shake '– we *are* going to have to go public about the money.' Word had got around about The Angel being stripped out – the police doing their door-to-door thing had made sure of that – but Gabe had suggested silence regarding the money until the police and the bank had had a chance to consider the situation and give their views. He'd said it would be easier to face the inevitable and understandable questions if they had at least *some* idea of the answers.

He sighed. 'But you know that. Tubb's agreed we can call a village meeting in the pub for Saturday.'

'Yes. But I was hoping we'd get the money back first . . .'

Alexia rang off with a feeling of doom. Perhaps she'd read too much crime fiction but somehow she'd expected the police to catch the miscreants and restore all they'd stolen. She hadn't let herself consider the consequences should they refused to be caught, but now, as she let herself out of the noisy house and into the comparative quiet of her car, she had to face the fact that there was a nasty mess to clear up and she and Gabe were the ones left holding the mops and buckets.

Christopher Carlysle couldn't wait to disassociate himself from The Angel and all who sank in her. Benign landowner lending his estate for fundraising events had been his chosen role. Hapless victim held no attraction.

Jodie, after taking several days off to cope with the misery of Shane's perfidy, had returned to her job in a Bettsbrough coffee shop and had to be coaxed and cajoled into doing her part in providing what the police and the bank needed. Having to admit that Shane had emptied her personal accounts had made her more silent and withdrawn than ever.

Alexia drove to the glazier and then home through pelting rain, realising she could no longer ignore Elton's *How's it going? Let's make plans* emails.

The police were not going to pull off a miracle.

The village meeting in two days' time would have to go ahead. If Alexia had ever considered running away, now was the time, before that meeting, but she knew she'd never leave Gabe to face it alone. At least it should make up for any business the wrecking party might have cost

The Three Fishes as a lot of stiff drinks would be required when the news broke.

Alexia didn't know if or when she'd be in a position to add a dazzling altruistic touch to her portfolio via The Angel. Her heady vision of restoring The Angel to its former glory, all glittering glass, glowing wood and flowing lines, was under a giant black cloud. With a heavy heart she let herself through her front door, shucked off the red raincoat that usually made her feel cheery and, taking a deep breath, picked up her phone to call Elton.

He answered instantly. 'About time, too! What's going on with you? I absolutely stole a Streatham property at the auction today. It's a small block of studio flats with shower rooms but they have their own *balconies*, Alexia . . . in *Streatham*! I'm my investor's golden boy today because young professionals will lap them up.'

'If the ceilings are high you might be able to put in mezzanine sleeping platforms to maximise the space,' Alexia suggested automatically, before remembering she hadn't called for a creative ideas storm. She sighed. 'Actually, I'm calling with bad news.'

Instantly, Elton sobered. 'What's that?'

He became progressively quieter as Alexia explained.

'So that's about it,' she wound down eventually. 'We've worked through the aftermath with the police and the bank, which has got us precisely nowhere, so I can't give you an idea of when or how I'm going to get the project underway. We're still reeling from the shock.'

If she'd harboured any glimmer of hope that Elton would react with, 'Oh, no! You poor guys. Don't worry Alexia, make your portfolio as fantastic as you can and include The Angel as "work in progress" and I'll present it to my investor now,' she was destined for disappointment.

First came a pregnant silence. Then Elton swore viciously. 'How the hell did you let this happen? I can't present you to my investor applauding your outstanding project-management skills when you've just let a builder do you up like a kipper!'

Alexia's leaden heart sank towards her boots. 'But—'

Elton snapped, 'Don't ask whether we really have to tell her. Because yes, we sodding do. Otherwise I'd be putting my nuts on the chopping block. She expects scrupulous honesty.'

Instantly, Alexia felt her hackles rise. He was making it sound as if she'd been found out doing something awful and was looking to Elton to lie for her. 'And you couldn't just tell her *honestly* what's happened and get her views on whether she wants to see my portfolio anyway?'

A pause. 'She also expects me to act professionally.'

Alexia swallowed. 'I see.' A wave of anger almost stole her voice. 'Disappointing.'

'Not kidding. I thought I'd have you on board by New Year. We could all have made a lot of money, you know. If things had gone to plan.'

'Being mistaken over someone's support is unpleasant,' Alexia said, through her teeth. She waited for Elton to get the irony and realise he ought to say something sympathetic or even apologetic. When all she got was further griping about Elton's plans being ruined, she cut across him. 'You're going to be busy finding someone to take my place in the team so I won't waste any more of your time.' She ended the call, sick with disappointment and disillusion.

She sank her face in her hands and wallowed in self-pity. The worst had happened. No new job. No new home. No exciting regeneration projects or healthy bank balance. It hadn't been a black cloud threatening her project, more a swinging axe – wielded by about the only fellow-student who'd bothered to keep in touch with her after her short-lived time at uni. The one she'd thought was her friend.

By the time Saturday crawled around, Alexia was feeling very alone.

To start with, Jodie made it clear that facing the village meeting was not on her agenda. 'I just can't, I'm sorry.' Alexia stood at the window and watched her buzz off up Main Road in her little white Fiat knowing that Jodie feared bleeding from the cuts of a hundred accusing gazes because of her involvement with Shane. Though her only crime was to have been taken in by a conman, Jodie wasn't good at bearing anguish.

Christopher Carlysle hadn't even bothered replying to Gabe's notification of the meeting.

So that left Alexia and Gabe.

And, to her surprise, Ben, who arrived with Gabe at ten to seven. Alexia had barely seen him since the night his confidences had built a shaky bridge over the breech between them, but managed a wavering smile as she fumbled to do up her coat. 'Let's get this over with.'

Gabe gave her a bracing hug. 'They can only hang us once.'

The chill inside Alexia matched the bite in the October air as the three of them trudged up Main Road to the pub, which had already been strung with lights outside ready for Christmas and looked much cheerier than Alexia felt.

The Three Fishes was so full that they had to push their way in past the red and silver poster that invited them to 'Come and join us for a special festive dinner on Christmas Eve! Ask at the bar for details!' Alexia tried to smile as eyes swivelled in their direction. Reminding herself that these were people she'd known all her life, the same who'd enthusiastically supported the fundraising in the first place, she forced her chin up as she followed Gabe. Someone patted her on the shoulder and she flinched as if expecting a knife in her back until she realised it was probably Ben.

When they reached the polished wooden bar where Tubb watched events from behind the beer taps and beside a counter-top Christmas tree, Gabe gave Alexia a reassuring smile. 'Might as well get on with it.'

She nodded and they turned to face the rows of expectant faces. Alexia's hands began to sweat.

Without hesitation, Gabe boomed, 'Ladies and gentlemen.' The bar, which had been alive with hushes and mutterings, fell silent. Even the *thunk . . . thunk . . . thunk* from the dartboard paused.

Gabe made the grave announcement that the money the village had raised had gone and there was little prospect of it coming back. Before he could provide more details, the protests began.

'What?'

'How the hell—?'

'What do you mean "gone"?'

'Has someone got sticky fingers? Started their Christmas shopping early, have they?'

Gabe held up his hands for quiet but it only caused the volume to increase as people tried to shush those uttering protests, and the protestors protested at being shushed.

A loud, 'Please! If you *please*!' from Gabe did eventually reduce the clamour to an angry buzz. Meeting the stunned, hostile and suspicious gazes as Gabe explained everything they knew was the hardest thing Alexia had ever done. Her heart felt as if it were trying to escape her chest and

Gabe had to raise his voice again and again as angry muttering became angry talking, even punctuated by the odd angry shout.

Then Ben, who'd been watching in silence, leant over the bar and gave the last orders bell several energetic tugs. The clanging ripped through the uproar and left a startled hush in its wake.

He spoke quietly. 'Gabe can now take any questions you might have.'

People certainly did have questions. They asked loudly, louder, loudest, over one another, of each other, and Ben clanged the bell again. 'One at a time, please!' Thereafter he took control of the meeting, pointing at each person in turn, giving them the go ahead to speak.

Gabe did his best to answer. No, the police had no leads on Shane or Tim. In fact, there was no record of this particular Shane Edmunds or Tim O'Neill existing.

No, the police hadn't put out descriptions to other forces as the fraud wasn't considered big enough, but they had circulated pictures of Shane on the police national computer. No, that hadn't brought forward any clues. No, nobody knew what their real names were or how to stop people opening accounts with stolen identities.

No, it was unlikely that the bank would replace the money unless it could be proved that their organisation had been negligent.

Bracing herself, Alexia stepped in and took the next barrage, the flashing lights on the Christmas tree beginning to make her head ache. No, neither she nor Jodie had had any clue that Shane was anything but genuine or, obviously, they would have had nothing to do with him. Well, yes, she supposed they had made it possible for him to see examples of their signatures and snaffle cheques from their cheque books. And, likewise, Jodie must have allowed him to see her password as she typed it in. Yes, they did feel terrible—

Ben clanged the bell again. 'I know you don't mean to make this personal,' he suggested mildly. 'Jodie was taken in by a trickster. It could have happened to any one. Many of you met Shane. Hands up everyone who noticed he was a practised conman.'

No hands were waved and a charged silence took the place of heated questions, but few of the villagers seemed to want to meet the gazes of Gabe or Alexia.

Then, just as it seemed the worst was over, Carola pushed her way to the front of the pack. 'Nothing like this ever happened to the village hall.' Her triumph, though delivered in her silvery voice, carried as clearly as Tubb's bell.

Sick of the whole situation, Alexia jumped on her remark. 'Good. Because I wouldn't wish this situation on anyone. We've been betrayed and used and now we're left with the fallout. It's not just about the money the village raised. The Angel is Gabe's personal property and it's been thoroughly devalued by a pair of unscrupulous thieves. We couldn't feel any worse, so you're wasting your breath trying to make us.'

Carola's mouth shut suddenly.

When no one said more, Ben turned to the bar and ordered three double whiskies. Janice, no doubt at Tubb's prompting, began to take advantage of the crowded bar by trying to flog a few Christmas raffle tickets.

'I'm going home.' Alexia could hardly speak for the lump of misery in her throat.

Ben's eyes were sympathetic. 'The anger isn't really against you, it's against Shane and Tim. Stay for a drink and they might begin to thaw.' Passing along the whisky glasses, he gave them a mock toast. 'To Shane and Tim.'

'May it choke them,' responded Gabe.

They drank in glum silence. Gradually though, as Ben had predicted, a couple of people came to commiserate, a few to ask more questions, as if they could scarcely believe the baddies had got away with the loot. When the fifth person had said, 'Bastards. They ought to be strung up,' Alexia began to believe that Ben had been right. The anger wasn't really directed against her and Gabe.

Except Carola's. That had seemed pretty personal. Alexia didn't know what was wrong with her lately. Or rather she did – it was the village hall versus The Angel. With the village hall shut and her girls, Charlotte and Emily, being teens and increasingly self-sufficient, Carola didn't have enough to occupy her.

Gabe nudged Alexia from her thoughts. 'Whilst we're dealing with difficult things we should schedule a clean-up meeting.'

Alexia groaned. 'Is it worth it?'

Gabe's eyebrows met. 'I need to know where I stand.' He paused, scratching his nose uncomfortably. 'Christopher's made it plain he wants no more to do with The Angel. I'd completely understand if you and Jodie felt the same but I need to know because I've got to do something with the bloody place.'

Alexia almost choked on her whisky. 'Do you think I'd just leave you holding the baby – dirty and smelly as it is?'

He took a swig of his drink, looking relieved. 'Why don't you and Jodie come to Sunday lunch tomorrow? We can talk things over.'

'Great.' But Alexia felt a wriggle of doubt. 'I'll have to

check with Jodie, though.' Then, realising from his face that she'd sounded totally unenthusiastic, she gave Gabe a hug. 'I'll be there, of course. But now I'm going home to a comforting cup of tea and a good book.'

Thankfully this time neither Ben nor anyone else tried to detain her, although a few of the villagers managed sympathetic or sheepish smiles as she pushed her way to the pub's front door.

When Alexia reached the cottage Jodie's car was in its usual spot. Struggling out of her coat she called, 'Jodie?' When there was no reply she ran upstairs and tapped on the door to Jodie's room.

Jodie appeared, eyes red-rimmed and skin blotchy, hair unbrushed. She hovered on the threshold of her space as if on guard.

Alexia hesitated, slightly wrong footed by the door not being thrown open to enable her to step inside. 'Are you OK?'

Jodie shrugged. 'Suppose. What was the meeting like? Was it really hostile? I'm sorry I couldn't . . .' She gulped and any residual irritation and hurt drained away from Alexia's heart. When Jodie was down in the dumps she really went a long way down.

Not wanting to make her friend feel worse than she obviously did, Alexia tried to pass it off lightly. 'There was some anger and disillusion, but nobody threw anything.'

Jodie shuddered but still didn't invite Alexia into her room.

Trying not to mind, Alexia passed on Gabe's lunch invitation and when Jodie looked as if she was going to refuse, added gently, 'We can't just desert Gabe, can we? None of this is his fault and he needs to know if we can contribute to whatever happens next.'

Jodie's mouth turned down at the corners. 'OK. I'll come. I'm going to bed now.' With a tired smile she stepped back into her room and Alexia was left staring at a closed door.

Chapter Eight

Was Alexia surprised that she had to knock on Jodie's bedroom door the next day to remind her of the lunch date? Not really.

What she didn't anticipate was that when they reached Gabe's they'd find Ben ensconced in the kitchen, calmly mashing potatoes amidst the mouth-watering smell of roast lamb.

Jodie hesitated, turning an uncertain eye on Alexia.

Alexia was surprised, too, but if Gabe wanted to invite his nephew to Sunday lunch there wasn't much she or Jodie could do about it. 'Hi,' she said when Jodie remained silent. 'What can I help with?'

'Strain the veg while I make the gravy.' Gabe smiled at Alexia but it was Jodie his shrewd gaze followed as she flumped down in a kitchen chair.

Everyone else chattered over lunch, enjoying the creamy potatoes and discussing whether Yorkshire pudding was best crisp or stodgy, but Jodie hardly spoke – though she drank her share of the wine. She picked at her food and gazed at the unvarnished pine table top. Gabe and Alexia exchanged glances.

Presently, when Ben got up to clear away, Gabe kept Alexia and Jodie at the table. 'So far as I can see, we have the building but no money for the refurbishment.'

Alexia had no choice but to cast an even blacker shadow over the picture. 'In fact, we'd be starting the refurbishment from a negative position because we now need things that we thought we had, like floor tiles and roof slates. And there's a lot to make good where fireplaces and things were ripped out.' It made her feel queasy just to think of the desecration.

Then Jodie finally spoke. She rose slowly to her feet, her eyes full of tears. 'I can't help. At all. I have no money until I get paid from my current job. Shane took even the cash in my purse and everything of value from my room.'

'Oh, Jodie,' Alexia breathed. 'You didn't tell me that! I could have lent—'

But Jodie ploughed on without looking at her. 'If my rent to Alexia hadn't already left the account I wouldn't even have a roof above my head.'

Alexia reared back in astonishment. 'I wouldn't throw you out, Jodes!'

A tear slid down the side of Jodie's face and she swiped it away. 'Thank you. But it's all I can do to drag myself to work at the moment and I have zero energy to bring to The Angel. And zero inclination. In fact, if I ever see the place again it will be too soon. Gabe, I think you should set fire to it and claim the insurance money.' Her tears began to escape down her cheeks. 'I'm so sorry that all this is because of me but I just want to go home. Don't try and come with me, Alexia!' She flung out a hand as if to physically ward Alexia off as Alexia began to rise. 'I want to be on my own.'

She grabbed a paper napkin and, blowing her nose, stumbled out.

As the door shut behind her, Alexia remained on her feet, half-inclined to ignore Jodie's words and go after her. 'I've never seen her this down.'

Gabe shook his head sorrowfully. 'We'll just have to give her space to recover.'

Slowly, though still fighting an urge to run after her friend, Alexia resumed her seat. Gabe poured her a fresh cup of tea and added more sugar than she usually took, as if she needed it for the shock.

He folded his arms on the table top and regarded Alexia keenly. 'And what about you? You had no money invested in The Angel and I wouldn't blame you if you walked away.'

Alexia's eyes grew hot as she noted the new lines on his face. 'But the village still needs a café and friends don't just disappear in times of need.' Her breath caught as she realised what she'd said. 'Oh! I didn't mean Jodie.'

'She's as great a victim in this as anyone,' Gabe allowed kindly. 'She's at her limit, strength wise.'

Alexia nodded, watching Ben absently as he moved back and forth to the sink. 'Because I don't have a financial stake I'll make suggestions rather than recommendations. For one, if you have some money to add to whatever the insurance company pays out I could help you get The Angel up to a standard where you could at least sell it. But unless you have a lot of dosh, it won't be a sympathetic restoration, rich in original period features, as was intended.'

Gabe shook his head, seeming to sink into himself. 'There won't be an insurance payout. Giving a tradesman keys to the building and then him stealing from you is "theft by deception". It isn't covered.'

'But that's unfair! First the bank and now the insurance company say you just lose—'

Gabe held up a hand. 'Yes. I lose.'

Unable to speak for a moment without spouting a stream of unladylike language, Alexia took a shaky sip of tea. Poor Gabe! Talk about good guys coming last.

But then Gabe proved he wasn't going down without a fight. 'What about if I decide I still want the village to get its community café? Would you lend your expertise to the conversion? For as long as you're still in the village, anyway. I know you have plans.'

Plans that were in smithereens, but there was no point bothering Gabe with that right now. 'Of course,' she agreed dubiously. 'But it means more money. Buying the kitchen equipment, even if you can get some second hand, will take a chunk of change. We can streamline a bit but you simply can't run a café without certain equipment, and every surface in the food prep area has to be wipe-clean so we're talking a lot of tiles, stainless steel, glass splash backs and that kind of thing. You have to have separate sinks for different purposes and we'd have to get the new plans past the Environmental Health people because we can't just deviate from what's agreed and assume they won't mind.'

Eyes twinkling, Gabe managed a smile. 'I do have *some* money left.'

Ben returned to the table, drying his hands. 'If you'd let me invest, you'd have more. I sold my house and business before I came to Middledip. My share of that could provide the shortfall until the café begins making money.'

Gabe frowned him down. 'I've told you I'm not going to let you risk your capital. Alexia, what kind of money are we talking?'

With pleated brow and much drumming of fingers, Alexia took the pen and pad and listed all the major unavoidable purchases with ballpark costs. Without calling in proper quotes or checking prices on websites it took a long time and a lot of guesswork, doing her best to recall her original scheme of works from her memory and carve it up to suit the new circumstances. She tapped the pen on her teeth as she went up and down her list, trying to be sure she wasn't missing anything.

Gabe and Ben had conducted several quiet conversations, made more hot drinks and were halfway down them by the time she finally sat back with a sigh. 'Eight thousand for the kitchen workstations and equipment, even if you don't buy an espresso machine or a full oven. And then there's the groundwork, rewiring, plumbing and plastering. Easily another fourteen thousand, and that's only for work that we absolutely can't do ourselves. It could easily inflate.' She watched Gabe raise his eyebrows and puff out his cheeks. 'They're probably higher figures than you were expecting.'

Gabe managed to collect himself and turn his attention to her figures. 'You've listed next to nothing for the seating area.'

'Hopefully it won't cost much. I'm sure I can find an eclectic collection of chairs and tables for not much on Gumtree. My new plan will owe more to *The Scavenger* than *Grand Designs* and there's going to be a lot of painting and repurposing going on.'

'That's a fantastic idea.' Gabe summoned a smile. 'It will mean picking things up, I suppose, but we have Ben and his truck.'

Ben was silent for just a fraction too long. Alexia caught an odd expression on his face as his gaze rebounded from hers. No doubt he was realising that helping Gabe meant spending time with Alexia. 'That's right,' he answered, his smile bland. 'Evenings and weekends. No problem.'

Alexia began to feel awkward and defensive. Whatever that look on his face had meant it wasn't *Goody goody! What a fab time we're going to have!* 'I'll try not to call on you more than I have to,' she said stiffly. 'But I don't have a vehicle that will carry as much as yours.'

'Don't look a gift horse in the mouth,' Gabe chided. 'A big, strong, practical man with a truck will be a godsend, Alexia.'

'Of course.' Alexia tried to sound casual, absolutely not wanting Gabe to get a whiff of the whole getting-their-clothes-off-and-regretting-it scenario.

But Gabe was already gnawing on the next issue. 'I'd meant to offer Jodie the opportunity to still run the café, just as an employee rather than a partner. But in view of what she said . . .' His eyebrows knitted.

With a pang, Alexia nodded. 'She's not cut out for taking risks and things going wrong.' She tore the pages she'd been working on from Gabe's pad. 'OK, let me work on the plan . . .' She broke off as her phone began to ring. 'It's Jodie's mum, Iona,' she said in surprise. She hurried to answer, her stomach giving a funny swoop.

'I think it's only right to tell you,' Iona said, the instant the call connected, not giving Alexia time to greet her. 'Jodie's decided to come home to live at my house.'

Alexia's stomach swooped more violently. 'But I was with her a couple of hours ago and she didn't say a thing.'

'I know. She's just owned up to leaving without waiting to tell you herself.' Iona spoke in a low voice as if Jodie might be nearby. 'Yesterday she came and asked if she could come back here to live. What could I say? When

110

your kid's in trouble you do what you can. But I couldn't let you get home and just find her gone.'

'*She's gone already*?' Alexia's voice rose. Gabe and Ben paused in their conversation.

'I'm afraid so. She called me to come and get her, and she had everything in black bin bags when I arrived. She's up in her old room now with a bottle of wine and the door shut.'

Gabe's kitchen seemed to wobble slightly around Alexia. 'She must have been packing last night and that's why she didn't want to let me in her room. But why couldn't she tell me what she was going to do? Why . . . why *sneak* out, like this?'

Iona sighed. 'I knew you'd be upset. She says she's left you a letter.'

'Right,' Alexia said numbly. 'I suppose I'd better go home and read it, then.'

When she ended the call she found Gabe and Ben gazing at her sympathetically, obviously having gathered that all was not well. Economically, she filled them in.

Gabe shook back his ponytail in distress. 'What on earth's she thinking? Good gracious. I'll pour you another cup of tea.'

Blindly, Alexia halted him. 'Thanks, but I need to get home.' Her heart was pounding so hard that she felt as if it had drained all the blood from her face. Why would Jodie leave like a teenage runaway while Alexia's back was turned? A knot rose in her throat.

'Let me walk with you.' Gabe reached for his jacket.

But Ben was already on his feet. 'I'll run her home in the truck. She looks as if she might pass out.'

Alexia found herself being bundled into her coat and ushered out of the door. 'I never pass out,' she protested as her gallant knights steered her towards Ben's silver truck. But her voice was far from convincing, wavering thinly and pitched several notes higher than usual.

Gabe patted her hand softly. 'Let Benedict drive you so I'll know you reached home safely. I'll ring you later.'

It seemed easier to acquiesce. Her legs did feel as if they were made of string and she only gathered the strength to climb up into the truck because Ben stepped forward as if to lift her. She wasn't sure she could cope with having his hands on her again. Not right now.

Gabe waved farewell and soon they were bumping down the track and travelling the few yards along Main Road to her cottage. It took only a minute but it was long enough for Alexia to decide to put Ben in the picture.

It came out clumsily the moment he drew the truck to a halt outside her house. 'I won't be leaving Middledip now.'

He didn't pretend not to understand. 'I wondered. You didn't mention a commitment to a new job while you were outlining your plans for The Angel.'

She leant her head back on the headrest and closed her eyes, exhausted by the dramatic turns her life was taking. 'Opportunity lost.'

'But maybe not lost permanently? You just need to find an alternative community project—'

She rolled her head to indicate the negative. 'Not so far as Elton's concerned. I've besmirched my project-management CV by allowing a builder to "do me up like a kipper", apparently.'

'Oh.'

'Yeah. Maybe I should have downplayed that side of things. But Elton was such a prick about it I'm not sure I want to work with him now.' She forced herself to open

112

her eyes and straighten her spine. 'Anyway. Not your problem. What I started out to say is that I'm staying in the village. You and I weren't ships that passed in the night so much as two that ran aground on the same sandbank. I'd like to pretend it didn't happen, especially if you're to be involved to some extent with The Angel.'

She turned to find Ben looking at her with a strange expression. 'You've just stolen my speech.'

'OK, good. Unflattering, but good.' She felt for the door handle.

'Likewise. Would you like me to see you into your house?'

'I'll be OK, thanks.' Alexia let herself out onto the pavement, summoning up a smile and waving farewell as she fished for her door keys.

It wasn't until she got inside her house that she let the tears out. They poured down her face as she gazed around, realising that Iona had not somehow got the wrong end of the stick. No longer did Jodie's coats clutter up the hooks behind the kitchen door or hang askew on the newel post at the foot of the stairs. Her haphazard DVD stack was missing from beside the TV. There was no sign of the jumble Alexia had teased Jodie about since the days when Jodie's school bag had needed tipping out just to assess its contents.

On legs that shook as she absorbed the magnitude of the betrayal, Alexia climbed the stairs. She had to take several breaths before pressing down the handle to Jodie's door. When it swung ajar she saw a room that looked as if her childhood friend had never shared her home. The bed stripped. Every shelf and surface cleared except for the chest of drawers, on which lay a single sheet of paper.

As if in a dream, Alexia crossed to pick it up and read Jodie's rounded handwriting.

Dear Alexia,

I've decided it will be better if I live with Mum for a bit. I need a clean break from everything that happened with Shane, not to live in a room that I shared so often with him.

I wish I'd never met him. I wish you'd never made him and Tim the contractors at The Angel. Everything's got too much for me and you know how I am.

If you can find it in your heart to give me back some of my rent for this month I'd appreciate it. This mess isn't all down to me.

Jodie x

Alexia sank down onto the bare mattress, the letter quivering in her hands. Hurt tears flowed harder, flooding down her face and landing on her hands in her lap.

It took her a long time to dry her eyes. Then she fetched her laptop, opened her online banking app and returned the entire month's rent to Jodie. The system wouldn't allow her to send it without typing something in the box designed for a reference so she typed in a single full stop. It seemed appropriate. And so much more dignified than typing in what she was really feeling.

Chapter Nine

A pair of sessile oak trees needed to come down. It pained Ben not to try treating them first, but they were showing advanced symptoms of acute oak decline and jewel beetle infestation. As some more distant stands of oak weren't yet affected and these stood near Carlysle Hall, Christopher Carlysle was firm that they should come down and the local authority had agreed. Now was the ideal time as the approach of winter meant the tree sap would have fallen, along with the leaves.

Ben zipped up his heavy jacket, his breath hanging white on the air. He needed to fell the trees in sections to keep the house safe and affect the garden as little as possible, Cassie, Christopher's wife, being a keen gardener – although she'd admitted she wouldn't be wielding her secateurs much so long as the cold weather lasted.

While Ben stepped into his harness, put on his hardhat and visor and wielded the screaming chainsaw from a mobile elevated work platform, two estate workers used a flat-bed truck to cart the timber away to be pulverised by the wood chipper. Another estate worker, a man called

Ted who Ben had ensured had the necessary training in manual handling, aerial rescue and first aid, usually worked as the mate that safety dictated Ben have.

Despite the chilly autumn damp, it was hard and dusty work. By Friday afternoon Ben was pleasantly tired, glad to oversee the clear-up then head for home. He drove slowly up the track to Woodward Cottage, trying to enjoy the prospect of warming his frozen limbs in a hot bath without remembering Alexia in it. They'd each warned the other off so he had to do as she requested and forget their night together.

But when he unlocked his front door he halted with one foot over the threshold. His mail was lying on the doormat and his heart skipped a beat as he recognised the handwriting on one letter.

Lloyd's.

Stepping over the mat, he discarded his damp boots and hi-viz jacket and tramped up to the bathroom. Half an hour later, now refreshed and in clean clothes, the letter was still lying where he'd left it. He made himself coffee and let Barney out of his tub to play on the kitchen floor.

At twelve weeks, Barney's fluff was beginning to be replaced by soft speckly grey and gold feathers and he had a squeaky-door call underlying his *hehhhhh*. Ben wasn't particularly looking forward to the full-blown screech adulthood would bring but at least he'd be out in the aviary by then and less likely to wake Ben at dawn, when Barney should be out hunting.

Freed, Barney made small circles with his head as he peeped at Ben. Then pounced on Ben's toes.

'Ouch, mind your damned talons,' Ben grumbled. He reached for the tiny teddy that usually kept Barney company in his tub and bowled it a few feet across the

116

floor. Barney flung himself after it, fly-hopping energetically, right wing beating but the left hanging at his side. His flapping bounce allowed him to land on his 'kill' with surprising speed. His head rotated on his neck and his black eyes checked on Ben as if to say, 'Good, wasn't I?'

'Well done.' Retrieving the battered teddy, Ben tossed it across the floor a few more times, each time Barney pouncing as if his life depended upon it – which, in the wild, it would. Watching Barney cope with his wretched wing, Ben didn't know whether to be glad that he'd never flown so couldn't miss it, or sad he'd never know freedom.

Finally, Ben backtracked to the front door and the letter. He stooped to pick it up then hesitated with it in his hands, tempted to rip it up.

Instead, he ripped it open.

Dear Ben,

I know Mum and Dad are trying to get you to come and see me but you don't want to. I understand. But I've been talking to a bloke in here who is a counsellor 'on the outside' and he advocates clearing what I can from my conscience, so I need to tell you this: I didn't have an affair with Imogen.

Ask Imogen what I mean, and she might explain – if you don't come over all straight edged on her.

I was scared of making things worse for myself so I didn't explain before I was sentenced and everything's difficult while I'm in here anyway, but see Imogen.

Best,
Lloyd

Ben's coffee grew cold while he read and reread his brother's words, trying to make sense of it. If he couldn't or wouldn't explain then why suggest Ben dig it all up again with Imogen when they were less than two weeks from their divorce becoming absolute?

Did he really believe that Lloyd felt the need to clear his conscience? His mind circled around the puzzle while he prepared his dinner, frying steak, onions and potatoes in a big pan and heating a tin of peas.

As he ate his meal and darkness fell outside, his phone began to ring. When he saw it was his mother calling his hand hovered over the handset. Usually he let calls from either parent go to voicemail, listening to the message then replying with a text. But this time . . .

This time he picked up.

His mother sounded surprised but pleased. 'Ben, darling! Is everything OK at your end?'

Ben made a sudden decision. 'I'm thinking of coming down to Didbury this weekend.'

'Why – I mean that will be *lovely*,' Penny stammered. 'Are you . . . Um, what's . . .' She paused, then seemed to gather herself. 'I'm thrilled, Benedict. Please do come. Your old room is always ready for you. How long will you stay?' She sounded almost tearfully pleased.

'Not sure.' He was already half-regretting his impulse. His mum being obviously emotional at the prospect of seeing him again made him feel guilty about staying away. He tried to imagine being in his childhood home, eating meals with his parents, sleeping in his old room. Being expected to behave like a guest. 'I could always go into the Travelodge or Premier Inn. It might be easier.'

'Don't be silly. It's not hard to have you stay. Your room's waiting.'

Ben had meant that staying in a hotel would be easier for him. It might be easier for his dad too, not to have to go to the trouble of hiding his preference for his golden eldest son while, via some convoluted reasoning, silently laying blame on his youngest.

But Ben could imagine how agog Penny's friends and neighbours would be if word got about that Ben had been in Didbury and had stayed at a hotel. That crowd from her gym could be far too bloody nosy. And if Imogen's family found out . . . Wow. The gossip. The sly digs.

'OK,' he said abruptly. 'All right for me to arrive tomorrow afternoon?'

'Yes, *definitely*. It will be *lovely*. *Really* lovely.'

'Good.' With mixed feelings of apprehension and guilt, Ben said his goodbyes then texted Gabe to ask him to owl-sit for the weekend.

Ben woke early the next morning, his mind gnawing on the events of the evening before.

His mum had been in one of her overemphatic moods, he thought, lying back on his pillows and staring at his bedroom ceiling. Ben had never quite understood what it meant when she was so bright and brittle. Even as a teen he'd sensed the strain behind it but had come to see it as a fact of life that he had a mum who sometimes crackled with nerves and a dad who was grumpy for no apparent reason. As he'd matured he'd sometimes wondered if his parents' marriage was troubled, but there seemed no point lying in bed hunting for insight now.

He yawned his way into the shower and, once dried, packed a change of underwear, his toothbrush and a clean T-shirt, the absolute minimum necessary for an overnight stay. It took longer to pack Barney and his food up ready to drop him off at Gabe's on his way out of the village.

Gabe was waiting when Ben drove up the track, the

wind blowing his ponytail over his shoulder. 'So you're going to see your parents?'

Ben heaved out Barney's tub from where he'd wedged it in the footwell of the truck then pulled out Lloyd's letter. 'This arrived yesterday.'

After unfolding the sheet of paper, Gabe scrunched up his forehead. 'My goodness. Fancy Lloyd seeing a counsellor. He doesn't seem the type.'

'My thoughts too. My visit to Didbury is a fact-finding mission.'

'Ah.' Gabe refolded the letter and handed it back. 'Good luck. Let me know how it goes. You know where I am if you need me.'

Warmth crept through Ben. 'I do know. Thanks.'

Ben's journey took him south and west, pootling along roads clogged with traffic. When he finally turned off the M40 towards Reading he needed no signposts to take him along the lanes towards Didbury.

Finally, he parked by Didbury Town Football Club, which had been alone on the edge of town when he was a teen but now had a supermarket and a retail park for neighbours. He took out his phone.

Imogen answered his call on the second ring. 'Ben?'

Ben could hear tentative pleasure in her voice but he kept his neutral. 'I'm in Didbury and I'm hoping we can talk.'

A catch in her breath. 'What about?'

'Can we meet up?'

'Well, yes! When?' She sounded as if she were smiling.

Though troubled that she was probably reading non-existent subtext into his suggestion, he remained focused on his aim. 'I could pick you up now. We could have lunch.'

She hesitated. 'I'd rather meet you somewhere.'

'You're OK to drive?' he asked carefully.

'I have an adapted car now.'

'Right.' She didn't sound as if she were asking for sympathy so he didn't offer any. 'I noticed a chain pub called The Crow's Nest on the outskirts of Reading.' Far enough from Didbury to make stumbling upon family or friends unlikely; so new that they'd never been there together.

They agreed the details and an hour later he was waiting inside a pub that seemed entirely lined with wood and faux ship's rigging. Unlike The Three Fishes, The Crow's Nest hadn't given itself over to Christmas yet and there wasn't a tree or strand of tinsel to be seen.

To ensure he didn't miss Imogen's arrival, he'd chosen a seat in a slightly raised area named the Lower Deck (further flights of stairs led, according to the signs, to the Upper Deck and the Crow's Nest).

Imogen arrived promptly, stepping through the big double doors and glancing around. She looked too slender, almost fragile, in a loose, long-sleeved top in a shade of gold that complemented her chestnut hair. She was wearing her hair longer than he was used to – probably to hide the scarring on her neck. Her eyes were still wide and blue, her lips a perfect bow. He lifted his hand to get her attention and a smile broke over her face as she glided up the steps to join him. The way she moved awoke memories of happier times. Hard on the heels of those memories, though, followed all the reasons they'd become tarnished.

He rose to meet her, suddenly realising he had no idea of the etiquette of greeting someone you used to be married to. When Imogen had first been injured, hugging or even kissing cheeks would have been physically uncomfortable for her so they'd never begun a pattern. Even now she might not like him coming into contact with the arm that hung crookedly from her shoulder as if she were ninety-four and arthritis had gnarled the limb. She was probably self-conscious about it and it was a glaring reminder of the accident that led to the end of their marriage.

Much better to simply smile and say, 'Thanks for coming.'

'Too intrigued not to,' she answered honestly, taking her seat.

Lunch proceeded along civilised lines. One glass of wine each. Salad for Imogen. Steak sandwich for Ben. Imogen propped her injured arm on the table and ate with her fork in her right hand, pointing out, unnecessarily, that her left arm was 'pretty screwed'. The skin on the back of that hand looked smeared, like brush strokes in an oil painting. That's what happened when you were the passenger in a car that landed on its side and dragged you along the ground and into a hedgerow littered with rocks and tree roots.

Ben was reminded forcibly of Barney. Two beautiful creatures with similar injuries, unable the live the lives they should have had a right to.

Her smile was bright, though. 'How are things going for you? I hadn't expected . . .' She paused, sipping her wine. 'It's good to see you. You look in great shape. Have you joined a gym?'

He shrugged, feeling awkward at the warmth in her voice. 'Just doing the same kind of work I've always done.' He told her something about working for the Carlysle Estate, trying to keep things light and friendly. She knew Middledip itself from visits to Gabe, of course.

It was over coffee that he brought up the purpose of his visit. 'I've had a letter from Lloyd.'

Imogen's teaspoon halted mid-stir. The shutters came down over her eyes and her earlier animation drained away. 'Oh.' Then she changed it to, 'Oh?' as if in polite invitation for him to continue.

Ben cleared his throat. 'He says you and he never had an affair and I should ask you again what happened.'

Her gaze dropped to her coffee and she recommenced her stirring.

'So . . . I'm asking,' he pointed out, after the silence had stretched into several seconds.

Her gaze had fallen on her hand. The left one. 'There's no point to this, Ben.' Her voice was low and dreary.

He waited. The colour had leeched from her face and yet she was still beautiful. He pitched his voice low. 'You told me you weren't having an affair and I'm afraid I found it hard to believe. But now, as Lloyd seems to feel strongly enough to write and suggest it, I'm here to ask you again. If you weren't having an affair then what were you doing with Lloyd and why did you lie to me about your plans for that weekend?'

Listlessly, Imogen stirred and stirred at her coffee, a tiny frown pinching the skin above her nose. 'We've done all this. My word wasn't enough for you before so why should it be now?'

'Perhaps if you told me what you were doing. Rather than what you *weren't*.'

She half laughed. 'Airing the rest of the story isn't going to improve things between us now.'

He made an effort to meet her suddenly penetrating gaze but couldn't find it within himself to disagree. The gulf between them was too great to be bridged, whatever she disclosed. He was pursuing the truth because he felt he deserved it and the need to know was like black bile lapping inside him, not because he was going to suggest stopping the divorce.

She rose suddenly, tucking her handbag awkwardly between her bad arm and her body. 'Sorry, but I have urgent need of the ladies' room.'

Though churning with frustration, Ben had little option but to watch her hurry down the steps, pausing to ask something of a waitress then nod her thanks and set off purposefully into the depths of the pub.

He drank his cooling coffee thoughtfully. Until he'd mentioned the letter she'd seemed positive, even anticipatory. He'd evidently upset her and he was beginning to seriously suspect that he'd even dashed her hopes. But if he'd been unable to live with her secrets before then why would he be able to now? Trust, to him, was a minimum requirement in a relationship, but she couldn't trust him with the truth and he no longer trusted her at all. He checked his watch.

Minutes ticked past. After a quarter of an hour he felt concerned enough to approach the long bar on the lowest level and ask a female staff member to enter the Ladies to check that Imogen was all right. 'No problem,' the girl told him brightly. She was about twenty and wore her hair in a ponytail that hung over the shoulder of her black polo shirt.

Both sets of ladies toilets were duly checked.

No Imogen.

'I see.' Ben felt like an idiot. 'Is there a back way out of this pub?' The front door had been in view all the time he'd been waiting.

The young barmaid's widening eyes suggested she was

beginning to get the gist of what had happened. 'To the beer garden, yes.'

His cheeks burned. 'I'd better pay the bill for table twenty-one.'

She skipped back behind the bar and tapped a few buttons on the till. 'Erm . . . it's been paid.'

Anger licking inside him, Ben muttered his thanks and turned away, eager to escape the interested looks he was attracting from the other bar staff. He could imagine them giggling over the pints they pulled for punters after he'd gone.

Probably it was a blind date and he was acting like an idiot.

Yeah, probably got him off Tinder. She should've swiped left.

She paid the bill before she legged it. She must have really wanted not to hear from him again.

He wondered whether even one of them would say, *'But why didn't she just tell him she was leaving? Sneaking off isn't cool.'*

He thrust his way through the doors. Once back in the truck he yanked his phone from his pocket. Not trusting himself to call in case he said something he'd later regret, he fired off a text.

Ben: *WTF?????*

Then he snapped the radio on and seethed for ten minutes until his phone bleeped on an incoming message.

Imogen: *I'm sorry. Just leave things as they are. No idea why Lloyd should start raking stuff up now. It's stupid. x*

Ben sat on, phone gripped in hand, angry and baffled. Through the windscreen he watched people arriving, leaving, selecting their parking spots or squeezing in or out of their cars. Confronting Imogen had only left him with more questions and no answers.

The need to know the truth ate at him. For the first time since the sentencing he gave serious thought to visiting his brother in jail. He tried to imagine going through the process he'd seen on TV: handing over personal effects, being ushered through doors that were immediately locked in his wake. Talking to Lloyd across a table in a stale-smelling room filled with other inmates and prison officers in uniform. Lloyd looking diminished by his incarceration but, knowing him, trying to pretend prison was a perfectly OK place to be.

But since when could he rely on the truth from Lloyd? He was good at putting a spin on things to make you see what he wanted you to see.

He started the engine, relieved to have talked himself out of it.

Chapter Ten

His parents' house, a 1930s double-fronted detached, looked exactly as it had as long as Ben could remember – a cube with bay windows topped by a pointed roof. He parked on the drive, pulled his bag from behind the seat and jumped out before he could change his mind.

Out of habit he made sure not to step on the inset of herringbone tiles on the front step. Penny liked them to shine. The door key still swung on his keyring so he let himself in. Before he could call out that he'd arrived, his mum bustled out of the kitchen. 'Ben! It's good to see you.'

Her hug was warm enough. He had to stoop to return it, feeling a tug of guilt that he hadn't visited, that in the nearly six months he'd been living in Middledip he'd avoided calls and been lax in replying to messages. 'It's good to see you, too,' he said gruffly.

Then Victor, his father, was in the hall, taking Ben's hand in a firm grip. 'Benedict.'

They all paused to look at each other. So much to say. Or so little.

Penny fluttered into action. 'Let's have a cup of coffee. I bought Jaffa Cakes. Did you know they do black cherry, now, Ben? Dad loves them. Don't you, Victor?'

So his mother was in bright and brittle mode again. Ben followed her into the kitchen. 'It was Lloyd who liked Jaffa Cakes.' He took a seat at the oak table at the side of the room. Then, in case he'd sounded childish, added, 'But I'll give one a try.'

The discussion of Jaffa Cakes and whether Ben had ever liked the original orange variety took three minutes. Three minutes in which Ben wondered why he'd arranged to visit for the weekend when he could so easily have made the trip in a day. It wasn't that he didn't love his parents. He did. But resentment had built a wall between them and he might just be about to build it higher.

Then he looked at his mother's smile and his conscience gave him another hard dig. He'd spent so many months feeling aggrieved that he'd made no allowance for human frailty. Yes, his parents had suggested that if he'd acted differently Lloyd and Imogen wouldn't have been in that car together, but people made unguarded comments when upset.

He made up his mind to treat this trip to Didbury as a normal family interaction: a son visiting his parents. Build a bridge for once instead of a wall. They could enjoy a nice afternoon and evening. He was pretty sure his mum would have something in mind that, if not fatted calf, would constitute a special meal. If it proved to be one of Lloyd's favourites instead of his he wouldn't remark on it. He'd sleep in his old room tonight and tomorrow he'd leave with a smile.

Decision made, he opened his mouth to apologise for being out of touch.

128

But Victor got in first, rolling out one of his great sighs. 'I suppose you heard I was asking for you in Middledip as you've been so damned coy with your address?' He shifted in his seat, his brow gathering in familiar furrows. 'I'm glad you've made the effort. Each time we see Lloyd he asks when you're going to see him.'

Ben closed his mouth again. All his good resolutions vanished as surely as if he'd opened the shiny flip-top bin in the corner and shoved them in.

He pulled Lloyd's letter from his pocket and tossed it onto the table.

Slowly, Victor smoothed it out and he and Penny pressed themselves shoulder-to-shoulder to read it.

'Now what's he done?' whispered Penny as she sat back. There was no sign of her earlier smiles.

Victor sent her a look. 'Don't go borrowing trouble.'

Ben glanced from one to the other, scalp prickling at the oddness of their manner. 'Why should he have done anything?'

Victor refolded the letter and offered it back to Ben, granite-faced. 'No reason in the world. Your mother worries.'

Fingering the folds of paper Ben thought hard, trying to make sense of the sudden change in the atmosphere. 'I confronted Imogen today. She still won't admit they had an affair.'

Victor rose restlessly to prowl to the window, jamming his hands in his pockets and looking out over the garden where the leaves were drifting onto the lawn. 'Then maybe they didn't.'

'But until this letter Lloyd's never protested his innocence.' Ben switched his gaze from parent to parent, taking in his father's frowning restlessness and the way his mother's fingers were covering her mouth. 'What's conspicuously absent is an explanation of what they *were* up to on the night of the accident.'

Penny gave a tiny gasp. Victor returned to his seat beside her, taking her hand in his. Neither of them spoke.

'Do you know what "it" is?' Ben pressed.

Like puppets controlled by the same strings Victor and Penny shook their heads.

Ben's hands curled into fists as he fought down a hot surge of anger. 'Don't you care? Imogen and I are getting divorced. Lloyd's in prison. How could the truth make things any worse?'

'Sometimes,' Victor said hoarsely, 'it's best to let sleeping dogs lie.'

Ben laughed harshly. 'Best for Lloyd?'

'Not just Lloyd.' Victor glanced at his wife.

Penny's gaze was fixed to half a black cherry Jaffa Cake on her plate. 'I don't even know why we're protecting him any more,' she whispered.

Victor sighed, his eyes still on her. 'We always agreed—'

'But it's such a strain, and it might be doing more harm than good.'

Ben's temper glowed red at this opaque exchange. 'Why are you protecting Lloyd? Why's it always Lloyd? I sometimes wonder if you only had me in case he ever needed a kidney,' he added bitterly.

Victor's face set in its habitual harsh lines. 'We tried to protect both of you.'

Penny began to cry.

Ben, though he watched his father slide an arm about his mother's shaking shoulders, steeled himself against her tears. 'I never noticed you protecting me.'

130

Victor gathered Penny closer, pressing a kiss upon her hair. 'You not noticing was the idea. We covered it up when it started and the time never seemed right to uncover it. Your mum got so upset every time.'

Penny gulped. 'We didn't want anyone knowing. And it made things all right for you. You didn't have the worry.' She wiped her eyes on the sleeves of her cardigan, fumbling in her pocket for a tissue so she could blow her nose. 'This time, all we know is that there's *something*. We recognise his behaviour when he refuses to admit he's done wrong. I'm scared for Lloyd.'

Ben sat frozen, his heartbeat thudding in his ears, while Penny dried her eyes. The tantalising sensation of being on the cusp of significant discovery consumed him. He had to rein in the compulsion to roar, 'WHAT did you cover up? Just TELL ME!' and thump the table. Fury was never the way to solve an issue with his parents. His mother would cry and his father would get loud and defensive. It was why he'd developed the habit of simply withdrawing, leaving them to focus on Lloyd. It had seemed easiest.

But that had been when he was a teenager. Now he was an adult and it was time his parents began treating him as one. He imagined his throat made of silk to coax out a voice, reasonable and calm. 'It seems really important, what you're trying to tell me. Can one of you begin from the beginning, so I understand?'

'I wish you'd leave it alone.'

'I can't.'

With a sigh, Victor rubbed his forehead as if it would help him marshal his thoughts. 'It began when Lloyd was fifteen. You were nine. There had been –' he paused to clear his throat '– *incidents* before that.' He swallowed.

131

'Lloyd was questioned at school several times about stealing but there was never anything but circumstantial evidence and Lloyd always protested his innocence.'

'Stealing?' repeated Ben blankly. 'Lloyd?' He almost wanted to pinch himself to check he wasn't imagining the words. *Lloyd* had been in trouble at school for stealing? Lloyd the golden child?

Penny took up the story. 'We didn't want you to know. We thought it was a phase, and there was no reason to make your brother look bad in your eyes or for you to share the shame.' She had to pause to wipe her eyes again. 'Then a substantial sum was involved. It had been collected for a school trip and the teacher had to run out of the classroom to help a child who'd fallen down some nearby stairs. All the kids had crowded out into the corridor but then a teacher with first aid qualifications arrived to help the student and Lloyd's teacher was back in his classroom faster than Lloyd had bargained for.' Her voice dropped to a whisper. 'He was caught red-handed.'

Victor took up the tale once more, voice bleak. 'We were called to the school. We begged the head teacher not to get the police involved or expel him. He agreed, so long as Lloyd apologised and saw the school counsellor about his behaviour.'

'Mrs Ives.' Lloyd had gone to sixth-form college by the time Ben moved up to senior school, but she'd been school counsellor then, too.

Victor nodded. 'What came out was that he was stealing to fund playing on the fruit machines. Those gambling machines should be banned, out there in public where children have access. It was a hell of a job to keep Lloyd away from them. Mrs Ives suggested we keep him as fully occupied as we could so I used to take him to football, rugby, whatever he was good at.'

'You used to coach his teams,' Ben supplemented.

'It kept me involved.'

'I hardly saw you.'

Victor's eyes, grey like Ben's own, grew defensive. 'I used to try and get you to come along sometimes. You were resistant.'

'Because, "Why don't you come along and support your brother?" wasn't particularly appealing. Not like, "What would you like to do today, Ben?" might have been.'

Victor rubbed his eyes tiredly. 'Benedict, we were at our wits' end with Lloyd. I'm sorry if it meant I didn't spend much time with you. You were not much more than half Lloyd's age so I couldn't invite you to train with his team, could I? And Lloyd kept saying, "Don't tell Ben," and I thought it was a good thing that he knew you'd be ashamed of him. That somewhere inside himself he did know right from wrong. You looked up to him in those days.' Victor began to sound as if admissions were being ripped from him. 'Then money began to go missing out of his team-mates' bags. Nothing was proved against him,' he added, hastily. 'But all my attention was taken up with trying to keep him away from those damned machines.'

'Holy shit,' Ben murmured. If his parents had confessed Lloyd to be a unicorn he could scarcely have been more surprised. 'I do remember holidays where he sneaked off to the arcades and you were furious. I used to kick around while you did the family counsel thing, bored stiff, wishing I was on the beach or the cliffs.'

Penny had stopped crying, though she still clutched her tissue. 'You were such an easy child in comparison. You never got in trouble and you were happy doing your

133

outdoorsy things. You seemed so self-sufficient, oblivious to what we were dealing with.'

Ben thought he caught a whiff of reproach. 'Being kept in the dark isn't the same as being "oblivious". I felt ignored.' He heard the old sense of injury echoing in his voice but he couldn't suppress it. 'Everything seemed to be about Lloyd and I didn't understand. If I did get your attention I knew it could be withdrawn at a moment's notice.' He took in his mother's white face and the shock in his father's eyes. 'Sorry. That was blunt. But it's how I saw things. All Lloyd's sporting trophies were evidence that he was your golden child.'

He jumped up and started making more coffee, needing to occupy his hands. 'Only Gabe seemed to have time for me. Even before he had his smallholding, when he still lived with Auntie Rona, he helped me build a tree house in his garden and bought a rowing boat that we took on the river.' Coffee granules spooned into each cup, he poured on steaming water and added a dash of milk, setting mugs in front of each of his parents.

He took his seat again. 'But, to move on: how on earth did Lloyd manage to go from lifting other people's money to being a lawyer?'

Victor wrapped his hands around his coffee mug. His hair was beginning to thin rapidly now, and his sixty-two years seemed to be weighing down the flesh of his face. 'To be honest, when he wanted to go to university and study law we were delighted.'

'We thought it meant he'd reached the end of a weird phase and was ready to grow up.' Penny sounded wistful. 'We used to read books about dealing with teenagers and they all talked about "phases" and "bad patches". That risky behaviour was about the way some adolescents' brains change, affecting their ability to reason. That they'd learn the difference between wrong and right sometime in their twenties.'

Victor chipped in. 'And he was never caught doing anything wrong again.'

'Until the accident,' Ben pointed out.

His parents nodded sadly.

Silence fell. Ben was not at peace with his thoughts. His parents had created fictions and hidden secrets but what he'd seen as an isolating lack of attention they'd considered to be shielding him from unpleasant truths. Ironically, his reaction had been to create shields of his own, such as visits to Gabe and outdoor activities; the venture scouts while he'd been a schoolboy, then a countryside management and environmental studies course at college.

Unwittingly or not, Ben had been contributing to the gulf that was ever growing between them all the time his parents had been battling to keep his brother from permanent disgrace. Trying to keep it all hush-hush.

Regret almost took his breath away. 'I suppose it's the squeaky wheel that gets the grease,' he said, almost to himself.

'Yes!' Penny smiled eagerly. 'Exactly. Lloyd was the one who needed our help.'

Ben had been thinking from the perspective that it was the one who made most noise that got the attention, but he didn't contradict her. Instead, he elected to try to erase some of the distance he now regretted by introducing a happier topic. 'It's your birthday soon, Mum. How about I take you both out to dinner tonight? Where would you like to go?'

Penny's eyebrows flipped up in surprise. A hint of colour returned to her cheeks. 'Dad and I sometimes like to walk down to the Thai Garden and drink Tiger Beer with our dinner. How about that?'

'Perfect.' Ben grinned because he'd expected her to preferences to lie with a little bistro or maybe a jazz bar. 'Let's do that.'

Victor managed a rusty smile of his own. 'Better take your credit card, boy. Mum can guzzle her way right through that set menu.'

'Aren't you going to tell us about what you've been doing in Middledip?' broke in Penny tentatively.

Recognising that he wasn't the only one making an effort, Ben settled back in his chair and told them about the Carlysle estate and helping Gabe at The Angel, about the money disappearing and that only one of the original party had stuck by Gabe. A picture of Alexia flashed into his mind, widening her eyes at him like Betty Boop. For some stupid reason he felt his cheeks heat up.

His parents didn't seem to notice, though. They listened with so much interest that Ben almost relaxed and began to believe that the heart-to-heart, uncomfortable as it had been, had heralded an era of understanding between him and his parents.

That is, until that evening when the three of them were strolling into Didbury towards The Thai Garden and Penny took his arm. 'I am sorry if you've ever felt you've been treated unfairly, Ben. But, when it comes right down to it . . . well, you're all right, aren't you?'

He saw no reason to pretend. 'I haven't been all right for the past couple of years, no.'

'Oh, dear. I'm sorry if we didn't support you as we should.' Then Penny brightened. 'You're through it now, though, aren't you?'

With a rueful shake of his head, Ben gave her hand a

squeeze. 'Shall we reserve judgement until we find out what Lloyd and Imogen are trying to hide?'

Penny halted so abruptly that Ben almost tripped over her, her eyes wide with panic. 'What's the point of trying to find out? You said yourself, the worst has already happened.'

Victor loomed protectively over Penny, his mighty frown taking over his forehead. 'Remember what I said about sleeping dogs, Benedict.'

The three of them stood gazing at each other on the pavement in a street of ordinary houses where ordinary people lived, Ben's mother in her 'going out' uniform of black trousers and a pretty top, his father wearing a tie because, to him, a shirt didn't look right without one. Ben sighed. 'But following your logic that the worst has already happened, then what's to be lost by knowing the truth?'

Penny adjusted her glasses uneasily.

It was Victor who enlightened Ben. 'Lloyd's automatic release date's coming up. He'll serve the rest of his sentence out on licence.'

Ben felt suddenly lightheaded. 'And?'

'He'll be subject to supervision. If he breaches his conditions he'll be back in jail.' He eased his collar. 'Obviously, were some difficulty to come to light . . .'

'He'll be back inside, back in court, and his sentence might be extended. And you're worried in case whatever happened that night fits the bill.'

Ben felt sick as he realised that it wasn't just that his parents didn't know what Lloyd had done.

They didn't want to know.

Chapter Eleven

Alexia knocked on Gabe's door, glad he'd invited her for a Sunday afternoon pow-wow because, although Jodie had occupied Alexia's spare room for only a few months, Alexia now felt very conscious of her absence. Had Jodie moved on in an open, friendly way, or if Alexia had realised her plans to move down into the Greater London area, Alexia knew things would have been different. There would have been a plethora of texts and phone calls instead of the current pronounced silence. Alexia hadn't tried to contact Jodie because she needed a little more recovery time before she'd trust herself not to say something she might regret, but she could only speculate why Jodie hadn't got in touch with her. Shame? A sense of grievance? Alexia hadn't even caught sight of her around the village.

'It's open!' Gabe's voice called. 'But don't let any cats in.'

Alexia checked the vicinity and could see only one cat, Luke, black with a white paw, and he was on the windowsill of an outhouse, curled up in the sun as if he didn't intend to move for anything less than an earthquake.

Assuming Gabe's caution would prove to concern one of his chickens, brought indoors for attention, she opened the door and stepped carefully into the warmth of the homely kitchen. But it was no chicken that met her with a beady stare. 'Barney?' Alexia closed the door behind her as the young owl jumped down from the open door of Gabe's dishwasher and sidled up to check her out with a flap of his good wing, like a villain swirling his cloak.

Gabe looked over his silver-rimmed glasses from the paperwork strewn across his kitchen table. 'I didn't realise you two had met.'

Alexia hung her bag on the back of a chair then stooped to let Barney investigate her fingers with his beak, glad Ben didn't seem to have shared the news of his and Alexia's encounter with his uncle. 'Ben let me feed him once. Has Barney moved in with you?'

Barney lost interest in her and floppety-hopped off to pounce on one of Gabe's wellies, which stood by the back door. The boot wavered and then toppled onto the floor, causing Barney to flutter quickly clear before spinning round to give the fallen boot an appraising stare.

'He's just on a weekend break here while his human's away.' Gabe shuffled a pile of paper together. 'If you'd like a cup of tea, feel free to put the kettle on.'

Alexia took the hint, scooping up the kettle from on top of the range cooker. As she filled it at the tap she searched for a way to ask where Ben had gone without looking too obviously interested. 'Barney might have liked to be included if Ben's flown off on his broomstick.'

Gabe poised his pen thoughtfully over a big pad of lined paper. 'Wizards fly on the backs of eagles, don't they? Barney might be intimidated.' He noted something down then frowned at a column of figures on his pad.

Alexia tossed a big scoop of fragrant tealeaves into the brown teapot in which Gabe liked to brew proper brown tea and poured milk into bright red mugs bearing line drawings of Kit-Kats.

'Ben . . .' began Gabe, when she deposited one of the steaming mugs at his elbow and seated herself. He paused, turning his frown on a stack of bank statements.

Hands cupped around her mug, Alexia hid her impatience as she waited for him to find his thread. From a fresh perch on the lowest tier of the pan rack, Barney called loudly, '*Hehhhhhh!*' then turned his head ninety degrees sideways to treat Alexia to his most owlish look.

'Aha.' Gabe pulled out a statement before he recalled that he had a sentence to finish. 'Ben's gone to see his parents and Imogen so he asked me to look after Barney for a couple of days.'

'Oh.' Alexia sipped her tea, though it really wasn't cool enough. It gave her an uncomfortable feeling to think of Imogen because a picky person might say Alexia had been wrong to spend naked time with a man who wasn't absolutely divorced. Without disclosing the fact that she had, she'd no real reason to show curiosity about Ben's life or, particularly, his wife. Ex-wife. Soon-to-be-ex wife. 'That's nice.'

Barney hopped out from the pan rack and scuttled off to pounce again on the fallen Wellington boot, flapping his good wing energetically, then turning to check that Alexia was admiring his prowess.

Gabe lifted his eyebrows. 'Hmm. Nice? I wonder.' With a weighty sigh he sat back, pulled off his glasses and picked up his mug of tea. 'Crunching the numbers, I think I can scare up enough dosh for the rewiring and replastering and to outfit the kitchen if we take your low-budget approach. Any deals you can strike that don't require large deposits so the cost will be spread over however long the whole job takes will be appreciated.'

Stomach giving a nasty roll, Alexia gazed at him. 'Are you sailing close to the wind? Would it be better to sell The Angel now and put whatever you can salvage safely back in the bank?'

Gabe smiled but rubbed his forehead anxiously at the same time. 'As two great chunks of money have just disappeared from a bank I'm not certain about the word "safely". Moreover, if I sell The Angel now I'll cement in a loss. Some property developer would come along and make a killing. That's the kind of thing you'll do in your new role, isn't it? You'll be like Lucy Alexander from *Homes Under the Hammer*.'

'She might be a shade more successful.' Deciding now wasn't the time to re-examine the depressing truth about the other unusually silent person in her life, Elton, and the missed opportunity, Alexia circled back. 'By selling now you'd cut your losses.'

Gabe popped his glasses back on and returned to his numbers. 'What self-respecting bank manager would cut his losses when he could see a way not to make any? I plan to end up with a functioning building that's risen in value and can be occupied by a coffee shop that makes money. It's just a matter of managing cash flow and budget.' He looked up to twinkle at Alexia. 'So all you have to worry about is how to get the work done as economically as possible.'

She managed a laugh but in her mind her worries multiplied like vermin. Gabe hadn't asked for any of this mess. Jodie and Alexia had led conmen Shane and Tim to Gabe and made it possible for them to fleece him good and proper. A hideous feeling of culpability prompted her to assume an air of vigour that she hoped might be reassuring. 'So let's see if we can firm up the budget, then we'll go down to the Angel and decide on a strategy. I've brought my camera and a pad.' She patted her bag. 'Then I can make the detailed costing I promised, and if you're still happy you can see if you can make it work on your budget. It's only ten weeks until Christmas so let's not waste time.'

It was dark by the time they were happy they understood the figures, had fed Barney and shut up the chickens for the night. Alexia zipped her coat and stamped her feet while Gabe made sure Snobby had his pony rug on – not that such a hairy little barrel should be feeling the cold – then they set out for Port Road, hurrying to keep warm.

At the great silent presence of The Angel it seemed as if time had stood still since the events of the wrecking party weekend. Alexia wrestled the padlock off the ugly temporary front door and they fell inside, where it was no warmer than outside. Flipping the light switches, Alexia tried to sound positive. 'At least Shane and Tim left us the light bulbs.' A veteran of working in empty unheated houses, she pulled her fingerless gloves on in the hopes of keeping her hands warm enough to wield clipboard and pen. 'I think we should concentrate on the ground floor until we've hit the target of opening the café.'

Gabe hunched into his coat and gazed sadly around the stripped out Bar Parlour. 'And you truly think it can be done by Christmas?' He smothered a sneeze and had to blow his nose.

Alexia clicked her pen as she glanced around. 'There's a lot to do but I promise you that, with a bit of management, I can produce an interior all ready for tinsel and baubles. But, to get back to the here and now, I *do* recommend a whole-building approach to plumbing, wiring, plastering and making good where fireplaces have been ripped out. You wouldn't want the water or electricity turned off while the café's trying to trade, or plasterers traipsing through the foyer while your customers are trying to relax with a chocolate brownie.'

Gabe sighed. 'But it will take longer.'

'It'll save you money in the long run.'

'Yes, yes,' replied Gabe in the testy kind of voice that suggested he knew it but didn't have to like it. 'But can we open the Saturday before Christmas?'

'That's still the aim,' said Alexia, cheerfully. 'You'll love Christmas as much as I do when the twinkling lights are up and the café bursting with customers.'

They paused at the sound of the outer door opening and closing. A figure strode into the space where the Bar Parlour door ought to be, if Shane and Tim hadn't stolen it, hair blown by the wind and grey eyes watchful. 'I saw the lights and I thought I'd better come in and check everything's OK.'

'Ben! How were your parents?' Gabe asked.

After greeting Ben, Alexia thought she might as well carry on while they had their catch up. She wrote *Bar Parlour* at the top of a clean page, underneath listing *damp membrane, concrete, screed to floor*. She glanced up at the ceiling, thankful there were no bulges or other indications of impending problems and that Shane hadn't made an attempt to get the plaster roses down, which would almost certainly have ended in a disastrous level of damage.

Then she heard Ben say, 'Why don't I hang around? There might be jobs I can put my name down for to save money.'

143

Alexia's pen paused. Putting That Night behind them would be a sight easier if Ben went back to secluding himself in the woods. Still, it would be wrong to block anything that saved Gabe a few quid so she looked up with a polite smile. 'There are always ways of saving the tradesmen work, which will keep the bills as low as possible.'

Gabe boomed, 'Hurrah for smaller bills!' so loudly it made him cough.

Ben looked at Alexia and smiled faintly, as if both reading her thoughts and sharing her feelings.

She chose to focus on what she could influence. 'Gabe, are you happy for me to have a fairly free hand with choosing tiles and things? I'd normally offer clients ranges of materials at every stage but it'll be way quicker and easier if I don't have to. My aim is to do things as cheaply as possible but where "cheap" means "inexpensive" rather than "shoddy". I'll be looking for bargains and I know where to look.'

Gabe agreed with alacrity. '"Bargain" is my new favourite word and I trust your taste implicitly.'

They progressed from room to room, Alexia listing work to be carried out and equipment to be purchased, making sketches and taking pictures. Ben, plainly under occupied, asked a lot of questions. Alexia was sure he liked to thoroughly understand any project in which he was involved but reached exasperation point when he wondered aloud whether she should measure the rooms. She snapped, 'Or, as I did a detailed survey months ago, I could just consult that?'

He had the grace to look abashed. 'Sorry. Whether running my own business or working for the Carlysle estate, I'm more used to leading a team than being part of someone else's.'

He managed to prowl silently after that except for putting his name down for a multitude of jobs such as wallpaper stripping upstairs and knocking unsound plaster from walls. He'd also complete the clearing of the grounds.

When Alexia reported that it wouldn't be long before Dion began on the roof, having ordered the scaffolding and located sufficient recycled blue black Welsh slate, it was Gabe's turn to stick his oar in. He wrinkled his nose. 'Is recycled OK? It won't last as long as new slate, will it?'

Alexia smothered a sigh. 'It's not just cost. The rest of the roof's not new so recycled will blend better.' Suddenly tired of the way they stamped their feet and clapped their hands to keep warm, preventing her from getting fully absorbed in her task, she said, 'Right,' brightly, as she snapped her pad shut. 'I've enough information for the costing and schedule of works. Give me time to get estimates.'

Looking relieved, Gabe consulted his watch. 'Good timing. I told Tubb we'd probably be along for supper because Janice's stew and dumplings is on the menu this evening. You'll join us, Ben, won't you?'

Ben looked uncertain. 'Oh, I—'

Gabe clapped him on the shoulder. 'Come on, you've got to eat. Let me buy you supper to thank you for your help.'

Ben let Gabe and Alexia walk in front of him to The Three Fishes, Gabe's silver ponytail flipping in the wind. Ben wasn't sure he'd ever enquired about Gabe's actual age but he knew him to be older than Ben's mother by some years. Until he'd conceived the idea of plunging into the restoration of The Angel, Gabe had seemed perfectly happy

145

pottering about on his property with his chickens and his old pony. He ought to be enjoying the same peace of mind still, not scraping the bottom of his financial barrel to retrieve a situation in which he'd been ripped off. Ben would quite like to get his hands on the unscrupulous bastards who'd put him through all this worry.

As he couldn't, he turned his gaze to Alexia. She was being a bit buffeted about as well, and not just by the wind swirling up Main Road. Back at The Angel she'd exhibited signs of tetchiness. He felt guilty that his own restless energy had exacerbated that. Alexia had never wavered in her support of Gabe. Even though they'd obviously been friends for ages and there was liking and trust on both sides, she didn't *have* to give Gabe untold hours of her time in a salvage operation.

He emerged from his thoughts to find they'd reached the pub and Alexia was holding the door open for him while he gazed at her like a moron. 'Sorry,' he said, jumping forward to take the door. 'I was miles away.' She gave him a look that was not quite an eye roll.

By the time they caught up with Gabe he'd secured a table in the dining area and was checking with Janice that she'd reserved him at least four dumplings. Although Alexia was more restrained on the dumpling count, it wasn't long before they were all addressing aromatically steaming plates of stew. Alexia followed Gabe in choosing a pint of Adnams to wash it down. Ben had to hide a smile, not for any sexist belief that women should drink decorous halves, but because the glass looked the size of a bucket in her delicate hands.

Watching her take the first draft, Ben decided to try and improve things between them, partly because they were going to be falling over each other at The Angel but

146

mostly because of her support for his favourite uncle. 'Sorry I fired off too many questions when you were trying to concentrate,' he said. 'Waiting patiently with my mouth shut while someone else takes the lead doesn't come naturally.'

Alexia managed a smile that vanquished some of the worry from her eyes. 'The lead's yours if you want it, I'll do the sweeping up.'

'No, no,' Ben backtracked hastily. 'I'll just offer muscle power and my truck.'

Janice, passing by, fanned herself. 'Muscles and a truck? The wizard just gave me a hot flush.' She grinned knowingly at Alexia. 'And I haven't even begun think of his magic wand.'

Alexia flushed scarlet and Gabe coughed. 'Perhaps now would be a good time to change the subject. What did your parents say about the letter?'

'Much more than I ever expected.' Ben saw no reason to avoid speaking of family matters in front of Alexia, as she knew his brother was in prison, and recounted the whole story of Lloyd's problems in his teens. 'It completely took me by surprise. I'm still having trouble absorbing the fact that Lloyd was capable of that kind of dishonesty.'

Gabe shook his head gravely. 'His teenage delinquency is as much a surprise to me as it is to you. It explains a lot about why your parents gave him so much attention, though. And it's very like Penny to have desperately hidden the pilfering and gambling from everyone.'

'True. And it doesn't shed any light on what Lloyd and Imogen have been up to. I confess I couldn't think of much else on the drive home.' Ben didn't miss the quick look Alexia gave him before returning studiously to her meal. He was pretty certain it wasn't the crackling of the logs in the fireplace that brought a sudden flush to her cheeks.

Without really understanding his compulsion to garner her views, he waited until their plates were empty and Gabe had gone to the bar to buy another round of drinks, then told her of Imogen's extraordinary behaviour in the pub. Her big dark eyes grew larger and rounder. 'She just left you sitting there?' she breathed. 'Just *left*? Without even texting you from the car park?'

'Just left without even texting me from the car park.'

Ben had time to note each expression that flitted across her face: astonishment, dismay, anger, compassion. Finally, she leant in and dropped her voice soft and low. 'Are you all *right*?'

It was a simple enquiry but Ben's heart seemed to collide with his chest wall. Imogen had demonstrated that whatever was worrying her was more important than Ben's desire for the truth; likewise, his parents' confession regarding the truth about Lloyd's past had been focused on Lloyd, even while they'd been acknowledging its impact on Ben.

So often Ben's emotional resilience was taken for granted. Alexia's unaffected concern made him feel as if something around his heart quivered and began to peel away. 'I don't know,' he heard himself reply. 'Perhaps because of her injuries, there were no shouting matches or tearful recriminations around our agreement to divorce, so it was a shock that she'd bail like that. What the hell can she be hiding? I feel as if I want to pound on the door to her parents' house and demand to know.' He found himself wiping his palms up and down his jeans and realised that he was sweating. Then what felt like a rock jumped into his throat. 'Crap. I'm getting emotional!' he growled in horror.

Luckily, Gabe had been drawn into conversation with a group of people he obviously knew at the bar, the fresh drinks standing untouched at his elbow.

Beneath the table, Ben felt Alexia's hand come to rest tentatively on his knee. Her voice was full of understanding. 'It's all right to be emotional. What Imogen did was bizarre and hurtful. Undeserved.' She hesitated. 'To be betrayed is a horrible experience. It changes everything you thought you knew.' Then she got up and snaffled their drinks from beside Gabe, giving the older man a grin and obviously encouraging them to finish their conversation. She carried the two glasses back to the table and pushed Ben's Pepsi into his hand so he could raise it to his lips and ease the ache in his throat.

'Thanks,' he said gruffly. And though Alexia hadn't asked, he found himself adding, 'The astonishing thing is that until I brought up the subject of Lloyd's letter Imogen seemed unexpectedly happy to see me. I think she might have thought . . . well, the divorce becomes absolute at the end of the week and it's possible she thought I wanted to stop it. But if I'd ever entertained a single doubt about our marriage ending, I don't now.'

Alexia regarded him gravely over another pint glass. 'Is that good or bad?'

He wished he'd had the foresight to order a big fat pint of his own. He could have left his truck here and walked back for it in the morning. 'Good,' he decided. 'I think the marriage must be more over than we'd realised. There's something even more fundamentally wrong than I thought for her to treat me that way.' He summoned a smile. 'Thanks for listening. It's not as if you don't have problems of your own.'

Her return smile was fleeting. 'Let's not get into a "my

crap's worse than your crap" contest, because I think you'd win. Once I've helped Gabe limit the damage at The Angel, I'm OK.'

He wondered if this was her usual modus operandi, to reassure others. It seemed as if she did it automatically. 'You're making light of it but what happened with Jodie must have really stung. And Elton let you down. I know you were so looking forward to that new opportunity and leaving the village.'

Alexia gave a rueful eye roll and he realised Gabe had returned and was standing transfixed, obviously having overheard. He sank heavily into his chair and turned his gaze on Alexia. 'Isn't your new job going to come off?'

Alexia pulled a face. 'Doesn't look like it.'

'My dear, I'm so sorry. I had no idea.' Then understanding washed over his face, digging lines of sorrow in the flesh beneath his eyes. 'Because of what happened at The Angel? Surely not?'

For a few seconds Ben thought that Alexia was going to deny it. She'd already dredged up a reassuring smile. Then, perhaps unable to grab a plausible alternative explanation out of thin air, she let it slide away again. 'Elton wasn't impressed,' she admitted. She told him about Elton getting all flinty and not wanting her working on his team any more.

'What a shit,' Gabe eventually decreed. 'I'm so sorry. I'm beginning to think that The Angel is really a wicked witch who puts a curse on everyone who has anything to do with her. If I thought I could get away with it I might do what Jodie suggested and burn her down.'

'Maybe she's an angel with dark moments,' Alexia acknowledged. 'But in ten weeks she'll be dressed in new finery, even if it's a bit more boho than she's used to, and

150

she'll start replenishing your poor ravaged bank account. We'll love her again by Christmas, you'll see.'

'Then I'll burn Elton's house down instead. Little prick.' Gabe threw his arms around Alexia for a big hug, making her squeak and giggle in surprise.

'I'll drink to that.' Ben raised his glass with mock solemnity and Alexia and Gabe joined the toast.

The relieving of feelings seemed to cheer them all up and they were just deciding on whether to have a final round of drinks when Carola, who Ben remembered as the grumbler from the village meeting, approached.

Alexia sighed audibly.

Carola looked thin and white and pinched by the cold. 'Is this a council of war? Or are you about to announce you've found the missing money?'

For once, Gabe lost his customary cool. 'As you didn't put any in, it's none of your damned business. Come back when you've got something to contribute other than salt for our wounds!'

Carola's mouth opened. And shut. Then her eyes filled with tears and she turned and hurried away, gaze fixed to the floor until she'd gained the door of the pub. In a moment it had swung closed behind her.

Alexia and Gabe looked at each other. Gabe's eyebrows almost disappeared into his hair. 'Did I just make Carola *cry*?'

Alexia's eyes were very wide. 'I think so,' she agreed uncertainly. 'Wow. I thought she was made of iron. But she's been acting strangely since the village hall closed. She hasn't got any fetes to organise or committee meetings to chair and I think that those things were all she did, aside from being a mum and wife.'

Gabe's look of horror was comical as he pulled on his

151

old duffel coat. 'I'll have to apologise to her. Get me another drink, someone.' And he hurried to follow Carola out through the door.

It was Ben's round and so he went to the bar for two more pints and another Pepsi. When he returned, it was to find Alexia's ex-boyfriend, Sebastian, had arrived.

'Why don't we just try it?' Sebastian was asking Alexia. He might be described as a bear of a man but a teddy bear rather than a grizzly.

Ben resumed his seat. 'Don't mind me.'

Sebastian evidently did mind as he gave Alexia a wistful smile and made for the bar.

Alexia shook her head as she drank the foam off yet another pint. Where did she put them all within her half-pint frame? 'He's just tried the "let's just go out together as friends until you leave" angle.' She rolled her dark eyes. 'I didn't have the energy to tell him I'm not leaving and then have to fend off his attempts to make us a couple again.'

Ben winked. 'I could tell him about our night together if you think it would put him off.'

'Don't be an idiot!' Alexia looked pained. The flush on her cheeks reminded Ben of when no frown had crinkled her brow or worry clouded her eyes and she'd worn only a smile as she'd shared her body with him in the dancing light of the fire. He knew he shouldn't have reminded her of what had happened but when images of her naked breasts hung in his mind's eye and the memory of the feel of her skin made his fingertips tingle . . .

Gabe burst back into the pub, wiping rain from his face, hurrying to rejoin them. 'Brr, I got soaked. It's raining cats and dogs.' Hanging his coat on the back of his chair, he edged it closer to the fire. 'Damned woman wouldn't let me apologise. Said I was right and I'd given her something to think about. Now I feel worse than ever.'

Ben fell to sipping his drink and listening as Alexia and Gabe discussed the oddities in Carola's behaviour, glad Gabe had bumbled back in to break the spell, and shaken to realise he'd quite like to put Seb off Alexia.

And had been about to say so.

Alexia returned home from the pub exhausted, but her mind was too busy to allow her to sleep.

Both Sebastian and Carola had unsettled her. And Ben! When he'd told her what Imogen had done her heart had felt as if it were literally trying to reach out to him. Then he'd offered to tell Seb about their night together and she'd returned abruptly to the more familiar state of feeling twitchy irritation with him. To top it off, he'd then lapsed into a state of silence for most of the rest of the evening.

Once in her favourite cosy pyjamas covered in little paw prints, Alexia climbed into bed and propped herself on her pillows. Setting up her laptop, she began firing off emails. First to Dion the roofer, giving him the go ahead to buy the reclaimed tiles and trying to woo him into starting her job the moment he had them in his possession. She moved on to plasterer Freddie, ground worker Hayden and electrician Phil, outlining the work for which she needed estimates and requesting site meetings.

That done, she checked her inbox. The several work-related emails could wait until the morrow but her cursor hovered over one from Elton. She clicked and watched his email fill the screen.

Alexia,

  Sorry our last conversation ended on a sour note.
I might have something for you, if you're interested?
  Elton

She drummed her fingers. Resentment told her to click
delete but common sense grabbed her clicking finger before
she could do it. When she'd thought she was going to
work with Elton she'd kept only enough work-related
irons in the fire till Christmas to smooth her transition
from one geographical area to another. Now Jodie was
gone she had no rent coming in so she needed more irons
and a much hotter fire. Whilst her mortgage wasn't as
overwhelming as some people's it did need paying.

The bleak fact was that she couldn't afford to be choosy,
even if it was Elton offering.

  What kind of 'something'?
  A

The clock read nearly midnight, but she still felt too
keyed up to sleep. Probably working on emails tonight
had been a bad idea because all the problems associated
with The Angel and her pique at Elton were now buzzing
like a swarm of insects with names such as *doubt, fear,
worry, anger* and *pressure*. Unlike Pandora's Box there
seemed no corner reserved for *hope*.

She decided to read for a while. She was halfway through
a great romantic comedy that had been keeping her attention for the last few nights.

Somehow, though, curiosity guiding her fingers, instead
of picking up her paperback she typed into her search
engine *Lloyd Hardaker*. The first item that came up was

from the *Reading Chronicle* and was headlined: *Woman Dies in Head-On Collision*. Uncomfortable now at her own interest, she skimmed the account of Lloyd taking a corner on a country road half in the wrong lane and the collision with an oncoming vehicle, flipping Lloyd's car on its side. Of the other car careering out of control into a tree and its driver not surviving the impact, and Mr Hardaker's blood alcohol level being nearly three times the legal limit. Her heart ached with her knowledge of the pain that underlay the passing mention at the foot of the column. *Mrs Imogen Hardaker, passenger in Lloyd Hardaker's car and wife of the driver's brother, Benedict Hardaker, received life-changing injuries.*

A later article covered Lloyd's sentencing at crown court. *Guilty! Lawyer in the Dock* rehashed the previous article and contained a 'no comment' comment from Holloway Menton & Partners, solicitors and Lloyd's erstwhile employers, and an emotional 'I hope he rots in jail' quote from the husband of the poor woman who'd died.

The next searches simply listed links to Lloyd's Facebook and LinkedIn profiles, all no doubt leading to *page unavailable* messages or out-of-date information.

She was about to close down her computer when her curiosity got the better of her again and she typed *Benedict Hardaker* into the search engine.

Top of the list was a website for the company Hardaker Tree Management. The company had changed ownership earlier in the year but it looked to be a thriving business full of smiling employees wearing hard hats with raised visors. Clicking on *Blog* and searching the archives from before the company had changed hands she found several entries about Ben very visibly heading up his own company. Ben at the tops of tall trees, Ben travelling to work at stately homes. Ben in a dark suit receiving an award for entrepreneurship from the local chamber of trade, a beautiful woman at his side in a blue-green shiny cocktail dress that looked as if it should be made of mermaids' tails.

Feeling guilty at poking her nose into Ben's past, she closed the machine.

As she tried to sleep though, one thought kept spooling through her mind: Benedict Hardaker had once had a ready smile. The kind that actually made him look happy.

Chapter Twelve

The rest of Alexia's week passed in a whirl of work. Issues arose on the basement conversion job and made it hard to keep it on track time-wise. Mood boards had to be prepared ahead of meetings with clients. Noting the thinness of her order book in November and December she emailed five people who'd previously sent enquiries to explain that she was not now relocating and would be happy to discuss their needs if they hadn't yet found a decorator. These, and all the other tasks involved in running a business, particularly one that had hit a bump in the road, took care of the day job.

The Angel took care of every other spare moment. On Tuesday the scaffolding had gone up so Dion could begin work on the roof early next week and Alexia had squeezed in site meetings with Hayden and Phil. Another was arranged with Freddie for Saturday morning.

Roughly, the schedule said Hayden and his mate Toby would get the ground floor to screed level while Phil the electrician and Malc the plumber worked upstairs. In their wake, Freddie and Nick would plaster and Alexia would make decisions on joinery. There would be a lot of drying out time before tiles could be laid and walls painted. She was already combing Gumtree, eBay and Bettsbrough Freecycle for whatever she thought she could use. Good kitchen equipment bargains were particularly hard to come by but Gabe had blanched at the cost of a commercial espresso machine first time round, let alone now their budget was a shadow of its former self.

By Friday she was shattered. Even spending the afternoon on a mood board based around lilac checks and apple green floral for a pitch to a small hotel on the edge of Bettsbrough wasn't the joy it should have been. She spent the evening working on how much of the walls of The Angel's cavernous kitchen should be tiled and estimated the square metreage needed over the entire ground floor, along with grout and adhesive. At least when she fell into bed, she slept.

On Saturday morning, refreshed, she whizzed off to The Angel to wait for Freddie to turn up so they could decide on plastering needs. Ben arrived at just about the same time, which meant Freddie could tap walls and point out unsound plaster to Ben. All Alexia had to do was make notes and establish that Freddie would manage the areas of brickwork to block up what had been fireplaces.

Freddie pulled a regretful face. 'You're not putting the fireplaces back, then?'

Without looking up from her notes, she shook her head. 'Not necessary. No money. No fireplaces.'

'Shame.' Freddie settled his hands in the bib of his dungarees. 'I expect all the fire surrounds were original, were they?'

'Yep. Cast iron and Victorian tile. Worth nicking.'

Freddie tutted and went back to tapping walls and

making sure Ben knew how to use a hammer and bolster to chop off unsound plaster. Alexia hid a smile that someone was questioning Ben for a change.

Once Freddie had eased himself back into his van and trundled off Ben followed Alexia into the Bar Parlour. 'So shall I begin on the unsound plaster?'

Alexia scuffed the floor with the toe of her boot. 'How do you feel about breaking up this old lime mortar instead? We need to get it up for the damp proof membrane to go down.'

'OK. I don't have a sledgehammer or pickaxe but I think Gabe has. Be right back.'

With the sound of his departing truck in her ears, Alexia was free to pace around the ground floor with her pad and pencil, opening her mind to possibilities.

The huge kitchen worried her. The floor was OK as at some time heavy-duty vinyl had been laid. Shane hadn't deemed it worth the effort to rip it up and steal whatever lay beneath and if the loos and pantry were anything to go by he would have found only workaday quarry tiles anyway. There wasn't much remedial work necessary in the kitchen but the amount of equipment they could afford would be lost in the huge room, and tiles for the work areas plus emulsion for walls and ceiling would cost.

She wandered back to the Bar Parlour and studied the spot where the bar had been. If they simply sectioned off that area they could get everything in behind a counter: refrigeration, food preparation, storage and sinks. She made a series of rapid notes to discuss with Gabe, the environmental health officer, the electrician and the plumber, and made rough sketches.

When Ben returned she asked him to begin on the floor of the Public so she could continue undisturbed.

She immersed herself in her ideas to the rhythmic thump of the sledgehammer and scrape of the shovel in the next room. When she reached the stage of needing the software on her computer to produce a proper drawing, she poked her head into the Public to tell Ben she was leaving.

He paused to remove his hat and safety visor, leaning on the sledgehammer and breathing heavily, dust on his clothes and lower part of his face. The mortar was broken up around his feet and more was piled up behind him. 'Do you know if it's safe to go up in the loft?'

She stepped a little further into the room. 'The timbers are sound according to the survey Gabe had done when he bought the place, but it depends what you're planning. At the back there's only the tarpaulin between you and a long drop.'

'Understood.' He wiped his face on his sleeve, balanced the sledgehammer on its head, reached for a bottle of water and took a couple of thirsty gulps. 'I'm trying to think of ways to monetize this place. I wondered whether it was possible to rent out the upstairs and, if so, worth converting the loft to make additional living space.'

'It would make an amazing two-floor apartment and we're in such easy commuting distance of Peterborough, young professionals would love its history and dormers overlooking the village. And those fantastic wide floor-boards and moulded plaster ceilings. Maybe a Juliet balcony.' She laughed. 'But there's no money for a new kitchen and bathroom upstairs let alone a loft conversion. Maybe when the community café's up and running . . . but it will take time to accrue capital.'

He grimaced, swiping up his sledgehammer again and hefting it in both hands. 'If he wasn't such a stubborn old sod there would be money. I'd invest. Or lend, if he let me.'

Alexia stretched and yawned. 'I'll leave you now to frown over that problem while I go home to frown over my computer. Then I think I'll have earned a couple of glasses of wine this evening.'

Ben pulled his hardhat back on, obviously ready to convert more of the mortar to rubble. 'I was thinking along similar lines. Why not let me buy you a drink?'

'I didn't mean I'd earned wine from you!' she protested, her face feeling warmer than the frigid air inside The Angel warranted.

'And I didn't take it as a heavy hint. I'm offering to buy you a drink in appreciation of you going above and beyond the call of duty in helping my uncle out of a tight spot.' He flipped his visor down so it was harder for her to see his face. 'Also my final divorce papers arrived this morning and I feel as if I should somehow mark the event. I only really know you and Gabe in the village. And Gabe's had a rotten cold all week.'

Alexia found herself laughing. 'So I'm your last resort?'

He grinned. 'Or nearly my first choice, if you want a more positive spin. But don't worry if it doesn't appeal. I'm man enough to go for a pint on my own.'

He turned back to his work but Alexia's conscience twanged as she imagined him spending the evening alone when such a seismic shift had occurred in his life. To be married and then single. So, as she turned to leave, she tossed back casually, 'It's not good to drink alone. I'll meet you in The Three Fishes about eight.'

At home, once settled with a pot of tea – she must be catching teapots and loose-leaf tea from Gabe – and her computer, Alexia was soon absorbed in creating plans and digital rendered models until an email from Elton pinged into her inbox. Knowing she'd be unable to sink back into her work until she knew what he had to say, she clicked on it.

Alexia,

The 'something' would be doing job costings for me. I'd do all the design but it would be great if you could get the estimates in, make recommendations, collate etc. All done by email, obvs.

He suggested fees that were pretty much the going rate. Alexia glared at the screen, longing to send back:

Stick your rotten work where the sun don't shine, you shitty little git. That's the least enjoyable and rewarding part of the role you originally offered me. And 'all done by email, obvs' just emphasises that you don't want me sullying your sites with my 'done up like a kipper' presence.

But she didn't have the luxury. None of the enquiries she'd followed up this week had elicited replies and the sad truth was that most people likely to use someone like her would already be fixed up for the short term. She'd set most of her regular team to work on The Angel anyway so anything she might pick up would probably have to be the kind she got her own hands dirty on. Such decorating-only jobs were generally short but sweet, which meant you needed a lot of them.

She printed her drawings out for Gabe, knowing he preferred paper to a screen, then, chin propped despondently on fist, pecked out a reply to Elton.

OK, send it over when ready.

Though she knew her missive was brusque and ungracious she couldn't bring herself to sound grateful. As soon as she could get her order book into its usual satisfactory state she'd tell Elton he'd have to do his own costings. Hopefully, she'd be able to choose her moment – the one that would cause maximum inconvenience to him and make him fully aware of what a diamond he'd let slip through his fingers.

Down in the dumps, she snapped shut her computer and prepared comfort food of beans on toast smothered in cheese followed by digestive biscuits spread with Nutella and settled down to binge on property programmes on TV.

Ben left the frosty evening behind him and stepped into the warmth of The Three Fishes. Alexia was there before him, laughing and joking in the middle of a group beside a Christmas tree someone had felt the need for though it wasn't yet the end of October. He hesitated. Alexia looked so much at one with her own tribe; following the eddying conversation and using names with easy familiarity.

He recognised the skill of fitting in. There had once been pubs in Didbury where he'd exercised it himself. Ben shifted the weight of the messenger bag on his shoulder. He didn't feel the need to wear that puppy-dog look that Sebastian was wearing at the fringes of the group, but he had to acknowledge Alexia looked good, hooking her thumbs in the pockets of her jeans and leaning on the bar while she listened to a woman with a rope of red-blonde hair, tilting back her head and laughing.

Just when he was giving serious thought to reopening

the door and fading back through it, Alexia caught sight of him and waved. As she didn't make a move to join him he had little choice but to skirt the edges of the group to reach her.

'Come and meet my friends,' she urged. 'This is Ratty and Jos, from the garage by The Cross, and Tess and Miranda.' She introduced about another half a dozen people but, apart from the men from the garage, which Ben passed whenever he drove or walked to Gabe's, he knew he didn't have a hope of remembering names. They were drifting off, anyway, reminding each other that they had a table booked in the dining area.

Ratty lingered, hand-in-hand with the woman with the long plait. 'Are you the wizard in the woods?'

Ben shrugged. 'Can't be. No pointy hat.'

The woman, Tess, gave Ben a soft smile. 'But you have an owl? One of Gabe's rescued creatures? He told me about it. The thing is . . . well, I'm an illustrator and it would be brilliant for me to get some sketches of a baby owl. I work on children's books. Heavy hinting going on here . . .' Her smile turned winsome.

Ben laughed. Several minutes later he found he'd agreed to Tess visiting him at Woodward Cottage armed with her sketchbook, had taken her card, given her his phone number and promised to tell Gabe from her that he was to get better soon.

Ben stared after her as she and Ratty wove their way between the backs of Saturday evening drinkers and were lost to view. 'I hardly know anyone in the village but they seem to know me.'

Alexia shrugged. 'Don't come to an English village if you crave anonymity.'

'At least the villagers seem friendly tonight.'

She rolled her eyes and fanned her face with her hand. 'And that's a huge relief, let me tell you.'

They turned to the bar. Alexia requested a 'big cold glass of chardonnay' and he ordered a pint of Courage Best as a nod to his Reading-area roots.

When they'd settled at one of the nearby brass-topped tables she raised her glass. 'Happy Divorce Day, for good or bad.'

He returned the toast. 'I'm not sure "good" or "bad" are the right categories. Let's just say it's for the best in the end, no going back, blah blah.' Putting down his glass he flipped open his bag and drew out a dusty book. Its cover showed patches of its original blue but most of it had faded to grey. 'I went up in the loft after you'd left and found these old photos of The Angel when she was still a pub. They look like professional shots.'

Lips parting in awe Alexia took the album with gentle, reverential hands and opened it. Each page bore one or two photos, black and white but yellowing with age under their gloss. 'Wow. Gold dust.' She turned a page. 'There are eleven people in this shot and only one of them a woman. Her blouse and skirt cover her from neck to ankles.' The men wore caps and high-buttoned jackets and held large tankards. All stood, unsmiling and unnaturally stiff, around the polished bar with its acid-etched glass screens.

Ben followed Alexia's progress through the pages. 'The album certainly reinforces what was lost when Shane and Tim's thieving hands wrenched that history away from its rightful home.'

'Too true. See this picture of the bar in the Bar Parlour with all the bottles on the back wall and the advertising mirrors? We had some of those mirrors until Shane did his dirty work.' Slowly she travelled the pages, careful not to touch the photos themselves. 'I wish we were still able to give The Angel the sympathetic restoration she deserves. By Christmas she'd have looked like this again – with a little updating of things like gas lamps.'

And Alexia would have had the future she deserved, Ben thought. The project would have become the cherry on top of her portfolio and she'd have followed her career curve to pastures new, fulfilling her potential in a way she never would here in Middledip.

They could have more easily forgotten their one-night stand. But then no one would have asked Ben, 'Are you all right?' and seemed to care about his answer and Ben would probably have had no one to share a Divorce Day drink with.

'Look at this group shot!' Alexia giggled, stirring Ben from his thoughts. 'They're all lined up behind the bar so I think they must be the staff. The women look like nurse-maids and the men have winged collars under their waistcoats and aprons. Look at the moustache on this guy; it would do a walrus proud. And the chef's hat is about two feet tall! Do you think this woman could be the landlady? She looks a scary old grump, doesn't she?'

'She does.' Ben craned his neck to view the photo in question. 'I can imagine her rapping out, "Time, gentlemen, please!" and everyone meekly shuffling off home. I think the same lady's in some framed photos I left in the Bar Parlour because they're so fragile. There's a great one of men in the yard, too, rolling barrels around, lots more droopy moustaches in evidence.'

A man from the next table interrupted. 'What have you got there, 'Lexia? Old photos? Wow, is that what The Angel used to look like inside?' The rest of his table were soon crowding round oohing and ahhing, underlining Ben's earlier point about the villagers having seemingly returned to their usual levels of friendliness. Tubb appeared with the air of one who considered everything in the pub to be his business and soon half his customers were jostling to view the album too. Alexia, refusing to pass it around for fear of damage, slowly turned the pages for them.

Ben sipped his pint and watched her chatting and laughing and joining in the hazarding of opinions about the people in the pictures and whether anybody present could claim to be a descendant. Was it entirely bad that Alexia had failed in her bid to transplant herself from this village? The friendship and fellowship this evening wasn't granted to everyone, no matter how long they'd lived in a place or how small it was.

Eventually the interest died down. People drifted back to their seats and Alexia shut the album, giving the cover a last stroke before handing it back. 'Have you shown Gabe?'

'He was too stuffed up and croaky to be bothered. I bought the village shop out of Lemsip and cough syrup for him and ended up promising to feed his animals for a few days. It means getting up early to get over there and let the chickens out.'

Alexia's brow crinkled in concern. 'Poor Gabe! I hope it's not flu. I can let the chickens out in the mornings, if you like, and do the feed and water. Does he have enough food for himself?'

'He says he doesn't fancy anything and just wants to be left alone in bed. Wouldn't listen when I tried to tell him what else I found in the loft, told me to bugger off and do what I wanted with it.'

Her eyes sparkled as she laughed. 'What else did you find?'

167

This was what Ben had been waiting for. He fished in his pocket for his phone and called up his camera roll. 'It's a bit of a treasure trove. I guess it belonged to the landlady who died.' He tilted his phone so Alexia could see for herself. 'I believe some of this ceramic stuff's Clarice Cliff. And there's a proper old trunk, the kind that people used to take on long sea voyages, with a wedding dress in it. Then there are oil paintings, silverware and I don't know what else.'

It seemed Alexia's evening for saying 'wow' and she said it over and over again while she swiped through the images he'd collected. 'Presumably it all belongs to the old landlady's relatives?'

Ben took a draught of beer. 'Not at all. Gabe was definite about that, between bouts of coughing. Because the relatives didn't want to clear anything or send in a house-clearance company Gabe bought the property with contents. It's all his now.'

Dark shining eyes lifted slowly to Ben. 'This stuff must be worth money.'

Excitement fluttered in Ben's chest. 'I'm sure it is. I'm going to contact the specialist auction house in Peterborough for valuation. I reckon it could add thousands to Gabe's pot. Anything the auction house turns its nose up at I'll list on eBay.'

'Oh, Ben,' Alexia breathed, 'this could make a real difference.'

It took Ben a second to kick his brain into gear to answer. That breathy *Oh, Ben* had transported him back to their encounter. 'Let's hope so,' he managed 'Anything that brings in money has to be good.'

'Especially as he doesn't want you to risk your savings.'

Ben frowned. 'I'm tempted to pretend the stuff from

the attic fetches more than it does and get some money to him that way.'

Alexia snorted a laugh. 'Sort of reverse stealing?'

Unwillingly, Ben found himself smiling. 'It sounds crazy put like that.'

She became serious. 'But the situation makes you consider just about anything, doesn't it? I've been researching getting The Angel on a property makeover show.'

Ben's attention was caught. 'Is it worth a shot?'

Draining the last of her wine, Alexia glanced round at the bar. Tubb caught the glance and raised his eyebrows, pointing at their glasses. Alexia nodded, and, in seconds, refills stood on the bar. All she had to do was hop up and pay for the round, carry them back to the table and pick up the conversation. 'There are a lot of property shows still around, even though the bubble's supposed to have burst. All of them require the subject of the programme to have their own budget. *And* they all work with the subject's main dwelling, not commercial property.'

'Ah. Nothing to be gained.'

She shook her head, propping her chin on her hand. 'There's even a programme that specifically rights builderly wrongs but, again, works with householders who have their own budget. So unless you can do a bit of abracadabra, Wizard of the Woods, it's a non-starter.'

'I forgot my book of spells.' He sighed. Around them, the pub buzzed with Saturday evening chatter. Because it was a nice pub in a nice village the only raised voices came in the forms of bellows of laughter or good-natured barracking around the dartboard. Ben stretched out his legs beneath the table and settled deeper into his seat. 'Has The Three Fishes ever had a bar brawl?'

Alexia glanced around with an affectionate smile for their surroundings. 'Not to my knowledge. It's pretty cosy. Aren't there pubs like this where you come from?'

'Not really. Didbury has its fair share of rough diamonds.' *Like Imogen's family*, a little voice reminded him, making him smile ruefully to himself.

Imogen. He was officially divorced from Imogen. Realisation hit him anew. He was no longer a married man. It took a bit of getting used to. He was sitting across a table from a woman he'd already . . . encountered, and he need have no guilty conscience about it. He could officially date. Officially take himself off to wherever the nearest club was and see who he could pull. Go home with. Get naked . . . And thoughts of getting naked brought him back to Alexia who, he suddenly realised, was gazing at him, one eyebrow arched.

'What?' he demanded, hoping he was managing to meet her gaze without thoughts of her nakedness showing on his face.

'Me, what? You, what! The weirdest expressions have been crossing your face. Do you have stomach ache?'

'Sorry if I zoned out. I was just taking a reality hit I suppose.'

Instantly her expression softened. 'We're supposed to be marking your divorce but we've hardly mentioned it.'

'I don't need to talk about it,' he put in swiftly.

She dimpled at him, eyes narrowing. 'I could really make you uncomfortable by asking avidly if you're on the lookout for someone new, couldn't I?' The absence of wine in her glass suggested that she'd been letting the alcohol do its job in terms of relaxation. A slight flush edged her cheekbones and her eyes were dancing. 'You'd think I was either going to put myself on your list of hopefuls or start matchmaking between you and my mates.'

It was so exactly what he did think that Ben was surprised into a laugh. 'Some people see divorce as a sign that they're not cut out for relationships.'

She was obviously enjoying teasing him. 'But you have money in the bank. When you've finished your contract on the Carlysle estate you could buy a house or another business. Find another wife.'

'What about you?' he countered. 'You could look for another boyfriend.'

Her eyes looked nearly black in the soft lighting of the bar. 'I don't want a boyfriend. The Angel's refurbishment is still going to gain me commercial experience and a lot of urban properties have commercial premises on the ground floor and residential above. By the time The Angel's up and running I'll have a record of working with the local planning authority on non-residential and adapting to a changing situation in getting the new kitchen plans passed by the Environmental Health Authority. I haven't given up on finding the vehicle to ride out of the village on.'

Surprised, probably because of his own assumptions that her plans going to hell would mean she'd stay in the village, he went to ask more, but a woman with a dripping umbrella hurried in and interrupted with a flurry of low-voiced exclamations. 'Alexia, would you talk to Jodie, darling? She's so down. She won't talk to me but she says she'll talk to you if I fetch you.' Her beige coat was beaded with raindrops and she wiped her damp, dyed-blonde hair back from her face.

Alexia hardly moved, aside from her eyes cutting left to regard the woman. 'Jodie and I haven't talked to each

171

other since she left nearly two weeks ago, Iona, and I'm having a drink with a friend at the moment. Ben, this is Iona, Jodie's mum.'

'But—' Iona began, obviously more focused on her mission than on observing social niceties.

With a little shove Alexia sent her wine glass across the table towards Ben. 'Your round, isn't it?'

Ben, having no confidence that he could commune wordlessly with bar staff, rose to order drinks in the traditional way. 'Would you like a drink, Iona?'

'No, thanks.' She scarcely looked at him. All her attention was focused on Alexia, a perplexed frown above her eyes.

When he returned to the table Iona had gone. 'All right?' he asked cautiously, observing Alexia's set expression.

Tonelessly she replied, 'Fine, thanks.'

He set himself to distracting her from what were evidently difficult thoughts by fishing out the album of photos again and passing uncomplimentary remarks about the long-ago po-faced people in the pictures, but he didn't get much of a reaction.

In fact, the happy, teasing Alexia seemed to have vanished along with Jodie's mum.

Chapter Thirteen

Alexia woke with the heaviness of head caused by drinking four large glasses of wine. She also knew a heaviness of heart from acknowledging that she could have been nicer to Iona. She'd contact Jodie later.

A pint of water and a couple of paracetamol helped the head, and the heart was buoyed by a pot of tea and a bacon sandwich. She pulled on her coat and boots and braved a gusty morning to let Gabe's chickens out of the coop. Once they were contentedly clucking and pecking at the feed she cast around their run she knocked on Gabe's door.

No answer.

She knocked again then tried the handle. It wouldn't budge.

She tried his phone. No answer.

Heart picking up uneasily, she texted Ben.

Alexia: *Have seen to hens. At Gabe's door but can't get reply . . .*

Ben: *On my way.*

She whiled away an anxious ten minutes peeping fruitlessly through windows, pausing to pet Luke the cat, who was pacing outside the back door as if fully aware he ought to have been let in by now. Luke was the kind of cat who'd let you stroke him if it made you feel better and Alexia felt a shade calmer for smoothing the glossy black fur and hearing Luke purr like a distant engine.

As if in reply came the sound of another distant engine, though rapidly nearing. Ben's truck appeared, jolting along Gabe's track faster than looked comfortable. He pulled up, shut down the engine and hit the ground running.

Hair blowing into her eyes in the wind, Alexia jumped back to give him access to the door. Neither spoke as Ben fumbled for the right key and got it to turn.

Bursting into the silent and unusually chilly kitchen Ben crossed straight to the door to the hall calling out behind him, 'You'd better stay here. He'll be mortified if you charge in and he's not decent.'

Alexia slithered to a halt. Although she couldn't argue with his reasoning, the hurrying of her heart echoed the receding sound of his feet racing up the stairs and she felt as if he was keeping her out in case something bad had happened.

To occupy herself she located Luke's food in a cupboard, spooned some out and topped up his water. The black cat settled down enthusiastically to the task of emptying the dish, curling his tail delicately across his paws.

Alexia opened the door to the hall and strained for noises from upstairs. After a moment she caught Ben's voice, muffled but calm, and breathed more easily. For Ben to be speaking, Gabe must be capable of hearing. But then came an explosion of coughing, the endless, gasping, helpless kind that made you feel sick to listen to. Gabe.

Alexia hurried to put the kettle on but found the range out, which explained the frigid air. A quick investigation proved that the ashpit was full to bursting. Gabe must have been ill for days and not felt like attending to the clinker and ash. She felt a lurch of guilt for not making time in her busy week to check whether he needed help.

Rather than pausing to clean out and light the cooker she turned to the little electric hob Gabe kept for when the range wasn't in use in summer and set the kettle on one of its rings, then, while waiting for it to boil, raked out the ash from the range. Before she could do more than screw up a few pieces of newspaper and criss-cross the sticks ready to relight it, Ben thundered downstairs. 'Going to get some advice from the NHS helpline. I'll use the landline because it's more reliable.'

He snatched up the phone that perched on Gabe's kitchen windowsill between a pot of chives and a letter rack. Alexia set a match to the paper and listened as, once he'd got through, he explained that his uncle's heavy cold had developed into a high temperature and racking cough. 'He's experiencing terrible sweats, isn't eating but is sleeping all the time and can barely get out of bed. Yes, I'll hold.' After a short pause he explained it all again, presumably to someone new, ending with, 'Thank you, I'll wait to hear,' and replacing the phone with a clatter. A frown line cut between his eyebrows. 'A GP's going to ring back. They want me to get as much fluid down him as possible. I gave him water while I was up there but I need to try him with more.'

Alexia put out a hand to stay him as he made as if to dash off again. 'What about a hot drink? And food?' She winced as the sound of another jagged bout of coughing floated down the stairs.

Ben raked his fingers through his hair. 'We can try him with a cup of tea but he says he has no appetite.'

Gabe normally loved his food. Alexia was alarmed as she found a clean mug and washed out the teapot. Suspicious of the open milk in the fridge, she took the lid off a new bottle. 'And he's been lying there all alone not wanting to ask for help?'

'It sounds as if he's barely woken up since I saw him yesterday.' Ben took the tea Alexia made upstairs, reappearing in the kitchen only when the landline phone began to ring again.

Meanwhile, Alexia had heated another kettle so she could deal with the washing-up abandoned in the sink. She tried not to clatter while Ben talked to a GP, reciting the facts for a third time. He was frowning once again as he ended the call.

'The GP wants another report in four to six hours, particularly if Gabe's no better.' Ben rubbed his chin anxiously. He hadn't shaved that morning, judging by the whisper of rasping stubble. 'I'm going to stay here with him but I need to grab a few things from home first.'

'I can stay till you get back.'

'I was hoping you'd say that.' Ben slipped an arm around her shoulders and pressed a kiss on her temple.

Everything paused for an instant.

Then he was in motion once more. 'I'll be as quick as I can.' Snatching up the keys to his truck, he shot out of the door.

'Right. OK,' Alexia said to Luke, who had finished his meal and was washing his paw. 'That was new. Ben and I don't kiss.' Or not apart from on That Night, when they'd kissed a lot. Over a wide area.

She got the range going and binned a piece of mottled cheese and the bottle of suspect milk from Gabe's fridge. Creeping upstairs she peeped into Gabe's room, but he was an unmoving lump beneath the quilt, breathing noisily. At least he wasn't coughing while he slept. She crept back downstairs, answered Luke's imperious meow to be let out to patrol his domain and then settled herself at the kitchen table and turned to checking her phone.

Elton had responded to her last email:

OK, cool, hope this is some consolation.

In reply Alexia pulled her ugliest face while waving two fingers violently at the phone before stabbing *delete*. The rest of her mail was an unexceptional mix of newsletters and notifications.

When she'd read or deleted them she sighed and, feeling stupidly apprehensive considering the length of their friendship, texted Jodie.

Alexia: *Saw your mum last night and she mentioned you'd appreciate a chat with me. If so, I should be available later today.*

A reply pinged right back.

Jodie: *I thought you'd come last night.*

Alexia quashed a desire to point out that Jodie had no right to such expectations after the way she'd sneaked off. Alexia had taken her in when her marriage crashed against the rocks and expected better treatment than she'd received. She typed again.

Alexia: *I was busy.*

While she waited to see if Jodie would respond she browsed Facebook and saw that Jodie had checked in from work a couple of times in the last few days and also from the swimming pool in Bettsbrough yesterday afternoon. Evidently she hadn't, as Alexia had half-expected, turned herself into a room hermit. The phone sounded an alert.

Jodie: Mum said you were just hanging out at *The Three Fishes.*

Alexia: That's right.

Alexia refused to address what she knew to be the subtext, which was that hanging out at The Three Fishes could easily have been abandoned in favour of rushing off to see what Jodie needed. But Jodie's recent behaviour had opened Alexia's eyes as well as bruised her feelings.

Jodie was needy, that was no secret, and her warmth and humour vanished when she was under pressure. Alexia had always showed understanding; knowing the 'real Jodie' would be along again soon. But maybe, by accepting Jodie's behaviour, Alexia had been telegraphing that being high maintenance was OK and nobody else's feelings mattered. If so, Alexia really needed to learn from that mistake.

A long text silence followed. Upstairs Gabe exploded with a fresh paroxysm of coughing before settling again. Alexia checked both Facebook and Instagram before her phone tinged to signal the arrival of another text.

Jodie: I'm sorry I haven't been a very good friend to you recently. Can you come over now?

Thawing slightly, Alexia tapped 'reply'.

Alexia: Not right now. I'm hoping to be free later, though. Shall I text you when I am?

Jodie: Yes, please. I'd appreciate it.

Maybe the warm Jodie was ready to reappear?

As Ben still hadn't returned, Alexia checked Freecycle and was delighted to be able to secure two kitchen chairs and a small pine table to be picked up from the other side of Bettsbrough. Two legs were trying to drop off one of the chairs and the back was unstable on the other, reported the donor. *Not a problem*, she typed in a message, and arranged to be in touch regarding when to pick them up once she saw the rest of her day more clearly, wanting to be on hand to support Gabe if necessary.

Ben, when he swept back into the house an hour later, seemed to have everything firmly under his control though. He'd brought an overnight bag and a fresh supply of cough syrup and Lemsip from Booze & News.

He also had Barney's tub in his arms, with Barney screeching happily to himself inside.

'All OK?' He was panting slightly with the exertion of carrying so much.

'Gabe has been coughing a bit but he seemed to be sleeping when I checked.' Alexia relieved him of the tub and peeked in as she lowered it carefully to the floor. 'Hello, Barney Owl.'

Barney elongated himself to peer at her, tilting his head and opening his beak. '*HEHHHHHHH!*' His call was noticeably louder and creakier than the last time Alexia had seen him.

She glanced at Ben, who was opening his overnight bag. 'Barney's grown!'

He took out a silver laptop and deposited it on the kitchen table. 'He's only feeding twice a day now, but bigger portions. He's spending a bit of time in his aviary too.'

Alexia put her hand into the tub to let Barney nibble at her fingers. 'Outdoors already?'

'Parent barn owls kick their offspring out into the world at fourteen weeks, which is about now, so he's actually taking advantage of my better nature.' He gave one of his half-smiles as he fired up his computer. 'He'll get out of his tub in here and be a nuisance, hopping up onto things, particularly as he's getting smellier and poopier, but I don't want to leave him in his aviary at Woodward while I'm here.' He seated himself before his computer and trained his gaze on whatever was happening on the screen. 'Anyway,' he went on vaguely, as if most of his mind were already on a planned task, 'my grateful thanks. I hope we haven't taken up too much of your Sunday.'

'Oh. OK.' With the definite feeling of being dismissed, Alexia shrugged on her coat and found her bag, taking an uncertain step towards the door, unsettled by the Ben now before her. Maybe this was how he processed worry? Holding himself aloof and withdrawing? Brooding had been his persona when they'd first met, after all.

But he seemed to process any anxiety about Gabe perfectly well earlier . . . Until the kiss, brief and light as it had been.

Another step towards the door. 'I'm glad I could help. Let me know if you need anything. To do with Gabe, I mean,' she clarified hastily, her cheeks heating. Not that Ben noticed as he seemed to be looking everywhere but at her. It *was* the kiss. He was wishing it undone. She paused with her hand on the doorknob, feeling self-conscious all at once. 'Would you mind letting me know what happens when you speak to the doctor again?'

'Of course.' He kept his eyes trained on his screen. He raised his voice so it would follow her as she stepped outside. 'Thanks again.'

Alexia closed the door behind her, feeling awkward, almost as if she'd made a huge gaffe that had made Ben wish himself free of her presence. Which would have made a lot more sense if she'd been the one doing the kissing.

180

Chapter Fourteen

Alexia felt cross and out of sorts as the wind blew her home. Not only had she never known Gabe suffer more than a sniffle before, but until now it would have been Alexia and Jodie making sure he had what he needed. Now Ben was using his status as blood-relative to dismiss Alexia, and Jodie wasn't showing signs of caring about anybody but herself. Everyone in Alexia's life right now was unsettling her.

And that included Ben. He'd been the only one-night stand of her life. Now, instead of moving out of the village as planned and leaving her uncharacteristically wayward behaviour behind her she was obliged to stay for the time being. It meant facing what she'd done every time she and Ben met, which, because of his relationship to Gabe and The Angel, was often. The spectre of That Night floated between them and it was always going to if the stupid man reacted to a stupid excuse for a kiss – a *peck,* not even a proper kiss – with such a painfully obvious with-drawal.

Marching up her garden path and into the house, she

resolved to make herself too busy to brood on the negatives of her life. 'Keep busy, keep out of trouble,' Grandpop used to say. OK, then.

With the rest of the day now at her disposal, she messaged the person on Freecycle and arranged to drive over to pick up the table and chairs after lunch. If she took the seats out of the multi-purpose vehicle her day job made practical, she was pretty sure she could squash the table and chairs in.

Then, after waggling her phone between her fingers while she pondered, she sent another text to Jodie:

Alexia: I have to go to Bettsbrough for 2.30 p.m. to pick up some stuff. Want to come with?

Jodie: I'm not feeling 100%, can you come here after instead?

With a sigh, Alexia replied that she would. She was lonely for her friend. They hadn't gone a two-week stretch without speaking since they'd met in the village primary school.

After a quick sandwich, overdue as she'd never got around to breakfast, she drove off to make her collection, the blinking blue dot on her phone app guiding her.

The table and two chairs stowed in her vehicle with a bit of pushing and shoving, she drove back to Middledip with them rattling in the back. She could call at Iona's house to see Jodie on her way into the village as they lived at the top end of Port Road. Their house stood with its back to the estate still known as the 'new village' though it had been up for at least fifteen years.

Jodie answered the door when Alexia rang the bell. She seemed hesitant and unsure. 'Hey. Thanks for coming.'

'What's up?' Alexia stepped into the familiar cluttered home that she'd visited a thousand times. A pile of coats swamped the newel post at the foot of the stairs, a curtain had become unhooked at one end and a pile of boxes and bags awaited some purpose unknown. Iona Jones always had stray scarves wafting about and cardigans slipping off a shoulder and her house reflected something of her colourful disarray.

'Mum's not in. Let's go up to my room.' Jodie began up the stairs.

Alexia followed, skirting the laundry basket left at the top of the stairs as if to remind someone that the washing needed attending to. As the basket was overflowing, 'someone' obviously hadn't taken the hint.

Jodie had returned to the room she'd once shared with her big sister, Jaynie. Her bed was unmade and Jaynie's old one was covered in discarded clothes. Black plastic sacks had been shoved haphazardly around the walls, presumably still packed from when Jodie hurriedly vacated Alexia's spare room. They'd unpacked a similar-looking set of bags together when Jodie had moved out of her matrimonial home and in with Alexia.

She wondered whether they would ever have been unpacked if Jodie had been left to her own devices.

Now, Jodie flung herself onto her bed, propping her back against the old-fashioned quilted headboard and pulling the duvet over her feet. Alexia hesitated before settling herself cross-legged on the foot of the same bed. It was that, clear a place on Jaynie's bed or sit on the floor.

Jodie took a deep breath. 'I'm sorry I left like I did,' she said in a rush, her gaze on her hands. 'It was horrible of me and I don't blame you for not coming last night.'

Alexia propped her elbows on her knees. 'I was having a drink with someone and so I told your mum I'd get in touch.'

Jodie peeped at her. 'Mum thought it was Ben the wizard you were hanging out with.' Alexia didn't confirm or deny it so Jodie left that tack in favour of offering her the ghost of a hopeful smile. 'Are we still friends?'

Alexia fidgeted. Sitting cross-legged was already making her back ache. 'I hope so, Jodes. Until two weeks ago I would have said *of course* we were friends and nothing would ever alter that. But . . .'

Jodie scooted down the bed, her eyes huge with unshed tears. 'I'm sorry. But I'm in trouble and I don't know what to do.'

Heart softening, Alexia said gently, 'I understand that you're in trouble. It was terrible what Shane did, stealing the money and stripping out The Angel. We've all ended up in trouble over the missing money and the state of The Angel. It's had a disastrous effect on my career and Gabe—'

'No,' Jodie interrupted. Her face had paled so much that her skin looked almost transparent. '"Trouble" in the way our grans would have meant it. *In* trouble. Pregnant.'

The room seemed to stand still. Alexia stared aghast at Jodie's woebegone expression, at the tears now sliding down her face. It hadn't occurred to her that Jodie could have piled another problem on her teetering stack of problems. 'Oh.'

Jodie nodded. '"Oh". Oh, dear. Oh, shit. Oh, what am I going to do?'

Alexia swallowed. 'Did Shane know?'

Miserably, Jodie nodded. 'I told him about a week before he did his moonlight flit. He was obviously shocked but then he seemed to come round to the idea and suggested we make it our little secret for a few weeks so we could sort of hug it to ourselves. There was me, drawing castles in the air, dreaming of us being a happy family, and all the time he was plotting to bring his horrible scam to a successful conclusion.'

Alexia's mind flew back to the evening of the barbecue, when Jodie had been so tipsy. 'You drank a lot of alcohol for a pregnant mum.'

A sob tugged at the corners of Jodie's mouth. 'I honestly only had one beer, Alexia! He must have spiked it. Then he gave me all that limoncello on top.' She took a big gulp of air. 'He risked his own child so I'd pass out while he cleared out the accounts. He left us both with nothing, that bastard! I think it was me telling him about the baby made him hurry the execution of his plans. I didn't tell you at the time . . .' She grabbed a handful of tissues from beside the bed and stopped to blow her nose, gulping back tears. 'He left a note. I didn't find it straight away because it was stuck inside my laptop. It said, "You shouldn't have tried to trap me, girl. Anyone can avoid pregnancy. You think I don't know that?" But we used condoms, every time! He took responsibility for contraception himself. What did he think I did? Kept a used condom to inseminate myself?'

Then she put her head down in her hands and began to howl. Alexia gathered her up, feeling ready to explode at the extent of Shane's ruthlessness. 'Shh, shh,' she whispered, rocking Jodie like a child. 'Shh, shh.'

It took a lot of hugging and a couple of cups of tea before Jodie calmed enough to speak in anything but sobs and half sentences. She sipped dolefully from a big blue mug, pulling her duvet around her and shuddering with the aftershocks of her storm of tears. 'I left your place because I'd started throwing up in the mornings and I didn't want you to know I was pregnant. I didn't know if I was going to keep the baby.'

'I wouldn't try and talk you into or out of an abortion!' Alexia protested, hurt.

'I know. It just seemed easier to make the decision if nobody knew and I didn't really think about being fair to you. I didn't know if I could survive the grief and humiliation Shane left me with. I thought I was going off my rocker.' She managed a watery approximation of a smile. 'Or more off my rocker than I always am.'

She sniffed. Her eyes were red and swollen. 'Mum's been great. She says she'll help look after the baby so I can work at least part-time. She hopes it's a daughter so we'll be three generations of women living together, loving and supporting each other.' She half-laughed but fresh tears leaked from her eyes at the same time. 'You know what an old hippy my mum is. She'll want me to call the baby Love or Treasure or something.'

For once, Alexia didn't blurt out, 'And you know I'll help. I'm always here for you. We've been friends forever.' It wasn't because she was bearing a grudge. In fact, she could see exactly how Jodie had made the decision to leave Alexia's house without telling her to her face.

It wasn't because she felt Jodie had brought her problems on herself and, unintentionally, on everyone else. She'd been duped by a good-looking, practised rogue with, apparently, not a single scruple in his make up.

It was because she suddenly saw that hers and her friend's lives were about to diverge. Jodie was making a lifestyle change of magnitude, just as Alexia would do when she left the village – which she still hoped to do, somehow, some time.

They were growing apart and their friendship would be affected. It would have been affected if Shane hadn't been a bastard and they'd formed a family, too. Or if

Alexia had taken up the wonderful job with Elton. It was a fact of life, Alexia thought an hour later, driving home after ministering cups of tea and satisfying herself that Jodie was OK to be left alone. In fact, she felt that Jodie had summoned up some inner strength from somewhere. Maybe it came from the baby.

When she reached home she backed her vehicle up to the workshop and opened both sets of doors. The chairs didn't take a moment to pull out and line up inside but the table wasn't quite so easy. Although it wasn't large, it was fairly heavy.

She was considering whether to try it on her own when a figure came to the end of the drive and hovered as if waiting to be noticed. With a sinking heart, Alexia realised that the figure was Carola. She sighed. A lecture about the responsibilities of fundraising wasn't what she wanted to round out a fun day.

Apparently Carola couldn't read sighs because she marched across the flagstones as if invited. 'I'm sorry you and I have been at loggerheads lately,' she began unexpectedly. 'I think a lot of it has been my fault.'

Alexia tried not to look astonished. Carola generally set her eyes on a goal and then expected others to help her achieve it. Alexia had never seen her offer any kind of apology for that. 'The village hall means a lot to you, I know.'

'Yes.' Carola bit the word off as if there was more she could say. 'Anyway, what Gabe said about me helping – or not helping – struck home. He's right. My husband always said I'm only ever happy if I'm Queen Bee. I'd sort of like to prove him wrong so I've come to offer to be a . . . what do you call bees that aren't the queen?'

'Drones?'

187

Carola wrinkled her nose. 'Oh, no, I don't think that's very me.' She whisked out her phone and tapped and swiped until she'd pulled up the relevant information. 'Drones are male. "Worker bees" are the females who aren't queens. I'll be a worker. Part of the hive.' She returned her phone to her pocket and beamed expectantly.

'Oh.' It had been a long day and Alexia wasn't sure she was correctly interpreting Carola's remarks. 'What is it you're offering?'

'To help you with The Angel. I'm very good at decorating and whatnot. I've done a lot.'

'So I've heard.' Alexia smothered a grin. Carola's decorating was a village legend. She loved makeover programmes and learned skills to utilise liberally on her house up in the new village – or Little Dallas as it was less kindly known. Villagers insisted they were worried that if they let their kids visit Charlotte and Emily they'd come out stippled or stencilled. 'Erm . . .' Alexia tried to think of a way of saying, 'We don't want all those nineties paint techniques all over the place, thanks'.

Carola tilted her head. 'I can let someone else lead a project, you know. And I need something to keep me out of mischief.'

'That's true,' Alexia agreed, perhaps too frankly. 'OK, welcome aboard. Would you like to help me get this table out, please?'

Although she looked surprised to be given a job there and then, Carola looked pleased, too. They pushed and pulled the table to a point where they could manhandle – or womanhandle – it into the workshop.

Carola gazed about, taking in Grandpop's tools racked on the wall and Alexia's pots of brushes. 'I didn't realise you kept your grandfather's workshop up.'

'It's going to get a lot of use over the next few weeks while I collect unwanted tables and chairs and refurbish them for The Angel. We're short of dosh, in case you hadn't heard.'

Carola acknowledged the hit with a laugh. 'But these chairs have had it. The back on that one's all drunk.'

'The glue was probably never much cop and it's dried out.' Alexia cast around until she found her rubber mallet. 'Stand back.' Turning the chair upside down so its seat was on her workbench she gave it several judicious taps. The back parted from the seat, then the components of the back parted from each other. Jumping up on the bench, Alexia grasped the rungs and heaved. Without too much protest the legs and rungs parted from the seat as a unit and from there it was easy to twist and knock until they were separate too.

'What we have now are chair parts. I'll do the same to the other one, then the whole set needs rubbing down.'

Carola looked absolutely rapt. 'And what then?'

'I'll paint them, probably a sea green that will look just right in the café. I know where to get trade paint and I can mix it myself. It won't matter that all the tables and chairs I scavenge are different shapes and sizes because they'll all be the same colour. It will be an eclectic look.'

'Oh, may I do it too?' Carola clasped her hands beneath her pointy chin as if she was prepared to beg if necessary.

It wasn't. 'You absolutely may,' said Alexia quickly, before the older woman could think better of it. 'And if anyone tells you they're getting rid of suitable tables and chairs, ask if we can take them. Whatever's wrong with them, I can salvage.'

'Fantastic,' Carola breathed happily. 'We ought to go into business and call ourselves Scavenge and Salvage.'

Alexia tried and failed to imagine herself going into business with Carola. 'Mm. Let's concentrate on this for now. If we swap phone numbers I can let you know when I'm beginning on these. Maybe tomorrow evening, after work.'

Carola looked discontented. 'Do I have to wait till then? How about I visit a couple of recycling centres tomorrow and see if I can pick anything up?'

'If you want.' Alexia stacked the chair parts on the bench and began switching off lights, ushering Carola out ahead of her. She suddenly felt as if she could sleep for a week. 'But we have almost no money and recycling centres generally sell rather than donate. Why don't you begin by asking Melanie at the shop if you can put a notice up asking people if they have any old stuff they want to get rid of? Put a note on the village Facebook page, too. Some people just stick things in spare rooms if they don't have a vehicle big enough to take them to the tip.'

'I could use my husband's Land Rover Defender to pick stuff up. It's pretty roomy.'

Alexia glanced at her as she locked the workshop door. Carola's husband was a shadowy figure in Middledip, away for long periods and commuting to London the rest of the time. Presumably he had such a vast vehicle just because he lived in a village. 'That would be fab if he doesn't mind you using it.'

'He's never here to mind.' Carola zipped up her coat. 'Let me know about tomorrow evening.' She marched briskly away in the direction of the new village, her fine blonde hair blowing in the wind, leaving Alexia free to let herself into the warmth of her cottage and run a hot bath.

190

Chapter Fifteen

Ben scraped most of Gabe's meal into the scrap pail for the chickens. Gabe had eaten about four mouthfuls then, in his words, 'coughed them up again'.

When Ben had finished washing the supper plates he picked up his phone. He'd promised to contact Alexia but he cringed whenever he thought of this morning. He'd casually kissed her and her scent and warmth had reached out and clonked him over the head. It wasn't only his head affected, either. He'd driven home with discomfort in the jeans department like an out-of-control adolescent.

And he had no idea why he'd kissed her except that she was helping Gabe and for an instant to drop a 'thank you' kiss on her head had seemed comfortable and natural. A heartbeat later it had seemed bizarre and moronic. When he returned from picking up his stuff he'd continued to act like a moron, all distant and busy as if Alexia were an inconvenient caller holding him back from an urgent rendezvous with his laptop. In fact, all he did when she'd gone was look at the website for Spring Hill Prison and wonder how Lloyd was managing to exist cooped up in there.

He sighed. She'd probably agree with him. He was a moron.

He dialled her number and was almost relieved when she didn't immediately answer. He'd even had time to decide that the call would go to voicemail and was starting to compose a brisk message . . . when Alexia picked up.

'Hello.' She sounded breathless. Beneath her voice was another sound, faint but unmistakeable. The sound of water lapping.

'Is now a good time to give you a Gabe update?' he asked tentatively.

The sound of water again, this time louder, a distinct slosh, and a squeak followed by a muttered 'Oh, shit!' Then, 'Are you still there? I almost dropped the phone in the . . . um.'

In the *bath*? 'Can you talk?' he asked, imagination whirring into action to produce images of Alexia wet and naked. In fact, he didn't need his imagination as he had those images all ready in his memory bank.

'Absolutely. I've treated myself to a glass of wine and it's probably made me clumsy. I've been anxious about Gabe. How is he?' she gabbled, as if keen to steer the conversation on to safer waters.

The distracting image evolved to her naked, wine in one hand, phone in the other. Wet. Rosy with the warmth. He had to moisten his lips before he could reply. 'I took stock a few hours after you left –' that's right, make it sound as if you didn't hint her out of the door '– and Gabe seemed worse rather than better.'

'Oh, no!'

'I'm afraid so,' he answered grimly. 'I called 111 again

and a doctor came and diagnosed a severe upper respiratory infection. He left a prescription for antibiotics so I had to hotfoot it to Bettsbrough to get that filled out. Gabe's had the first dose and the second's due at bedtime. I'm hoping he shows signs of improvement by the time I have to go to work tomorrow.'

She hesitated. 'What will you do if he doesn't?'

'I've been wondering the same. I can give him one dose before work but I'm worried about him rousing enough to take his medicine in the middle of the day. I suppose I could ask the bailiff at the Carlysle estate if it's OK to take a day's holiday or unpaid leave but I have a team lined up to work in the coppice out on the other side of the home farm so it wouldn't go down well. I think I'll just have to ask for a long lunch hour to rush back in, instead.'

'I could swing by between one thirty and two. I have an appointment in Bettsbrough in the morning and then in Crowland in the afternoon.' Another faint sloshing of water.

He broke out into a mild sweat. 'That would be great! But I wasn't hinting just because you're self-employed. I know being your own boss means less spare time rather than more.'

'But my time can sometimes be administered flexibly.' That watery sound again but louder this time. A distinct splash and an 'oops!'

Words came out of Ben's mouth uncensored. 'I'm sorry, have I interrupted you at a bad time? I should have texted first.'

'No, it's all right.' She cut him off hastily. But then a giggle escaped. 'OK, it's not the best time.'

He felt an answering smile tug at his lips. 'Would you have answered this if I'd made it a Facetime call?'

This time she laughed out loud. 'No! Stop trying to embarrass me and tell me where you're going to leave the key for me tomorrow.'

Ben did so, and that he'd see to the chickens in the morning, as, staying temporarily with Gabe, he'd be on the spot, and hopefully Gabe would soon be capable of chicken wrangling again himself. He rang off, still smiling.

A rustling from the tub told him that Barney was awake and Ben watched him launch himself at the smooth sides of the tub until he finally managed to scrabble his way out, pausing to settle his feathers and check Ben had noticed he was now a hard owl to keep down. Ben laughed. 'Don't look so smug. I already knew you could do that. Just try not to make too much mess.'

'*HEHHHHH!*' said Barney. He tipped his head on one side to give Ben a last look before hopping across the floor to pounce on a shoe. Then he looked up at the kitchen door as if waiting for the handle to move.

Ben folded his arms. 'If you're waiting for Alexia, she won't be here tonight.' Barney turned his head right round to stare at Ben as if in disbelief. 'Sorry if you're disappointed. I'm pretty sure she's in the bath. I'm trying not to think about it but as that's where our "encounter" began I have some pretty reliable footage in my memory. And it's running riot.'

'HEHHHHHHH.'

Ben sighed. 'You're right. I need to control my thoughts. But I didn't know she was going to hang around looking desirable and being kind to my uncle, did I? She should have had one foot out of the village by now.'

Barney spread his good wing out like a mantle to cover the shoe then poked his head underneath to peek at it.

Ben pushed away from the kitchen cupboard he'd been

leaning on. 'She's an unusual person. No matter how much she has on her plate she seems to be able to pile it a little higher if other people need help.'

Barney folded his good wing and hopped off the shoe to sidle up on the scraps pail.

Ben groaned, scrubbing his hand over his eyes. 'I'm knackered. I've seen to the chickens and that grumpy bloody pony but I can't veg out in front of the TV till I've filled the range and seen if Gabe wants anything. And I ought to tell Mum that he's ill. After all, she's his sister.'

But Barney had lost interest and was making himself very tall – for a barn owl – to peer into the scraps pail.

Once he'd moved the pail outside to save himself a clear-up job when Barney inevitably knocked it over, Ben went upstairs and crept into Gabe's room. It smelt musty and stale. Gabe stirred at his approach. 'How are you doing?' Ben whispered.

Without lifting his head from the pillow, Gabe nodded, his hair lying in untidy strands around his face. ''Bout the same. I'll be all right.'

'Great.' Not feeling particularly reassured, Ben refilled Gabe's glass with fresh water then left him in peace to doze.

Back downstairs, he rang his mother. She sounded pleased to hear from him but wary at the same time. He supposed he couldn't blame her. Their agendas, unfortunately, weren't neatly aligned but at least now he felt he was making the call under a truce, uneasy as it might be, so he didn't have to brace himself as he would have a few weeks ago.

'I just called to tell you that Gabe's not well.' Quickly, he ran through the events of the past couple of days while Penny said 'oh, dear' a lot.

'Am I needed?' she enquired delicately, when he'd finished.

He debated. If his mother came to Middledip to keep house for her brother for a few days it would release Ben to disappear back into the comfortable and solitary world of Woodward Cottage and the woods. He could put Barney in his new aviary for significant periods each day and they'd both be more comfortable.

But then Gabe's property was not the well-kept house on the edge of town his mum was used to. He tried to envisage her cleaning out the chicken house or shoving Snobby out of the way when he stubbornly blocked the path to his hayrack and tried to eat the hay out of your arms instead. Even keeping the range burning could be a mission. 'Thanks, but I can cope for now. Shall we keep that idea in reserve? Uncle Gabe's got his medicine so by the time you've settled here he could feel a lot better.'

He moved on to the next subject. 'But while I've got you, has Lloyd's release date been confirmed?'

Instantly Penny's voice became guarded. 'He's got an automatic release date – which normally comes around the midpoint of a sentence – so he can serve the remainder in the community, but I'm not sure how definite anything is until it happens. You know. Behaviour has an effect.'

'Is he getting in trouble inside?' Ben was pretty sure Lloyd was too savvy to do anything that would increase his sentence even by a day. Out of the corner of his eye, he watched Barney as he began today's assault on Mount Pan Rack, good wing beating to propel him onto the first level and bad wing and the resident saucepan getting in the way of him achieving it. Settling back down onto the floor, Barney pooped, as if to signal his displeasure.

'I didn't say that.' A pause, then Penny added, 'Do you mind me asking why you want to know?'

'I think I ought to speak to him – but not until he's out.'

A longer pause. Barney rotated his head to gaze at Ben as if checking whether he'd noticed the poop. Penny drew in an audible breath. 'I was hoping you'd . . .'

'Just let it go?'

'Not rouse any sleeping dogs that might send your brother back into jail,' Penny corrected softly.

Ben imagined her biting her lip, the strain of having a son in prison etched on her face. He preferred to picture her as she'd been at the Thai Garden when the subject of Lloyd had been cleared out of the way and she'd chatted instead about her gym buddies and what was happening at work, a couple of Tiger Beers helping her to relax. His dad had watched her and smiled. How nice it would be if she looked that way more often. 'I'll try my utmost not to do that,' he promised.

When he'd ended the call, and as he was getting out the kitchen roll to clear up the owl poop, he resumed his chat to Barney. 'Once he's out, I don't see anything wrong with asking him for the truth, do you, Barn? I'll just do it where those sleeping dogs won't be able to hear his answer.'

Ben settled down in Gabe's rocking chair and switched on the little kitchen TV for company. He'd fed the range half a scuttle of coal and was reluctant to go to the additional trouble of lighting the fire in the lounge.

He picked up the pad Gabe always kept on the window-sill and began to write.

Dear Lloyd,

Just to update you, Imogen chose not to share information with me. I do feel entitled to that information so maybe you and I can chat in due course? Mum tells me your release should be coming up. Do you know the exact date yet?

He chewed the end of his pen for a minute then, conscious that this was the first time he'd written to his brother in all the time he'd been in prison, filled the rest of the page and most of the next with chat about Uncle Gabe being under the weather and Ben's visit to Didbury, carefully omitting any mention of the stunt Imogen had pulled, until he could sign off with a clear conscience.

Then he opened his laptop, picked up Gabe's wifi and went online to see what the Internet had to tell him about a prisoner's release. It broadly coincided with what Penny had told him, speaking in terms too general to be really helpful about 'supervision' and 'conditions' when a prisoner was released on licence. Burrowing down further, he discovered a list of likely conditions and they did, indeed, involve good behaviour and not undermining the purpose of the licence period. Finally he found the information he'd been searching for – that a person could be recalled to prison if they were to commit another crime or be charged with another crime. He could see why his parents and Lloyd would be keen that no whiff of hitherto unaccounted for problems should come to the noses of the authorities.

Pen still in hand, he gazed sightlessly at the Sunday evening drama on the TV, turning over in his mind the consequences of Lloyd's drink-driving offence. Lloyd had paid for his crime with the loss of his liberty, incarceration and an uncertain future. To Victor and Penny it meant the worry and stigma of having a child in prison. Imogen had lost her physical perfection and her marriage; her career had been radically affected. Ben had paid for Lloyd's mistake with his wife – not just the relationship, but the bitter conclusion that she wasn't the woman he'd thought her, even if he wasn't yet sure what she actually was. He was uneasily aware of being changed by suffering collateral damage and though his real self was emerging once again, it was a slow process.

Was it unreasonable that Ben thirsted for the knowledge that might provide the key to it all?

He slapped his hand on the chair arm in frustration. His promise to his mother not to wake sleeping dogs and set them on Lloyd had been given automatically but now he was bound by it, which could well hamper his getting at the truth for at least the next couple of years.

His heart gave a giant beat. On the other hand, if he did get at the truth he might be faced by a dilemma, of possessing the kind of knowledge that would send his own brother back to jail, cause his parents more agony . . . and even implicate Imogen. Was that possible? He concluded that he didn't know it to be *im*possible.

Suddenly he had more sympathy for his parents not wanting to know what had taken Lloyd and Imogen out into the countryside, drunk, in the middle of the night.

He supposed that all he could do was wait. Sooner, rather than later, Lloyd would be out.

To give his thoughts a happier direction Ben took out his phone and went to the folder of photos of the treasures he'd taken from Gabe's loft. He could begin listing some on eBay until it was time to feed Barney, wake Gabe for his next dose of antibiotics and then seek out the bed in the spare room.

Chapter Sixteen

By the first day in November Alexia had reason to feel optimistic as she hurried through the frosty evening – the ground glittering and crunching beneath her winter boots – beaming, despite being late for the meeting she'd arranged with Gabe and Ben. She arrived in Gabe's kitchen in a flurry of frozen breath and apologies. 'Sorry, but for once something good's happened and I'll tell you about it later. How are you, Gabe?'

Gabe's reply from his rocking chair, wrapped in a blanket, was to explode with a coughing fit that went on for a worryingly long time. 'About the same,' he gasped, when he'd finally managed to draw air into his lungs. He was thin and white, his hair lifeless. 'I just can't shake this damned chest infection.'

Ben pulled out a kitchen chair for Alexia, frowning in concern. 'His GP came out and says he doesn't know why he's not shaking this off. He's prescribed different antibiotics.'

'I might have to have . . .' but Gabe exploded into another coughing fit, his eyes wide and almost panicked as he tried to get his breath. 'A chest X-ray,' he wheezed before the next coughing bout.

Conscious of an uncomfortably cold feeling, as if all her earlier elation had turned to ice and sunk to the pit of her stomach, Alexia jumped up and, finding the kettle warm from the range top, made him a drink of warm water and honey to try and soothe him.

Gabe looked about ten years older than usual as he thanked her for it then leant his head on the chair back and closed his eyes.

The frown on Ben's forehead deepened. 'I hope the new meds work.'

Alexia could only agree. Ben looked tired too. He still wore the dark green trousers and sweatshirt she knew to be the garb of the Carlysle estate workers and washing up stood in the sink. He'd never actually gone back to live at Woodward Cottage since Gabe had been ill. Alexia had helped where she could, checking on Gabe, cleaning out the chickens or mucking out Snobby's field shelter. She'd even taken Snobby out on a leading rein like a big dog because he was getting no exercise without Gabe to drive him in the trap. Gabe, between racking coughing episodes, had seemed more worried about The Angel than his own health so she'd continued to devote the rest of her spare time to keeping that on track.

With a big sigh, Ben flopped down at the kitchen table. His hair looked as if the wind had been tossing it around.

'Been up in the trees today?' she asked.

He pulled a face. 'Wish I had. All week I've been stuck either in the estate office or walking the estate talking Christopher through what I've planted where and why and what else needs doing. I'm more than halfway through my year's contract so he wanted an overview. One good

201

thing, though.' He brightened. 'He's let me take the stuff to make a portable enclosure for Barney from the estate stores. I put it together when I got home and Barney's busy investigating.'

Gabe stirred slightly. 'Be better for him than being stuck indoors.' He coughed again, violently, then let his head roll so he could open his eyes and look at Alexia. 'How are things going at The Angel?'

She had her report all ready. 'Roof complete and watertight. Concrete went down on the ground floor today so they can screed soon. Plumbing and electrics have begun upstairs but they can't move down while the floors are wet. As you know, Carola's got the bit between her teeth with the café furniture—'

With a wave of his hand, Gabe interrupted. 'You are all such good friends to me, especially you, Alexia. Do exactly as you see fit with everything, and thank Carola for me.' He ended on another bout of coughing.

'While we're swapping news, I have some,' Ben mentioned. 'The auctions have come to an end, both at the local auction house and for the stuff I listed on eBay, and they've made over three thousand between them. It's all landing in my accounts so I'll be able to transfer it over to you, Gabe.'

'Three thousand!' gasped Alexia. 'That's going to make life a lot easier.'

'Fantastic, thank you. Use it as you need it, Alexia.' Gabe's breathing was laboured and too quick. His hands lay on the blanket that covered him. They were beginning to look thin and knotted.

'There's more to list,' Ben promised. His voice reflected nothing of the consternation in his eyes as he watched Gabe closely. 'I've just been keeping it manageable.'

With a tired nod, Gabe coughed again. 'What is it you were going to tell us, Alexia?'

She remembered her good mood when she'd bundled in through the door, before finding Gabe looking frighteningly worse. She followed Ben's lead and kept her fear from her voice, though. 'I've had some good luck. Do you remember me telling you that I heard one of the local radio presenters, Quinn Daly, complaining on air that she'd fallen out with her interior decorator and wouldn't get their ground floor decorated in time for her big family do at Christmas?'

'You emailed and offered to start right away.' Ben nodded.

A little bubble of excitement fizzed up Alexia's spine. 'The only benefit of everything that's happened was I could make myself free, especially as their job's decorating only. At the weekend I met Quinn and her significant other, Ruby. The last decorator has taken all his mood boards with him, but that suits me fine. They had a lot of materials ready for me to work from so it doesn't mean too much strain for me but there's a bit of wiggle room to bring in my own ideas, too. It's very hands-on so I'm getting paint in my hair and generally enjoying myself.'

With another paroxysm of coughing, Gabe had to lean forward and crow for breath before he could speak. 'I think I'm going to have to go back to bed.' Beads of sweat had broken out on his forehead.

Ben rose to help him.

Alexia realised she was losing her audience. 'Just a second. The reason I'm telling you this is that I told Quinn about The Angel and she's asked me to go on an afternoon radio show she's planning about refurbishment and restoration. I want to do it, of course, because it's brilliant promo for me, and I need it. But I'd like your permission to talk on air about The Angel and what happened, Gabe. Quinn thinks the fact that we're overcoming the difficulties by adapting to them gives the story a lot of human interest.'

Gabe had half-risen from his chair, Ben at his elbow, but now he fell back again. 'That sounds like a good idea, though it's interesting use of the word "we" as I'm currently contributing precisely nothing.' He coughed again, ending on a wheeze. 'Go for it,' he added breathlessly. 'The facts should be out in the wider world. The programme might help others avoid being conned.' He coughed so hard that it almost shook the blanket from his shoulders. When he'd overcome the spasm he turned to Ben. 'Will you take over for me?'

Ben glanced around the kitchen. 'With what?'

'The Angel. I'll give you access to the bank account because Alexia's going to have to make payments to tradesmen soon and I just can't arsed, to be honest. Any chance?'

For a moment, Ben looked as if he'd argue. Then his expression softened. 'Of course. But you'll soon be back on your feet.'

Gabe laughed, but it turned into a cross between a crow and a gasp. 'Ever the optimist.' He let Ben help him up and, managing a fragment of a smile for Alexia, dragged himself through the door to the stairway. The sound of his coughing diminished as he climbed slowly. Then Alexia heard the creak of footsteps overhead and Ben's voice.

Thinking she might as well make herself useful, she rinsed the plates and a saucepan in the sink then did the washing up, automatically putting the kettle on to boil as she hadn't managed a cup of tea before leaving home. She

204

made tea for all of them but it wasn't until she'd delivered one to Gabe and told Ben there was a cup waiting for him downstairs that she realised it might seem that she was creating reasons to linger. She was just debating whether to commit the sacrilege of adding cold water to hers so she could drink it quickly, or pour it away so she could leave right away, when Ben bounced back down the stairs.

'Is it going to be a problem?' were his first words as he returned to the room.

Alexia blew on her tea. 'What?'

'Gabe asking me to act for him. I could hardly say no but I'll have to ask questions if I sort of deputise for Gabe. I wouldn't want you to take that as a criticism.' His grey eyes looked apologetic. 'I'll be keeping him in the loop and involving him if there are particularly knotty problems.'

'If he can hear you over the coughing?' Alexia grinned. 'It's OK. Welcome aboard. In fact, how would you like to bring your truck to pick up the floor tiles on Saturday from a warehouse in Peterborough? They're so damned heavy it would take two trips in my vehicle.'

With a yawn, he dropped into Gabe's rocking chair and tipped his head back tiredly, much as Gabe had done earlier. 'It's not as if we have anything else to do, eh?'

'I'll make the two trips if you're busy—'

He waved that idea away, closing his eyes. 'Why don't you bring me up to speed on everything so I get a sense of whereabouts in the project we are.'

'We're seven and a bit weeks away from opening.'

His eyes flipped open. 'Seriously?'

'We've got to be. I told Gabe to give me till Christmas, so we're opening on the Saturday before.'

'But when you said that the ship hadn't been attacked by pirates.'

She smiled at his picturesque analogy but managing a project meant focusing on reality. 'Do you know how much business rates are? Gabe needs to get money flowing in instead of out. Your eBay money is a godsend.'

'Good.' He sounded so weary that rather than recite the schedule of works to him Alexia just sipped her tea and watched as his breathing grew slow and deep, his chest lifting beneath his folded arms. His face relaxed in sleep, a shadow of stubble defining his determined jaw, his permanently windswept hair falling to one side. He looked like an off-duty Prince Charming taking a nap because Disney didn't need him in this scene. She finished her drink and quietly deposited the mug on the table, prepared to creep away so as not to disturb him.

But then he jerked awake and sat up. 'Sorry. You need to tell me when I'm being self-indulgent. Or grumpy. You've got just as much on as I have, if not more.'

Although his tone was light she caught an undertone of impatience with himself. 'We're all entitled to a touch of grumpiness now and then. You're worried about Gabe.'

'Deeply. But so are you.' He stretched his way out of the chair and pulled Barney's tub out from a corner. 'Want to see Barney's new home? I'm just going to bring him in. It's stupid – as he's an owl – but I don't quite feel comfortable with leaving him out at night yet.'

Alexia pulled on her coat and accompanied him into the raw darkness. She held the torch while he opened the side of the low-slung mesh run and coaxed Barney back into his tub. Barney screeched gustily but it seemed more for the fun of it than because he was objecting in any way. While Ben shut the run up again Alexia watched over Barney in case he tried to flutter straight out of his tub and onto the ground, then they carried him back into the kitchen where he screeched continuously from the safety of the tub.

'He's getting really loud,' she observed, pulling her zip a little higher and moving back to the door, ready to go home.

'Not kidding. I'm thinking of wearing ear plugs when I'm trying to sleep.' He checked the clock on the wall. 'I'm going to stretch my legs for ten minutes. How do you feel about me walking back with you if I promise I'm not going all Sebastian on you and "walking you home"? I just want to get some fresh air.'

She laughed. 'OK. I'll show you the chairs and table we've done, if you like.'

Ben locked the kitchen door behind them and they set off in the darkness, using their torch apps to light their way along the ruts of the track. 'Is Carola still helping?' he asked as they picked their way towards Main Road.

'I can't believe I'm saying this but she's a boon. If she carries on as she's begun she'll make my life considerably easier because she finds rubbing down even awkward things like spindles the height of good fun. Also, she's found someone she says will take Snobby out on the leading rein. Unfortunately, that someone's Seb.'

She was aware of him turning towards her, even in the dark. He hesitated as if choosing his words. 'Is it a genuine offer?'

She sighed. 'It could be that he thinks it'll mean us spending time together but his sister's always had ponies so he would be useful. Poor Snobby needs some company and it would stop him turning into a tub of lard.' They turned into Main Road, a fresh gust of wind almost sending Alexia flying.

Ben huddled into his jacket. 'Give me his number and I'll call and talk to him. If it's just a ruse to get close to you he'll backtrack if he realises he'll probably be dealing with me and that will be the end of it. If he will do it then it'll be useful because with my job, Gabe, the chickens and The Angel I don't really need to add taking a pony for a walk to my list.'

'Let's try that.' Conscious that more and more tiny threads were connecting their daily lives Alexia made her voice businesslike as they reached her cottage. 'Let me open the workshop up so you can see what I'm doing with the furniture.' She fished in her pocket for her keys.

The interior of the workshop seemed calm after the squalling wind outside, even with the door still ajar. She exhibited the table and chairs she'd secured through Freecycle already in their top coat of blue-green plus two wheelback chairs rubbed down and undercoated.

'I like the colour.' He ran his fingers over one of the chairs. 'It's like an unsettled sea.'

Alexia was pleased. 'That was pretty much the effect I went for. This is only the beginning. Carola's been promised another table, circular pine with four chairs. One of the chairs needs a new leg but I know a joiner with a copy lathe so that should be OK. The problem's going to be storage as we collect more, especially as, now you've been clever enough to add a bit of cash to the pot, I won't feel so reluctant to buy from charity shops or house clearance places. Actually,' she went on, 'now you're the guy with the purse strings I need to talk to you about the kitchen at The Angel because I need to brief the electrician. Can we arrange a time? I know you're too tired now.'

Giving the finished furniture a last glance, he turned away. 'I'm not too tired if you give me coffee but I ought to be back at Gabe's in an hour to make sure he's woken to take his last dose of meds for the day.'

'That would be great. I only need your initial reaction.' She closed up the workshop and led him into the house, shucking off her coat and making him coffee and her tea while he wandered into the sitting room. He looked about himself with curiosity, half-expecting it to bear testament to her profession and be starkly monochrome or be full of strange-shaped furniture and odd art. Instead, she'd used a colour on the walls that wasn't green or white but somehow in between, then plain bold colours for curtains, different for each room.

It was warm and bright and at least half as large again as Woodward Cottage. The stairs rose from a proper hall rather than out of the sitting room and he knew there were at least two bedrooms because of Jodie having been her housemate. She left him on the sofa while she fetched her drawings then settled a decorous few inches away from him.

'Here's the original plan.' She handed him an A3 sheet of paper. 'The kitchen was going to be where it was when The Angel was a pub, with both the Bar Parlour and the Public abutting it. We've always known the kitchen's too big. Even with our original budget our equipment would have only filled a corner, and now we're strapped for cash I think there's a better way.' She unrolled her new drawing and spread it across their laps. 'I see this as an efficient and economical alternative – expanding the counter area in the Bar Parlour and housing our now more modest equipment needs behind it. It would mean carrying drinks and snacks through to the Public instead of passing them directly from the kitchen. Or we could make a hatch.'

'Neither seems insurmountable. How much money will it save?'

'Lots.' She gave him a brief contrast of costs between the two schemes. 'It would give rise to the issue of what to do with the existing kitchen though.'

'Shut it off until some unspecified time when it's needed again?'

'Construction's never that simple. That room has to come into the scheme of works so far as the electrics and plumbing are concerned. Loosely speaking, both work on a principle of circuits.'

He'd edged closer to her to get a better view of the drawing, and the warmth of his leg was brushing hers, banishing any residual chill from hurrying from Gabe's. He continued to study the drawing. 'Do you have a suggestion?'

'Before we even get to the suggestion stage there are things to think about. For example, that room's big enough, especially as it has its own pantry, to be a working kitchen in its own right, so maybe we could rent it to a local business. Someone who bakes cakes or packs lunches to sell around the offices.'

'Are there many offices in Middledip?' He turned his teasing smile on her.

'No, there's that big industrial estate just on this side of Bettsbrough, which must contain a lot of hungry mouths to feed, but I'm just throwing ideas around. The point I'm getting at is that *if* we thought that room would *ever* be a kitchen we need to know now. Commercial ovens are high-powered electrical appliances and require a circuit with a high rate, or even three-phase. We don't want to be burying the wrong cable in the plaster and then have to redo it all. In any event, it would probably be best for that area of the property to have its own circuit.'

210

'Right.' He stooped to pick up his coffee mug from where he'd left it on the floor. 'So, to summarise, you can save money with one hand but we have to spend it with the other.'

She shrugged. 'No. You can have that room as anything you want. Make it and the pantry into a studio flat and rent it out as domestic. That would work well with your plans for accommodation upstairs if you can get it past the planning authorities but, again, you'd want it to have its own circuit for billing purposes. You could keep it commercial but make it into a gift shop – customers can access it through the Public already. I'm just saying that it would be helpful to have some idea of where we're heading before rewiring downstairs, and that room could be made to earn its keep.'

He turned to look at her but there was no laughter lurking in his eyes this time. 'You're good at this.'

Pleasure prickled up her spine. 'I expect you're good at looking after trees.'

'True. But they only occasionally prompt quick decisions. One of the few predictable things in my life.'

Alexia read sadness in the set of his mouth. 'How are things with you apart from your worry over Gabe?' The thought popped out as words before she realised she was going to voice it.

He looked back to the drawing across their laps. 'You mean Imogen?'

She felt that wriggle of something again when he said Imogen's name. Not guilt precisely, but regret. And not regret that their night together had ever taken place, but that it had been so quickly and thoroughly tarnished.

She'd looked no further than the fact of his imminent divorce, heedless of the complexity of it or him, but their

211

level of physical intimacy must have been in stark contrast to the degree of emotional engagement. Before that night Alexia hadn't experienced a post-coital polar-change of attitude and now she knew what to look for she'd be a lot more wary of the 'I'm up for a no-strings thing' conversation. It did mean no strings, despite its disguise of caresses and gentle words.

She gave herself a shake. So she didn't want anything heavy but she didn't like the consequences of 'no strings' either? 'Not just Imogen – I suppose I meant everything. You haven't had a great time.'

He smoothed the drawing with both hands and took so long to answer that she expected him to look at his watch and make going home noises. Instead, he watched his hands smoothing, over and over. Finally, he smiled a crooked smile. 'I worry about my family and its dynamics. I see a dilemma on the horizon with Lloyd. Imogen has phoned to apologise for abandoning me in that pub and hinted she'd misread my invitation to talk. When I demanded – her word – more information, she ran away from the situation.'

'She's been through a lot.' Alexia tried to sound sage and sympathetic.

He nodded, still absently smoothing the drawing. 'It was her who said that if I couldn't forgive her I ought to divorce her but I got the impression she'd been hoping . . .'

'. . . that you could forgive after all? I suppose it would be an easy conclusion to reach.' Playing devil's advocate on behalf of Ben's particular devil wasn't a role Alexia relished. Gently, she pulled her drawings free of his hands while they still had some ink on them.

He turned to watch her roll them up. 'Living in Woodward Cottage I sometimes have a romantic vision of myself as an animal hiding out in the woods to lick my wounds. Yet when I talk to you I see myself more as a bear with a sore head.'

She blinked at him, feeling the back of her neck gather in indignation. 'What? Why? It's you who called yourself grumpy! I didn't mention it. I've been *nice*.'

His eyes smiled. 'Nice or not, when I talk to you I see my own shortcomings in your generosity. Considering our history you'd be quite justified in telling me to shut the front door about my ex-wife. Instead, you ask me if I'm OK and seem to care whether I am. I find such big-heartedness rare. You're caring towards Gabe, Carola, Jodie and the village as a whole at the same time as soldiering on with everything that happens to you. I admire you for it at the same time as feeling bad that it doesn't occur to me to return the compliment.'

He hooked his elbow on the sofa back and turned in his seat to face her. 'So now I'm asking. Are *you* OK, Alexia?'

For a stupid moment her eyes burned. She could have laughed it off with a 'Fine, thank you!' But something about the warmth of the moment trickled through her, soothing and comforting, encouraging her to answer honestly. 'I'm coping,' she said. 'But I'm finding life a bit tough. Building up my order book, keeping everyone going full guns on The Angel. Getting used to Jodie not being around.' She told him about Jodie's pregnancy and the note Shane had left about Jodie trapping him. 'I haven't told Gabe while he's poorly. It's interesting background information but it doesn't make any difference to the situation we're facing.'

His eyes narrowed. 'Shane's a total shit.' He hesitated. 'If you get another opportunity to leave the village, will you take it?'

213

She beat back a compulsion to demand, 'Why? Are you thinking of lining up another no-strings thing as a parting gift?' Instead she answered, 'It would depend upon the opportunity. I'm not desperate to leave but I do regret losing the chance to work with that property investor. I liked her ethos – not doing a bodged job then flipping a property full of problems to make a quick buck. She could be tempted by the odd quirky project, too, like turning old industrial properties into contemporary residential. And I would have been happy to contribute to her portfolio of smaller properties for families in need.' She sighed but forced a smile. 'But other opportunities might crop up.'

He was watching her gravely. 'I really hope they do, if that's what you want.'

Touched, she tried to repay his kind thought. 'And if you want to patch things up with Imogen at some time in the future, I hope that it happens for you.'

His eyebrows snapped into a frown. 'I just want the truth. "Closure", as they say.' He rolled to his feet in an easy movement. 'Nearly time for Gabe's meds. See you soon. Thanks for the coffee.'

Alexia listened to him letting himself out, allowing herself to wonder, just for a minute, what might have happened if she and Ben didn't have an ill-advised one-night stand and his pain over his ex-wife between them.

Chapter Seventeen

'Oh, go on, let me come.' Carola wore a streak of sea green satin paint in her blonde hair and liberally on her hands and clothes. The culprits, the four wheelback chairs, gleamed prettily under the lights of the workshop, as smart as . . . well, paint.

Alexia inspected them critically. 'They're wearing more paint than you, though I think it's a close-run contest. You've done a fantastic job. Even the fiddly bits don't have a single run in them.' Having spent most of the year in a hostile stand-off, Alexia was still getting used to the friendly and enthusiastic Carola who turned up most days to rub down or paint a steady procession of pre-loved chairs and tables.

Carola glowed with pride, scratching a speckle of paint off the end of her nose. 'So you're going to take me on the radio with you as a reward?'

'How can I? You're not invited. There are two guests on the show, each talking about a different angle to property improvement. It's not in my gift to invite you,' Alexia protested, glancing at her watch. She'd only paused at the workshop on her way out to check how Carola was doing. She'd never been on the radio before and, tingling with nerves, had taken pains with her outfit and her make-up, which was stupid as nobody outside the radio station would be able to see her.

Carola dropped her brush into a jar and grabbed a cloth to wipe her hands. 'I'll just come into reception and wait while you're on air. I won't be pushy, I promise. I've always wanted to visit a radio station.'

Alexia smothered a sigh. 'But I don't have time to wait for you to get cleaned up.'

Beaming, Carola rubbed her hands more vigorously. 'No need! We can go in my car so I don't get paint on your seats. Nobody's going to care what I look like.'

This time the sigh found a way out. 'Come on then. You can drive me to Cambridge in your husband's country-side status symbol.'

'Hurrah!' Carola grabbed her keys.

Alexia was shocked when Carola opened the door to the Land Rover and jumped into the driver's seat without even a dustsheet. 'You're getting paint all over the leather! Look at that steering wheel! Your husband's going to go mad.'

'It was painty already.'

It was true. The driver's seat, the steering wheel and even inside the driver's door were spattered liberally with sea green satin and white undercoat, reflecting Carola's progress in furniture refurbishment.

The passenger seat was unsullied so Alexia climbed in and they bowled off on the hour's drive across the county to Cambridge.

All went well until they arrived at the radio station and couldn't find a parking spot. Carola reversed the oversized vehicle out of the car park – and into a street sign. 'Oops!' Changing gear and waving away Alexia's yelp of horror with, 'It's OK. I didn't knock it down,' she whizzed off to find street parking.

Alexia jumped out and tried to check the damage to the corner of the Land Rover but Carola cried, 'We'll look at it after; you can't be late!' So they ran back, arriving at BBC Cambridge out of breath just in time for the producer to come in search of the afternoon show guests.

Alexia puffed out her name and the producer held the door wide in welcome. 'You've got time to catch your breath; one of the guests hasn't turned up yet. And is this your friend? Would you like to come through and watch through the glass?'

Carola beamed. 'I'd *love* to!'

Leaving Carola on a sofa near the producer's workstation while music played to the listeners, the producer ushered Alexia into the studio. Glass formed one side and the rest of the walls were covered in what looked like red carpet. Quinn, earphones clamped over her long dark hair and plus-sized figure nestled comfortably in a plus-sized chair, waved and grinned and did something on one of the computer screens before her. Alexia, heartbeat trotting excitedly, seated herself at the guests' side of the desk.

Quinn stopped clicking her computer mouse and beamed, pulling off her headphones. 'Hiya! Great to see you here!' She gave Alexia a quick briefing on what to expect, waving at the equipment with, 'Just ignore this lot. You're on the green mic.' She glanced at the clock as she slid her headphones back into place. 'We're waiting for a lady who's restoring an old mill near Waterbeach.'

As if on cue the producer stuck his head into the studio. 'Lady with the mill won't make it today, Quinn. Currently waiting for roadside rescue. Car conked out.' He ushered another figure into the room. A small, blonde figure bespattered with sea green paint. 'But this lovely lady is Carola who works with Alexia. She says she's happy to step in.'

'And it looks as if she's working her hard, judging by the state of her!' Quinn treated Carola to her thousand-watt smile. 'Can I get you on blue mic then, Carola? Thanks so much.' She glanced at the clock again and began to move sliders up and down the console. 'Here we go everybody. I'll do the weather, then we go to traffic, then we'll get you on.'

Carola wriggled in her seat, wearing a huge grin. 'I wasn't pushy, honestly,' she mouthed at Alexia. 'He asked me.'

Alexia shook her head in mock despair, but she was secretly quite glad for the friendly presence.

In no time they were caught up in the singular experience that's radio, cocooned by Quinn's ability to create rapport with her guests and draw out their stories.

Alexia went first, talking about the original plans for The Angel and the brutal way they'd been forced to change direction.

Quinn was all sympathy. 'Oh, no! How terrible. I had no idea that stripping a building could be that profitable.'

'If you pick the right building. There can only be so many genuine Victorian cast iron fireplaces. And as for the etched glass! Irreplaceable. With so much gone, we had to rethink.'

Quinn turned to Carola. 'And where do you come in, Carola? Have you and Alexia been working together all along?'

'Gosh, no. We began at loggerheads.' Carola beamed

cheerfully. 'We were hardly speaking. I thought their fund-raising was inappropriate and we had a couple of public fall outs.'

Alexia's jaw dropped at Carola's blunt reply.

'Oho,' said Quinn, beaming right back at Carola. 'Fall outs? Tell me what naughty Alexia had done.'

'Nothing *wrong*,' Alexia managed to put in hastily, with visions of bad publicity instead of the good she was hoping for.

Carola laughed her tinkling laugh but, to Alexia's relief, was quick to deny Quinn the controversy she'd perhaps scented. 'It wasn't Alexia's fault. I'd just been involved with our village hall for so long that I wasn't keen when another community project came on the scene. It's only recently that I've begun to work for The Angel. Alexia's doing an amazing job and I count it a privilege that she gives me the run of her workshop while she's out being a wage slave.'

So the baton was passed back to Alexia and, relaxing, she began to get into the swing, contrasting what they were doing to the sympathetic restoration they'd hoped for at The Angel, managing to weave in information about her work as an interior decorator with the familiar explanation of how that differed from being a) a painter and decorator and b) an interior designer.

Carola jumped in to disclose that she was currently covered in sea green paint in her quest to repurpose sufficient chairs and tables to fill both rooms of The Angel and Alexia jumped in with, 'And you should see the inside of her car!' Soon it had become the Alexia and Carola show with Quinn only putting in occasional questions and witticisms to keep the ball rolling.

The chat was punctuated with music tracks, weather,

traffic, and messages coming in from listeners, and when Quinn handed over to the presenter in the next studio and took her headphones off with a 'phew!' Alexia couldn't believe an entire hour had flown by.

'That was brilliant.' Quinn smiled her beautiful white smile, coming out from behind the desk. 'You two have such a fab human interest story and I'm sure we've alerted listeners to the conmen out there.' With a quick hug each she handed them back to the producer at the studio door, the producer ushered them back the way they'd come and in startlingly short order they were outside, blinking in the daylight and breathing in fresh air.

'That,' pronounced Carola with satisfaction, 'was *thrilling*. And I've googled recycling centres and there's one in Butts Lane, only nine minutes from here. Shall we go and see if they've got any tables and chairs while I've got the Land Rover?'

Alexia followed Carola's eager footsteps back towards where they'd parked, suddenly feeling a fondness towards the other woman who was not only giving up so much time and labour to The Angel but had also just resisted Quinn's fairly open invitation to have a little dig at Alexia. 'Don't you ever run out of energy?'

'Not really.' Carola looked surprised that anyone would think she could.

Chapter Eighteen

Ben answered Gabe's door expecting the caller to be Dr Worthington, Gabe's GP, who was due to call after his surgery at the clinic. Middledip only got a doctor's surgery on Wednesdays so Ben had had to take an hour off to be there. It was frightening how the weight was dropping off Gabe, leaving him looking too frail to battle the cough that threatened to shake him apart.

But it wasn't Dr Worthington who stood at the door. It was Alexia's old boyfriend, Sebastian, wearing a cautious expression. 'I've come to walk Gabe's pony as per our text conversation.'

Ben stared at him. 'But it's dark. And Snobby's black.' The way Sebastian looked past him into the kitchen confirmed Ben's earlier suspicions that his volunteering to walk Snobby had been much to do with catching a glimpse of Alexia.

Sebastian shifted from foot to foot. 'I work during the day. Don't worry. I'm used to ponies. Snobby's got a high-vis rug, hasn't he? I'm wearing a high-vis jacket and he'll only be near the traffic for five minutes if I walk him straight across The Cross and into the bridleways. It's a clear night so we'll see our way OK. Snobby knows me.' Then he added, as if he couldn't resist trying to stake a claim. 'I came here with Alexia enough.'

Ben debated no longer. It wasn't his business whether Seb's offer came from a genuine desire to help Gabe or a grasping at the straws of encountering Alexia. Gabe had already okayed Sebastian as a pony walker and, even as elderly as Snobby was, it didn't seem fair to keep him cooped up in his paddock when there was an offer of company and a chance to stretch his stubby legs. 'He's wearing his head collar. I'll get the leading rein and rug.'

Ben grabbed what he needed from the barn and a carrot from the store then the two men hurried through the chill to the paddock. Once aware of the bribe Snobby was perfectly amenable to being caught and Ben had only to spectate as Sebastian folded the reflective rug to place over Snobby's withers.

A car rumbled slowly up the track. Ben turned to check it out. 'I think this is the doctor.'

'Go, I can manage one little old pony. Tell Gabe to get well soon. We all miss seeing him round the village.' Sebastian fastened the straps across Snobby's shaggy chest. The pony nuzzled Sebastian as if frisking him for additional carrots so Ben felt that Snobby was comfortable with his walker. Tossing back brief thanks, Ben loped up the track, catching up with the car as the doctor climbed out, bag in hand.

Dr Worthington was a pleasant, direct man, not given to wasting words. 'How are you finding your uncle now?'

Ben let him into the house, his stomach giving the unpleasant kind of lurch that went with voicing worries. 'Worse. Still coughing up a lung every few minutes, burning with fever, sleeping all the time.'

222

Dr Worthington raised a brow. 'Is he in bed? I'll go up.'

Minutes later, having taken Gabe's temperature, examined his sputum and listened to his chest, Dr Worthington sat down beside the bed, his expression at once grave and comforting. 'It's turned to pneumonia, Gabe. No wonder you feel lousy. I'm going to hit it with more antibiotics but you might have to go into hospital if you deteriorate further.'

Gabe coughed until he retched, then gasped, 'Rather stay here.'

'We'll try and keep you at home.' Dr Worthington pulled a prescription pad from his battered bag. 'But it's very important that you keep your fluids up, get plenty of rest and take the antibiotics exactly as prescribed. I'll leave you four of these in this little pot so your nephew doesn't have to go out to Bettsbrough to fill the prescription tonight.'

'OK.' Gabe lay back on his pillows, exhausted and shining with sweat.

Dr Worthington patted Gabe's shoulder and rose, pausing to speak to Ben. 'I'd like you to continue to keep an eye on him. I'll come back on Friday, after my Port-le-Bain clinic. If you're worried between then and now, ring 111. Are you staying with him?'

Ben watched the doctor's pen skate across the prescription pad. 'Yes. I'm wondering whether to get my mother up here, though – Gabe's sister. She's offered and I work Monday to Friday and can't always get back for his lunchtime meds. If she can come up I'll move back to my own place so she can have the spare room.'

'I try and wake up but I can't always rouse myself,' Gabe rumbled from the bed, coughing harshly, then turning weakly on his side and apparently falling straight to sleep.

He looked awful. His cheeks had sunk with the loss of weight and he hadn't felt much like washing his hair so, free of its ponytail, it lay in dull strands across his pillow. Dr Worthington watched him for several moments before he left his bedside.

His troubled expression fuelled Ben's anxiety. Immediately he'd seen the doctor out, Ben snatched up the landline phone from the windowsill and dialled. While he listened to the ringing tone he one-handedly filled a nearby mug with water and sloshed some into the pots of herbs lined up behind the sink. They were looking almost as dry and gaunt as Gabe.

'Hello?' said someone at the other end of the phone.

Ben paused, mug poised over the coriander. The voice wasn't his mother's. It wasn't his father's. But he knew it well.

'Lloyd?'

A hesitation. Then, 'How are you doing, little brother?'

Carefully, Ben returned the mug to the draining board. 'Are you home on a ROTL?' Instantly, he corrected himself. 'No, you only come out on *temporary* licence for weekends. So you must be out? You've served the custodial part of your sentence?' *And nobody told me. Mum might have known last time I rang.* He tried to count the days in his head. It was probably about a fortnight ago.

'That's right. My house has a tenant in it, and as I'm not currently gainfully employed I need the rent. Mum and Dad said I could stay here so it could be written into the terms of my release.' *Then Mum definitely knew last time I rang.*

In the background, Ben heard his mother, her speech rapid and high. He kept his own voice even and neutral. 'How long have you been home?'

224

'Five days.'

Emotions roared up inside Ben. Anger and hurt that, even supposing his mum had been frightened of jinxing Lloyd's release date by stating it aloud to Ben on the phone, she'd had *five days* since Lloyd got out. Sadness that Lloyd had had *five days* to call Ben himself and offer to continue their conversation.

Following more sedately behind came relief that Lloyd was free.

He opened his mouth to vent but just as quickly sucked the words back, shoving the emotion on the back burner because Gabe had to be his priority for now. Would Penny agree to leave her golden child to travel to Cambridgeshire and look after her older brother? Was Ben even going to ask it of her?

But what of Dr Worthington's uneasy expression as he'd watched Gabe sleep? What would be best for Gabe?

'So, how are you?' Lloyd asked in his ear. Then, when Ben didn't reply, 'Did you want to speak to Mum? Or Dad?' Another pause. Lloyd's voice dropped. 'Are you still there, Ben?'

Penny's anxious voice asked something. Lloyd's voice fell away. 'I can't hear him. You try.'

Penny's voice came on, tentative and worried. 'Benedict? Is everything all right?'

'Yes.' *No, it isn't.* 'Well . . . the doctor's been to see Uncle Gabe because he's much worse. I feel as if he's fading away in front of my eyes.'

'Oh, dear.' She hesitated and Ben waited for her to repeat her offer to come. Insist that she should, even. But she said, 'Give him our love and tell him we hope he gets better soon.'

'Will do.' Suddenly resolved, Ben ended the call without

asking her to come. That way, nobody would be hurt if Penny refused. Cracks in family relations wouldn't be widened. Ben wouldn't be more disillusioned that he was already.

He wasn't even surprised, he realised as he filled the mug with water again, noting that it trembled as he lifted it to his lips and drank, cooling his thoughts, easing the tightness in his throat. An explosion of coughing came from upstairs and he gazed at the ceiling as if he could see through it to check on Gabe as he lay in bed. The thought that Gabe's care was down to him made him feel as if someone was filling his stomach with ice.

He wasn't frightened of much but he was frightened of making a mistake with Gabe.

He picked up his mobile to call Alexia.

She answered on the second ring. 'What did the doctor say? Pneumonia? Oh, no!' She sounded appalled, scared, all the things Ben himself was. 'Can I come round?' Then, as if anxious she had to justify the request, 'I've got a little prezzie for him and we can work out how much of the next couple of weeks we can cover between us. Jodie or Carola might even pitch in a bit if Gabe can put up with them.'

'Come,' Ben responded even before she'd finished speaking. Again he wasn't surprised at the answer he'd received – but this time in a good way.

Waiting for her to arrive, he helped himself to a handful of digestive biscuits and a cup of coffee, putting out two clean mugs and the teapot for Gabe and Alexia ready for when she arrived.

While he ate he wished his family could have heard Alexia and perhaps have learned how people reacted to the serious illness of someone they held in affection: with warmth and kindness, breathless with concern, putting aside their worries, perhaps even their hidden agendas and secrets, to help.

Within ten minutes she was bursting into the kitchen, unwinding her scarf and bringing with her the scent of a frosty evening. 'Flipping Seb! He was on the track and I almost slipped over on an icy puddle when he suddenly spoke! He said he wanted to tell me that he'd just put Snobby back in his paddock but somehow that turned into a lot of sighing over "the old days". I got him to leave Snobby's rug on because I nearly turned into an icicle while he kept me chatting. Brr.' She gave a theatrical shiver, dumping Snobby's leading rein on the quarry tile floor. 'Is that all you're having for dinner? I haven't eaten and was hoping to scrounge something a bit warmer and more satisfying than biccies.' She flung off her coat and hung it beside his on the door hook. 'I've brought Gabe some wondrous tea from a posh new shop in Bettsbrough.' She tugged the packet out of her bag, finger combed her spiky curls and turned on Ben an anxious smile. 'How is he?'

Ben felt his muscles unscrunch just in reaction to the energy Alexia brought with her. It was impossible to feel alone when she was near. He updated her on Gabe's condition against a paroxysm of coughing from upstairs, adding, 'If I raid Gabe's supply of frozen pizzas and bung some in the oven and you brew a pot of your special tea we can take Gabe some while the pizzas cook.'

Plan followed, they carried their drinks upstairs to keep Gabe company. Despite the earlier coughing he'd fallen heavily asleep again and Ben had to wake him to drink his tea. He drank half, listened to them chat for a few minutes, then his eyes gently closed once more.

227

Alexia placed her hand on his forehead. 'You could fry eggs on him.' She sounded very subdued.

Sombrely, Ben nodded. 'It must be the fever that's burning the flesh off him. If he doesn't turn the corner soon . . .' He wasn't sure what would happen but it was with a feeling of dread that he led Alexia back downstairs.

When the pizzas were bubbling and golden – one pepperoni and one Hawaiian – Ben cut them into slices and they sat at the table to munch, burning the roofs of their mouths on the molten cheese.

Ben allowed himself to be distracted from his anxiety by Alexia's tongue darting out to capture stray strings of cheese as she *mmmed* appreciatively and made her first slice vanish in short order. 'By the way,' she said, when the second slice had followed the first and she'd slowed her consumption rate from starving to merely famished. 'I can work from here tomorrow and Friday so you needn't bother haring back at lunchtime. I've got a big costing to do for Elton. He asked if I could rush it so I moved some other stuff around and put a premium of 20 per cent on what I'm charging him. Ha!' She looked as triumphant as a woman could when wiping tomato from her chin.

'Thanks,' he said with real gratitude. 'I'll be here evenings and at the weekend so that's all four doses of Gabe's meds covered for four days.' Surely by then he should be showing some improvement? 'You're a friend,' he added.

Her glance was so fleeting that he would have missed it if he'd blinked, but *something* flickered in her dark eyes and then was gone. She picked up another slice of pizza and became absorbed in the even distribution of its pineapple pieces.

Awareness see-sawed through him. Did she dislike the

label 'friend' after they'd been lovers? Shying away from such a grey area filled with landmines he told her about Lloyd picking up the phone at his parents' house.

She wiped her hands on a piece of kitchen roll. 'Wow.' If he'd thought she'd been having trouble meeting his eyes then apparently she was over it as her gaze was openly compassionate. 'How do you feel?'

He chose to interpret her question as 'What are your conclusions?' 'My parents must really want me to let sleeping dogs lie. If Lloyd intends me to know something, then he wants Imogen to be the one to tell me. Or he doesn't want Mum and Dad to hear.'

She sat back, brows knitted. 'It seems to me it would be much easier for him if you were simply never to know.'

'True. But now he's got me deeply curious.' Ben picked up his phone, flat and black in his hands.

She paused. 'Are you going to make a call? I could leave.'

'No.' He sent her a smile. 'I'm just going to poke a sleeping dog. Or two.' He composed a text:

Ben: *Now the custodial part of the sentence is over, there's nothing to prevent you from telling me the truth about what happened that night, is there?*

He sent it to Lloyd and to Imogen, then showed it to Alexia.

She raised her eyebrows. 'A text is easy to ignore. Wouldn't a visit pay more dividends?'

'I don't think the text will do anything but make them slightly uncomfortable,' he admitted. 'But it will have to be enough for now because I can't leave Gabe to go chasing off after their secrets.'

She got up and reached the tea down from the cupboard, demonstrating an easy familiarity with where things were kept in Gabe's kitchen. 'I could spend the weekend here, if you want to go.'

He stared at her back, slim and straight, the fit of her blue jumper following the indent of her waist. 'Aren't you full on with The Angel and supervising Carola?'

A pause. 'Yes.'

'Then I don't think so. But thanks.'

In silence she completed the making of the drinks and returned to the table with a steaming mug in each hand and a smile that seemed to him more distant than before. 'Actually, we ought to have a business meeting. I need a decision about the electrics.'

Ben watched her not looking at him and a prickle ran up his spine. He'd learned enough about her by now to know that when she didn't look at him it tended to relate to their night together or to Imogen, as though she wanted to keep him from reading her feelings. Which sort of suggested that her feelings about them were something to do with feelings for him. Unwanted feelings, he was pretty sure.

He felt the same. He wanted to obey the pull between them, that frisson of awareness when they were together. But he also wanted to resist, put it in a compartment in his heart marked 'too difficult' or 'if only things were different' or 'give me time'. So he resisted. He wasn't going to risk his heart. He wasn't available. Okay he was *available*, in that he wasn't in another relationship. But not emotionally available.

Alexia, as if to validate his choice, became particularly businesslike. 'I don't think you can justify the expense of putting in fifty-amp cables for commercial ovens unless you're committed to letting it out as a commercial kitchen.'

'I agree. But I took on board what you said before

about the possibilities of letting, so I think it should have its own circuit. If that's more expensive then at least it's justified.'

Nodding, she made an entry on the Notes app of her phone. 'The screed's gone down so we'll be able to walk on it just in time for the plumber and electrician to get into the Public and the Bar Parlour. It's good that the consumer units were going in the foyer anyway and weren't affected by the floor. OK for me to move the plasterers in upstairs now?'

'Shit.' He scrubbed his face with one hand, tired by the number of balls he had to juggle. 'I haven't finished knocking the plaster off the last wall Freddie marked up.'

'Then they'll have to do it.'

'No, it won't take more than half a day. Let me do it this weekend. By the way,' he added, to try and lighten the atmosphere, 'I had a look at those boxes of tiles we unloaded. Did you mean to buy several different colours?'

Her eyes crinkled as she tapped another note into her phone. 'If you buy from end-of-range tile warehouses you have to be adaptable. They'll be laid randomly. Ivory, cream, brown, and a beautiful sea green to match the chairs. Our look will be eclectic.' She put down her phone and stretched, easing her back.

Ben tried not to look. Then he absolutely looked because he was a man and that's what men did. And he was cautious about women, not blind to the amazing shape of this one.

'I'd better go,' she said. 'If I'm going to work here tomorrow then I need to get my stuff together tonight.'

He rose too. 'Is that the business meeting over? I'll come out with you and check on Barney. He's old enough to stay outside but I get antsy about him.'

She brightened. 'Then I can say hello to him before I go.'

They zipped themselves into their coats and Alexia wound her jaunty green scarf around her neck while Ben got the torch to illuminate the area between the house and outbuildings before they headed out and crossed the yard to the temporary owl house. With the torchlight wavering it was hard to see Barney for the shadows cast by the branches Ben had wedged at various heights between the walls of mesh.

'Brr, he must have gone into the nesting box part to get away from the cold,' Alexia observed, pushing her hands in her pockets and hunching her shoulders. 'Look at the frost on the twigs.'

Ben stopped short. 'The door's open!' He blinked several times, as if that would magically clear his vision and he'd realise his eyes had been playing tricks.

'Oh, no!' But Alexia could obviously see exactly the same as him. 'How on earth did that happen?'

'It must be the wind.' Ben rattled the door in its frame and sure enough the simple catch began to drop out with the vibration. 'Crap! This is my fault.' He raised the torch to make absolutely certain that Barney wasn't in the run or nesting box.

And then '*Hehhhhhhh!*' Gold-grey feathers glowing in the torchlight, Barney flappety-hopped out from behind the run like a child triumphantly revealing himself at the end of a game of hide and seek.

'Barney!' Alexia cried thankfully.

Ben felt almost weak with relief. Unable to take off, Barney would have had no defence if a patrolling fox had caught his scent. 'Let's stick him back in the run for a minute while I fetch his tub. He'll have to stay indoors tonight.' Barney didn't at all object to being shepherded back into the run and Alexia stayed to check the door didn't blow open again while Ben jogged to the house.

By the time he returned, Alexia's teeth were chattering and Ben made short work of popping Barney into the tub. 'You get off home. I'll settle Barney then give Gabe his meds and see if he wants another drink.'

They said their goodnights. Ben shone his torch to help her see her way down the track; a small figure bundled up in her coat, hurrying to get out of the cold.

After watching her disappear from sight he went indoors, fed Barney, saw to Gabe, then fell into bed, glad to close his eyes.

Chapter Nineteen

In the morning a hoar frost fringed every twig and blade of grass in her garden. Alexia paused to notice how pretty Main Road looked as the early light seemed to coat the houses in glitter.

'Come on!' urged Carola, hopping from foot to foot to keep warm.

'Sorry.' Shivering, Alexia fumbled with the key as she opened up the workshop, knowing Carola was anxious to begin on the preparatory work for painting a tall narrow corner dresser someone had donated. 'You've picked up another scratch on your husband's Defender.' It made a matching pair with the ding Carola had picked up at the radio station.

Carola didn't even glance behind her at the unfortunate vehicle. 'It's not very big. It was one of those little posts in the supermarket car park. Stupid things.'

'I'm getting worried when you park next to me,' Alexia joked.

'I wouldn't bump into your car.' Carola followed Alexia into the workshop and turned on both heaters.

'You can't this morning because I'm driving it to Gabe's so I can take my laptop and everything.' She took a good look around the workshop and the sea green tables and chairs crammed into the available floor space. 'You're doing a fantastic job. I need to make more space for you to work in but I don't think I can, yet. The plasterers will be working at The Angel or I'd ask Ben if he could move some of it there in his truck.' She heaved a sigh. 'We might have to halt production until this lot can be moved but we've only got about half of what we need.'

Carola turned an appalled face on her. 'Stop?'

'I don't want to,' Alexia assured her hurriedly, taken aback by Carola's horror. Once Carola had committed herself to The Angel she'd certainly put her whole heart into the project. Alexia gave her a consolatory hug, not wanting to damage their blossoming friendship by breaking disappointing news. 'But you can't stack stuff up when the paint's so fresh because it will stick and mark.'

Carola jutted out her chin. 'I'll start taking them up to my garage at home in the Land Rover. It's a double and I hardly ever put a car in it.'

'Great, if you don't mind that.' Alexia disengaged herself and glanced at her watch. 'I'll see you later. If you want to leave, just lock up and stick the key through my front door.'

Fastening her scarf a little tighter, she braved the cold once more and grabbed everything she needed from the house to pile into the car, shivering as she drove the short journey to Gabe's.

She arrived to find Ben tying up the door to the temporary owl house with string.

'I wish I'd done this last night instead of bringing Barney in,' he said grimly. 'Now he's able to hop out of his tub he's crapped all over the kitchen. Bloody bird.'

'*Hehhhhhhh*,' Barney added, hopping up onto a branch.

'And how's Gabe?' Alexia lengthened her step to keep up as Ben strode back across the yard to the house.

'No better. Worse, in fact. Most of the fluids I get down him are coming back. This infection seems to be eating him up.' He looked at Alexia and she saw the fear in his eyes. 'Even though you'll be here I think I need to come back at lunch to see how he is. Maybe get some advice from the NHS helpline.'

Alexia's blood ran colder than even November frost warranted. 'Do you think . . . he's actually in danger?' Her voice came out high and small on the crisp morning air.

For several moments Ben didn't respond. Then, 'That's what I'm scared of,' he admitted hoarsely.

Silently, they stepped into the warmth of Gabe's kitchen.

Ben gazed around with an expression of despair at the pungent white splotches on the floor and some of the other perches to which Barney's hops could propel him. 'And I've got to clean this lot up before I go to work.'

'I'll do it,' Alexia volunteered immediately. 'Don't be late, especially if you have to try and wangle enough of a lunch break to get back here. It won't take me long.'

He turned his grey gaze on her. 'Really?'

'Really,' she replied firmly.

With voluble thanks, and instructions to ring him if she needed him, Ben hurried out. After a few moments Alexia heard his truck start up and then the sound of his engine grumbled off down the track. Sighing, she found the anti-bacterial spray and spent the next twenty minutes cleaning up owl poop, glad that Barney's fluttering hops couldn't spring him as high as the worktops or table. At least the kitchen smelled a little sweeter by the time she gave her hands a good wash at the end.

With a glance at the clock, she hurriedly fed Luke, who'd begun to rub around her ankles, his usual hint that his belly was rumbling, then carried a cup of tea up to Gabe, creeping into his bedroom, which was really beginning to smell like a sick room. 'I've brought you a drink.' She gazed down at the man she'd known for a good part of her life, the man she called a true friend, the man who would normally be pestering her to make him mince pies by now, and her heart did a nosedive.

He looked terrible. His cheeks were sunken, his hair lank and snaggly, his heavy breathing punctuated by peculiar squeaks. 'Gabe,' she said, more loudly, her heart doing a panicky little flip.

Then Gabe stirred and opened his eyes. 'I'm not well.'

Relief flooding through her that she'd been able to rouse him, Alexia lodged the mug of tea on his bedside. 'You're certainly not. Ben said you have to have lots to drink.'

Gabe exploded with coughs, covering his mouth with one hand and holding his chest with the other. His eyes widened as he crowed for breath then, gradually, the coughing calmed. 'My chest hurts. Ow.' He sucked in another whistling breath. 'It hurts down my sides, too.'

'Do you fancy a cuppa?' Alexia asked gently.

'I keep water down better.'

'I'll get you a fresh glassful.' She had to rouse him again when she returned a minute later.

He sipped from the glass after raising himself weakly on one elbow. 'It's not time for my medicine, is it?'

'Not till lunch time.'

Gabe sank back down and closed his eyes again.

Horrified by this weak and wobbly version of the Gabe she knew and loved, Alexia cast about for ways to help. 'Do you want the TV on? Or me to read to you?'

'No.'

'Shall I sit with you?'

'No.'

Alexia trudged back downstairs with foreboding as heavy as rocks around her heart. If anything were needed to convince her that Gabe's condition was grave it was the omission of those pleases and thank yous. Their absence was as alien as Gabe's unwashed hair.

With Luke for company, sleeping off his breakfast in Gabe's chair, Alexia set herself up at the kitchen table and tried to become immersed in collating estimates from bricklayers and damp-treatment specialists. It was hard to settle, though, and she kept creeping upstairs every time Gabe finished one of his wracking bouts of coughing to check he was still in one piece.

When she heard the sound of the truck lurching up the track shortly after one, she jumped up, ready to meet Ben at the door. 'I've given him his next dose of antibiotics but he coughed until he was sick right afterwards. I think you need to speak to someone.'

Ben didn't even run upstairs to check for himself. He nodded once, went very white, and crossed the room to ring 111, bouncing off the furniture in his haste. Within twenty minutes Dr Worthington had rung him back and within two hours the ambulance arrived.

Although the green-clad paramedics, one male and one female, were unhurried and calm, they were swiftly about their business. They clipped a thing on Gabe's finger to measure his oxygen levels then gave him oxygen via a mask and used words like 'cyanose' and took readings again. It wasn't until they'd 'got his sats up' that they reached agreement to move him.

Friendly and cheerful, they explained what they were

going to do then moved Gabe smoothly onto a big sort of chair thing and strapped him in. Down the stairs. Into the ambulance. Checked his oxygen saturation again.

'We're going to take a steady ride to Peterborough City Hospital,' the male paramedic told Ben. 'Want to hop in?'

Ben did.

In no time Alexia, shivering despite her coat, was watching the big vehicle dip and lurch down the track, her stomach feeling as if she'd lunched on concrete. When the ambulance had vanished from sight she trailed back to the warmth of Gabe's kitchen and gazed about with no idea what she should do.

She couldn't settle to Elton's stupid costing.

There was no one to make tea for.

No one to check up on or give meds to.

No point banking up the range because she didn't know when anyone would be staying here again.

From old habit she tried to ring Jodie, thinking that maybe she'd cry, 'Come round to Mum's and we'll make you a cuppa. You can tell us all about poor Gabe.' Jodie had known Gabe just as long as Alexia had, after all. But Jodie's phone went straight to voicemail and Alexia didn't feel like leaving a message.

Numbly, she gathered up her things, threw them in her car and went home.

Chapter Twenty

Ben had never been in an ambulance. Now that he was belted into a seat on one side of one with no view out, he didn't particularly like it. It was probably the lack of visual references that made him feel vaguely sick as they followed the curves of Main Road out of Middledip, he told himself. Or the antiseptic and medicinal smell of the ambulance interior.

Or that Gabe lay on the other side of the vehicle, his face grey and beaded with sweat, the female paramedic sitting beside him doing observations. Gabe's eyes were shut. He was so unresponsive that, his noisy breathing drowned out by the rumble of the wheels on the road, only a growing and shrinking patch of condensation on his oxygen mask reassured Ben that life was not extinct.

At least the paramedic driving wasn't sounding the sirens or hammering around corners. Ben would surely then have been sick. From fear.

He cleared his throat. 'Is he OK?' He felt helpless with the width of the ambulance between him and Gabe.

The paramedic looked up with a reassuring smile. 'No deterioration. He's holding his own.'

Ben thanked her but he didn't find that very bloody reassuring. He wanted her to exclaim that a bit of oxygen had been all that Gabe needed. That the trip to hospital was a precaution and Gabe would be back in his own home by evening. He wanted Gabe to open his eyes and ask what all the fuss was about and demand to know who would feed his chickens.

He wanted reassurances that didn't come.

It seemed hours passed in the claustrophobic confines of the wallowing ambulance full of frightening equipment. Ben tried to read their labels to pass the time but that just made him feel sicker. Finally the vehicle stopped and the engine fell silent.

Ben was thankful to be able to take a deep breath of fresh air as the doors were flung open. 'Just give us a minute,' the male paramedic called, as the female reported Gabe's oxygen saturation levels before they wheeled him out of the rear exit. Happily for Ben's heart rate the female paramedic opened the side door to release Ben back into the real world without delay. 'Just stick with us while we get your uncle admitted,' she suggested briskly.

Just try and shake me, Ben thought.

The process of hospital admission seemed interminable. They began in the 'ambulance stream' – which had a lot in common with a trolley in a corridor – and Gabe's care was passed to a member of hospital staff who began the process of assessment as the paramedics said goodbye. Ben did remember to thank them, though he was preoccupied with trying to assess Gabe himself and watch what the member of hospital staff was doing. They quickly progressed to resus where someone else assessed Gabe, Gabe stirring every now and then to try and answer a question, Ben filling in the blanks. Every new medical professional Ben and Gabe encountered gave their name but didn't announce their role or title.

Things speeded up. A porter pushed Gabe along several corridors to X-ray, Ben walking alongside. There Ben had to wait outside, holding Gabe's old, holey slippers, wanting to find a Gents to use but frightened to leave in case Gabe was whizzed on his journey through the massive hospital and Ben lost him.

From X-ray the porter pushed Gabe to a holding bay to wait for a doctor. Gabe slept. Ben fidgeted. He could hear goings on in other cubicles but could see very little but the patient in the cubicle opposite, who was looking very apologetic that she couldn't produce a urine sample for a nurse.

Then a tall doctor with black hair and golden skin arrived and Gabe alternately roused and dozed through his examination.

'Is he going to be OK?' Ben asked at the end of it.

The doctor smiled. 'He's quite unwell, as you're aware. His X-ray shows severe pneumonia in both left and right lungs and he's obviously developed pleurisy, which is a common complication. As the antibiotics prescribed by his GP haven't helped enough I think we're going to have to keep him here for a while.'

'He often coughed the antibiotics back up.'

The doctor nodded. 'We can administer fluids and antibiotics intravenously. Someone will be along to get your uncle up onto a ward when a bed's available.' He shook hands with Ben and was gone.

'Was that a doctor?' Gabe croaked through his oxygen mask.

Ben moved swiftly to the head of the bed, glad to see Gabe had roused on his own. 'That's right.'

'But he was in his pyjamas.'

For the first time since he'd arrived at Gabe's at lunchtime, Ben grinned. 'They're hospital scrubs.'

'Oh. No white coat these days?' Gabe was asleep before Ben could reply and slept through his admission to a high dependency unit.

Hours later, from a chair next to the bed, Ben watched Gabe's still figure. Propped up on crisp white pillows, antibiotics and fluids flowed into Gabe's wasted arms through thin tubes that seemed to glow in the subdued lighting the hospital favoured in the late evening. Oxygen hissed comfortingly into the mask covering Gabe's mouth and nose, easing his breathlessness and marginally improving his colour.

A benefit of Gabe having an alcove to himself was that nobody asked Ben to respect visiting hours. He was able to simply sit, monitoring Gabe's breathing and remembering boyhood trips to watch birds or swim in the sea or climb to the top of a hill solely to see how the world looked from a new angle.

In those days, Gabe had been there for Ben.

And now Ben was here for Gabe. He'd listed himself as next of kin on the hospital records, even though he presumed that, as Gabe had no children of his own, Penny legally owned that title. But she wasn't here and Ben was.

Almost as if she'd read his thoughts across several counties, his phone vibrated on a text from her.

Mum: Do you think you'll be coming home for Christmas? Dad and I are hoping you will. Come for the week, if you like. We might have a NYE party. x

Ben read it twice. Checked today's date. He supposed mid-November wasn't too early to be making festive plans but it felt incongruous in this world of hissing oxygen, swishing trolleys and hushed nurses in the corridor outside. A number of pithy retorts sprang to his mind but he reminded himself that Penny didn't know her brother was in hospital.

Ben: Thanks for the invitation. Of course I'll see you at some point but I don't think I'll manage several days . . .

He paused to review that thought. What *would* he be doing at Christmas? So far he'd thought of it only as a date by which Alexia insisted The Angel would be open. Last year, though acutely aware of not spending Christmas with Imogen, he'd been living in Didbury so had visited his parents on Christmas Day. The atmosphere had been subdued, his parents sighing over Lloyd's second Christmas 'inside' and feeling guilty to be feasting on home-cooked turkey with all the trimmings. Ben had spent the rest of the holiday period working grimly on selling his business and the marital home. And the Christmas before had passed in a haze of pain in the aftermath of the accident.

This Christmas should be different.

He was no longer that melancholic brooder. In fact, he thought, watching Gabe stir to cough then lapse back into sleep, Christmas in Middledip could be warm and relaxing. He'd go for long walks through the woods. He could see Gabe for Christmas Day. Perhaps spend some of Christmas Eve at The Three Fishes. He might get to know more villagers and have people to chat to whenever he went in, like Alexia.

He finished the text:

. . . because I have plans in the village. I was about to text you: Gabe's in hospital with pneumonia. I hope he's not in danger but he's very unwell. x

'I was about to text you' was stretching the truth but

he had to segue from Christmas to illness somehow. While he had his phone in his hand, and as Gabe was still sleeping deeply and breathing loudly, Ben texted Alexia. He should have done it earlier. It was already nearly ten and he felt a pang of guilt as he imagined her waiting up anxiously for news.

Ben: *Gabe's finally settled and in bed. X-rays show pneumonia, both lungs, and he has pleurisy. I'll leave him soon and come back tomorrow.*

He pressed send. Almost immediately, his phone rang and the word *Mum* sprang onto his screen. 'I had no idea Gabe was that ill!' she cried. 'Are you with him? What's happening?'

Ben filled her in on everything he knew, ending with, 'Hopefully they can get on top of the infection here and then he'll be well enough to go home.'

Penny clucked and sighed, sounding genuinely worried. But she approached the subject of visiting diffidently. 'Do you think I need to come?'

Ben replied honestly. 'I suppose you don't *need* to. You could *want* to.'

'I'll talk to Dad.'

Ben knew from long experience that this meant 'I'm looking for excuses not to'. He was faintly surprised as well as disappointed. Before he could comment his phone buzzed and he took it away from his ear to read a new message.

Alexia: *I'll come to the hospital to fetch you. Taxi to the village will cost £stupid at this time of night. Setting off now.*

He returned the phone to his ear. Penny was saying something about whether Gabe had any pyjamas fit for him to be seen in. Ben interrupted. 'There's nothing you can do about it from there so just leave everything to me.' He tried not to sound sarcastic but as Penny immediately went quiet he guessed he hadn't succeeded. 'I'll update you tomorrow but Uncle Gabe's in good hands.'

'Thank you, darling.' Penny sounded relieved but Ben couldn't judge whether it related to Gabe being in good hands or Ben giving her an opportunity to end the call. When she'd done so, he rang Alexia. 'Are you sure about fetching me? It's late.'

'I'm already on my way.' Her voice sounded more projected than usual so she was presumably on a hands-free device. She sounded perplexed and he smiled, imagining her rolling her eyes that he'd ask. Alexia was really that uncomplicated. She wouldn't have offered if she'd minded fetching him – in contrast with his mother, who'd framed her question about coming to see her brother in such a way as to make the verdict Ben's responsibility.

Thirty-five minutes later, Ben huddled in his jacket beneath the big canopy sheltering the entrance to Peterborough City Hospital, his breath white on the night air. The car park and hospital grounds were quiet and Alexia was able to pull up right in front of him in her dark red MPV. He hopped into the passenger seat, glad of the warmth of the interior.

'How's Gabe? What did the doctors say? Is he going to be OK? Can I see him tomorrow?' The anxious questions began even before she'd pulled away. She drove quickly but competently, curls bobbing as she checked both ways at junctions, frowning as she winkled every detail out of Ben.

Then, when she finally seemed satisfied that Gabe was receiving the best possible care, she demanded, 'Have you eaten?'

Now she mentioned it, he had a big empty feeling where his stomach usually lay. 'Just a sandwich from a machine. The coffee shops and restaurant had all closed by the time I thought about it.'

She nodded. 'I made casserole and over catered so there's another portion I can microwave for you. You'll be nice and close to get your truck from Gabe's when you've eaten.' She indicated left and peeled off from the ring road around Bettsbrough to head for Middledip, her eyes glinting in the lights from other vehicles at the roundabout.

'The prospect of home-cooked casserole makes my mouth water. The pickings are slim at Gabe's house and mine.' He felt weary and strained and the promise of half an hour to relax and be fed was irresistible. 'Thanks.'

He sank more deeply into the passenger seat, grateful that nothing more onerous was required of him than to half-close his eyes against the twinkling of lights threaded through garden trees and listen as she tossed out ideas for how they were going to manage hospital visiting, Snobby, the chickens, Luke and their jobs while Gabe was away. She called it 'away' as if she held a superstitious belief that using phrases such as 'in hospital' or 'ill' empowered the evils of reality.

When they reached her place she ushered him indoors and sat him at the kitchen table while the plate of chicken casserole and mashed parsnips rotated in the microwave and began to emit a mouth-watering smell. In a few minutes she placed the steaming plateful in front of him, got them each a glass of red wine and plonked herself in the seat opposite his, dark eyes sparkling.

'Now I know Gabe's not in immediate danger I can tell you my news. Something fun has happened.'

Blowing on his first forkful, impatient now to move the

fragrant mouthful into his stomach, he raised his eyebrows. 'To you?' He transferred the food from fork to mouth and the taste of chicken gravy exploded on his tongue.

Her eyes sparkled. 'I think so. You know Quinn Daly, the radio presenter I've been working for? She's left me a voicemail.' She took her phone out of her bag and tapped at the screen for a few moments. Then she held it up so he could listen.

'Ooh, Alexia, you won't be late tomorrow, will you?' the voice from the phone said. 'I can't wait to tell you something! Well, I *can* wait because I'm not going to tell you until I can see your face. But, majorly, it's going to be *so* much fun.'

He swallowed his mouthful, just herby enough to warm him from the inside out. 'Mysterious. But she does sound convinced about the fun.' He thought about everything that had happened recently. 'I seem to have forgotten how to have that.'

She deposited her phone on the table. 'You don't find it fun to knock plaster off the walls of an old pub?'

He almost laughed as he took the next mouthful, which could have had the disastrous consequence of firing casserole down his nose. 'If that's fun, there's an abundance. You come in for quite a lot of it yourself.'

'True. I'm almost seeing sea green paint in my sleep. Goodness knows how Carola must feel about it. Which reminds me.' She reached for her laptop from a nearby stretch of worktop. 'I've identified the minimum kitchen equipment I think we can get away with. I'd like to use a local catering-equipment provider in Bettsbrough because they have a fitter they can recommend. So if you'll OK the purchases I can make the order. I'll need you to pay the deposit from Gabe's account.'

248

'Seriously? We're having a business meeting? Don't you ever switch off?' He took a mouthful of chicken and parsnip to demonstrate his intention to continue with his meal.

'Well, we're going to be busy while Gabe's away, aren't we? If you're absolutely *sure* he's OK where he is –' she paused to regard him keenly, as if checking him for updates '– then I can't do anything to help him other than keep my promise. He gave me till Christmas to bring this project in, if you remember.' She tapped and clicked a few times then angled the machine so Ben could see the screen. Then she dragged her chair around to his side of the table and perched alongside him to talk through her plan, sipping wine, switching between drawings of the kitchen area to explain what went where.

She smelled nice, even above the food. He supposed it was her hair, as it was down at his nose level. It brushed his chin once or twice as she edged closer so that the screen could be at a comfortable angle for both of them. Her voice was quick and light as she explained the importance of an espresso machine in today's café. 'We need a place for when it can be afforded. You know what everyone's like with coffee these days, wanting froth and sprinkles.'

She turned to glance at him. Her eyes were big with enthusiasm. She was wearing no make-up and he could see a handful of faint freckles running over her nose. 'Did you say you have more loft stuff to list on eBay? Could those funds go towards the espresso machine?'

He dragged his mind back to kitchen equipment. 'I think so. I haven't taken the photos yet, though. There are a lot of plates with shire horses on, a couple of lamps with glass shades and—'

'Don't list the lamps until I've seen them.' She did that enthusiastic thing with her eyes again. 'If they're attractive it might be better to hang on to them for the café.'

He nodded, finishing up the gravy with a last scrape of his fork and a lot of regret. 'That was delicious, thank you. Maybe you ought to cast your eye over all the loft booty before I list it. I don't want to find I've let anything go that would be more use to The Angel decoratively than financially.'

She grinned and her eyes crinkled at the corners. 'You're really getting the hang of this scavenger business model. If we didn't have to wait for the screed to dry we could really get the project going. Six weeks and one day to opening.'

'Do you think you're going to make it? Last time I saw The Angel there were channels chopped out of the walls everywhere.'

'For the cables. The rewiring will be well on the way in a week. Plumbing's almost done. It probably doesn't look like it because the radiators haven't been hung, but all the pipework's in. Once the electrics are finished I can bring the plasterers in and you won't recognise the place. The carpenters will follow with the skirting and architraves and to hang the new doors. It was sacrilege that Shane nicked those doors.' She shook her head sadly. 'The screed shouldn't be green by then and I can tile, hopefully while someone else is sloshing cream emulsion everywhere – someone a lot like Carola. If we've got the kitchen fitter lined up he can fit out the kitchen area in two days. We move in tables, chairs and kitchen equipment and we're ready to open the Bar Parlour, Public and foyer.'

'You make it sound a breeze.'

Her nose wrinkled. 'It's not hard. It's only a question

of craftsmen and money. I just draw pretty pictures and boss everyone around.' She changed tack suddenly. 'I fed your owl, by the way. I made sure I tied the door of the run up again.'

With a shock, Ben realised he hadn't given Barney a thought since before he took the slightly uncomfortable seat inside the ambulance beside Gabe, all screwed up with worry and shock. 'I totally forgot about the poor little guy, so thank you.'

The smile faded from her face and she turned to say, 'Do you think Gabe—' just as, grateful for the way she picked up all kinds of slack without ever being asked, and with a sunny smile at that, he made to drop a kiss on her temple. It felt more natural now, as if they were becoming close enough that he should express his thanks with warmth. But with her turning to him and him turning to her, and her looking up as he looked down, the kiss ended up at the corner of her mouth.

She said, 'Oh!'

He said, 'Erm . . .'

But neither of them moved away.

If he'd had to explain why he did what he did next he'd probably have to say that the barriers he'd erected for really good reasons swayed dangerously in the wind of weariness and emotion. It was only for a moment . . . but that's all it took for him to take a step. When so many people in his life seemed unsupportive, Alexia was the opposite. He'd never been able to get their encounter out of his head and he'd always had a thing about Betty Boop. Alexia was soft and pretty. And her mouth was so close.

He angled his head slightly. And slowly brought his lips to hers.

Just as slowly, she joined in. Questioningly, tentatively,

her lips warm and soft. It would have taken superhero restraint not to deepen the kiss, not to encourage her lips to part so he could touch his tongue to hers. It was restraint that, in that weary, emotional moment, he did not have.

Instead, he brought her into the curve of his arm and kissed her again, one hand caressing the dip of her waist. Her arms wound around his neck as if to prevent him breaking away until she was good and ready. She needn't have taken the precaution. His compulsion was all about pulling her closer, kissing her harder.

It was only when she squeaked that he pulled back. 'Did I hurt you?'

'No. Maybe you took me a bit by surprise.' Eyes half-closed, she gave him a smile of the utmost sweetness and eased his head back down to hers so he could kiss her again.

It was difficult just to get his breath. His heart raced even faster than his thoughts, which were all about making love to her. The prospect of losing himself in her body, leaving behind all the worry and aggravation, swamped him. All he could think about was the feel of her in his arms. No, actually, two things – also the tightness of his jeans.

He struggled to his feet, banging his leg on the table, bringing her with him as he slid his hands into her clothes and encountered a whole woman's worth of hot, smooth flesh. He groaned against her mouth. Her spine was a perfect slope. He traced it with his palm, moving on to her sides and the curve of her stomach.

Then he realised she was freeing herself and stepping away.

Reluctantly, he let her go.

'Do you want me to go home?'

Chapter Twenty-one

The relief he felt when she replied, 'No. I think this could be exactly what we both need,' was indescribable. She linked her fingers with his and led him out of the kitchen, up the stairs, pausing on the landing with a questioning look, as if offering him a last chance to escape. Never a more willing captive, he stroked her bottom to encourage her to believe it.

Her eyes sparkled but she assumed an air of mock solemnity. 'I have condoms,' she announced.

He pulled her close enough to kiss again. 'I'm more impressed by you every time we meet.' He carried condoms in his wallet all the time now, but he wasn't going to admit it and spoil her moment.

She pushed open a door and, still entangled, they drifted into her personal space, Alexia fumbling with a lamp just inside the room until a halo of golden light lit the bed. He would have been happy with the full overhead light option as he was a visual kind of guy but he was just glad she wasn't a lights-out girl. That would have been a damned waste.

They undressed each other. He tried not to rush her, particularly when her pauses included tours of his torso with her mouth, but he was glad when his jeans finally joined hers on the floor and he had every inch of her nakedness in his arms. Sinking down, he took a nanosecond to note that she apparently bothered with bedmaking, which was a waste because he just flung the duvet aside and rolled them both down onto the coolness of the sheet.

She was anything but passive, rubbing against him as he kissed her, pushing her breasts into his hands as he caressed them, reaching down and stroking him with her fingertips, her palm. When she got a rhythm going at the same time as taking tiny, gentle nips of his neck and collarbone his heart hammered so hard he thought it was going to beat its way out of his chest.

'Holy hell,' he breathed as he rolled onto his back, carrying her with him so he could bring her breasts to his face, knowing he had to take control or he would lose control. 'You are beautiful.' He might have added that this moment was beautiful, too, but it sounded too cheesy. It stayed in his mind, though, as she responded, kiss for kiss, caress for caress.

It was only when he was convinced she was ready to join him in the race to the finishing line that he reached for the condoms – one of his, because he had preferences – and, finally, sank into the velvet heat of her with a groan of relief. He began smoothly, slowly, but she dug her fingers into his buttocks and urged him on. Presuming that she knew what she wanted, he was happy to co-operate.

Afterwards they collapsed into one another. She dragged up the duvet and he snuggled her more closely to him and, finally, exhaustedly, shut his eyes.

He slept deeply for hours. Then jerked fully awake.

It was just past 4 a.m.

Tonight, though, his wakefulness was nothing to do with a night terror and everything to do with a set of delicate fingertips tracing patterns on his inner thigh. 'Alexia,' he murmured, not because he had to make sure but because he was glad it was her, glad he was glad, glad there had been no sickening moment of confusion and guilt.

'Sorry,' she whispered, not sounding sorry. 'I didn't mean to wake you.'

'Disappointing.'

She laughed, moving her hand slightly north and discovering that he was indeed awake. 'OK, I absolutely meant to wake you.' And proceeded to show him why.

The morning light was creeping in through the windows when Ben awoke again, this time because his phone had bleeped a text alert.

Gabe: Any chance you could bring me in more PJs? Thanks.

Ben: Will do. How are you doing?

Gabe: It's noisy here.

Although relieved and reassured by the pragmatic little exchange Ben could imagine Gabe finding a hospital alien compared to the peace and quiet of his own house in the middle of his own land. It was an uncomfortable thought and made him restless. As he had to go to Gabe's, he might as well see to the animals before he dashed home to change for work. No one would be living full time at Gabe's so it was time to give Barney the full-time freedom of his big aviary at Woodward, too.

If he didn't get out of bed soon he'd also end up ringing

the estate bailiff and explaining why he was going to be late for work again. He turned to look at Alexia to find she was awake. Hair flattened by sleep, her naked shoulders were escaping the embrace of the quilt.

He angled his head to drop a kiss on her face, making her smile. 'I have to leave.'

'OK.' Beneath the duvet, her hand stroked down from his stomach.

His eyes drifted shut again. 'I do have to leave.'

'OK.' She gurgled with laughter when, instead of leaving, he rolled on top of her.

He ended up ringing the bailiff to explain why he was going to be late again. Moreover, when he did finally arrive to join the team taking out a diseased elm before it spread its nasties, he was so keen not to create even a hint of bad morning-after etiquette this time that he texted Alexia before he jumped out the truck.

Ben: Last night was amazing. xxx

It was lunchtime before he had a chance to check for a reply.

Alexia: Yes, it was . . . 😊 xxx
Alexia: *Blush* x

Ben grinned as he put his phone away, feeling more light-hearted than he had for a considerable time.

He was well into his busy day when he realised he'd never had replies to his texts to Imogen or Lloyd. He took out his phone to follow up, then hesitated. If they hadn't replied to the first message they wouldn't reply to a second. He stuffed the phone back in his pocket and jumped in the truck to drive to the hospital. One thing at a time.

Alexia had whizzed through her shower and run wet fingers through her hair in lieu of styling before dashing to Quinn's house in Yaxley, the other side of Peterborough, leaping from the car with seconds to spare before the agreed ten o'clock 'at the latest' rendezvous.

Quinn threw open the front door before the doorbell had reached its last echo. The winter sun made her mop of dark hair gleam. 'I thought you weren't going to make it. I have to leave in ten minutes because I'm recording an outside broadcast on my way to the radio station.'

Alexia's cheeks grew warm. 'Sorry. I, um, stayed in bed longer than I meant to.'

'Come in and let's cut to the chase, then.' Quinn dragged her through the door and beamed. 'How would you like to be in a video?'

In her wildest dream Alexia hadn't expected that. With what had happened last night with Ben she'd suddenly stopped wondering about Quinn's intriguing voicemail. She groped for the right words. 'I don't know. I've never given it a thought.'

'Think about it now.' Quinn chivvied her down the hall and out into the conservatory, which she and Ruby were currently using as their lounge. Alexia was part way through transforming their sitting and dining rooms to an ethereal green that reminded her of light filtering through water. Feature walls of bold stripes in the dining room and stylised peonies in the sitting room would be breathtaking once Alexia used their accent colours to pull everything together.

'Sit, sit, hurry, hurry,' demanded Quinn. 'If I'm going to sign you up I need to get on with it. It's only because someone dropped out that I can ask you at all but I know you'll be good. And you won't turn to jelly, because I'll be with you.'

With a laugh, Alexia obediently took a seat in a cane

chair. 'I'm exploding with curiosity. What are you talking about?'

Quinn slapped two pieces of paper on a small black table as if exasperated Alexia couldn't read her mind. 'OK – bullet points. There's a homes and interiors show at the East of England Showground on Wednesday for which I've agreed to put together a panel of experts to discuss home improvements. It's being filmed for YouTube. You'll be great to consult about decorating and refurbishing. Do say yes! You'll be fab and it's got to be good exposure for you.'

'Oh. It would be if—'

'If . . . ?'

'If you really think I won't be a disaster,' Alexia ended feebly, grappling with a scary vision of glaring lights and staring cameras.

Quinn planted her hands on her hips. 'Would I ask you if I thought you'd be a disaster?'

'I suppose not . . .'

'So you'll do it?' Quinn tapped the paperwork.

'Um . . . I suppose so. Yes, OK.' Alexia's head felt all big and floaty. She wasn't sure if it was because of this extraordinary suggestion coming out of the blue or the fact that she'd skipped breakfast but she did recognise that she was being offered a rare opportunity. 'So long as everyone knows I've never done anything like it before.'

'You'd never done radio before but you were a natural.' Quinn's round cheeks quivered on either end of her huge smile. 'All you have to do is ignore the camera, chat to the interviewer and other panel members and answer questions. The footage will be edited before it goes online so it doesn't matter if you waffle or need to cough. The team will extract what they want.'

258

'I've been to the homes and interiors show once or twice. Is it in the Peterborough Arena again?'

Quinn nodded, turning her pieces of paper towards Alexia. 'The main event's in the Exhibition Hall but there will be several media stages in the Atrium, and that's where we'll be. Gorgeous light quality in there.' She tapped the pages. 'Read this, this and this, then sign *this*, and the release, if you're happy. I've got to run but if you have any questions or decide not to go ahead can you text me? I'll have to look for someone else.'

Quinn's tone suggested she absolutely didn't want to look for anyone else and Alexia found herself supporting that wish. In the last two minutes a wave of excitement had carried her from never entertaining an ambition to be filmed to wanting desperately to have this new and exciting experience. By the time Quinn had wriggled her feet into thick boots and dragged on a royal blue overcoat Alexia had scan-read the documents, which seemed very simple, and signed on the dotted lines with a flourish. 'Here you are!'

'Fab!' Quinn swept up the pages. 'I'll find out what happens about passes and stuff and email you. Toodles!'

In two minutes, Alexia was listening to Quinn's car roar away, her heart still beating fast enough to make her feel unreal.

After climbing into overalls, she hummed to herself as she put up her wallpaper table. Work was beginning to pick up, although some of it consisted of Elton's damned costings, and The Angel was coming along. Now she had this YouTube film to look forward to. And last night had been . . . well, her legs still didn't feel as if they belonged to her.

All she needed now was for Gabe to start getting better.

Her task for the day was wallpapering the feature walls so she forced any YouTube-related butterflies to settle and mixed the paste. Careful with her plumb line because vertical stripes were reliably more regular on the paper than the wall to which the paper was applied, she soon found her zone. Her pasting roller moved in long slow strokes, letting each fall of paper soak for exactly the same amount of time so as to avoid uneven application. Not wanting Quinn and Ruby to return home to find she'd put the paper up crooked, she only allowed herself to think about Ben when she took her breaks. This meant a break was called for when he texted, mid-afternoon.

Ben: *Have seen Gabe and he seems slightly brighter and even checked up on our treatment of his animals. He says you can visit him any time. xx*

The City Hospital was almost on her route between Yaxley and Middledip. She put a spurt on and by the end of the day had papered both feature walls, cleaned her roller and bucket, and tossed them in the back of her MPV along with her overalls. She slid into her coat, slightly disappointed that neither Ruby nor Quinn had arrived home in time to admire the contrast between their bold and lively wallpaper choices and the ethereal green walls.

Rush hour traffic dogged her through Farcet into Peterborough, then she had the hassle associated with parking, but it was all worthwhile when she reached Gabe's ward and found him awake. He turned his head on the pillow when she stole into his room.

'How are you feeling?' she whispered.

He pulled a face. 'Damned sore. Pleurisy hurts. I can't cough or sneeze without saying "bastard".'

Alexia grinned. 'But you're more wakeful than I've seen you for days.'

He nodded and held up a pair of crossed fingers. 'Early indications are that the antibiotics in the drip are working. I asked Ben to bring me more pyjamas and he bought me four new pairs. Do you think he was trying to tell me my old ones had seen better days?' Then he hunched his shoulders, covered his mouth and went into a paroxysm of coughing, *cough, cough, cough, COUGH, COUGH*, and finished up with, 'Uhh . . . bastard!'

Trying not to giggle at his coping technique, Alexia began bringing him up to date on progress at The Angel.

Gabe, though, wasn't attentive. Mainly he sank into his pillows and coughed until he could groan and gasp 'bastard!' so, although she'd been cheered to perceive a small improvement, Alexia kept her visit brief and was soon hurrying to her car through icy rain for the drive back to Middledip.

When she entered the village, rather than stay on Main Road after she'd slowed for the speed camera – which someone had added a flamboyant twist of silver tinsel to – she turned right along Ladies Lane and then left into Port Road to call in at The Angel to check on the progress of the electrician and the plumber.

She picked her way across the dark drive and unlocked the door, stepping into the reassuringly familiar musty smell of drying plaster. Flicking light switches as she went, she found wiring and plumbing complete and that plaster patching had begun. There was still some to do and she texted Freddie to ask him to concentrate on the toilets and foyer and leave the pantry till last. With a few days' drying time she'd be able to apply the mist coat of watered down white emulsion to seal the raw plaster in the area they needed finished in order for The Angel Community Café to open. She glanced at the screed on the floor. As it was to be tiled over she could use a roller for the mist coat and spatter wouldn't matter.

She wandered into the Public to assess the number of chairs and tables they'd need in there. If she could see one on Freecycle within easy fetching distance she might put a sofa and a long, low coffee table against the back wall. Dark brown or black, preferably, so that when Mums 'n' Tots met in here it wouldn't show if someone was careless with a crayon.

The mist coat would begin the exciting part of the transformation, she thought, gazing about with satisfaction. Soon would follow emulsion, tiles, doors, window dressing and shiny kitchen fittings.

Mind working on when they could get the light fittings in, she meandered back into the Bar Parlour – and nearly jumped out of her skin to see the figure of a man coming towards her.

It was Ben and he was frowning. 'Snobby isn't eating properly,' he said without preamble. 'I've no way of finding out whether he's grazing but his hay net's scarcely been touched.' His eyes seemed darker than usual in the brash light of bare bulbs. His gaze was fixed on her, but he halted a few steps away.

Alexia's heart gave a couple of extra beats but she followed his lead with an all-in-a-day's-work tone. 'If he's drinking I think we could perhaps leave him a day or two. Then we'll need to talk to a vet if we're still concerned.'

He accepted her idea with a nod. 'Perhaps he just needs company. We could take him for a walk?'

It sounded like a question so Alexia answered, 'OK. I'll take my car home and get my boots.' It seemed a pragmatic sort of conversation with which to greet each other after a night notable mainly for the amount of sex they'd packed into it.

She was conscious of a gentle sinking sensation, unable to discount the memory of their first morning-after-the-night-before – and afternoon-after-the-night-before, for that matter – when Ben had behaved like an arse. She watched him uncertainly, searching for signs of that same uncomfortable distance in his face.

But then he held his hand out for hers and closed the distance between them. Stopped. Stooped. Touched her lips with his, his tongue tip quivering along her bottom lip, and pleasure flooded through her like liquid heat. He pulled back to look at her. 'I think you have wallpaper paste in your hair.'

'Wouldn't be the first time.'

He grinned, then led her back out into the evening as if they'd walked hand-in-hand a hundred times before. 'Let's go on a date with a lonely pony.'

Vehicles parked outside Alexia's cottage, they walked up Gabe's track. 'I wonder how we'll catch Snobby if he's off his food,' mused Alexia. 'Generally you have to make it worth his while before he'll let you approach.'

'I'd be happy to give him ten handfuls of carrots if it meant I knew he was eating.'

However, Snobby just mumbled over the proffered carrots and let them fall, allowing Ben to attach the leading rein to his head collar without even a show of tossing his head out of reach or hiding it between his hocks.

'He's *not* himself,' Alexia declared, warming one hand on Snobby's neck as they traversed The Cross and turned into the bridleway. 'He must be missing Gabe.'

Ben stroked Snobby's greying mane. 'Another reason for us to hope Gabe gets home quickly.'

Although Snobby's ears flicked back and forth at the rustlings and noises of the night-time hedgerow he didn't even bother to pretend to spook at shadows just for the entertainment of pulling people off their feet. They tried trotting him and he did reluctantly break into a bit of a shamble, but almost immediately fell back into a walk, as if anything else was just too much trouble.

Even Alexia breaking the news about the YouTube filming didn't grab Snobby's attention, though Ben was gratifyingly interested and congratulatory.

The only time Snobby showed any real animation was when they escorted him back up Gabe's track. He dug in his toes and pricked his ears as he stared in the direction of the house. Then he blew out what sounded suspiciously like an unhappy sigh and allowed Alexia to lead him through the muddy patch into his paddock. He held still for the lead rein to be detached then mooched disconsolately up to his field shelter, drank briefly, then stood with his head hanging.

As Ben and Alexia hadn't joined Snobby on hunger strike, they paused only to feed and water Luke then strode off to The Three Fishes, staking their claim on a table near the fire for a supper of lasagne with crusty bread.

Beginning on a pleasingly golden pint of lager, Alexia sat back with a contented sigh.

Ben's knee was warm against hers beneath the table. He leant close, his breath tickling her ear. 'Sebastian's behind you. He's staring at you so longingly I'm surprised his gaze isn't burning your back.'

She groaned. 'I won't look over because I'm not sure I can cope with him this evening. He makes me feel guilty for not returning his feelings.'

Ben sat back to allow Janice to set their steaming meals

264

before them, then passed Alexia a set of napkin-wrapped cutlery and unwrapped his own. 'I'm not sure what there is to be done. You can't feel to order just to make him happy.'

She broke through the baked cheese topping to the lasagne with her fork, allowing fragrant steam to escape. 'True, but poor Seb. He's the original Mr Nice Guy. But also, unfortunately, Mr Possessive.'

Ben tilted his head thoughtfully. 'You can pretend you don't know he's there unless he actually comes over. Then we could say we're having an early night, if you want to get away.'

Alexia almost choked on hot cheese as Ben hadn't lowered his voice and a couple of nearby conversations paused expectantly. He grinned but spoke more quietly as, beneath the table, he slid his hand lightly onto her thigh. 'Or am I being possessive?'

She drank a mouthful of her beer so she could speak again. 'Not exactly.'

Subtly, his expression altered, as if reading a lot into those two words. The expression of gentle amusement in his eyes died. 'Ah. I've taken too much for granted in assuming there's more bed in our future?'

'Not exactly that either.' Alexia watched the expression in his eyes, trying to find the right way to share what was on her mind. 'I'm hoping there is but . . .' She hesitated awkwardly. 'At the same time, I'm hoping we don't have to hang too many labels on whatever's happening between us. It's not that I don't want it to be happening,' she added hastily. 'I just want to—'

'Let it happen?' he suggested.

She took his hand. 'Now I feel as if it's me writing all the rules. How do you feel?'

'Happy to keep things light,' he answered promptly, giving her fingers a squeeze.

'I could probably keep things light for at least a decade before I tired of it. Possibly longer.'

His eyes crinkled. 'Thanks for the clarification.'

In case he thought she was joking, she kept her voice serious. 'Something I was never able to get over to Seb is that I can enjoy the *zing!*, that tingly magnetic pull towards someone without wanting to be part of a Couple with a capital C. I'm truly happy as things are.' She waited for him to react. To show some sign of being slighted that she didn't demand the labels and commitment that everyone seemed to think all women wanted.

But he just lifted her hand and kissed it. 'Don't panic. Let's just enjoy the *zing*.'

Chapter Twenty-two

Although she had a lot to occupy her days – Gabe was still making only slow progress, the plasterers were almost finished at The Angel and she continued to enjoy feeling tingly with Ben – Alexia felt that the Wednesday of the YouTube filming took a long time to come around.

Carola had been beyond excited when Alexia offered her the companion pass she received along with her own. Alexia had briefly considered offering it to Jodie to cheer her up but it was Carola who'd earned the treat with her unstinting work on The Angel's furniture. Now the day was here Carola had insisted on driving Alexia to the East of England Showground as a mark of gratitude. 'This is going to be amazing!' she crowed, almost bouncing with joy as they left the car park and joined the crowd filtering into the foyer and Exhibition Hall, relieved to be out of the wind that tore across the 250 acres of showground.

Alexia laughed, feeling pretty bouncy herself. 'You deserve it. I'm surprised you're not seeing chairs and tables in your sleep, you've tarted up so many. I'd be a month further back without you.'

They eventually reached the front of the queue and had their passes zapped with a bar code reader. Then they were free to surge into the bright lights and exciting hum of the main hall where colourful stands and light boxes vied for their attention. Alexia wasn't required to report to Media Stage 2 until 1.45 p.m. so, after she'd texted Quinn to confirm her arrival, they had the morning in which to please themselves.

Carola was like a child given the run of Toys R Us, trying out software on which to design her dream kitchen, getting into earnest conversation with a woman about the benefits of a water softener, drooling over fine white towels that purported to dry you in no time and never discolour, and tossing back her blonde bob to consult a physical trainer about what she'd require from a home gym, should she ever feel the need.

Alexia was inclined to observe rather than interact. She watched a couple of demonstrations involving new paints and browsed room sets to check out upcoming styles and colours. Innovations in smart home technology absorbed her for an hour because she'd had a lot of home-loving clients who were gadget lovers, too.

Deliberately not telling Carola where she was going because she was beginning to get a very fluttery attack of butterflies, she toured the Atrium with its two media stages, sponsors' hubs and 'theatres' where those interested could sit and watch a rolling programme of talks and demonstrations. The media stages were very plain, comprising a dais with a white background and black seating.

But Alexia gulped when she saw enough plastic chairs to seat an audience of twenty. She'd assumed a facility that would enjoy the seclusion of Quinn's radio studio but with a camera as well as microphones. Although the audience numbered only three for Media Stage 2's current community radio event she left the area with her butterflies in a frenzy.

By lunchtime both she and Carola were glad to take the weight off their feet. Carola dug into roast vegetables and corn-fed chicken while Alexia picked at a sandwich and drank three cups of tea. Ben, Gabe and Jodie all sent her good luck texts and she got so caught up with understated replies about feeling slightly nervous that she got a horrible shock when she caught sight of the time.

'I'm due at Media Stage 2 in five minutes!' All her butterflies simultaneously looped-the-loop and went into tailspins. 'I haven't left enough time to get to the loo and I've drunk about a bucket of tea.'

Carola glanced at her watch and her eyebrows shot up. 'Gosh. I'll find you a loo. Come on!'

She almost had to drag Alexia and her trembling legs along, locating a Ladies behind a wall of stands and shoving her through the door. A queue of patient women waited in front of an inadequate number of stalls.

'Oh, no!' Alexia ground to a hopeless halt. She'd never attend to business in time to arrive for the filming on time if she waited her turn but if she didn't attend to business she'd very likely be bug-eyed and cross-legged by the time the filming was complete.

Undeterred, Carola simply carried on to the head of the queue, smiling charmingly. 'Could you possibly put up with my friend cutting in? She's due at a filming in three minutes and is desperately desperate. I wouldn't ask if it wasn't an emergency.' A cubicle door opened, a lady came out and Carola shoved Alexia through it so hard she almost greeted the toilet on her hands and knees.

'Thank you!' Alexia shouted over the stall to the waiting queue. 'I'm really sorry.'

She could hear Carola's voice continuing, soothing, apologising and thanking in such a long and grateful stream that nobody really got a chance to protest. Mission accomplished, Alexia shot out of the cubicle, washed her hands, ran her fingers through her hair in the hopes that it would make it a bit less as if a child had scribbled it around her head, applied a lightning coat of lipstick then shot out into the Exhibition Hall.

Carola caught her up, linking arms firmly to swing her around. 'You're fine. Absolutely bang on time. Don't run all the way there and arrive out of breath and sweaty. Let's look at you.' Carola checked her out. 'A tiny touch of powder? You're shiny.' She produced a pale green compact from her bag and dabbed at Alexia's nose. 'Straighten your collar. Good. All set for a relaxed stroll.'

'When did you become a media styling expert?' Alexia felt her knees turn to soup as they passed into the Atrium and she could actually see Media Stage 2 and several people in black polo shirts surrounding two cameras topped with spongy microphones.

Carola laughed. 'It's not much different to getting everyone settled before the village fete, is it? Last-minute nerves. People needing a bit of a tidy up before their photos are taken.'

'Alexia!' Quinn waved from the stage, rocking a navy blazer over what looked a lot like a bodycon dress under stress. 'You're nice and punctual. The other guests haven't arrived yet. Come on the stage and Avril will mic you up.'

Carola gave her an encouraging pat and promised to look after her bag. 'I'll sit back a bit. Have fun!'

The relaxed attitudes of Quinn and Carola had their desired effects. Alexia's knees hardly wobbled as she ascended two steps to the carpet-covered stage and met

Avril, a tiny girl with big boots who seated her in the middle one of the three guest seats and clipped a tiny microphone to her jacket lapel and shoved a battery pack at her back. Quinn chatted to Alexia as if they were the only ones there while Alexia tried not to think about the gathering audience. The other guests arrived, both men. One was grey-haired and smelled slightly of beer, the other looking as if he did this sort of thing every day. 'You're a rose between two thorns,' he said cheerily to Alexia. 'I'm Eddie and I advise on solar heating.'

The other man reached over Alexia to shake hands with Eddie and said, 'Brian. Floor covering.' Almost as an after-thought he shook hands with Alexia, too.

Quinn chatted with each guest in turn while the camera crews talked about levels and readings, then one of the crew, a woman who Quinn had identified as the floor manager, said, 'Ready when you are,' to Quinn.

Alexia felt her nerves again for a few seconds as she realised that not only were two cameras gazing at her like one-eyed robots but that all twenty of the audience seats were filled and a similar number of people were standing behind. Local presenter Quinn obviously commanded a lot of interest. She took a steadying sip of the water provided on the low table in front of the panel.

'OK.' Quinn took a last glance through her notes. 'We're going to carry on chatting, just as we have been.' She glanced at the floor manager and nodded then looked into Camera 1 and smiled. 'I'm Quinn Daly, a self-confessed home improvement junkie. It's a delight for me to have the chance to chat to some industry experts today and pick their brains. Welcome along, everyone.' She included them all in a wide, welcoming smile. 'Eddie,' she began, homing in on the self-possessed man, 'your area of expertise is solar panels. What's so good about them? Should I be marring my beautifully tiled roof with an array? I've seen them around residential neighbourhoods but I'm not sure how I feel.'

Eddie, obviously used to this type of enquiry, gave a practised spiel about the pros and cons of solar panels.

Quinn turned to Alexia. 'But what do you think, Alexia? Do you have solar panels on your house?'

With a jolt, Alexia remembered that they weren't just supposed to be answering questions on their own subjects. She moistened her lips. 'I don't have an array. I like solar power's green credentials but I don't have the money to invest.'

Eddie came back with financial information about the Feed-in Tariff, i.e. the government paying you for surplus power generated.

Alexia nodded and said, 'That's interesting,' although she knew about FiT already and added, 'To be honest, I'm not keen on how the panels would look on my stone cottage.'

Eddie nodded back. 'I think people will worry about that less and less. Twenty or thirty years ago we looked askance at every satellite TV dish. Now we hardly notice them.'

'Would she need planning permission?' Quinn's head tilted as if to show how hard she was listening. Eddie explained the rules then Quinn turned to Brian to begin a debate about hard floors versus carpets.

By the time it came to Alexia's segment she felt fairly at home on the little stage. The audience had even laughed at a couple of her comments. Quinn began by asking in general terms about beautifying the home.

Then she slipped in a question Alexia hadn't anticipated.

'Alexia, I'd particularly like to talk to you about your recent experience with cowboy builders. We're all scared of them. How did you, an experienced professional, get so thoroughly ripped off? And how can people avoid the trap you fell into?'

The audience stirred and turned expectantly towards Alexia.

It wasn't remotely what Alexia had been led to expect and she felt as if Quinn, discovering the existence of a corn on her toe, had stamped upon it.

What the hell? How dare Quinn make her sound as if she were incompetent? *And* try to lead her into criticising the very tradespersons she needed in her professional networks? It was hardly the positive exposure she'd been encouraged to hope for.

For a moment, all she could do was gape. Quinn leant forward in her seat, looking like an investigative reporter scenting blood. Maybe it was Alexia's blood because that suddenly roared into her face, making her feel hot and barely in control of the words that began to pour from her lips.

'Well, Quinn,' she snapped. 'Let's talk about the term "cowboy builders" for a start. I, for one, get sick of hearing it. Instead of being reserved for the person in a thousand who pretends to be qualified when they're not, or tricks customers into expensive options they don't need, it's used far too often against competent and honest tradespersons. For any "offence" from asking perfectly legitimately for a deposit to be paid, bills to be settled on time, architects to share correct information, keys to be left where promised and kids and dogs to be kept off-site, these craftsmen find themselves referred to as "cowboys".'

A man in the audience gave a quiet cheer, and the audience laughed.

'You're a prime example,' Alexia ploughed on as Quinn opened her mouth to interrupt. 'You told me you were "let down" by your last interior decorator. In fact, all that happened was he made a simple mistake with dates. Yet you had no hesitation in telling me he was "some cowboy" without making any allowance for a normal human error.'

'Oh! I didn't really—' Quinn began, clearly taken aback.

But Alexia wasn't ready to bat the conversational ball into Quinn's court yet. 'If you want me to provide tips for how to find the best tradesperson for you, and how to work with him or her to make the experience go as smoothly as possible, I'm well qualified. I'm the person who stands between the tradesperson and the client, explaining that if you want a wall knocked down it will make a bit of dust, or that building regulations are not some tiresome trick the builder has created to give you a hard time. Or that he's not actually responsible for the existence of VAT. *But*,' she went on loudly, as Quinn's mouth opened again, 'to answer your original question, what happened to me was not about cowboy builders but about conmen. Criminals. Conmen operate in all areas and these two just happened to be builders.'

Quinn sat back, her smile, for once, absent as she ceded control. 'Why don't you tell us what happened.'

So Alexia launched into the torrid tale of The Angel, from the inception of a sympathetic restoration to the horror of realising the money had gone along with 'all the beautiful original features – ripping those out was a crime in itself', and then how they'd all pulled together to 'create a different Angel, but one we hope will save my friend from losing all the money he has left. The conmen only *think* they took everything from us because . . .' She paused

274

as if hearing an imaginary drum roll. 'The Angel Community Café in Middledip opens on the 23rd of December.'

The audience burst into applause. With a last hard look at Quinn, Alexia stopped speaking and sipped from her water glass instead.

After a dazed instant, Quinn switched the conversation back to Brian and Eddie and soon they were wrapping up the session. Alexia couldn't believe an hour had flitted by.

'My goodness.' Eddie grinned at Alexia as he unclipped his mic. 'You were impressive.'

'She talked more than the rest of us put together,' Brian said sourly, dropping his microphone carelessly on the table as he got to his feet before jumping down from the dais.

Quinn looked at Alexia uncertainly. 'I'm sorry if my question caught you off guard. It's just that I was asked to keep things lively.'

Now her adrenalin was subsiding Alexia felt as if she'd been blasted into space in a rocket and returned to earth without a parachute. She rose slowly. 'I'm sorry if my replies caught *you* off guard.' She couldn't quite keep the edge from her voice even though Quinn and Ruby were clients. 'You told me I was coming here to answer questions about decorating. I know I talked freely about The Angel on the radio but I never used the term "cowboy builders". It would have been unprofessional and it would have alienated all the great craftsmen I work with. If you'd come clean about your line of questioning then we could have agreed what was off limits.'

'It was interesting and powerful, though,' said a man Alexia hadn't noticed until now. His eyes gleamed from behind blue-framed glasses and his hair was clipped very close to his head.

275

As he wore a black shirt Alexia assumed he was one of the film crew. 'Oh, good,' she said, with a hint of sarcasm.

But the man produced a business card. 'I'm Antonio Cabrio. I happened to be close by because I work for a production company that's preparing for a slot on Media Stage 1. I'm also working on another project, a series called *Lemonade from Lemons* for a satellite channel. Have you seen those programmes like *Top Gear* and *The F1 Show*, where the audience stands around the discussion that's going on between pundits and experts, and some of them get to ask a question? It's a similar format but selected people in the audience tell their stories of something positive coming from something negative. We've just lost a guest we thought we had in place for our "Crooks and Conmen" programme and you'd be perfect. So articulate and impassioned and with an individual perspective.'

Carola, who'd come up to hand Alexia her bag, promptly backed him up. 'You would be great, Alexia. And you never know, you might stop other people falling for conmen.'

'Well . . .' Alexia began, all uncertain again.

Quinn hovered closer. 'That does sound interesting.'

'At least let's talk about it, Alexia.' Antonio turned his shoulder to Quinn in an obvious intimation that she wasn't the one being courted. 'Let's find a corner where I can tell you more about what's involved and you can ask any questions you might have. Which would you prefer – a cuppa or a glass of wine?'

'Both,' Alexia replied frankly, suddenly glad that Carola had offered to drive.

She said a cool goodbye to Quinn and soon Antonio, Alexia and Carola had claimed a corner of a bar and

Alexia was letting herself be talked into an actual real life TV appearance. One that included a car to deliver her to the studio and take her home. 'And just think,' Antonio enthused, 'your account of what happened might even ring bells with viewers and lead to Shane and Tim being caught!'

'Well, OK then, but I'm not the kind of person who usually goes on TV,' Alexia said, taking a great gulp of Pinot grigio.

'The team will look after you,' promised Antonio, checking his phone quickly as it beeped an alert. He speeded up his delivery. 'Filming for the "Crooks and Conmen" episode takes place one week from this evening, 22nd November, and it airs four weeks later, 20th December. Someone will be in touch about the car and what you should expect. I don't mind telling you that it's a great relief to me to secure a replacement guest. Excuse me if I rush, won't you? Needed on Media Stage 1.' He jumped up grinning boyishly, dropped luvvie kisses on the cheeks of both women and strode off, already on his phone and looking important.

Carola pedalled her feet, as excited as if she were the one to be on telly. 'You're a media star!'

Alexia drained her wine. 'And I've got another week of being on pins! If you've seen everything you want to, please can we get home to a bit of sanity? The queues to leave the showground will be immense later.'

Although she sighed, Carola acquiesced. Soon they were hurrying across the great open car park. Carola was driving her husband's huge Land Rover Defender once again. The mud-spatter pattern emanating from each wheel arch made it look as if she'd been off-roading in it.

Alexia had to fight with the zip of her coat as she climbed in because her phone began to ring. 'It's Ben,' she said before she answered, suddenly feeling self-conscious. She hadn't had much practice speaking to him in front of others since their relationship-or-whatever-it-was had changed a week ago and was conscious he might say something she wouldn't want Carola to overhear.

She began in an unnaturally bright babble. 'Hiya! I'm in Carola's car and we're just about to leave the showground.'

Ben sounded amused, obviously getting why she'd want him to know that she wasn't alone. 'How did the filming go?'

She filled him in while Carola reversed the behemoth vehicle from its parking space as if she didn't care whether she hit things or not, raising her voice to chime in when Alexia got to the part about *Lemonade from Lemons*. 'She's going to be marvellous. Tell her.'

'You're going to be marvellous,' Ben agreed. 'Maybe you can supply images of Shane and Tim and turn it into a mini *Crimewatch*. Get the bleeders caught.'

'We're not allowed to go quite that far. Carola suggested it.' Alexia sighed regretfully. 'Wouldn't it be fantastic, though? Not only would Gabe and Jodie get their money back, but The Angel would get all her lovely etched glass and polished mahogany returned. Oof!'

Carola had created a shortcut into the queue for the showground exit by bouncing over a kerb.

'Sorry,' said Carola, unperturbed.

On the subject of The Angel, Ben had his own information to impart. 'I've been in today and the plaster's dry. Just in time –' he paused theatrically '– for Gabe to come home and see it!'

Alexia whooped with joy. 'I began to think they'd never bash that infection on the head.'

'The doctor who saw him today says he's really turned the corner. I expect he'll need a while to get over the fatigue but then it's going to be a challenge to stop him from doing his winter digging or taking Snobby out for a drive.'

'That,' said Alexia fervently, 'will be wonderful.'

She ended the call just as Carola biffed another kerb; an ominous scraping noise suggesting that one alloy wheel was now less beautiful than before. 'Is your husband particularly understanding about his car?' she teased, tucking her phone away.

A pause. Then Carola replied flatly, 'He's not particularly understanding about anything.'

Alexia glanced at her, shocked to see that all of a sudden Carola was blinking hard. In fact, she had to stop the car in its slow progress along the queue to fish in her pocket for a tissue and blot her eyes. 'Damn,' she muttered. Then she began to edge the vehicle forward once more.

Alexia gawked. 'Carola? What's up?'

Carola offered only a silent shrug. Reaching the head of the queue, she indicated right and joined Oundle Road in the direction of Nene Parkway. Giving little sniffs as she gazed through the windscreen with single-minded concentration she was very obviously *not* all right.

Before Alexia could decide whether to suggest stopping at the garden centre coffee shop at the bottom of Ham Lane, Carola heaved the steering wheel to the left and pulled up in a service road, putting the Land Rover in park.

Then she burst into big, noisy, gulping tears.

Chapter Twenty-three

Alexia laid a remorseful hand on Carola's shoulder. 'I'm sorry. I didn't mean to upset you.'

Shaking her head violently, Carola brought out the tissue again. 'It's not you,' she quavered. 'It's Duncan. My husband.'

Alexia was pretty sure she'd never heard Duncan's name before. Carola always referred to him as 'my husband'.

'Does he get shirty about his car?' Alexia hazarded, though she wondered why, in that case, Carola didn't look after it a bit better.

Carola found a clean piece of tissue in which to trumpet. 'He used to.' She wiped her eyes on her sleeve. 'He le-left me months ago. He dumped me and the village hall had to close, all in the same week. I felt totally sodding useless.'

Horrified, Alexia pulled Carola's slight frame into a gentle hug. 'I had no idea! I'm so sorry.'

With a long and mighty sniff, Carola regained control. 'Nobody knew. I haven't told anybody. Not even Charlotte and Emily know the whole story, but it turns out he's been leading a double life. All those nights he stayed in London at what he said was the company apartment he was actually shacking up with his girlfriend in a perky little mews house in Chelsea.' She tipped her head forwards so the wings of her silky blonde bob swung either side of her eyes, like blinkers. 'When he finally decided between us, he said he had to take my car for a bit. *Had* to.' Her voice wobbled pitifully. 'Because the Defender won't fit in her ga-garage and my sports car will. And mine's no good for the girls because it's a two-seater. His plan is to swap back when he's found a bigger place to park and I've found a car with four seats.'

'So that's why you've seemed so accident-prone lately. You've been letting his get dinged up on purpose.'

Carola nodded tiredly. 'I know it's vindictive and petty but he deserves it. Aside from dumping me, he hasn't asked to see Charlotte and Emily once. He's always been away a lot but does he expect them just to not *mind* that he's gone for good? He hasn't even asked to see them at Christmas. He's just sent me money to buy their Christmas presents as if it'll carry on being my department.' Carola managed a watery smile, her face displaying the kind of red blotches that seemed to occur whenever tears met fair skin. 'There's no Christmas Fair in the village hall for me to organise so The Angel's opening is the only part of Christmas I'm looking forward to. Then after Christmas I'll have to get a job.'

'That could be exciting, though. What sort of thing will you look for?' Alexia's heart ached for the woman she now thought of as her friend.

Carola sighed. 'I did a catering course and worked in a couple of small restos before I married. Part of the reason I was so against you all at The Angel in the beginning was that because I always quite wanted a coffee shop and thought Middledip needed one. But you got there first. You don't want to give me a job as a decorator, do you?'

'Not as a decorator.' Alexia had been withdrawing her arm from Carola's shoulders as the worst of the tear storm seemed over but she stopped short as an idea fired across her brain. 'Do you want to run the coffee shop for Gabe, though? He's going to need someone. It's a pretty important detail but one that's been left because of Gabe being ill.'

Carola pushed all her tissues into various pockets, still sniffing. 'But isn't Jodie doing it?'

'I'm pretty sure she's not.'

Hope began to dawn on Carola's still-blotchy face. 'I'd need to update myself with the hygiene certificates and stuff you see up on the walls of coffee shops.'

'It's all on the Food Standards Agency's website. Jodie used to do her training online.' Alexia was beginning to be glad she'd made Carola cry if it brought about this neat solution to the running of the community café. 'Shall I suggest you to Gabe and see what he thinks?'

'That would be wonderful!' Carola gave Alexia a beaming hug. 'Sorry to have bawled all over you.' She restarted the Land Rover, putting the blowers on full because the tears and hugs had steamed up the windows.

They drove back to Middledip talking of more cheerful things like stopping at Carola's for a count-up of tables and chairs and whether Carola fancied helping with the mist coat of the raw plaster at The Angel.

By the time Alexia left Carola's des res nearly two hours later they'd determined that if they had chairs and tables for about twenty more covers it would be enough for the Bar Parlour and the Public.

Alexia elected to walk home from Little Dallas, wanting

not just a breath of fresh air but to call in on Jodie on the pretext of confirming her intention not to run The Angel Community Café. Striding along New Street and rounding the corner into Port Road she was glad she had a reason to call on Jodie. A lot had happened for Alexia in the three weeks since Jodie had announced her pregnancy and they'd had a few text conversations but not a single real one.

She strode up the garden path and banged the black horseshoe-shaped doorknocker that she'd clattered regularly all her life. It was Iona who answered, fluffy hair escaping from its clasp. 'Alexia! How lovely.' She beckoned Alexia in and called up the stairs, 'Jodie, Alexia's here!' in the same cadence she'd always used. 'JO-deeee, ALEXia's here!'

In seconds, wearing the first normal Jodie smile that Alexia had seen for ages, Jodie ran down the stairs.

They hugged hello and Jodie immediately took her through to the kitchen so she could update Iona about Gabe's progress. Everyone in the village, Alexia imagined, knew he'd been ill.

Once she'd heard the good news that Gabe was on the mend, Iona said, 'I'll leave you girls to chat,' and melted away to some other part of the house.

Settled over a pot of tea, Alexia tried to give Jodie news of The Angel.

Looking suddenly self-conscious, Jodie diverted the conversation to maternity clothes. Evidently beginning to eagerly anticipate the arrival of her baby, she looked almost shy when she showed Alexia she was wearing her baggiest jeans but could no longer do up the button.

Alexia exclaimed over this development, recognising the pleasure lurking in her friend's eyes. She was happy and relieved to find Jodie so much brighter, her hair washed and her nails done but, after a while, not wanting the subject to be a no-go zone between them, she circled back to The Angel. 'By the way, Gabe's soon going to need someone in place to run the community café. A suitable person's cropped up but I just want to check it won't be treading on your toes if we go ahead.'

Pink bloomed in Jodie's cheeks. 'Of course not, but thanks for checking.' She took a breath, then visibly steeled herself to add, 'Especially when I left you in the cart. Will you still open in time for Christmas?'

Glad to be making steps in the right direction, Alexia just said, 'We're on course,' and then told Jodie about the extraordinary invitation to appear on TV. Jodie was instantly bug-eyed with amazement and they spent a happy half hour speculating about whether it would all be amazingly glamorous and creating increasingly unlikely scenarios based around Antonio's idea of viewers recognising Shane and Tim. It was almost like old times.

But not quite.

Oh, they laughed together but so much had changed. Jodie didn't grab a bottle of wine from the fridge to share. There was no current man in Jodie's life to whisper about – unsurprisingly.

Most tellingly, Alexia found she had absolutely no desire to divulge that there was 'a thing' going on between her and Ben. Maybe it was because the discovery of the scam had got in the way of her ever telling Jodie about that first night with him.

Or was it because it seemed unfair to Jodie, approaching unplanned single parenthood, to flaunt her relationship-or-whatever-it-was in front of her?

Or, Alexia realised as she walked home after a last cup

of tea, pulling up her hood because the evening was raw, because she simply no longer felt close to Jodie.

She had to stop walking in order to confront the idea, watching freezing drizzle eddying in the halo of light from the streetlamps. It was wonderful that they were friendly again . . . but the trust was no longer there.

Chapter Twenty-four

At home in bed, Ben struggled awake, realising that his phone was ringing.

By the time he'd fought off the quilt, sucked in his breath at the frigid air and staggered across the room to where he'd left the phone on charge, the ringing had stopped and the illumination from the screen was fading away.

His brain functioned sufficiently to fire off alarms. Was something wrong with Gabe? He was supposed to be going home in the morning. In his anxiety he fumbled, knocking the phone off the polished surface and then struggling to locate it in the darkness. He had to feel his way, shivering and cursing, to the light switch before he could locate it on the floor.

He sought the sanctuary of his bed before tapping the home button at the bottom of the screen. The phone lit up. *Missed call Imogen. 3.04 a.m.*

What the hell?

Burrowing further into the bedclothes he returned the

call, willing to run the risk that somehow she'd rung him in her sleep or it had been a pocket call.

After five rings, the line opened up. Then it was a couple of seconds before Imogen spoke. 'Ben?'

'I've just been woken up by a call from your phone. Is anything the matter?'

She sighed. 'I just wanted to say I'm sorry.'

He hesitated, trying to replay her voice in his head and capture what he'd heard there. 'Why are you sorry?' he asked more gently. 'What's up?'

A sound, perhaps the breath of a laugh. Or a sob. 'I'm sorry,' she repeated. 'I was being silly. I wanted to ask you something but I've been on a Netflix binge and I hadn't realised what the time was. Then I did, so I rang off.'

With more words to base a judgement on, he worked it out. Her voice was as controlled as she could make it but it was there in the over sibilance of the 's' sounds. She was drunk. 'As I'm up now, you might as well ask me whatever it was.'

'I'm sorry, Ben. I'm so, so sorry. I don't want to hurt you again.'

He screwed up his eyes as he tried to get a handle on what was going on. 'Well, I'm awake and listening so why not just go ahead and ask me?' He tried to sound encouraging, as if this were a perfectly normal time to chit chat with the ex-wife he'd only seen once in months, on which occasion she'd sneaked off and left him sitting alone in a pub like a prize idiot. He remembered his burning quest for knowledge that had consumed him then. Before Gabe got sick. Before he took on extra responsibility in the form of The Angel.

Before he began whatever he'd begun with Alexia.

She was silent for so long that he began to suspect she'd fallen asleep. When she did speak again, her voice trembled. 'Do you think – do you think there's even the tiniest chance that we might get back together?'

The world rocked slightly. What she suggested seemed such a foreign concept now. 'I thought we both agreed we should divorce.'

A sound like a sob trying to escape. 'I wasn't sleeping with your brother, I swear.'

Frustration roared back. 'Then what the fuck happened that night? I don't understand why you or Lloyd won't just tell me.'

Her voice began to shake. 'You haven't answered my question. If I know there's no chance, I'll know what to do.'

A great wave of pity swamped the frustration, doused it. Pity for the beautiful woman he'd loved, bearing the scars of a night that had changed everything for both of them. Searching for a phrase that would leave her in no doubt of the situation without being overly blunt, he made his voice soft. 'I've moved on.'

The sound of her breathing grew louder, quicker. 'Oh.' A hesitation. 'So you won't be hurt if I do the same?'

He tried to answer the question as honestly as he could. 'I expect it will feel odd but I think I've done all my hurting. And we don't live in the same town any more. We won't see each other.'

'But what if we did?'

'Then I would have to deal with it.'

'I see,' she whispered. 'Who is she?'

An annoying shaft of guilt shot through him. 'I think the divorce means you no longer have the right to ask me to explain myself.'

Silence. She'd ended the call.

He fell back on his pillows, irritated at ending up, once again, with more questions than answers.

Imogen's middle-of-the-night call couldn't just be about drinking too much. She was searching for something. Instinct suggested that it was something more abstract than truth. Encouragement? Hope? Permission?

Permission. His mind seized on that one. Maybe she'd simply met someone else and, on some level, needed Ben's blessing, as it were, to go ahead? The habits associated with being married could be hard to break, but why she couldn't just say 'I want you to know I'm seeing someone' was beyond him.

Except . . . he hadn't done that, had he? She'd given him the opportunity to tell her he was seeing Alexia and he'd replied obliquely, whether out of misplaced guilt at admitting such a thing to a woman he'd been married to, or a wish to avoid causing her pain.

He wished he'd stayed with Alexia tonight. Her warm body against his would make it easier to resist being the man who brooded on his hurts until they swamped him. Alexia the Uncomplicated. Apparently capable of giving and receiving affection without any subtext whatsoever.

On the other hand, the interchange with Imogen would've been a strange conversation to have with Alexia listening. 'Uncomplicated' didn't mean 'without feelings'.

Finally, he got out of bed, dressed quickly and drove to Gabe's to ensure the house was as welcoming as it could be for him. He changed Gabe's bed and turned on the ancient radiator, having to cajole the valve to open. He cleaned the kitchen, filled the range and also the scuttle beside it. Then, as it was still before six, he grabbed his coat and drove through the sleeping village to the twenty-four-hour supermarket in Bettsbrough and bought groceries to stock Gabe's fridge, freezer and food cupboard.

He drove back through the steely pre-dawn, patches of frost revealing themselves in the beam of his headlights. Nearing the turning into Gabe's track he saw light beaming from Alexia's kitchen window.

Without giving himself time to examine his actions, he pulled over.

She answered his knock cautiously, her hair on end and pyjamas peeping out from under her white fluffy dressing gown. 'Ben!' Not even questioning why he was there, she skipped back to let him enter. 'Coffee?'

He remembered the frozen food in his truck as he followed her into the warmth of her kitchen, which smelled of toast and butter, and slid his arms around her and pulled her body against his. 'No time. I just wanted to remind you that I should be fetching Gabe after doctor's rounds.' He couldn't think of a more convincing reason for his visit and was aware of a false heartiness to his voice.

Apparently, she heard it, too. 'What?' she said, nestling into him without taking her eyes from his face. 'What's up?'

So he told her all about Imogen's call. 'It was a bit weird,' he admitted. Then he saw a troubled light dawn in her eyes and wished he'd kept his mouth shut.

Especially when she said, 'Are you sure that you don't want to – to go and talk possibilities with her about this?'

'Yes.' He kissed her, holding her close. That's all he'd wanted, really. To hold her. 'How about celebration shepherd's pie with Gabe tonight? Or, better yet, why don't you come with me to pick him up?'

She smiled, though the hint of anxiety didn't completely leave her big Betty Boop eyes. 'I am working at home, so I could, I suppose. We could take my car. It would be more comfortable for Gabe than your truck.'

'Great. I'll ring you when he lets me know what time he's being discharged.'

He drove around to Gabe's track, wishing he hadn't suffered the moment of weakness and need that had prompted him to confide in Alexia. A few hours ago he'd been valuing the fact that she was uncomplicated and then he'd gone and complicated things.

He unpacked the shopping then pulled on his thick fleece and took himself off to continue his task of coppicing the willow copse. He'd arranged that his time off wouldn't commence until he got the call to free his uncle from the embrace of the hospital.

Cutting everything down to ground level was pleasant enough work on a brisk morning. His task would bring in money to the estate in one years' time when the new growth could be cut for basketry. He knew Christopher Carlysle was disappointed that this cut was only fit for fencing but neglecting the coppice for ten years wasn't the best way to make it generate money.

He worked energetically. Ted, the estate worker who was tying the brown willow rods into bundles for him and stacking them on the trailer, complained he could scarcely keep up. But his face took on a broad grin when Ben got the phone call he was waiting for. 'Tell the old git hello from me,' he said, gathering up the last rods.

'I'm ready for collection,' Gabe said over the phone, sounding as if he were a parcel. He also sounded thready and frail. Ben sent Ted off to deposit the willow rods in a shed and loped back to his truck, ringing Alexia as he went.

He was glad to find that she was her usual self as they drove to Peterborough. A frown only began to form on her forehead when they had collected Gabe and his bag and were walking with him through the corridors to the lift.

'You're shuffling,' she said to him accusingly.

'I'm knackered,' he protested. 'I've been ill.'

Her frowns persisted. 'If you brave the car park like that the wind will blow you over. I think you better sit in the foyer with Ben while I fetch the car.'

Gabe tutted, but he flopped down into one of the foyer chairs when they got there and they watched Alexia flying out of the door, the wind waiting to pounce on her and scramble through her hair as she jogged out of sight. Then he turned to Ben. 'I feel like I've been hit by your truck.'

Ben felt a wave of anxiety. 'Give yourself a chance. You've only this minute got up out of bed.'

'And I wouldn't mind going back there.'

Ben waited, but Gabe didn't laugh or even smile. 'Presumably the doctors feel you're well enough to leave, though?'

'Evidently.' Gabe sounded unconvinced.

'Well, we'll soon have you in your rocking chair by the range.'

'I'd rather go to bed.'

Heart heavy at this post-pneumonia wussy Gabe, Ben tried to be reassuring. 'Do that, then. But maybe you'll feel up to some soup for lunch first?'

Gabe shrugged.

On the way home, Ben sat in the back seat and watched his uncle in the front. Gabe looked at least two stone lighter than at the beginning of his illness and his ponytail hung like wool. Gabe might have embraced an individual sartorial style and personal appearance since he stopped being a bank manager but his hair was always brushed. He never looked like this.

Alexia chatted as she drove. 'Gabe, would you consider Carola to run the community café?'

He shrugged a shoulder. 'Sounds fine. She'll organise the hell out of the place.'

'I've already talked it over with Ben and I think it's a brilliant solution.' She went on to detail Carola's qualifications for the job but Gabe didn't even answer. Presently, he closed his eyes and appeared to sleep. Alexia glanced over at him and her flow of chatter ceased.

Gabe only showed any real animation when they turned up his track and Alexia drew her car to a halt by the paddock gate. Snobby stood in the middle of his field with the wind behind him, his tail blowing along his flanks and his mane streaming into his eyes.

Alexia gave Gabe's arm a pat. 'The old boy's been missing you, I think. He's not eating.'

Gabe actually looked interested. 'No!'

'Do you want to—?'

But Gabe was already struggling to open the car door, huddling into a coat that looked too big for him as he picked his way over the ruts to the gate. Alexia and Ben jumped out of the car and followed.

Snobby's head swung in their direction. Then lifted. His ears flicked forward. Then he whickered, wheeling his tubby body round and heading towards them at a trot.

Ben quickly unlatched the gate and pushed it wide enough to let Gabe through, standing back with Alexia to watch as Snobby slowed, still whickering.

Gabe held out his hands. 'Forgot the carrots.'

Snobby apparently forgave the omission as he pressed his face against Gabe's chest. And stood perfectly still.

Gabe crooned as he scratched the pony's neck. 'Look how much condition you've lost. Stupid animal. You need to start eating, idiot horse.' Ben felt his eyes pricking and when he looked at Alexia he saw her wiping her cheeks with the backs of her hands, quickly, as if hoping nobody would see. Then Gabe gave Snobby a last pat and said, 'See you tomorrow, Snobs.'

Snobby tossed his head as if he wasn't bothered either way and shambled off up the paddock to the field shelter. By the time Ben had seen Gabe out and closed the gate he could see Snobby pulling hay from his net.

Alexia drove Gabe the last stretch of the track and Ben followed on foot. He arrived in time to see Gabe shuffle into the house, reach his rocking chair and plop down with a great sigh of relief.

Luke the cat appeared and jumped lightly onto Gabe's lap, purring as he rubbed the top of his head on Gabe's jaw. 'Hello, you,' Gabe murmured. Then he shut his eyes and went to sleep.

Chapter Twenty-five

The next few days just seemed to evaporate. Alexia spent her days on the final part of Quinn and Ruby's job. Quinn hadn't, as Alexia had half-feared, kicked her off the job and turned difficult about payment. In fact, she seemed genuinely impressed that Alexia was going on actual television and was inclined to pretend the sharp interchange on the YouTube footage had never happened, which suited Alexia fine. Now she was concentrating her energies on making them a wooden chest with strap hinges out of two old doors from a reclamation yard. It was a while since she'd done anything quite so scavenger-ish, apart from rubbing down and painting endless tables and chairs for The Angel, and she loved using Grandpop's old treadle saw and brace-and-bit. She knew there were quick, efficient modern versions but there was something that felt right about old tools on old wood.

Carola pitched in eagerly, apparently not even bored by the tiresome job of stripping the old paint with a combination of paint stripper, scraper and elbow grease. As a reward, Alexia showed her Grandpop's old garden incinerator in the tiny yard behind the workshop and introduced her to his pet method of parting layers of paint from metal by getting a fire going then dropping the ironmongery into the flames.

Carola's eyes almost popped. 'What are you doing?'

'You'll see.' When the fire had burned down, Alexia fished the ironmongery out of the ashes and gave it a brisk once-over with a wire brush. 'There. Ready to be primed, painted and reused.'

Carola inspected the dirty metal. 'Awesome.'

Now, ironmongery painted dark grey and stripped wood finished with wax and wire wool, the chest had pride of place in Quinn's hall. Alexia had been slightly disappointed to learn that Quinn and Ruby were to keep their wellies in there but mentally catalogued it as not her business and just made a healthy addition to their bill.

The YouTube video went live and Alexia couldn't watch it. Ben could, and laughed at how she got Quinn on the run. 'You were amazing!'

Each evening she made sure to call in on Gabe, who was still dividing his time between bed/radio and rocking chair/TV with Luke bestowing his feline company. Snobby grazed contentedly and had returned to spooking at nothings when Alexia and Ben took him out on the leading rein.

Gabe did little more strenuous than stroke Luke's glossy fur, saying his legs felt like water and he didn't fancy anything to eat. Ben's gaze was anxious whenever it rested on him. He, too, called at Gabe's place every day, if not twice or three times.

At the weekend, it took the combined efforts of Alexia, Carola and Ben to apply the mist coat to the ground floor of The Angel. 'High ceilings mean big walls and painting raw plaster's never a fun job. It sucks up the paint like a towel,' Alexia warned them. And before long the smell of fresh emulsion filled the air and they were all wearing speckles of it, but the walls were, finally, wearing something too, even if it was just a blotchy mist coat.

Alexia enjoyed working alongside Ben. He wasn't Mr Chatty when concentrating on a task but she was conscious of a hum of heightened awareness when he was near.

Carola was ultra-industrious and quieter than usual too, because Charlotte and Emily had finally gone to stay with their dad and meet his new girlfriend and she was trying not to think about it.

They all ate their lunch together, munching sandwiches while they tried to imagine the glass globe light fittings Alexia had bought in a sale and the floor tiles, once they were in situ.

Monday and Tuesday Alexia drove to Bettsbrough to oversee the cleaning up of the basement conversion and then apply finishing touches, which, even those as small as directing the spotlights to maximum visual effect, were her favourite part of a job. A very satisfactory debrief revealed that the clients were thrilled with the end result – and even more thrilled to be able to move back in. Alexia was equally thrilled to be able to send in her final invoice.

By early afternoon on Wednesday, while Carola was beginning the second coat of emulsion at The Angel, Alexia was on pins about the filming of *Lemonade from Lemons*, waiting for the car to pick her up and take her down to east London for her six o'clock call. She'd half expected the casting producer's assistant to get in touch and say she should get the train to King's Cross and they'd send a car to meet her there, but it seemed that emergency guests received special treatment. The car duly turned up – an ordinary minicab rather than the stretch limousine her overexcited imagination kept conjuring up – and all Alexia had to do was sit in the back and relax as the day darkened and the driver eased the car down to join the motorway, passing through Bettsbrough where illuminations in the shape of snowflakes had been hung over the main street like a demented blizzard.

For the first time since the job she'd so yearned for had slipped through her fingers, Alexia thought pleasurably of London. She was only being ferried to the studio in Greater London like a delivery but, nevertheless, excitement stirred as her taxi's headlights followed a thousand others towards the general area in which just a short time ago she'd expected to start a new life and the Christmas illuminations she'd become familiar with would have been the sumptuous ones London was famed for suspended over Oxford Street and Piccadilly Circus.

Glad the taxi driver wasn't the talkative kind, she let her mind play back over those heady expectations of exciting projects with real money behind them. Of always aiming to attain the ceiling price for the locality and carefully selecting exactly the right materials to attain that with no waste. Opening up small rooms to go open plan, dividing large spaces to make additional rooms. Being part of a team that made money for the investor. And for themselves. She'd expected to emulate Elton's designer clothes and upmarket lifestyle within a few years.

Instead, she was living in the village where she'd grown up, with all the same people – plus Ben – and doing exactly the same job – plus The Angel (unpaid). Like poking a cracked tooth with her tongue she tried to imagine what sort of place she might have been able to buy for herself and whether she'd have gone minimalist or traditional on the refurb. She imagined quartz worktops and porcelain tiled floors, a chrome and glass staircase up to a master suite in the attic, a glass wall and a terrace on a flat-roof extension.

It could all have been so fabulous.

But it wasn't. And it was the fault of Shane and Tim. Bastards.

Eventually the taxi driver said, 'Should be here somewhere,' and turned into an industrial estate-like complex that reminded her of an airport drop off point. They pulled up outside a white building.

After thanking the driver she was collared by a black-clad young guy with a clipboard, who introduced himself as part of the studio crew and passed her on to a likewise black-clad girl deeper into the studios to give her a wristband and show her where to lock away her handbag. The girl shepherded Alexia along a corridor. 'Here's the cloakroom. You can wait in the staff café, OK? Get yourself something to eat and drink while you're waiting. The producer will take you through at seven twenty-five.' Then she grabbed Alexia's arm to detain her, although Alexia hadn't so much as moved a muscle, frowning fiercely at a piece of paper in her hand. 'Oh-*kay*! Hang *on*! The producer will come for *you* at seven because you've got a story to tell, haven't you? So you need a bit more of a brief, OK? We go live at eight.'

'OK,' agreed Alexia. Once freed, she went to the café as directed, so cheap it must be subsidised, and read on her Kindle app while she consumed a cup of tea and a scone.

A few minutes after seven, yet another black-clad man – she was beginning to get the idea that the black was a requirement for the crew – arrived to call her, along with two other women and a man. 'Hello, he*llo*.' He flashed them all a smile that exhibited an array of snaggly teeth. 'I'm Warren and I'm the producer today. Thank you all for coming. Could you follow me, please, and I'll tell you what's what.' He trotted down a corridor into a studio that looked like a warehouse hung with black curtains. Its black walls were slightly squishy to the touch – Alexia couldn't resist giving one a prod.

From up on high a grid of lights shone down, and uplighters created pale blue columns of light at intervals around the edge of the room. In the centre of the studio, a single chair and a curved bench were upholstered in a deeper blue than the columns. A few people were perched there uncomfortably or standing about looking bored, uncertain or both.

Warren launched into a practised spiel. 'Thanks for coming today to share your stories. The lady in the red dress is Kelli, our presenter. The people with her are our "experts" –' he made inverted commas in the air with his fingers '– and they'll be on the guest seating. As today's programme is Crooks and Conmen the "experts" are . . .' He consulted his notes. 'A police officer, a lawyer, and a representative from Citizen's Advice. Kelli will begin with a general discussion on the theme and the "experts" will define their roles.'

He flashed his smile again. 'When the rest of the audience arrives I'll run through where to stand, when to move and where to move to. I'll position each of you in the audience and make sure Kelli knows where you are. When it's time for you to tell your story, a runner will bring you a roving mic. Kelli will ask you questions, set the pace and gently steer you. I know you all have fascinating stories but it would be great if you'd let her dictate when your spot ends. Right!' Big smile. 'Come over and meet everyone.'

While they were being introduced to Kelli and the experts – Alexia forgot their names as soon as she heard them – the audience area behind and to the sides of the central stage began to fill. Kelli was a striking black woman with sympathetic eyes. She shook all of their hands and repeated their names, then Warren spaced them regularly around the audience where they stuck their arms in the air so Kelli could memorise their locations. Alexia was positioned just left of centre, front row. She was to be the last guest to speak, which gave her a whole hell of a lot of time to do battle with her butterflies. She swallowed down an impulse to beg, 'Can't I go first and get it over with?'

It was only by reminding herself of the outside chance of the programme leading to information about Shane and Tim that Alexia was able to nod and agree.

Warren began running through audience information using phrases such as 'in shot' and 'back of head shots', explaining what the floor crew did and who the floor manager was, that everyone was dressed in 'studio black' to be as unobtrusive as possible, even though the crew were often deliberately in shot. 'And there's the director and other people out of sight in a place called the gallery. The floor manager can hear the director through his headphones but you don't need to worry about them.'

'*Most importantly* . . .' Warren beamed around at everyone. 'We're going to tell you when to clap.'

The cameras were larger, more obtrusive and scarier than the ones used for the YouTube video, with crew seemingly attached to each by invisible umbilical chords.

Floor manager, presenter and experts conferred. Smiling

and nodding. Smiling and nodding back. Cameras shifted and shunted. Alexia's butterflies shook out their wings ready to go wild.

Eventually, Warren held up his hands for absolute hush. Then he gave a signal, the floor crew who didn't have their hands otherwise occupied burst into applause and the audience joined in. Although audience eyes were supposed to be trained on Kelli, as she clapped Alexia could see a monitor with credits scrolling over a long panning shot of presenter, panel and applauding audience. She didn't try to pick herself out. That would give her butterflies heart attacks.

But once they were underway properly, it wasn't too bad. After introductions, Kelli and the panel of experts held an interesting discussion on what constituted deception and that everyone and anyone could become victims. Then the audience clapped and they went to a break. It didn't seem as if the audience was allowed to leave the studio unless in an ambulance so they stood still while nothing much seemed to happen apart from more conferring and a make-up artist powdering the noses of Kelli and two of the experts.

The next segment dealt with the stories from the audience. A lady old enough to be Alexia's grandmother had been ripped off by a bogus holiday-bond company to the tune of £18,000; another had been deceived by his wife who, rather than divorce him and divide their assets in the usual way, had waited until he'd inherited from his parents, grabbed all the money and run. He'd been left with a house mortgaged to the hilt and a car on which she'd let payments lapse. Alexia was astounded by the cruelty and the man's blank shock even now, a year after the event. Each story earned a round of sympathetic applause.

The experts let Kelli lead them through a spirited commentary, and then contributed advice on how others might avoid their fate, and then there was another filming break. Alexia shifted on aching feet, the base of her back beginning to feel compressed. A few of the audience squatted down or even sat cross-legged on the floor so she obviously wasn't the only one, but she felt too keyed up to follow their example.

Filming recommenced with a woman relating how she'd been conned by someone claiming to guarantee the granting of a green card to work in America. The result had been nothing more than a few official-looking documents that proved to be counterfeit. 'I parted with thousands,' the woman kept saying, lips set grimly.

The panel began by pointing out kindly that instead of clicking a link in an ad on the Internet she should have searched through recognised channels and pretty much ended by saying that good conmen were hard to find when they didn't want to be found but when you only dealt with them electronically you were moving up a level from 'hard' to 'nearly impossible'.

Alexia quite wanted to say, 'FFS! What were you thinking?' to the woman instead of clapping, but apart from it no doubt getting her thrown out, her butterflies were bouncing off the walls of her stomach. She could quite clearly hear the *ker-BOOM* in her ears.

Then suddenly a figure in studio black handed Alexia a mic and Kelli was smiling caringly, introducing Alexia to the 'experts' and the viewers at home. She commenced drawing out the whole sorry tale of The Angel.

Though her palms sweated and her voice held the tiniest tremor, Alexia managed most of the interview calmly.

Kelli made the tiniest shift in her upper body, which

Alexia had noticed her doing as she went to ask the final question to each guest, as if to signal her withdrawal. 'Alexia, what I'd really like to know is how has this deception affected you going forward?'

All the brooding on the car journey suddenly flooded back. 'They've taken the future I'd planned,' she burst out. 'After adding The Angel to my portfolio I was supposed to be recommended for a job by a so-called friend, Elton –' she had a fleeting regret that she'd outed Elton by name but, hey, he'd earned it '– to the property investor he works for. I was lined up to work on both the folders in her property portfolio: the money-making refurbishments in trendy up-and-coming areas of south and east London, and her altruistic affordable rental property scheme in Kent.'

'I really hope something else comes along for you.' Kelli made another tiny turn away.

But the runner had left the microphone with Alexia, probably to allow her to say 'thank you' and shut up.

Alexia ignored the hint and Warren's earlier instructions to let Kelli wind things up and carried on. 'My *friend* dumped me instantly. He refused to even tell the investor what had happened. He was too frightened of my victimhood –' she wasn't sure that was even a word '– contaminating him, like lice.'

'I am *so* sorry,' Kelli repeated firmly, then turned to the police officer on the panel and the runner wrested the microphone from Alexia's hand.

The members of the panel had plenty to say on how other people could avoid the same fate. The police officer, a big burly bald bloke whose name, amusingly, was Bill, managed to get in a comment about the police force having very limited resources.

Then it was over.

Lots more clapping. Alexia joined in automatically, adrenalin draining abruptly away. A few of members of the audience said 'Well done' or 'Hope you get sorted' or just patted her arm as they filed past.

Depleted by being keyed up for so long, Alexia couldn't wait to get back in the taxi and be driven back to safe old Middledip. Especially once she had retrieved her phone from her handbag and could read a text from Ben.

Ben: *Were you brilliant? Did you enjoy it? Want to be dropped off at mine and stay tonight? xx*

Alexia: *Gah! Think I came over as an over-emosh female who walked into a trap set by a smarter man. Would love to stay at yours. Please have whisky ready. xx*

She must have fallen asleep as the wheels of the car turned soporifically because she jolted awake as the driver called, 'Sorry to disturb you, love, but I need to know how to find this place you want dropping and then get off home before the snow sets in.'

She sat up and blinked to see that he'd paused the car at The Cross – and that tiny snowflakes were shimmering in the light from the street lamps. 'Oh, pretty,' she yawned, then woke herself up enough to provide directions, gazing at the snow as they bumped up the track that branched from the back entrance to the Carlysle estate to the rear of Woodward Cottage.

'Blimey,' said the driver. 'A wicked witch doesn't live here, does she?'

Still yawning, Alexia felt for the door handle. 'No, a wizard.'

She scrambled from the car on stiff legs. The taxi turned round to lurch back the way it had come. Alexia caught sight of Barney on a branch in his aviary on the back of the cottage but, attracted like a moth to the light streaming from the cottage windows, she made straight for the front door.

It opened before she could knock. Ben stood there in a sweatshirt and jeans.

He opened his arms and she stepped into them. 'I made a proper tit of myself. If anyone ever wants to put me on TV again remind me to know my limitations and just stay home with a glass of wine.'

Chapter Twenty-six

Ben laid awake feeling Alexia's sleeping breath stir his body hair and mulling over her simple 'Glad *that's* over' reaction to her evening. He knew Imogen would have sought endless reassurance. Alexia, after recounting events at the TV studio, had curled up beside him to watch the snowflakes through the window, her arm lightly across his chest and her cheek on his shoulder, and dropped soundlessly into sleep.

He hadn't even had a chance to tell her that Carola wanted to order enough invitations to the 23rd December opening of The Angel Community Café to put through the door of every house in the village. That the date depended on things like the screed being dry enough for Alexia to tile so the kitchen fitter could fit, she'd waved away. 'Alexia says we'll do it! Don't fret.' The invitations were to be 'as sparkly and Christmassy as possible' and she had already bought decorations, tinsel and a tree with the necessary baubles for the opening, so great was her faith.

Finally, lulled by Alexia's breathing, he closed his eyes. His last thought was that this was the first time they'd slept together and just slept.

In the morning they rose before the late-November sun. Alexia had to go home to ready herself for her day. Ben needed make the most of the daylight to top a load of conifers that had been planted to create a windbreak for Carlysle Hall's kitchen garden but were now spoiling the view and casting shadows. Just enough snow had fallen to make the landscape glitter like a Christmas card.

After a quick slice of toast each, Ben unlocked the truck but Alexia hung back. 'Can we say good morning to Barney? I haven't seen him much lately.' Barney was completely at home in his aviary now, hopping up and down the branches and stumps Ben had set out for him as a sop to having lost his superpower of flight.

But Ben could hear a vehicle approaching from the direction of the estate, which almost never happened unless he was in the vehicle as it wasn't a right of way. 'You do that while I see who this is.' He strode off through the trees, his work boots crunching the crust of snow. Narrowing his eyes against the morning mist rising off the lake, he watched in astonishment as a small white van hurried up, backed up to the water's edge and, from the other side of the vehicle, a white and blue plastic carrier bag flew into the air.

It landed in the water with a splash.

The van accelerated swiftly away but Ben's attention was on the bag.

No doubt water was already seeping in but, tied at the top, enough air had been trapped to allow it to float for the moment. As he stared, the bag seemed to shiver. Perhaps because it was a still and frozen morning, a high-pitched noise reached him where he stood.

'For fuck's *sake*!' he roared, charging towards the lake. Without hesitation, he performed a shallow dive into the sparkling khaki water.

Its iciness took his breath away but it was too late to wish he'd thought things through. Still, in an inelegant flat crawl that was the best he could manage, hampered by his coat, he struck out for the bag, which was half-submerged now. Weeds dragged at his legs and he slowed his efforts to try and slide clear. And failed.

Shit. He'd made a mistake.

Anger had taken over and he'd disregarded everything he'd ever been taught. Now he was finding it hard to draw air deep into his lungs. It seemed to reach the base of his throat and then freeze, the cold water pressing on his chest and his shallow gasps ringing in his ears.

His coat was trying to pull him down but his hands were already too cold to unzip it. The weight of his work boots increased with every kick he tried.

The bag would probably be under water by the time he reached it. If he reached it. He wouldn't have the puff or use of his limbs to dive down and bring it up.

He'd been an idiot.

Pausing to tread water, he tried to suck in a proper lungful of air. All he could manage was a series of shallow pants. His legs tried to pedal harder but were losing the unequal fight with his boots and the weeds. And the cold. It was numbing. He had to tip his head back to keep his mouth clear of the surface.

He was in trouble.

Then came the sound of an engine and he blinked water

from his eyes in time to see his truck being driven along the edge of the lake to the point closest to him.

Alexia scrabbled out, slipping in the snow. 'Are you *stupid*?' she bellowed.

He didn't have the breath to acknowledge that he was. He devoted all his strength to keeping his mouth above the surface, one eye on the carrier bag riding low in the water and the other on Alexia as she grabbed one of his ropes from the bed of his truck, looped it around the tow ball and, taking a dramatic, cowboy-like circle or two above her head, flung the rope out towards him.

It fell short.

Before he could even try to reach it, she was hauling it in again.

This time she whirled it underarm, screaming, '*Get there!*' after it, to urge it on its way.

It almost made the distance.

Three floundering strokes and he was able to tangle it around his forearm, kicking as best he could while she leant back and heaved on the rope with him flopping on the end like a half-dead fish. His passage took him within arm's length of the carrier bag and he took one hand off the rope to wind his frozen claw into its plastic folds.

Then his knees were colliding with the muddy bed of the lake, his arms in the slushy margin. If it hadn't been frozen solid, his heart would have hammered with relief.

Alexia waded in, dropping the rope in favour of hauling on his arm. 'You are the stupidest, most moronic man I've ever met,' she gasped, tears – probably of fury – on her cheeks, slipping and splashing as she tried to keep her feet. 'Can you get up? Then GET UP and GET IN THE TRUCK!' With a strength he didn't think she'd possess, she somehow dragged and heaved his numbed and shivering self to the

310

passenger door and shoved him through it, his hand still tangled with the carrier bag, then slipped and slid around to the driver's seat. Twisting to look over her shoulder, she reversed the truck the way she'd come, zigzagging inexpertly as the wheels struggled for traction.

She backed over his climbing rope and dragged it along in their wake but he decided that now was not the time to mention it. Instead, he fumbled with numb hands at the bag, freezing lake water pouring down his freezing legs. 'Kit-kittens,' he managed, through chattering teeth.

Alexia spared a glance for the sodden, feebly moving mass in his lap. 'Some people need shooting.' And the engine complained as she recommenced the wavering back-track to Woodward Cottage.

There, she half-dragged Ben out of the cab again, although he'd almost got his breath now and was able to stagger under his own propulsion. Flinging his front door open, in grim silence she pulled him across the sitting room, up the stairs and into the bathroom. Turning the shower onto hot, she shoved him under the spray, swiping the carrier bag full of kittens out of his hands in passing.

Content that Alexia had rescued his rescue attempt he closed the shower door and gave himself up to the bliss of hot water raining down on him. It took minutes to thaw sufficiently to get himself out of his clothes and boots, wiping portholes through the steamy glass in order to watch Alexia gently dry kittens with his bath towels, laying them in a row on the bathmat like toys. 'Five,' she said, with a tiny shake of her head at a world where kittens could be hurled into icy water to perish.

She left them briefly to rummage in his airing cupboard, locating sufficient handtowels and tea towels to make each kitten a cocoon.

'May I have a towel, too, please?' He'd been under the shower long enough that his voice emerged almost without his teeth chattering.

Alexia threw him a darkling look. 'You stay there and get warmer, moron. I need to ring your uncle for emergency kitten care.' She pulled her phone out of her pocket and turned her back on him. He decided to obey because she hadn't passed him a towel to wrap up in and she was right. Morons had to prioritise getting their core temperature up.

As she talked rapidly into the phone he surveyed his saturated work boots, which would take days to dry out, and sighed as he noticed the bump in his jeans pocket that he knew to be his mobile phone. He took a smidgeon of comfort from the fact that it might be dead but the kittens were alive.

Finally Alexia fetched him a towel and opened the shower door. 'Gabe says to take the kittens to him. He's hand-reared litters before and he's boiling the feeding bottles ready for when we get there. He'll give them dilute milk for now but one of us has to go to the pet place and buy some formula stuff.'

Ben turned off the shower and began drying himself, realising, now Alexia was standing up, that her jeans were soaked to mid-thigh. 'You need to get warm and dry, too.'

She nodded impatiently. 'Get dressed and you can drop me off on the way to Gabe's.' She didn't look at him.

He grabbed her hand as she turned away. 'You were fantastic.'

'You were a moron.'

'I was.' He pulled her against him, realising that she was shaking. 'I think you just saved six lives.'

'One of them risked his.' She pulled away. 'We've got to get those kittens to Gabe.'

312

He fell in with her plan, fumbling into a thick fleece pulled over his clothes and taking the driver's seat while she held what had been Barney's tub, now cradling five well-wrapped kittens. 'Do you want me to come in with you?' he asked as they pulled up outside her cottage.

'No, I think you should get the kittens to Gabe. It would be ironic if you took that stupid risk and let them die anyway.'

'The irony to me seems in being in the doghouse for saving kittens!' But he received no answer. She was already climbing out of the vehicle and wedging the tub full of kittens into the footwell. Ben glanced into it. 'I hope you guys are grateful.'

Then he drove off to deliver them to Gabe's tender care.

Indoors, Alexia stripped off her horrible wet jeans that clung, freezing cold, to her legs. She jumped into the shower, as hot as she could bear it, thinking how much worse it must have felt for Ben, to be soaked head to toe.

Idiot.

She'd nearly had a heart attack when she'd heard his bellow of rage and rushed to the front of Woodward Cottage, only to see him trying to swim through that frosty murk. Her legs gave as reality melted her bones and she slid down the wall until she was sitting on the floor of the shower.

Ben could have died.

She trembled to remember the blank horror on his face and his obviously restricted movements. In a moment of stark terror she'd feared she'd have to stand there and watch him go under – until she'd forced her shocked brain to work, and she'd run for the truck on legs that didn't feel as if they belonged to her. Thank goodness he'd already put the keys in the ignition and hadn't dived in with them in his pocket. Then she would have been reduced to grabbing the rope and running.

It would have wasted crucial seconds.

A great hand squeezed her chest. Then a sob burst out of her, followed by another and then a whole series more. *It's the shock,* she told herself, heaving convulsively. *Give yourself a minute and you'll be fine.*

It was several minutes, as it turned out, plus getting dried and dressed. Even then she had to sit and drink two cups of strong tea, the words *Ben could have died* circulating endlessly in her mind. Ben *could* have died. And apart from the horror of bearing witness she'd have lost a lot more than she'd been admitting, she realised.

They might be keeping things light, just enjoying the *zing*.

But it was *zing* she didn't want to lose.

Eventually she was sufficiently recovered to drive around the corner and up Gabe's track, careful over the slippery ruts and potholes. By the time she let herself into the kitchen she was her normal brisk self – at least on the surface. 'I'll drive to the pet shop in Bettsbrough for the formula stuff. I'm working on a costing today so I'm pretty flexible.'

Gabe looked up from the tabby bundle of fluff on his palm that was sucking at what looked like a doll's bottle. For the first time in ages, his eyes had some life in them. 'That would be grand. These little fellows will need a lot of TLC for a day or so. I'm guessing they're about four weeks old.' A box lined with newspaper and towels was already standing near the range and three kittens, now freed from their individual cocoons, were cuddling up together. Judging by the fact that they were fast asleep, they'd already been fed.

Ben sat on a kitchen chair with the last kitten, ginger

and white, and another doll's bottle. He looked at her with wary grey eyes. 'Are you OK?'

She found it hard to look at him as she watched him gently deposit the kitten with its brothers and sisters. *He could have died.* 'Nice and dry, now. I'll get going.' There didn't seem much point in taking her coat off and getting comfy. Ben was OK. The kittens were OK.

'You're both heroes.' Gabe glanced at his kitten, which looked as if it was just drifting off to sleep. Gabe, too, was sinking into his chair as if he wouldn't be long awake himself once the last kitten was in its box.

It seemed a good time to exit but Alexia only got as far as just outside the back door when a pair of arms came around her and turned her around. Then she was pulled into a hard hug. Ben was warm and well and surrounding her with his embrace. 'Thank you,' he murmured. 'No point worrying Gabe with what a close call it was. You were the real saviour today. You kept your head when I lost mine.'

She tried to laugh but it hiccupped out more like a sob. 'I thought you were going to drown.'

'The thought crossed my mind, too. The relief when I saw you coming with the truck . . .' He pulled her harder against him.

'I'm sorry I called you a moron.'

'I forgive you.' His laugh reached her through his body as well as through her ears. Then he pulled back so he could see her face and his expression sobered. 'I put you in danger, too.'

He tried to kiss her and she wanted to relax and enjoy it but she had to pull away because tears were trying to come again and they blocked her nose so she couldn't breathe. To cover it up, she laughed. 'I'll see you later.'

It wasn't until she got back in the car that the tears broke her barriers, swamping her with their intensity as she reacted to the shock. From her left came the sound of the sudden opening of the car door then a large, warm body was in beside her, cuddling her close, while gentle hands stroked her hair and a deep voice murmured, 'It's OK. We're all OK.'

Alexia cried more loudly, hit hard by what she'd almost lost.

Chapter Twenty-seven

In the warmth of Gabe's kitchen Alexia turned one of Carola's cards over in her hands. Edged with silver holly leaves it bore a picture of a cake stand full of cakes – including one shaped like a Christmas pudding and one like an angel – on one side and the invitation on the other.

YOU ARE INVITED
to the opening of
The Angel Community Café!
From 10 a.m. Saturday 23rd December
Help us celebrate!
Opening Day offer ~ complimentary drink with any
cake purchased

'You're going to deliver one of these to *every* house in the village?'

Glasses on the end of her nose, Carola looked up from her laptop on Gabe's kitchen table where she was getting all pink and excited about making an order to the food wholesalers. She'd already bought crockery by the crate load as more money had come in from Ben's latest offerings on eBay. 'Well, yes. It's only the 13th so I have ten days. And the girls will help me.' In the past weeks she'd completed her food-handling certificates, helped to paint the last chairs and roller emulsion on the walls and ceiling at The Angel. 'Charlotte and Emily and I have done some of the New Village already and we're going to start on Port Road tomorrow. I need you to finish the tiling this weekend so the kitchen area can be fitted out. Then we can have a giant clean up, throw all the furniture in and put up the lovely jolly Christmas decorations. I've bought about a mile of tinsel.'

Out of the corner of her eye Alexia saw Gabe grin and Ben roll his eyes. They all knew Carola would be great at running the café but she could be a teensy weensy bit bossy.

December 23rd marked the crossover point when The Angel refurbishment project became The Angel Community Café. Alexia's role would naturally end and Carola would get into her stride so Alexia decided not to bother pointing out that she was aware, thank you very much, having set the programme of works herself. In fact, she'd already grabbed an hour at The Angel today, inhaling the smell of fresh emulsion, stroking the newly varnished doors (not as gorgeous as the originals) and planning the tiling. She couldn't wait to get going on that! She'd measured out and drawn the centre lines along the floor in pencil so she could dive in on Saturday.

But now Alexia was feeling nervous and hoping Carola's chatter about the opening would make everyone forget the time and date.

Gabe, however, though still frail, proved to have too good a memory. 'Time to turn the TV on for Alexia's programme.' Reaching over the kittens currently climbing up his trouser legs, he swooped on the remote control.

Damn. Alexia would much rather have watched the first airing of *Lemonade from Lemons* alone. 'Maybe I ended up on the cutting room floor,' she said hopefully. Her face heated up just at the memory of yet another red-faced rant.

'Here it comes.' Ben nodded towards the TV, taking her hand reassuringly. In the last two weeks, since Ben had rescued the kittens and Alexia had rescued him, there seemed an unspoken need to touch each other more.

Alexia covered her eyes with the other. 'I can't watch. You know Tubb's putting it on the big TV at the pub, too?'

Ben laughed and winked. 'Lots of people don't get satellite TV so he's hoping you'll be good for business.'

The first part of the programme when other people were airing their stories wasn't too bad. Alexia was in shot enough that the others got tired of exclaiming, 'There you are, look!' Carola turned back to her order and Gabe looked as if he might be dozing, despite the tabby kitten still swinging from his trousers.

But after the commercial break something seemed to go awry with the timeline of the programme as she remembered it, because the person who'd told her story third never got her moment in the sun. Instead, the camera went straight to Alexia with a voice over from Kelli that must have been edited in post-production about the story being especially relevant with the approach of Christmas.

The camera zoomed in on Alexia and she had to look at herself, eyes huge with fear in her white face. She groaned. 'What a rabbit in the headlights. I can't watch.' And she screwed up her eyes and stuffed her fingers in her ears.

The others were glued to the TV until the credits rolled.

Then Ben pulled her hands from her ears and pressed his lips to her forehead. It left a little warm feeling. 'You were great! A real hatchet job so far as Shane and Tim are concerned.'

'Really excellent!' chimed in Gabe. 'Everyone was so indignant on your behalf.'

'Did they show me get all shouty? I didn't shut up when Kelli hinted I should.'

Carola laughed. 'You were animated! You were amazing. I wish I looked that beautiful when I get angry, sparks shooting from my eyes. I just look like a grumpy elf.'

Then Alexia's phone began to ring. Family and friends rang, her Facebook notifications showed selfies of her friends, the TV on over their shoulders.

Then Jodie rang. Alexia felt a starburst of pleasure that Jodie had remembered to watch *Lemonade from Lemons*. 'If you're calling to tell me I acted like a diva, I know,' she groaned.

'Erm . . .' Jodie hesitated, apparently nonplussed. 'I'm ringing to say I've been to the police station today. They've got Shane and they wanted me to identify him from his mugshot, which I was *totally, totally, totally* happy and willing to do. Have they rung Gabe?'

'I don't think so.' Alexia swung around to look at Gabe. 'The police haven't been in touch, have they? Jodie says they've got Shane!'

She went back to Jodie. 'No, Gabe's shaking his head. Was it the TV programme? How could it be? It's only just this minute aired.'

Gabe, Ben and Carola all began talking and Alexia had to jam her finger in her ear to hear Jodie's report.

Finally, she rang off to pass on the news. 'After all that

it was nothing to do with the programme. Apparently it was a terrific fluke they got him – something to do with a driving offence and going through an ANPR camera. Bad luck for him, he probably thought he was in Lincolnshire because he was up by Wisbech somewhere but he'd crossed into Cambridgeshire. A patrol car got behind him and the automatic number plate recognition kicked in so they tried to stop him. He panicked and drove off so he was arrested and taken to a police station and suddenly everything the Cambridgeshire police know about him began to match up. His real name's Niall Radstock. The police are going to be in touch with you, too, Gabe, because they've got to put their case together.'

She took a deep breath, hardly able to believe what she was about to say. 'But, potentially, there's some prospect of you getting some of your property back.'

Everyone sat and stared at one another.

Only Carola looked discontented. 'All that work we've done to refurbish The Angel on the cheap and now you might get some stuff back and want to make changes again.'

Alexia stifled a giggle. 'Gabe will want to buy matching chairs and tables.'

'Nooooo!' Carola covered her eyes.

Gabe unhooked the kittens from his trousers and returned them to their bed. 'Now when did I ever care if everything matched? It would be nice to get some of that money back, though. *That* would be a Christmas present.'

'It would be great for Jodie, too,' Alexia agreed. 'It must be scary having no reserves with a baby on the way.' Then she rang Jodie back to go through the whole story again, just in case she'd missed anything out in the excitement of the moment and to loudly agree when Jodie said 'I hope they put the bastard behind bars'.

Later, she and Ben walked back to her cottage, huddled into their coats against a persistent sleet. She pointed at the halo around a streetlight. 'Look at the tiny spicules glistening. Aren't they pretty?'

'Why would I be impressed by that when I have a hot TV star beside me?'

She giggled as they turned up her path. 'So you've got a thing about angry women?'

'When you're not angry with me.' Then he cupped her buttocks through her jeans while she opened the front door and they fell into her hallway, laughing, before halting abruptly at the sound of a woman's voice. '. . . I'm certain I recognise myself from your description so I hope you'll call me.' The voice reeled off a telephone number and a click and a beep followed.

'Someone was leaving a message on the machine. I wonder what they were on about?' Alexia pulled off her coat and gloves then crossed to the machine to play her messages. The first two were from villagers being complimentary about her five minutes of fame.

The third was the message of which they'd caught the end. The unfamiliar voice seemed to fill the hall. 'I hope you don't mind me ringing,' the voice said. 'I took your number from your website. I saw you on *Lemonade from Lemons* tonight and was astounded. I'm a property investor and the man who heads up my team is called Elton. My name's Verity Hart and his name's Elton Cley.' Alexia caught the turn of Ben's head as he shot her an enquiring look and she nodded to indicate that Cley was indeed Elton's surname. The voice went on: 'I'd like to talk to you about what happened.' Then followed the snatch they'd heard as they entered.

'Wow.' Alexia gazed at the now-silent machine.

'Yeah.' Ben gazed at it, too. 'What are you going to do?'

Slowly, Alexia hung her coat over the newel post. 'I suppose I'd better ring her back.'

'I'll die of curiosity if you don't.' He dropped an encouraging kiss on her neck.

Heart pattering right up in her throat, Alexia dialled, more than half expecting a recorded message to block her access to the person that until now she'd thought of only as 'the money woman' or Elton's investor.

Instead, it was answered promptly. 'This is Verity.'

'This is Alexia Kennedy.' Alexia paused to swallow. 'I was on my way into the house as you left your message. So I'm ringing back,' she ended weakly.

'Thank you! Am I right? Do you think you were talking about me?' Alexia hadn't, as far as she could remember, said anything rude about Elton's investor so replied, cautiously, 'Potentially. The Elton I referred to is Elton Cley. I met him at uni. He lives in Ealing now,' she added as a cross-reference.

'It all fits. He said he wanted to bring in someone to do the project management and I told him it had to be exactly the right person. The team we have is finely balanced and I didn't want to disturb that. Suddenly he said it wasn't going to work out and we dropped the idea.'

They talked on and on, Alexia filling in the blanks in the story Verity already knew, perching on the stairs with the phone. 'I didn't mean to get Elton into trouble,' she said at one point.

Verity sounded surprised. 'Who said he was? I just want to understand the situation.'

By the end of the conversation Alexia had formed a good opinion of Verity Hart. 'I do like her approach. I kept having mad thoughts about asking her to give me a second chance,' she sighed wistfully as she returned the phone to its stand.

A hesitation, then he smiled. 'You could always call back. It would be great if you got what you wanted after all. You deserve it.'

She batted the suggestion away. 'But that would mean working with Elton and then I'd always be waiting for a knife in my back. I have my hands full with The Angel until Christmas, anyway. It's too early to think about what happens after that.'

The days ticked down to the opening of The Angel Community Café. Alexia couldn't wait to see The Angel not only complete but decked in her Christmas finery.

Thursday and Friday Carola delivered invitations while Alexia and Ben were at work. Then Ben took the rest of his annual leave to take him up to Christmas and let him share kitten-care with a still easily tired Gabe. Alexia took a risk and followed suit.

From then it was all systems go. Tiling such vast expanses of floor as the Public, the Bar Parlour and the foyer made Alexia's back and neck seize. Ben took over the grouting of the floor so at least she could stand upright and tile the kitchen area walls ready for the fitter. She and Ben madly grouted that together, using the waterproof stuff environmental health recommended and cursing when it wouldn't easily wipe off the faces of the tiles.

'It looks fantastic!' Alexia gave Ben a joyful hug when they were finally able to step back and admire the random mix of shades of cream and brown with the occasional accent of sea green.

Ben's gave her a smile. 'You're really going to bring this project in on time. You're amazing.' Then he went off to begin laying a flagstone path outside ready for the customers they hoped would pile in while Alexia and Carola gave the bathrooms a white emulsion facelift.

When the kitchen fitter arriving on the 19th, Alexia, Ben and Carola, instead of spending every spare moment at The Angel, had two days when they'd only be in the way if they turned up there. To celebrate, they, along with Gabe, met for a bacon butty breakfast at Alexia's. Once her stomach was full, Alexia sighed. 'I have done *no* Christmas shopping.'

'Nor me,' admitted Ben, wiping around his plate with toast. 'I'll have to hope I'm still in time to have things delivered as I don't see myself getting down to Didbury to visit Mum and Dad before Christmas.'

Gabe patted Ben on the back. 'No worry. I've invited your parents to the opening on Saturday.'

Ben looked blank. 'Why?'

'Because they're my family, too. And I'm really not feeling up to dragging myself down to Didbury.'

A strange look stole over Ben's face. 'Is Lloyd coming?'

'He's invited.' Gabe regarded Ben keenly. 'Have you spoken to him lately?'

Ben turned away. 'I've been busy.'

When the others had gone, Carola dropping Gabe at home before picking up her girls for a shopping trip, Alexia slid her arms around Ben's solid torso. 'If Lloyd comes at least you'll have the chance to ask him what you want to know. Finally get your curiosity satisfied.'

'Suppose so. With Gabe being sick and then it being all hands on deck at The Angel I suppose I haven't had so much time to think about it.'

His closed expression didn't encourage her to ask whether he'd heard any more from Imogen. Ben hadn't mentioned her for ages and Alexia found she didn't want to bring her name up.

When they'd cleared up she drove them both to Peterborough, where they split up to do their shopping. The Queensgate Centre was heaving with shoppers even though the schools wouldn't break up until that afternoon. Every hall and shop window sparkled in red, green, gold and silver. Christmas songs played in every shop and jolly cut-out Santas grinned from behind red-nosed Rudolfs and jingly belled sleighs.

Alexia bought a new dressing gown for her mum and a framed charcoal drawing of Peterborough Cathedral for her dad. She found an angel made of spun glass for Carola and was so pleased with it that she bought another for Gabe. She wasn't supposed to buy for him because he said he had 'enough stuff cluttering up the place' but she'd never been a do-as-you're-told woman. She bought Jodie a Clarins gift set, reasoning that nice moisturiser might not be affordable for a while. She blazed a trail through The Body Shop for school and village friends and made a mental note to send electronic vouchers to her brother, Reuben, and his wife, Hanna, in Germany.

Which left her with Ben to buy for.

Hmm. What did you buy the man you were sleeping with, who you had *zing* with but no labelled relationship, whose contract would be up in May so he might move on and who you suspected had unpacked baggage about his ex-wife? After an hour's drag around the shops she chose him an experience day at a falconry centre because of the owls pictured, as well as a tree made out of Maltesers, because how could that possibly be wrong?

Then, remembering the night they'd met, she bought him two crystal whisky glasses because she admired their beautiful lines. Too much? Not enough? Determined not to fall for the trap of judging the depth of one's affections by thoughtfulness and cost of gifts, as Seb always had, she paid some girl guides raising money with a wrapping service to deal with the presents while she wrote the labels.

Then she remembered Christmas cards and bought for her parents, Ben, Carola and Gabe and decided to send a nice donation to charity in lieu of the rest.

With a sigh of relief she texted Ben and told him in which café he could find her while she caught up with her reading on her Kindle app.

He turned up an hour later, laden with carrier bags and wearing exasperation like a pair of shoes that pinched. 'I'm going to opt out of Christmas altogether.'

Having consumed two teacakes and three cups of tea Alexia had mellowed. 'Shame. I was going to invite you, Gabe, Carola and her girls to a slap-up feast on Christmas Day.'

He glanced at her out of the corner of his eye and quirked an eyebrow. 'Kiss me and I'll accept.'

Alexia pretended to consider, then capitulated. 'It *is* nearly Christmas.' And puckered her lips.

Chapter Twenty-eight

At dead on ten o'clock Ben wiped away the frost on the glass of The Angel's new and elegant front door and stuck on a laminated notice.

The Angel Community Café
is OPEN!
WELCOME!
COME ON IN!

Carola added a twist of green and gold tinsel and Alexia cheered. Gabe put on his boomiest voice. 'I declare this café *open*!' Then they all blew on their hands and scurried back into the warmth of the Bar Parlour where anything festoonable had been festooned with so much green and gold tinsel it half hid The Angel's newly created beauty.

Ben hung back on the large room's threshold to admire the smooth, gleaming sweep of cream, brown and sea green tiles. Nobody would guess the finished product was the result of parsimony more than design. The eclectic collection of tables and chairs with their sea green coats of satin paint looked as if they'd always been destined to gather together in cosy groups. The old leaded glass lamps in shades of amber – Alexia said they were genuine Tiffany – graced either end of the room.

Alexia had brought the refurb in on time with an air of knowing she always would. Now, tying a black apron about her waist, she glanced his way, arching one eyebrow as if to query his dawdling. He returned what he hoped was a reassuring smile. Although he hadn't admitted it to anyone but himself, it would have been nice to simply enjoy the excitement of the café opening, which they'd all worked towards for so long, without another unpredictable episode in his relationship with his parents hanging over him today.

It wasn't as if he'd never seen them in Middledip, but then he, like them, had been a visitor. Now he felt part of the village that had proved a safe place to peel off the clinging tentacles of unhappiness found in Didbury.

And what if they brought Lloyd?

Lloyd, the brother he hadn't seen for two years, who was at the heart of Ben's divorce and who Ben had refused to visit in prison.

Behind the contemporary steel and glass counter, Carola darted about, uncharacteristically antsy. 'What if nobody comes?'

Alexia, who'd begun sliding biscuits onto cooling racks, was being admirably patient. 'You know your Charlotte and Emily will because you've told them you'll send all their Christmas presents back if they don't. Melanie from Booze & News is too nosy not to turn up. Tess, Ratty and all their crew are coming.'

Gabe, wearing a suit where both parts matched in

honour of the occasion, looked up from his task of making napkin bunny ears. He was a little stronger now, sleeping less, walking further and smiling more, but still thinner than pre-pneumonia Gabe. 'The Carlysles will be here because they'll want to be seen to lend their support – now the painful part's over.'

At that moment the front door rattled and Melanie from the shop proved Alexia right by barrelling in, red face matching red jumper. Despite her anxieties, Carola slipped promptly into her new role. 'Melanie! You're The Angel Community Café's very first customer.'

'I know.' Melanie beamed complacently. 'I'd better have angel cake, hadn't I?' She tittered. 'And my free drink's a cappuccino.' She'd barely fitted her capacious buttocks onto a sea green chair when the next customers arrived, claiming to be following the smell of real coffee.

Then followed a constant stream of villagers. Charlotte and Emily and their early-teen mates seemed delighted to have somewhere in the village to hang out, being too young for the pub and Middledip being too quiet for a McDonalds. Alexia's friends brought their kids. Tubb from the pub came to see what they'd done to the old place. Jodie and Iona came in for peppermint tea, Jodie round-eyed at The Angel's transformation and round-tummied as her baby grew inside her.

Carola and Alexia had baked dozens of gingerbread angels so Ben was kept busy dispensing giveaways.

At eleven Alexia glanced out of the window and saw such a big group of people chattering up the path that she gasped. 'Blimey, the Carlysles are here – and they've brought their friends. The Public had better go public. Gabe, can you check it's all OK in there?'

'Hello, hello!' called Christopher Carlysle, as if he hadn't avoided all connected with The Angel for the last three months.

And still more customers poured in, exclaiming over how pretty and shiny everything was and vocal in their reminders of the promised free drinks. Lunchtime brought an absolute influx and Alexia shot home to bake the cookie dough they'd had the foresight to slice and freeze. Hurrying back to her post behind the counter with a full cake box she gave Ben's behind a quick pat when nobody was looking.

He was just returning the compliment with a grin when Gabe called, 'Look who's here!'

Ben looked up to see his parents and his brother. And Imogen.

He felt his smile fade. He'd been prepared for his parents; he'd assumed there was a chance Lloyd would appear. But Imogen?

Gabe was already issuing greetings. 'Lloyd! Imogen!' Then, dimly, Ben became aware of Alexia putting down her box and sliding the plate of gingerbread angels from his hands. 'Why don't you go and sit with your family?' She smiled, but her eyes were no longer on him.

On automatic, Ben emerged from behind the counter to kiss his mother's cheek and shake his father's hand.

Then he turned to Lloyd.

He looked different. His hair was brushed back from his forehead, the sides cropped short, and he sported a beard. He was thinner, paler.

Lloyd stuck his hand out with no sign of his old ebullience. 'How are you, little brother?'

Ben had imagined this moment. But not the wary entreaty in his brother's eyes or the silent apprehension of his parents. Nor had he anticipated that his own heart would instantly weigh all the years Lloyd had been his brother against the most recent couple . . . and simply thaw.

It felt natural to accept the proffered hand, cold from the winter weather. 'Glad to see you –' he started to say 'out' then changed it to '– here.'

Then, awkwardly and face hot, ultra aware of Alexia's presence, good manners decreed that Ben should greet Imogen.

She turned up her cheek to be kissed. It was a surreal moment, his lips brushing the cool skin that was no longer familiar and yet not quite alien. The feelings of same and different collided with a jolt in his chest. It was as if a bubble descended on him and separated him from the room. Everyone was looking into his bubble from the outside. His family. Imogen. Even Alexia from behind the espresso machine.

Gabe grabbed a table in the corner, making jokes, taking orders. Everybody talked, asking Ben about his job, about Middledip, about Gabe's battle with pneumonia. As their drinks arrived Gabe told the story of The Angel's makeover, adding the recent chapter about Shane having been found and charged, though only in an undertone because if the fundraised money found its way back it was actually going to be a headache now The Angel was done.

The chatter went on around Ben as he sipped an Americano. He glanced at Lloyd and Imogen and, though it wasn't with the burning need of a couple of months earlier, wondered at them both being there. He turned his gaze to his mum, recalling the forthright opinions she'd once held about Imogen. And yet here Imogen was included in a family day out.

As if he'd been waiting for Ben's reflections to take him

to exactly that point, Lloyd nudged him. 'Walk outside with me for a minute?'

Ben nodded. Lloyd slid into his coat and followed Ben out. They stepped off the newly constructed path onto what would eventually be a hardstanding for cars.

Unwilling to give Lloyd the opportunity to launch into what no doubt would be a carefully constructed and reasoned speech, Ben looked into Lloyd's eyes, grey like his own. 'I'd like to know why Imogen's with you.'

The icy wind blew over them but to make an impression on Lloyd's gelled-back hair. 'Then get ready,' he said. 'That's what I'm here to tell you.'

Chapter Twenty-nine

Though occupied with serving steaming drinks and yummy cakes, Alexia saw Ben go outside with his brother. She glanced back at the table they'd just forsaken, at the sandy-haired man who'd looked for Ben at The Three Fishes and the tense-looking woman who must be Ben's mum. And the same beautiful woman she'd seen pictured with Ben on his old blog.

Imogen. Her hair shone, her features were fine-boned and her skin clear. As she wore a batwing top and an artfully swathed scarf, without prior knowledge of the injury Alexia wouldn't have noticed the way she coped with her damaged arm by propping it on the table.

Having her right here, in the building Alexia had poured so much into, was unsettling. Numbly, Alexia watched her watching the door Ben and Lloyd had disappeared through.

Minutes ticked by. Alexia continued to smile and serve. And watch. After what seemed an age she saw Lloyd return without Ben. He helped Imogen thread herself carefully into her coat before escorting her outside. Ben's parents exchanged meaningful looks and listened to Gabe with an air of not listening. Alexia smiled mechanically at four teens at the counter and began making them milkshakes.

Over their shoulders and through the window Alexia could see Ben outside, hands jammed in pockets. He must be freezing. His coat hung on the hooks by the door and she wished she'd thought to send it out with his brother.

The four teens took their milkshakes and were replaced by a tall woman in a smart coat. When Carola tried to serve her the tall lady fastened her gaze on Alexia. 'This is who I'm here to see. I recognise you from your website, Alexia. I'm Verity Hart.'

Alexia dragged her attention away from the tableau outside. 'Blimey! Hello.' Forcing herself to function in the new situation, she extended her hand. Then snatched it back and wiped it on her apron, wary of getting sugar on this stylish creature with her beautifully cut clothes and hair.

Verity laughed. 'I hope you don't mind. I saw the opening of The Angel mentioned on your website and my curiosity was aroused.'

Carola gave Alexia's arm a squeeze. 'I'll grab Charlotte and Emily to help me. You have a cuppa with your friend.'

Verity shucked off her coat. 'That sounds marvellous. May I have an espresso?' She paused to regard the old photos from the loft, which Alexia had hung on the walls. 'Gosh, are these this place?'

Alexia found herself nursing her mug of tea while she gave Verity a tour of The Angel, comparing the old photographs to the images on her phone of The Angel when she was sad and neglected, and even fetching down the original mood boards as she explained how it was all supposed to have been. She glanced out of the window several times but could glimpse just one side of Ben as he remained in deep conversation with Lloyd and Imogen.

Verity asked the occasional question but mostly listened. Finally, she selected a table in the corner of the Public and sat down. 'You've done an impressive job on a shoestring.'

Alexia was obliged to join her, not knowing whether to be glad or sorry that she couldn't see Ben's intense gathering from there. 'I do mourn the etched glass and the polished bar but I've learned to love The Angel's boho look.'

'Boho, yet stylish and intelligently designed.' Verity regarded Alexia keenly. 'I'd like to offer you a job – to head up your own development team, separate from Elton's. There's plenty of London and Kent to go around.'

It was as well Alexia was sitting down. The room seemed to recede, then return on a wave of tingling exhilaration. She laughed and it came out too high and excited. 'I didn't realise I was being interviewed.'

'That was the idea.' Verity began talking about retainers and profit shares while Alexia listened, feeling as if both eyes and ears were on stalks. It felt less and less real. Her own *team*? She wouldn't have to work with Elton, let alone for him?

She'd leave the village . . .

'Anyway,' Verity wound up. 'Think it over. Let me know.' She glanced at her watch. 'I need to head home, but I hope to hear good news from you soon and then we can get together to plan exactly how everything will work.'

Knees feeling as if they belonged to someone else, Alexia managed to scramble to her feet. 'I'm still in shock but thank you. It's a wonderful opportunity!' Although elated by that opportunity plopping into the palm of her hand, while walking Verity to the door and saying goodbye,

Alexia almost said straight out she was no longer sure about leaving. Through the trials of the last three months she'd fallen in love with Middledip again.

What she wouldn't have given for this to happen before Shane and Tim's dirty work, before being drawn closer to Gabe and Carola by adversity and producing from a sad, maltreated shell of a building and a few broken hearts this triumphant, glittering Christmas opening of The Angel Community Café. Before she and Ben got their *zings* together.

Her mind in a whirl, she turned her attention to clearing tables. And that's when she let herself look out through the window once more. From this angle she could see all of Ben.

And he was in a clinch with Imogen.

His arms around her body. Her right arm around his neck. Statue-still apart from the wind whipping their hair.

Alexia snatched her gaze away, heart thundering up into her throat until she felt sick.

Spinning round to present her back to the window she grabbed up empty mugs and balled-up paper napkins while the image of Ben holding Imogen so carefully hung before her eyes. Eyes that burned with tears. And now it was too late she knew it wasn't only Middledip she loved.

Ben. How had she thought she could keep her feelings for him light?

Stacking the dirty crocks on a tray she was forced to witness Lloyd and Imogen coming back in, Lloyd speaking to his parents, who went outside and didn't return.

Then he approached the counter to pay, Imogen silently beside him, a tiny smile playing around the beautiful bow of her lips.

'We wouldn't dream of charging Ben and Gabe's family,'

Alexia heard Carola cry, waving away Lloyd's money. 'Hope to see you again.'

It was another few minutes before Ben reappeared, shivering. He looked stunned. Not surprising, really.

Alexia had managed to carry her tray to the clear-up area without dropping the lovely new mugs onto the tiled floor she'd slaved over.

'Wow. That was intense,' he said, joining her behind the counter.

Alexia marvelled that her hands continued to load pots into the dishwasher without even a tremor. 'I hope things went well.'

'OK, I suppose. Mum and Dad are staying over at Gabe's so we can spend Christmas Eve together before they head home for Christmas Day.' He gave an odd laugh, then dropped his voice. 'And Imogen's cleared the way for me to get my life back in Didbury.'

Even having witnessed that poignant embrace, shock jolted sweatily through Alexia. She kept her head in the dishwasher. 'We've both had an interesting time, then. Verity Hart's been in here and offered me a job!'

'Really?' He sounded taken aback. Then he pulled her to her feet for a hug. 'Well . . . congratulations.'

She pressed her face against his jumper, cold and smelling of his shower gel. She noticed he didn't actually ask if she would accept. Just like she didn't actually ask if he was going back to Didbury.

He was quiet for the rest of the afternoon. Dazed.

Alexia didn't feel chatty, either.

Chapter Thirty

Christmas Day dawned with a hoary frost that made Middledip look like the December picture on a calendar. Alexia was awake to watch through the window as the early sun made everything glitter.

Ben had phoned last night to say he was 'caught up with family stuff' so Alexia had pretended she'd planned an early night after another frantic day helping Carola in the café. But then had scarcely slept. 'Family' included Imogen again now. She'd witnessed it with her own eyes.

Boxing Day would be soon enough to face all that. Today, having invited Ben, Gabe, Carola, Charlotte and Emily for Christmas dinner she must slap on a festive face and not spoil things by wondering miserably when Ben was going to break the news that he was leaving Middledip.

She shoved the turkey in the oven and took a shiveringly crisp early walk around the village, exchanging Christmas greetings with those already out to walk their dogs and wondered why she'd once thought it a bad thing to know everyone she met – and their dogs. Christmas tree lights blazed from windows and Alexia imagined happy families ripping colourful wrapping from exciting gifts.

Returning home alone she undertook the solitary task of beginning the feast she'd planned haphazardly in those last few halcyon days of getting The Angel ready to open.

She shouldn't be down, she told herself, her eyes prickling with tears while she peeled potatoes. She had a fabulously exciting job offer, one with the potential to provide everything she could possibly want.

Except Ben.

But you couldn't own people. She'd told Seb often enough. Nobody belonged to anybody. They might belong *with*, but that was a choice that had to be made by both parties. When the veggies were all prepared she went upstairs to change into a shiny red top and black trousers.

She'd grabbed the time a few days ago to fling up her twinkling Christmas tree and the decorations she'd made in previous years, but she didn't bother with her Santa hat.

Ben and Gabe arrived first, bringing with them cold air and a tub full of kittens. Ben stooped to kiss her but, as if shy in front of Gabe, she turned so it only landed on her cheek. If the kiss had landed on her lips she'd have felt as if she were stealing it from Imogen. She'd only ever had Ben on loan and Imogen would probably never know even that.

Carola and her girls arrived. Charlotte and Emily were glued to their Christmas iPhones while everyone else exclaimed about The Angel and how absolutely amazingly well it was going, that Carola would have to find help immediately and it had almost been a shame to shut for Christmas and Boxing Day.

They all helped in the kitchen and the meal somehow

turned out effortlessly fabulous. Maybe because Carola did everything Alexia forgot.

Ben carved the turkey and they crowded around the kitchen table because Alexia didn't have a dining suite, gorging on roasties and bread sauce, pulling crackers and laughing. Gabe enjoyed so much sherry he almost fell asleep in his chocolate mousse. The kittens awoke in time to climb up everyone's legs under the table, which was no fun for Emily who was wearing tights and a skirt.

After lunch Carola cried, 'Presents!' and led the charge into the sitting room where everyone had piled gifts beneath Alexia's little artificial tree. Carola had sportingly relabelled smaller gifts she'd bought for her girls so everyone had something for them.

'Oh, enchanting,' she cried, when she unwrapped the glass angel from Alexia, then snorted with giggles because her gifts to everybody were angels, too – little bronze ones.

Gabe had had a lady in the village make corn dolly angels. 'And we all thought we were being clever and original,' he beamed, pouring another sherry.

In the light of the Imogen development Alexia felt hot with embarrassment in case she'd bought Ben too much. When he looked pleased at the experience day and Maltesers and sent her a wink over the whisky tumblers, relief that she didn't have to be mortified made her drink half a glass of wine straight down.

He'd bought Alexia an angel, too, of the most delicate rose gold, dangling from an intricate chain. 'Oh,' she breathed as he fastened it around her neck, the touch of his fingers tingling across her skin. 'How beautiful.' The words came out all strangled and she felt her eyes burn.

'Hey, hey!' He pulled her gently into his arms. 'It's not meant to make you cry.'

She laughed through her tears as if she were just over-come with the gift, pressing her face bashfully against his jumper. It was typical of his kindness that he was letting Christmas play out happily before going home to Didbury.

But then it seemed she'd be denied even that crumb of comfort because over brandy – or lemonade if you were Charlotte or Emily – Ben announced plans to finish his contract on the Carlysle estate then start his own business once again. 'It'll take me a while to get everything in place because I let most of my equipment go when I sold up before but I've had enough of working for someone else.'

'Oh.' The exclamation shot out before Alexia could smother it.

He turned his gaze on her and she read consternation in his eyes. 'Actually, we need to discuss . . .' He fumbled awkwardly.

Her heart plummeted so hard it hit her toes. It was real. He was going back. Old life. Old wife. Old line of business. She was glad for him. Really. She was.

She could take that job with Verity . . .

Her heart gave a sickening squeeze. Could she leave Middledip now, when she had to give Ben up too? Even The Angel was on the brink of getting along without her. She wasn't sure she could lose everything all at once.

She jumped up. 'I'm gasping for a cuppa. I'll put the kettle on.' It was only a couple of strides from her sitting room to her kitchen but she was glad of the isolation to grab a ream of kitchen roll and blot her eyes.

Ben's voice came from behind her, making her jump. 'What's up?' Warm arms slid around her and turned her softly to face him.

She pinned on a smile. 'Nothing . . .'

He stared down, disquiet in his storm-grey eyes. 'I call

342

bullshit. Is it me starting my own company again? Sorry I launched it on you in front of everybody. I suddenly realised I should have told you first.'

'You don't owe that to me.' She sniffled. 'I'm three-glasses-of-wine emotional. I want you to be happy.'

'Oh-kay.' He paused. 'You crying doesn't make me happy. In fact –' he flushed '– it's taken the last couple of crazy days to realise what will make me happy.'

'It's all right.' She forced the corners of her mouth to turn up in an approximation of a smile. 'I know.'

He furrowed his forehead. 'About Kent?'

'*Kent*?' Alexia stopped trying to shelter behind a fake smile. 'What about Kent?'

He sighed ruefully. 'They do have trees there.'

'Obviously. But—'

'It would make me happy to base the business in Kent.' His words came out in a rush. He gazed at her stupefied expression for a moment, then his arms fell back to his sides. 'Shit. I've presumed too much. I know you find it suffocating to be committed but I thought if you were in southeast London, Kent would be close enough. For us to sort of give things a try.'

Her heart began a slow and heavy beat. '*Us*? What about Imogen?'

Ben shook his head and shrugged. 'What about her?'

'I saw you holding her as if she was made of something delicate and precious. You said she'd offered you your old life back. You were quiet and strange. You stayed away from me yesterday with hardly a word so I thought . . .' She took a steadying breath, tears gathering like a ball in her throat. 'I thought you'd patched things up. I assumed you starting up your business again was part of you returning to your old life.'

His eyes widened. 'Holy hell. If only you'd heard the conversation between me, Lloyd and Imogen yesterday! Nothing could be further from the truth. Lloyd and Imogen told me they're together now.'

Horror shot through Alexia, making her gasp. 'That must have been awful to hear. I'm so sorry.'

'Don't be. OK, it's uncomfortable, but things between Imogen and me went past the point of no return a long time ago.' He looped his arms more securely around her. His eyes were darkly intense. 'I admit to being dazed on Saturday but I didn't mean to shut you out. I couldn't just walk back into the opening day furore and spill my guts. I'd finally been told the whole truth and it wasn't pretty. I was trying to absorb it. When my parents hung on the extra day while Lloyd and Imogen went home I felt I had to try and provide some kind of quality Christmas time with them and Gabe. I wanted to involve you but you were helping Carola. I thought – hoped – I could introduce you to my parents another time. I knew I'd see you today and thought we'd have the rest of . . . well, whatever, to talk.'

Alexia felt her heart skip, remembering how she'd spent yesterday imagining Ben with Imogen. 'Imogen had already left the village with Lloyd?'

Carola burst through the kitchen door. 'We're all dying of thirst – oops, sorry!' At seeing them entwined, she turned smartly round and disappeared.

Ben rolled his eyes and, pulling Alexia with him, leant on the door so it couldn't be opened again. 'They insist they weren't having an affair at the time of the accident – though, privately, Lloyd admitted he'd been in love with her for a long time. He hadn't acted on it because of me.'

'Oh.' Alexia digested this information. 'That's good. Isn't it?'

He inhaled slowly. 'Suppose so. I've only just realised how hearing that would once have messed with my head. Now . . . I suppose it's just part of him finally coming clean. Welcome, but not my focus.'

He glanced away for a moment, as if it would be easier to say what came next without the weight of Alexia's gaze. 'They did have something to hide, though. Lloyd had begun gambling at online casinos. To fund his habit, he dealt in "legal highs" – substances that were escaping the letter of the law by not yet being classified as drugs. When that loophole in the law closed he still had a stash. He couldn't bring himself to destroy it so arranged to meet people he'd supplied in the past and sell it on wholesale.'

He took her hands and looked down at them, the pads of his thumbs brushing over her fingers. 'What I'm finding less easy to forgive is that he got Imogen involved. Apparently she was "burning out" owing to her pressured sales environment and he got her stuff that would help her relax. Then he began supplying it – via her – to her equally high-gas colleagues.' He glanced up, sadness in his eyes. 'She was as near a drug dealer as makes no difference. I understand why she was desperate to keep that from me. I hate that kind of stuff. Lloyd tells me I have "too many straight edges" but I could never have stayed with her if I'd known what she was doing.'

Alexia tightened her fingers around his. 'You don't have to tell me if you don't want to.'

'I want to. It's just that finally knowing the truth, and it being such a tawdry truth, has knocked me for six. It seems I wasn't married to the person I thought I was, which is a big adjustment. They went together to this party where Lloyd was supposed to do the deal. The so-called buyers waited till he was drunk and turned nasty about paying so he shoved Imogen into the car and put his foot down. Hence the accident.'

Alexia stared up at him, at the trouble in his face but the truth in his eyes. 'But your brother's a lawyer. "Legal highs" were always a grey area.'

He shrugged. 'Apparently to him the area was black and white. Either something's legal or it's not, even knowing that people collapsed and died on the substances in question.'

She frowned, trying to arrange the facts logically. 'Why did Lloyd write to suggest you ask Imogen about the truth? That doesn't add up.'

'I thought the same. But with our divorce going through, she'd been seeing him in prison. She'd felt the spark between them too, I suppose. He's a good manipulator and he devised it as a way of forcing the issue – making her see that the marriage could never be saved if I knew she was mixed up in supplying dodgy substances. It was a gamble because if she'd confessed and I'd informed the authorities he would have had more jail time. It's still a gamble because he's out on licence so I could get him locked up again.'

Alexia froze. 'And?'

He stooped and kissed the question off her lips. 'I might be straight-laced but I'm not going to inform on my brother and my ex-wife.'

She knew it was wrong to be relieved. Sending his brother back to prison was a burden Ben could do without, regardless of whether Lloyd and Imogen had already paid enough for their sins. 'Why did they come clean now?'

He glanced down at their linked hands. 'Imogen wanted to clear her conscience and the only way she'd commit to Lloyd was if he finally faced me. They want to go off and start again somewhere – hence her comment about the way being clear for me to go back to Didbury. You can imagine family occasions will be awkward enough with my brother married to my ex-wife.' He slid his hands up her arms and pulled her against him. 'Their story was pretty hard for me to hear but she wanted to part as friends. The hug you saw was a final goodbye. I wasn't holding her as if she was precious. I just felt awkward.' He grinned, suddenly. 'The space in my arms is Alexia-shaped.'

Heat flooded through her as she felt a genuine grin take over her face. For the first time all day she thought she might be catching Christmas joy.

'So yesterday was a bit sticky with Mum and Dad,' he murmured, pulling gently at one of her curls. 'They're blindly relieved that we've sorted everything out. The reason they didn't come to see Gabe when he had pneumonia was that they could see the way things were going with Lloyd and Imogen and hoped to put off the evil hour as long as possible. I tried to tell them the whole story but they still shied away from it. They love both me and Lloyd and they don't want to decide where to place their loyalty. Families are weird.'

Alexia watched his expression carefully. 'So you could go home to Didbury? When we first met you were so missing your old life.'

His eyes darkened. 'And you wanted to leave the village and take up a great new job. We can each have those things now.'

She laid her hand on his chest, feeling his heart beating through his shirt. 'If we want them.'

'I want to be where you are,' he murmured. 'I want it a lot. But only if you want it too. I don't want you to go from Suffocating Seb to Bossy Ben. That's why I suggested I base myself in Kent, close enough to you for us to see each other but not so close you can't breathe.'

She narrowed her eyes at him. 'What if Kent doesn't work for me?'

A bleak expression stole across his features. 'I suppose I'd ask what does work for you . . . but with diminishing hope.'

Slowly, she brushed his lips with hers, feeling his body heat enveloping her. 'If you want Kent I'll take the job. But, really . . . I want to stay here in Middledip. With you.'

Epilogue

Almost one year later

**You are invited to the opening of
THE SHOWCASE
the new function room at
The Angel Community Café
Christmas Eve from 6 p.m.**

Alexia was feeling ridiculously excited as she smoothed her new dress of forest green silk. 'It's only The Angel in Middledip village,' she scolded herself. Which was true. But the knowledge didn't settle her butterflies.

She looked round the brand new function room in what was once the kitchen of The Angel public house. Now it was literally a showcase – for a lot of things that had belonged to The Angel and had eventually been recovered from the illicit warehouse of one Shane Edmunds/Niall Radstock when he decided co-operating with the police might ameliorate the severity of his punishment, even to the extent of helping them pick up Tim (whose real name turned out to be Frank). Alexia's many photos of the features in situ had been helpful in Gabe getting his property returned.

What to do with the returned period features had been the subject of many a discussion between Gabe, Alexia, Ben and Carola. It would interrupt operations at The Angel to refit fire surrounds in the Bar Parlour or Public now the chimney accesses had been bricked up and, anyway, nobody wanted to mess with The Angel's new look. It was Alexia who'd come up with The Showcase idea.

She ran her fingers over the original polished bar that had stood in the Bar Parlour for well over a century, and had been recovered complete, to her joy, with its etched glass screens. Cast iron fireplaces graced the other three walls of the rooms. None of them was fitted to a chimney but they looked fabulous stuffed with flowers. Mirrors lined the walls and two imposing light fittings hung overhead. They didn't match because one had originally hung in the Bar Parlour and one in the Public, but that was a talking point. A section of panelling from an upstairs room was framed on one wall with another light, this time a three-armed wall sconce, shining down on it. Nearby hung the storyboards for the refurbishment that never was.

The room was decorated for The Angel Community Café's second Christmas but Alexia had stood firm that it shouldn't be with twenty-first century bling. Swags of real woodland greenery hung over the fireplaces and a Christmas tree stood in the corner, smelling wonderful because the only decorations Alexia had allowed apart from replica Victoriana such as smiling Santas, solemn cherubs and satin balls seeded with beads, were oranges threaded with ribbon and studded with cloves. Tiny white lights danced amongst the branches like fairies.

Under an arch of berried holly the old pantry was now a compact kitchen area for caterers to use when they brought in their crates and trolleys to provide for funeral teas or birthday parties. Today its shelves were groaning with angel-shaped cakes made by Carola, Jodie and Alexia, and Gabe had even risked the wrath of Tubb at the pub by obtaining a temporary alcohol licence to cover them for the wine, beer and fizz waiting in tubs of ice behind the bar.

Carola panted in. She'd been running in and out all afternoon, leaving Jodie – now working at the café part time – in charge. Happily divorced these days, Carola frequently climbed out of paint-spattered jeans or her smart catering smock and into more flattering outfits such as the navy blue lace dress she wore today in honour of the occasion. 'Got it!' Triumphant, she jumped up on a chair and placed a pious Victoriana angel on the top of the tree. 'Bloody delivery man had left it with a neighbour instead of in the stipulated safe place.'

She stopped and studied Alexia. 'You look fantastic.'

'Oh!' Alexia blushed hotly. 'My dress feels too short and too low.'

'Pfft!' Carola waved that idea away. 'You're too used to overalls.'

Ben came through from the Bar Parlour in a black suit that made him look as if he'd just stepped out of GQ. His gaze fell on Alexia. 'You look hot.'

She beamed as he hooked her to him. 'My dress isn't too short or too low?'

'It's both. That's why I like it.'

Gabe arrived at the same time as Charlotte and Emily, who were dressed in black, with aprons, to show they were responsible for circulating the cakes. From six o'clock

351

villagers began to flock in, all happy to ooh and ahh over The Showcase as they drank the wine and dug in to gingerbread and cakes of the angel-shaped variety. The level of noise rose and rose as more people trickled through the door until there was barely room to stand shoulder to shoulder let alone juggle glasses and plates.

Finally, Gabe climbed onto a chair and clapped his hands. He'd regained all the weight he'd lost in the grip of pneumonia a year ago and his ponytail was back to looking sleek and healthy. 'Ladies and gentlemen!' The noise died as everyone shushed each other. Alexia was reminded of that horrible night at The Three Fishes when Gabe had had to tell the villagers about the money and her stomach rolled.

But tonight was different in every way. Gabe was beaming. Ben's arm was around Alexia as he gave her a tiny wink.

'Thank you for joining us to celebrate the opening of The Showcase.' Gabe projected his voice impressively. 'Almost everyone knows the story of how and why this fabulous room has risen from the ashes of a terrible time for us.' Lots of nods. Jodie, who had shut up the café, slipped into the room, pulling off her apron to reveal a party dress. Alexia waved, knowing Jodie would soon want to run home to take over the care of seven-month-old Kaylee from Iona, who'd got her wish for three generations of Jones women to live happily together. Jodie seemed on a much more even keel these days whenever Alexia saw her around the village.

Gabe thanked Carola for her part in making The Angel the well-frequented and profitable business that it had become, before going on, 'I also want to use this occasion to update you on the events of the past year, beginning with a couple of people who are exceedingly dear to me. My nephew Ben has launched a new business, so you know exactly where to go when you need a little magic working on your conifers – Wizard Tree Services!' He paused for laughter. 'And Alexia, apart from overseeing the creation of The Showcase, will start the New Year heading up a new team for property developer Verity Hart, right here in Cambridgeshire.'

After waiting for the applause to die down, Gabe turned on his audience a more serious expression. 'I've never forgotten that so many of you raised money for The Angel. When we got a good portion of it back, I was worried what to do with it. There was no way of dividing it up and returning it so we've used it to create this function room, the showcase for what original features were eventually returned to us.' People began to clap again and Gabe had to raise his voice. 'And we have Alexia to thank once again for using her design and decorating skills to turn this room into a living storyboard.' Gabe had to hold up his hands for several seconds this time before the applause diminished.

'So the way I've chosen to give back the funds raised by the village,' he pronounced, 'is to make this beautiful and individual function room available for a nominal hire fee to anybody who lives in Middledip!'

The applause was louder than ever, people whooping and even calling out dates they'd like to book. Alexia looped an arm around Ben's neck, standing on tiptoe to get her lips close enough to his ear for him to hear her. 'I think they're pleased.'

He laughed. 'My uncle is a wonderful man.' He dipped his head and kissed her mouth.

'Mmmm.' Alexia snuggled against him and angled her

head to deepen the kiss, sure no one would mind. It was Christmas, a time for kisses, even if the mistletoe had been used up in the greenery boughs.

But Gabe hadn't quite finished. 'This is a very special day.'

Ben pulled back from the kiss to murmur, 'Can't argue with that. I love you, by the way.'

'I love you too,' Alexia whispered.

'So, ladies and gentlemen, please raise your glasses,' Gabe went on, raising his glass of fizz encouragingly, 'and drink a toast . . .' He drew out the moment for several seconds.

'To The Angel!' Carola cried, who'd never met a silence she couldn't fill.

'The Angel!' everyone echoed.

'AND,' boomed Gabe, 'to Alexia and Ben who got engaged this afternoon!'

'*What*?' Alexia cried, spinning around in shock. 'Gabe, it was meant to be a secret!'

'I know you didn't want to take the limelight off The Showcase,' Gabe agreed, beaming fondly at her. 'But I'm just so pleased that I want to tell the world.'

'Alexia and Ben!' everybody roared.

Then the happy couple were almost knocked off their feet by the wave of people who turned to congratulate them. Laughing, Ben shook a forest of hands over Alexia's shoulder. 'I kind of want to tell the world, too,' he acknowledged.

Alexia felt a huge hot rush of love. 'Telling Middledip is certainly a good start.' And she let herself be pulled into one enthusiastic hug after another from the people of the village she called home.

*

Much, much later, when it was actually the wee hours of Christmas Day, they finally locked up The Angel. Gabe hugged them both. 'Goodnight. Merry Christmas. See you for lunch tomorrow. Today, I mean.' Yawning, he turned towards his own home, huddling into his coat.

Alexia carried her party shoes, having slipped on her snow boots for the walk along the bridleways to Woodward Cottage, which Ben was renting from Christopher Carlysle now he was no longer an estate worker but heading up his own company once again. There had been a couple of light falls of snow in the last week and the estate had frozen into an eerie moonlit landscape that crunched beneath their feet.

Ben lifted Alexia over the stile so she didn't mess up her dress, then they walked on, glancing into the icy waters of the little lake as they passed. 'Fancy a dip tonight?' Alexia joked, though she shivered to remember the desperation on Ben's face as he'd tried to keep his head above water that day. The kittens he'd rescued had all been found good homes and Gabe had begun a 'Cats of Middledip' Facebook page so their owners could keep him up to date with their antics.

Ben gave Alexia's hand a squeeze. 'I'll give the swim a miss, thanks. Though I wouldn't mind the hot shower.'

By mutual consent, when they reached the cottage they walked around it to look in on Barney who, because he was an owl, was wide-awake and looking back at them with a regal expression. His '*HEHHHHHHH!*' was a thorough screech now. Aside from the permanently motionless wing, he'd grown into a handsome adult barn owl, his speckled feathers and creamy breast making him look as if he wore a jacket and smart shirt.

'And Merry Christmas to you,' replied Alexia as Barney

hopped down from a branch and scuttled towards them along the floor, his good wing flapping. They crouched down to say hi to him.

'You know,' Ben murmured. 'When Gabe asked me to rear Barney I thought he was trying to give me a message about Imogen. But I think now it was a message about me. About learning to live with things, even when they're bad. I don't think he realised how very, very good they were about to get.'

Alexia leant her head on his shoulder. 'For me, too. I didn't get what I wanted but what I got was so much better.' She took Ben's hand and began to rise to her feet. 'Merry Christmas Barney Owl, but excuse us. It's time I took my fiancé to bed.'

Loved *The Little Village Christmas*?

Then make sure you don't miss
Sue's other brilliant books –
guaranteed to brighten any day!

In theory, nothing could be better than a summer spent basking in the French sun. That is, until you add in three teenagers, two love interests, one divorcing couple, and a *very* unexpected pregnancy. . .

Escape with Sue Moorcroft in this glorious summer read! Perfect for fans of Katie Fforde, Carole Matthews and Trisha Ashley.

Available in all good bookshops now.

For Ava Blissham, it's going to be a Christmas to remember. . .